STAFFORDSHIRE LIBRARY AND INFORMATION
Please return or renew by last date shown

If not required by other readers this item may be renewed, in person, by post or by telephone. Please quote details above and date due for return. If issued by computer, the numbers on the barcode label on your ticket and on each item, together with date of return are required.

24 HOUR RENEWAL LINE - 0845 33 00 740

D1423333

A Garden Lost in Time

a&b

A Garden Lost in Time

JONATHAN AYCLIFFE

First published in Great Britain in 2004 by
Allison & Busby Limited
Bon Marche Centre
241-251 Ferndale Road
London SW9 8BJ
http://www.allisonandbusby.com

ISBN 07490 06870

Printed and bound by Creative Print & Design,
Ebbw Vale, Wales

Quem é que fala da morte
Docemente ao meu ouvido?

Who is it that speaks of death
Softly in my ear?

(From a poem by Antonio Botto, Trans. J.A.)

The Swan Summer

July 1916

Upon the brimming water among the stones
Are nine-and-fifty swans....
Unwearied still, lover by lover,
They paddle in the cold
Companionable streams or climb the air;
Their hearts have not grown old;
Passion or conquest, wander where they will,
Attend upon them still.
WB Yeats

Swans flew in that year from Tuscany or France, and spent a summer season on the lake, gliding between the Chinese pavilion and the boathouse. Up at the house, they spoke of them by way of portents.

'If they leave like they did last year and don't come back, we shall see another hard winter at the end of it,' said Mrs Penberthy, down in the laundry, her crisp sheets as white as magnolia or the down on a swan's back.

But, then, everything was a portent to Mrs Penberthy and the laundry maids. Swans were taken more lightly upstairs, by servants and gentry alike. The Trevelyans positively welcomed them, and made trips to the lake to watch them pursue their stately course across the water, the sun bright on their heads and the feathers of their folded wings like snow.

They were Mute Swans, white swimmers by day, ghosts crossing the air by night. They did not, as of habit, spend the winter abroad like other birds, but were happy to stay in England. They wintered on the lake, where they made untidy nests among the reeds. Normally, they hatched their cygnets in spring, and by late September had them up and flying. But the winter before they had all flown off at summer's end, and had not returned until the following June.

Perhaps these were not the same swans after all. Marion was convinced of that; she thought they were French swans, chased across the Channel by the fighting there, as though so much death had frightened them into the sky and back to the Swan Lake. She reminded the family that the Ancient Greeks thought much of the Mute Swan, and said they remained silent through their lives only to burst into heavenly song as they died.

There was a swan picnic one hot day in July, with ripe strawberries and fresh lemonade, and champagne for the adults. They invited friends from Porthmullion and further afield, the Wycombes and the Savages, the Fiennes-Bartons, the Shipperleys, and the Hope-Maddoxes. Lawrence Vulliamy attended with his bride of three weeks, and the young doctor, Quilty, came up from Porth Buryan with a bachelor called Bracewell. Vulliamy had been excused military duties on the grounds of poor eyesight, and had been given a white feather twice in Trafalgar Square for his trouble. As for Bracewell, no one knew how he had avoided service at the Front, but he had an old mother whom he looked after religiously, who was wholly dependant on him, and whose last will and testament promised him great future wealth.

At times, Bracewell let his weak eyes linger on Linda Mainwaring, whose husband had been killed on a French battlefield not many months before. She sat a little apart from the others, gazing wistfully across the lake throughout the afternoon, and not once did she lift her head when the swans rose above the water to test their wings. Everyone said she was very beautiful, and many declared she would not remain a widow long.

The day passed in a sort of dream. Swans, champagne, and sunshine became entangled in a reckless net of sounds and colours. The children were allowed to play on the goose lawn, and their excited voices formed a backdrop to the more sedate murmurings of their elders. No one spoke of the war. As though by mutual consent, this was a day out of ordinary time, for no other reason than to see the swans glide on the lake. It was remembered long afterwards; but perhaps that was because of what happened after. We remember our fears more than our pleasures: the pleasures slip away and are forgotten, the fears linger like ghosts, like white ghosts, like long white ghosts.

They say someone saw a ghost that afternoon, in the Cripplesease Woods, that stretch of forest that runs across the western flank of the estate and comes down almost to the lake shore. It's an old wood, mainly oak with several ancient yews that have grown there for more than two thousand years. When the trees are in leaf, very little light passes to the forest floor. Sometimes a wind blows through the branches and rubs them together, creating mystifying sounds and moving what little light there is in a curious fashion. Perhaps that is all he heard or saw. But there was almost no wind that day, and the branches did not move, and there was no light to catch anyone's fancy. But he saw something, that is certain. For weeks afterwards, he could not sleep, and in the end he had to have Dr Quilty attend him, who heard everything and sent his patient abroad for a long holiday. He never went back to Trevelyan Priors, even after the passage of many years, and he never again set foot in a wood or forest. Some say the ghost followed him out of Cripplesease Woods, and went with him abroad, and returned with him, for in all his life he never stopped looking over his shoulder when there was nothing to be seen.

Only the swans watched him slip among the trees, only they sensed his moment of blind terror when brought face to face with that thing in the woods, and only they were aware of his departure, stumbling and crying aloud, his sanity ruined, his heart broken.

Long-necked and thoughtlessly grand, the swans slid back and forth in silence, ignoring the picnic and the strange creatures bustling about on the banks of the lake. Further off, ducks quacked or swam in circles with their busy brood, sending ripples everywhere. The children threw pieces of bread to swans and ducks alike, and squealed with delight if the birds ventured closer to shore.

During those hours of liberty, not one word was said about the war. For all that, it was in everyone's thoughts, from the start of the picnic to its end. Someone had brought along a Monarch

Junior gramophone and a selection of recordings, dance music in the main. Hour after hour, the strains of the Victor Military Band and Conway's Band filled the air. The lilting tunes, *Pretty Baby*, *Chin Chin*, and *In the Beautiful Seaside Air*, scratchy and uneven, lodged in everybody's brain, but could not dispel the air of unreality, the dream-like mood that lay on grass and water alike.

The champagne was drunk in tiny sips, the caviar was spread with spoons of mother-of-pearl onto thin slices of toast, the strawberries and cream were spooned out into painted bowls of French porcelain. Smiles were passed round as easily as petits fours on trays. And their thoughts were with the dead and the living, with husbands, brothers, and sons, with those tens of thousands out on the fields of France performing a dance of death that seemed to have no end.

About a week after the picnic, Marion Trevelyan and Sir David were walking down by the lake when they noticed the swans take off and rise long-necked into the air. It was a long way from dusk, when the birds normally took to the sky. They stood listening for long minutes until they could make out a faint sound of booming or banging. It seemed to come from the sea, and it went on for hours.

'Artillery,' said Sir David, leaning against his ash stick. 'Heavy guns. Our guns, by the sound of it. 9.2 inchers. They'll be giving the Fritzes hell.'

Beside him, his wife sat as though wounded, her face pale, her eyes wide open. She was a woman between thirty and forty, thin, with a pinched face, above which her golden hair had been pinned in the latest London style. Her dress was fashionable too, and yet a disinterested observer, coming upon her then, might have thought her uncomfortable in both clothes and body. Only those who knew her better were aware that her face, in relaxation, could look radiant.

Like Linda Mainwaring, she did not look up at the swans as they left. She only paid attention when they returned at sunset; their wings as they descended to the lake were red, as though stained with blood. Marion Trevelyan closed her eyes and thought of white bandages laid out in the empty corridors of a

French hospital, and of red blood seeping through old bandages on broken limbs.

A day or two later, the first reports appeared in the papers of the fighting that had started on the Somme. On that first day, thousands of men on both sides had lost their lives. None of the friends to whom the Trevelyans related their tale thought it at all possible to have heard guns on the Somme from as far away as Cornwall. But the Trevelyans insisted, and no one wished to argue with them.

They had two sons at the front, James and William, both officers in the Devonshire and Dorset. James had turned thirty in June, William was twenty-five. They had spent the best part of the last two years in front-line postings, returning only occasionally to spend brief leaves at home. Each time they seemed more withdrawn. They never spoke about the war.

James had left behind a fiancée, a pale, elfin creature called Geraldine Fitzallan. She came from Arch Zawn, an elegant old house a few miles above St Mawes and a mile or so from Trevelyan Priors. Since James's departure, she had walked down country roads every Sunday in order to be with her prospective parents-in-law. They would tell her what news, if any, they had of James. Most weeks there was nothing to report, and the news from the front was generally so dispiriting as to render it, by mutual consent, out of bounds. Often enough there would be a letter, which Marion would read to her, carefully omitting any passages that might hint at her future husband's mental and moral distress.

They did not breathe a word to her about the guns they had fancied hearing that day down by the lake, nor about the white returning swans and their blood-stained wings. There was no letter in the week following, nor the week after that. Anxiety gripped both households. The swans sailed on the sun-flecked surface of the lake, drawing their reflections behind them like golden rafts.

On the morning of the twenty-ninth, a telegram arrived at Trevelyan Priors. They'd been well prepared for it by the guns. William was wounded and had been taken to the Hospice

Comtesse in Lille. James's body had not yet been recovered from the firing trench in which he and his men had been waiting to advance. It had been hit by a barrage of German shells.

'One of us should tell Geraldine,' said Sir David, hoping Marion would volunteer.

'I'll go,' she said. 'Better she hears from a woman. Stay here, and have Mrs Armitage tell the staff.'

'Very well, I'll see to that. I suppose I'd best speak to young Tom,' — he spoke of his youngest son, aged twelve — 'or would you rather do that yourself too, dear?'

'We'll break the news to Tom and Alice together.' Alice was their little girl. James and William were David's sons by his first wife. 'Perhaps we should do that now. I'll have Miss Benveniste bring them to the morning room.'

'Good.'

'And what about...?'

'We'll say nothing about that. William is still alive. If his wounds are not too severe, he may well live a normal life. Let us pray so.'

'Should someone go to France?'

He shook his head decisively.

'We should only be in the way, I think. The postal service is adequate.'

'What if he can't write?'

'I'll ring the War Office and see what I can find out. Now, dear, I think it's time we told the children.'

Everyone remarked on how composed the Trevelyans seemed, in spite of the magnitude of their loss, and all the uncertainty that still clung to young Mr Trevelyan. The longcase clock on the main stairs was stopped, and a severe silence fell on everything. Yards of black crêpe were fastened throughout the house: on picture frames and mirrors, on the door of James's bedroom, and on the portraits of his ancestors that lined the Great Hall. The flag on the Arundel Tower was gently lowered to half-mast.

Sir David stood by a tall latticed window on the third floor and looked out across the vast expanse of gardens that were the particular treasure of the house and its family. He was a big man, a head and more taller than his wife; yet today he seemed bowed and, more than that, diminished.

This had been his family's home for centuries, and Sir David dressed and talked and ate and rode with a natural affinity for his surroundings. He had been brought up to doubt nothing and to question nothing. In the mornings, he knew exactly what time to wake, and in the evenings he retired precisely to the minute dictated by his inner schedule. He knew what sort of haircut he needed, how to order a pair of boots from Lobb's, how much to tip a waiter in London, how much to leave for the servants when he visited another stately home, how to ride a horse and how to choose one, how to hunt and shoot and fish.

It was as though God had given him and his kind detailed instructions on how to live the cultured life. As a Jew knows how to wear his prayer shawl and *tallit*, what to eat and not eat, or how to behave in privacy with his wife, so David Trevelyan performed his slow waltz from day to day, through waking to sleeping, and so back again. But that day he seemed to stumble for the first time.

He noticed at once that the swans had gone from the lake. They would not return in his lifetime, he thought. The intervening winters would be long and hard.

Later that afternoon, Geraldine Fitzallan made her way slowly through the gardens of Trevelyan Priors. She did not make her presence known to anyone in the house, nor did anyone there notice her. The vicar had been brought up from St. Botolph's, and the household was assembled in the dining-room for prayers. No one, not even Marion during her visit, had thought to invite her: she was only a pale, elfin creature, after all, and of little significance in the world of the Trevelyans.

She went down to the lake and paused there for several minutes. There were footprints in the mud along one edge, a man's prints, large and deeply indented. She remarked to herself that the swans had gone, and like David Trevelyan she had little hope of their return.

She headed down through the gardens, passing the waterfall and the Hidden Valley before she set foot on the sloping path that leads down to Polzeath Head, where it looks across to the Sevensouls, and beyond to the open sea. Not far away stood the tall chimney-like structure of the shot tower. The men inside were at work. Perhaps no one had told them of the bereavement suffered in the house above. She could hear the sound of the newly-fashioned bullets as they thudded into the little pool of water at the chimney's foot. Crack, crack, crack, they insisted their way into the world.

How long she stood on the cliff's edge, gazing out over white foam and blue water, no one could guess. Perhaps she was listening for something more than the crashing of waves or the cracking of newly-forged shot; perhaps she expected to hear salvoes of heavy guns fired in far-away France, a country she had never visited. She never walked back up along the path. Her naked body was found three days later on the Strangles, the long beach of greenstone pebbles that runs along the cliffs west of the Head. Her clothes were nowhere to be found, and at the inquest it was recorded that she herself must have removed them and thrown them out to sea.

That same day, the head gardener at Trevelyan Priors, a knotty-headed man called Dick Tregideon, came across something unsettling by the lake side. One of the swans had died, and its body now lay on the edge of the lake, not far from one of the nests. It had died recently, he guessed, but already flies specked the linen white of its feathers, and spiders spun webs around its unseeing eyes.

He disposed of the remains in the incinerator, and given the sadness of the day, thought better of mentioning the swan to his master.

In the shot tower, molten lead spun through the hot air, to crash perfectly formed to the pool at its foot. Waves crashed against the Sevensouls. A light went on in the attic and did not go out again until dawn.

A Return to Trevelyan Priors

From the narrative of Simon Lysaght in his old age

14 July 1994

The house and the garden and the swans could be a hundred years away, if I thought of them as lost. But lost they are not; they still remain in that remote corner where I came upon them all those years ago. They are utterly changed, of course, and I expect anyone coming on them now with no more than a few faded photographs as his guide would find them quite unrecognisable. But I knew them in the first instant, the great trees towering over everything around, the house elevated, with its back to the sea, the shot tower, half in ruin now, no longer able to stamp its presence on the surrounding countryside. Its remains stood on the cliff top like a diminished beacon or a lighthouse of some kind, drawing the eyes of anyone at sea who happened to look up in its direction.

I passed them yesterday, quite by chance, and I ventured in a little way, wondering what I might see. Or hear. My courage failed me as it did that first time, and I went only a little way along the Glasshouse Path. Of course, it's grown over now, and I'm an old man who has to take care of himself. That's what held me back, if you must know. I'm not a child any more, I've seen bigger houses, more splendid gardens, rougher seas. But I've never come to fear a place like Trevelyan Priors.

I pretend it was chance that brought me there again, but that's a lie. We all like to have such pretences, to serve us in the daily re-creation of our worlds. As a matter of fact, I wanted to see Cornwall for the last time, it has been a particular ache inside me these ten years and more. During that time, I've been back to all the more exotic places to say my farewells, places where I've been happy, places where I've had to struggle to feel anything but despair: Paris, Venice, Rome, Florence, Nice. A last session of cante jondo in Seville. A performance of *La Forza del Destino* in Verona. The last concert given by Amália Rodrigues in Lisbon. That all sounds a trifle vain, a bit like name dropping, but they were, in their way, my very good friends once upon a time.

It was only after I'd finished the last of these visits — a month in Ravello, high above the clouds, incessantly dreaming, my heart ravished by the vast blue sea so far below — that it came home to me I had truly grown old. I made my way back to England in cold weather, and the winter that followed was of all seasons the least prompt to my dying needs. Spring came, and I revived, though I did not grow young again. With the coming of summer, it was time to visit Cornwall for the last time. I wanted to see Porthmullion again, and I had unfinished business at Trevelyan Priors.

I didn't see her yesterday, but then I only passed by without going in. She may have been waiting, indeed, I am sure she was, why wouldn't she be? The garden has turned to wilderness, so thickly overgrown it's hard to tell there was once a garden there at all. I saw the house at a distance only. It's been shut up for years, of course, ever since Marion died. I saw grey shutters fanned out across the front windows: it must be very dark inside. Ivy grows on it, and will in time cover it entirely. Birds have nested in the chimneys, they move in and out incessantly.

I went down to the village afterwards. It had changed less than I'd thought possible, and in the harbour the sea sounded exactly as it had sounded a lifetime ago. Gulls swooped down from Polzeath Head as though to welcome me back.

I found old Westerby's shop still doing a roaring trade (a miracle of sorts, all things considered). The window was full of glass jars containing brightly-coloured sweets and rock and toffee apples. I went in to buy a twist of tobacco for this wretched old pipe of mine. Dr. McRae is for ever telling me I should give the thing up, but where would be the point in that? I'm over ninety now — what do a few years matter at such an age, more or less?

I did not recognise the man serving behind the counter, but before I left I asked if he belonged to the family. He said he was George Westerby. That would make him old George's grandson. Robert's son. He's fifty-something now, I reckon. I told him I'd bought sweets from his grandfather and tobacco from his father. He smiled and said he didn't know anyone from that generation remained.

'I'm Simon Lysaght,' I said. 'You probably haven't heard of me.'

He shook his head, but I could see a little flicker of doubt move across his eyes. He'd heard my name before, of course he had, and it would only be a day or two before it came back to him. I didn't volunteer anything.

What would have been the point? He knew little enough of the house and what went on there. As much as anyone in the village. They all think they know a great deal, when the truth is they know next to nothing.

I caught a glimpse of a much younger man stacking jars at the back, and heard a woman's voice laugh from somewhere up the stairs. As though past and present were crushed together suddenly. As though, for one moment, they merged again.

I imagine the moment of death a little like that, the two ends of a single life brought face to face for the first and last time. Do we all die as newborn infants, as innocent leaving this world as we entered it? I imagine not. I cannot in all honesty think what it would be like to be innocent again. To set foot in Trevelyan Priors without taint or memory. Or fear.

15 July

I've decided to stay for the rest of the summer, or for as long as it takes to compile a coherent story of what happened all those years ago. I have my old journal, and letters belonging to my mother, together with others sent to her by Marion. I have my own memories, memories that have never left me, never leave me now. I was old enough to understand much of what happened, and matters that passed me by then I have understood most of my life. That has been the hard thing for me, the bearing of so many memories.

Even now, an old man, a hairless, gap-toothed remnant, I wake in the night, having dreamed badly, a nightmare or a memory grown out of shape — and staring into the darkness, I know she is there, there in the room, watching me. Once woken, I turn a table light on and sit up to say my prayers or just fiddle with the beads of my rosary; but as I pray, my eyes turn here and there, inspecting whatever shadows there may be, listening for a sound that will betray her presence. She plays tricks with me, horrid little tricks that sometimes go wrong. Once I heard her laughing, a coarse, cruel laugh unlike any she uttered when alive. And another time weeping as though her heart would break. That I could not bear. I had to rise and leave the room: I half slept on my armchair downstairs. And when I returned in the morning, someone else had been sleeping restlessly in my bed. Someone, something, it's all the same.

20 August

A month and more at my desk. I have found a hotel suitable for my needs. It used to be the Shipperleys' house: I still remember the trips we made to have tea there, the stilted conversations, my collar rasping against my neck, Tom making eyes at Dorothy Shipperley. From outside, it looks much the same, though somewhat sprucer than before; but the hoteliers have introduced massive changes inside, not all to my liking.

They call it a 'country house' hotel, and try in rather spurious ways to create the atmosphere of the sort of house that has largely died out across the English countryside, the gentry house, where the 'better sort' of person spent his or her time when in the country. In its favour, there is excellent service at all times of day and night, there is a smoking room, the restaurant, though a little formal for my taste, serves meals of very high quality. It all costs a lot, but at my age that scarcely matters half as much as my comfort. They pamper me. It's a long time since I was pampered, and I enjoy every minute of it.

I went up to the Priors again this afternoon. Just far enough to see the house. It is not in a state of ruin, not enough time has passed for that. But it has a deserted and unkempt look... and perhaps something more, a forbidding appearance. From where I stood, facing the front, it seemed that the house must be full of darkened rooms, unlit corridors, night-dimmed stairways, and silent furniture covered in dusty sheets. And no doubt that's

19

exactly how it is. Old furniture, faded carpets, wallpaper that has peeled away from damp patches on the walls, cobwebs stretched out between the glass branches of chandeliers, cracked windows that once shone in sunlight and came alive in firelight, now resembling old eyes with cataracts, tapestries left for the moths to eat, and a silence that goes on and on forever and eats, like moths, into the fabric of the soul.

26 August

The post brought me a bundle from France. My guess paid off, and I found myself unwrapping a treasure trove of papers and photographs. They've been in Heather's possession all this time, and no one knew. Heather is Quilty's daughter, of course, and getting on in years herself. I visited her many years ago, at her pretty house in Gascony, but she said nothing about her archive then.

Of course, I can't be sure how much she has actually sent, nor of how much remains with her. I pounced on her package when it came, like a child on a birthday present from a distant but generous aunt. But after second thoughts I realised it would take me a little while to determine whether Heather was being generous or not.

I've written elsewhere, to be sure, and I await the postman eagerly to see what he may bring me. I'm too old to traipse round the country in order to see these people in person, and I abhor the telephone in matters of this kind. Two disembodied voices squawking down miles of telephone wire to neither one's advantage.

Somewhere in the back of my mind a stern voice admonishes me. Why don't I look in the obvious place? Why don't I go to the house itself, to Trevelyan Priors, to the very heart of my story, and search for papers there? They may not be in bad condition. Not all the furniture or fittings have been taken out. There may be letters, estate papers, journals, who knows what in cupboards upstairs. I think I know exactly where to look, but… I prefer to stay here in my cosy hotel and read what I have from France, make notes, and doze off from time to time, while waiting for the next post and that exquisite trip downstairs for breakfast, in the course of which I shall pause casually at the reception desk and ask if there is any post for me.

30 August

Oh, very well — what's the point of beating about the bush any longer? The house is haunted. There, I've said it, and it wasn't so hard after all. Haunted. Ask anyone who ever lived there. They know, and if they're still alive, they'll tell you with a little kind persuasion. That's why I don't go there, why I don't seek out those boxes and files I know must still exist in one of those cold rooms.

The thing is... Yes. The thing... It is not a nice haunting. Not comforting or uplifting. Not to be spoken of in church or Sunday School. You would not want to come face to face with the thing that haunts our old house, our picturesque and ancient house. Believe me, you would not.

No, you definitely would not. Not even if you think this is your sort of thing. No doubt you've been to séances and never turned a hair. Or visited haunted houses in the company of a medium or a psychic guide, and whistled your way from front door to attic and back again. You've read all the ghost books, fiction and non-fiction, and you've scoured the photographs, wondering what that milky shape may be in the top left-hand corner. But you do not want to open that door, or walk up those stairs, or stand in the silence waiting.

Indeed, if you are at all of a nervous disposition, you should not be reading this record. True, you will not actually see anything or *hear* anything. You will not have to, and, indeed, if you read far enough, you certainly will not want to.

20 September

Some of what I hoped for has arrived. And there is more to Heather's bundle than I at first thought. Taken together, I think I shall have enough to start work in a few days. I estimate about a month to do the actual transcribing and writing. It's the end of the season here, and I've decided to move to a quite different place until I finish. It's a little seaside cottage, with a view out to sea. I've hired a girl to clean and cook for me. She'll go up to the hotel every day, just to check there aren't any letters or packets.

1 October

The nights are the worst. They always were. In the hotel, I felt safe, cushioned from my fears. There were always plenty of people around, even at night: my fellow guests, the staff, visitors. I think I may have made a mistake in coming here, in thinking I could stay in a place like this on my own. Sometimes it gets as bad as it ever did. Last night I lay in bed alone, whimpering like a child.

I cannot ask the girl to remain overnight. It would seem indelicate, and she might think I had designs on her. She's a pretty girl with an attractive figure, and I'm sure she has offers from boys her age, not to mention men much older. I have no such designs, of course, just a more basic need for company and reassurance. In any case, I doubt very much she could bear it any more than I can, that a single night under this roof would not send her scurrying for home. So I think I have to accept how things are and say no more about it. The hotel has closed for the season, and there are no others of any size within a reasonable radius of Porthmullion.

10 October

The girl — Rachel is her name — came to me this evening and handed in her notice. When I pressed her for a reason — for she had not at first wanted to give me one — she burst into tears and said she could not spend another day in the cottage.

'What's wrong with it?' I asked, knowing perfectly well what it was. 'Is it something you've seen? Something you've heard, perhaps?'

She looked at me blankly.

'Haven't you seen him, sir?'

I shook my head. Inwardly I felt a chill. There had never been a 'Him'. What was she talking about?

'Him?'

'The little boy, sir. You must have seen him. Surely, sir…'

I had seen no little boy.

'I really don't understand. I've seen no little boy.'

'Maybe not that little, sir. Fourteen or fifteen, I reckon. In the front room, sir. He always stands next to the window, looking out, looking out at the sea. He stands there crying softly, sir. I swear to you, on my mother's grave I swear I've seen him as I'm seeing you now.'

'Perhaps he's a real boy,' I said, clutching at straws, for I knew better than to suggest such nonsense. 'Perhaps he gets in somehow from the street.'

'He cries, sir. And he never turns his head. I tried to speak to him, to comfort him, as it might be; but not once did he look my way, and I was feared to go to him.'

'What does he look like?'

'The boy, sir? Like a boy. He'd be about fourteen or so, I reckon. Not so little, perhaps. But he's an old-fashioned boy, sir, he wears funny clothes.'

'What sort of clothes?' For I was growing anxious about this boy.

'He had on what you might call knickerbockers, sir. Old-fashioned sort of trousers, near down to the knee, and socks beneath that, from knee to ankle, yellow socks. They're expensive-looking trousers, sir; but on top he wears a heavy jumper, a fisherman's jumper of the old sort.'

And at that I thought my heart would die. It came to me with a jolt just who the boy was. It just didn't make sense, that was all.

I took Rachel's hand in mine.

'Rachel, you can rest easy. He's not a ghost.'

'He's not real, sir, I can swear to that.'

'I know you can. Nevertheless, he is not the ghost of any dead person.'

'Then, what is he, sir? He chills my blood just to look at him.'

'I know it does. Let me deal with him. I think I know how to send him away. Trust me.'

11 October

The boy is gone. I am alone now, without even Rachel's company. My papers have been collected in separate piles. My writing paper has been laid out. My pens are filled with ink and bristling in their stand. There only remains the task of setting down what happened all those years ago at Trevelyan Priors. Reading my old journal, the one I wrote in my days at the Priors and for years after I left Cornwall, I can see the shadows part and the failures of memory retreat. My old eyes blink and see veils lift away from the past. And my ears, half-deaf these many years, start to hear the old sounds, the clop clop of horses trotting, the creak of leather harness, the crack of a coachman's whip, the snap of an old gate shutting, and the cry of a dying swan circling high above the cliffs.

It's all over now, in a manner of speaking. But my ghosts have never been laid to rest. I have never been as afraid as I am now.

A New Arrival

The Journal of Simon Lysaght

From the Earliest Account in the hand of Simon Lysaght, dated 4th January 1917.

I arrived at Trevelyan Priors late yesterday afternoon, the third of January. The train carried me as far as Porthmullion, where I was met on the platform by the Trevelyans' chauffeur, a man of around thirty called Parkin. My baggage was very simple and took up little space on the car's luggage rack. We passed along narrow roads and muddy cart-tracks, our long motor vehicle more than once a subject for mirth or curiosity. I had never ridden in one before, but I affected to be entirely at my ease, and indeed, with time I took to it as the most natural form of transportation for a young man.

'What sort of car is this?' I asked — of course, I wouldn't have known one car from another, but it sounded grown-up to show an interest in their marques.

'It's a Silver Ghost, sir,' the driver answered. His name was Matthew, a young man whose father had been head coachman until recently. 'Made by Rolls Royce. You'll have heard of them, of course, sir.'

'Of course,' I lied, 'everybody knows of them,' my eyes scanning the knobs and buttons on the dashboard as I talked. I admired the way Matthew drove, using the gearstick and pedals in the most natural fashion.

'Have you always had one?'

He laughed and shook his head.

'This one's six years old, sir. You'd scarcely remember them coming in. Up until the war started, we had a German car, a Mercedes/Knight. A lovely thing, it was, and very smooth to drive, but nothing compared to this beauty. Once you're old enough to drive, you must ask Lady Marion to arrange lessons for you. A bright lad like you, you'll be up behind the wheel in no time.'

I hadn't even thought of it before, so poor were we and unlikely ever to own a car. Now, it became my first ambition.

'Matthew, may I ask you a personal question?'

'No harm, Master Simon. But I think I know what it is. You want to know why I'm not at the Front.'

I blushed to be found out so easily. But in those days, it was at the front of everyone's mind. So much work was done by older men or women, it came as a shock to see someone who seemed as fit as a fiddle, but who had stayed behind in England.

'It's my heart, you see,' he continued. 'The doctors don't think much on it. They say it may give out any time. Out at the Front, I'd be a liability. All it would take would be a heavy bombardment, or a shell exploding overhead, and there would be my old ticker getting all worked up one second and stopping work entirely the next. It wouldn't cost Fritz a bullet to send me underground for good.'

'Don't say that, Matthew. Surely it can't be that bad. The doctors are bound to find a cure for you, aren't they?'

'We'll see,' he said, and he smiled at me warmly, like a man long for this world, and we said no more about it.

It was a blustery day, with that grey abasement of the light that is peculiar to Cornwall. When I stepped down from the running-board, my feet crunching on the smooth wet gravel of the drive, I could not keep my wide-sleeved Ulster from billowing around me like a sail caught by high winds as it leaves harbour. Mother had given me strict orders about wearing it. 'You'll find it cold down at the Priors,' she'd said as I was leaving. 'You don't want to go down with something the minute you arrive.'

I looked steadily up at the house. The short drive from the main gate had already given me a chance to form an awed impression of the place. It was a stone building, most of which dated from the sixteenth century, with some parts going back to the twelfth. Sir Thomas Trevelyan had recently been appointed Master of the Rolls, and to enhance his new-found dignity bought the land and buildings of the old Augustinian priory of St. Endellion. His country house was soon set to rival any in the West Country, perhaps any in the land.

He left it half-completed on his death, a clumsy mixture of medieval and late Elizabethan, but his eldest son Charles and grandson Anthony scooped acres of stone from the little quarry in

Tremarin Woods and turned Trevelyan Priors into a perfect jewel of architecture. Thomas had chosen his setting well. The quarry returned to nature by and by, and before long it became the heart around which the famous gardens grew.

Until I arrived, I'd known all of that as nothing more than bare facts in a book my mother gave me. Now, as we drove down the last stretch of the long drive, I looked up at a great mirror of mullioned windows, and held my breath, thinking of how many rooms there must be, and how many corridors to be swept, and how many maids to sweep them... Suddenly, I noticed someone watching me from a window in what Matthew told me was the old attic storey. Whether a man's face or a woman's, I could not tell. Or a child's, I thought. It might very well have been a child's.

I'd left my mother like that, staring through a window after me into the cold Yorkshire morning. She had not moved her head the whole time of my departure, nor lifted her hand to wave at me, as I had hoped she would wave, until the very last, in the moments before the pony and cart were about to turn the bend and pass out of sight. I'd glanced back then and seen her, framed in the window like a votive painting, and I'd taken the image with me all the way to Trevelyan Priors.

So far, everything had matched my expectations. I'd smiled all through my departure, to show Mother she had no cause to be upset on my behalf, that I was handling our separation like a man. At fifteen, I could look after myself very well, or so I fancied. The rail journey, with its constantly changing scenes and unexpected sights, had distracted me well enough. I hadn't once opened the Homer that Mother had given me to read. The short trip from the station had seen me taken up with excitement just at being in a motor car.

It was only as my luggage was set down on the drive beside me and the car was driven off to the rear of the house, that the reality of my position fully sank in on me.

There I was, as alone as I could ever hope to be, cut off from anyone I knew and cared for, waiting to be admitted to that grim and forbidding place. I could hear the sea crashing hard against rocks nearby, and the sound seemed to me the very last word in desolation. I would not see my dear mother again for many months, perhaps not till the summer. She and I had never been parted for long before, except for a short time when her father had taken ill and died. I'd been taught at the local grammar school, Sir John Lowe's, for my parents did not have the money to send me to public school. My father had gone to Eton, but his fortunes had not brought prosperity, and we'd lived a simple life.

I almost sobbed as I stood there, thinking that I'd never see him again. At that moment, I missed him more than at any time since his death. He'd been killed three months earlier, shot while leading his men in one of the last offensives on the Somme. He was buried in France, in a cemetery at Hawthorn Ridge, near a place called Beaumont Hamel. A week earlier there'd been a memorial service for him in our parish church. The Reverend Westmacott said it was a celebration of my father's life, though I couldn't see that really. Westmacott spoke very little of life. His sermon was all about war and glorious death and the Empire, and the walls of his church were hung with tattered battle flags, faded scraps of red, white and blue. My father's friends paid for a marble monument to be put up in the church. It shows an angel wearing a chaplet of roses on its head and its breast adorned with garlands of gilded lilies. It says on it that he was awarded the Conspicuous Gallantry Medal. That was how I learned the word posthumous. And the angel carried a banner of war in one hand, and a sword in the other. I still don't know why an angel can be dressed to kill.

I was still thinking about all this when the door of the house opened and a tall man, very elegantly dressed, appeared in the opening. He was, I should think, aged about fifty. I'm not terribly good at guessing grown-ups' ages, mind you. My father was forty-five when he died. This man seemed a little older than that.

He detached himself from the doorway and started down the long flight of steps that led to the drive. I noticed that his hair was oiled back and that he wore a small waxed moustache on his upper lip. He was very dapper, and his movements were fluid and precise. There was a white orchid in his buttonhole, which seemed to have been recently watered.

Behind him trotted a little man in butler's uniform, and behind the little man a dog of some sort. I guessed that the tall man was not Sir David, whom I understood to be a gentleman of advanced years. I could not guess who this was, for I'd heard of no one in the household fitting such a description.

'*Monsieur Simon Lysaght, si je ne me trompe pas. Je suis très heureux...*' He suddenly broke off. 'But pr'aps you not speak French? Is Tongue of Angels, no?' His eyes seemed to spin in their orbits, as though positively dizzied by the thought. I stumbled to answer him as best I could.

'*Mais, oui, Monsieur. Je... je parle votre langue un... petit peu.*'

He snapped his fingers at the factotum and nodded at my bags. I made to pick up one myself, thinking it only polite, but the stranger hissed and frowned and shook his head disdainfully at me. Next moment, the little man — whom I later learned to be a footman of some sort, not a butler — beetled back up the stairs, my bags under his sturdy arms.

Nothing had prepared me for such an encounter. The wind whipped round us, blowing my long scarf out behind me like a banner. My mother had knitted it herself. It reminded me of how much she loved me, and as I felt it being tugged against me, so I sensed her pull on my heartstrings.

'Come,' the tall man said. 'We go to the 'ouse.'

He was dressed more for a soirée than a windy day in Cornwall. On his feet, he wore highly polished shoes with little silver buckles, and his trousers were held tightly to them by narrow straps that went under the sole. He was thin and severe looking, and his long jacket was cut as though to accentuate this. On his right lapel he wore a small enamel badge or medal in the shape of a lozenge, and a small silver cross fastened a sombre tie to his shirt front.

What most drew my attention, however, were the man's head and face. For all his thinness, his head was large and angular, and seemed to weigh heavily on his neck. His hair was thick and black, though touched with grey at the edges. It was held down by some sort of balm or unguent, and not even the wind could do more than toss it. Though elegant, he was by no means a fop. I sensed at once something innately spartan about him, a severity of spirit that would yield to nothing. He had long, thin hands that moved expressively when he spoke, and rested when he fell silent.

He led me ceremoniously through the front door and into the entrance hall. Dark wood walls encased a large open space that might not have altered since it was first built. My eye was drawn immediately by a large stone chimneypiece set to my right. The stone was carved into a wide variety of shapes and ornaments, including a dozen or more coats of arms, and the whole thing was framed by a wooden surround complete with canopies and little seats. Busts and small figures, some human, some animal, stood on marble columns placed along the walls. Ragged regimental flags hung on poles, dusty and moth-eaten, their colours faded, their histories long worn away. I was reminded bitterly of my parish church. Just below them hung rows of ancestral portraits. They gazed down at me like gargoyles, whey-faced and questioning, until I felt like turning and running from the place.

'The stairs, monsieur, the stairs. Quickly now, we must go up. Sir David he waits for you.'

The French man ushered me to the left, where a huge oak staircase wound its way upwards into the dimly-lit world of the floors above.

As we started our way up, a maid appeared, coming in the opposite direction. She seemed startled to see us, and for a moment I thought she was about to turn and hare back up the stairs. She continued down, however, looking very sheepish. In her hands she carried a mop, a galvinised bucket, and various cleaning things. As she was about to pass, the Frenchman barred her way. I though he was about to push her aside, but instead he drew back his hand and slapped her very hard indeed on the face.

She burst into tears. I thought he was about to strike her again, and made as if to protest. He said nothing to me, but the look in his eyes dissuaded me from ever thinking such a thought again. I was unsure of my place here, uncertain of my status in relation to the stranger. He turned to the girl. I guessed she could have been scarcely older than myself.

'How many times do you stupid girls 'ave to be told that you never, never use these stairs? Are you entirely out of your heads that you do such a thing repeatedly? I shall speak to Sir David about this. What is your name?'

'Please, sir, I never...'

'I ask you for your name. If you won't give it me, then set your pieces and bits down here, and leave this house at once.'

She gave him her name, Rose Hood, and he let her go, her implements clutched hard to her like talismans of the job she might now lose. He watched her go with undisguised disdain.

'You must learn, Monsieur Simon,' he said to me, 'to treat — what you say? What you call them — *les classes inférieures* — you must treat every one of them with true contempt. If not, they will cheat you and betray you. Take great care not to let them win your affections while you are here. Above all, never pity them. Let them live their lives, as you live yours. Now, we are late.'

I said nothing in reply. I had already made up my mind that I hated this pompous windbag, whoever or whatever he might be. My dislike for him troubled me less, however, than the thought that the Trevelyans, of whom my mother had spoken so warmly in the past few weeks, must treat him as their friend and, most probably, their confidante.

He clearly knew his way round the corridors of Trevelyan Priors. With no idea of where I was being taken, I followed him down a long passage, then a short one, and another long one. Everywhere, the riches of the place impressed themselves on my imagination.

I had thought about the house often enough in the days before my arrival, but nothing I had imagined or my mother had said could have prepared me for the reality of the place. It wasn't just that everything here was grander, or on a more magnificent scale than at home. Trevelyan Priors had been conceived differently. It belonged to a different race, not wholly human, perhaps not human at all. I had expected better things, and more — but not this irremediable difference, this presentation of fine art or cabi-net-making or plasterwork as a barrier rather than an invitation or an adornment and no more.

My escort knocked gently on a door of inlaid mahogany, and

without further pause, pushed it open. He bade me precede him, and as I went inside, he came after me, softly closing the door behind him. I realised he had not told me his name.

The room was a small one, much smaller than I had anticipated, judging by the scale of everything else I had seen. It had been built to a human scale and preserved in the style of the eighteenth century, with Etruscan figures and silhouette portraits on walls of painted silk. By the window, on soft, gilded chairs, sat a man and a woman, both dressed in black.

The man I took to be Sir David Trevelyan, by reason of his age and appearance. The woman must, then, I thought, be Lady Marion; but she seemed many years younger than he. He appeared old to me, sixty or more, though this I guessed merely on the strength of his prematurely white hair and the many things my mother had told me of him.

He stood and, without being introduced, stretched out his hand to me.

'You must be young Simon. How pleased I am to meet you at last. I'm David Trevelyan. I hope you don't think it was bad-mannered of me not to attend your father's funeral. I had wanted so much to be there, but as I explained, I was indisposed. Marion was obliged to remain here to nurse me.'

'You mustn't worry about it at all, sir. Lots of people couldn't make it. You have trouble of your own, you can't be expected...'

At that moment, Marion also stood and reached out a small hand in a fingerless glove of white lace. I guessed her age — correctly, as I learned later — to be little more than forty. In fact, she was forty-three. Uncle David was, according to Mother, sixty-six, which meant there was a gap of twenty-three years between them. That seemed huge, almost unimaginable to me.

'I'm Marion,' she said. 'You must be tired after your journey.'

'Not really, ma'am. Just a little hungry, that's all.'

'We'll take care of that at once. I think tea's due to be served. Perhaps you'll join us.'

'Yes, indeed, ma'am.'

'Oh, goodness — what's all this "ma'aming"? Call me Aunt Marion. And you must call the elderly gentleman you see standing next to me Uncle David. Elderly because he has lived longer than you and I. But he is very young at heart, I do assure you.'

Her eyes twinkled as she said this, and she smiled at me, as though inviting me into a small conspiracy. I tried to smile back, but felt constrained by the awkwardness of the situation. For all that, I took to her immediately and resolved to spend as much time in her company as possible. It was the first time in my life that I'd been won over by a beautiful woman. I felt tongue-tied and flattered.

'I see you've already met our esteemed ally,' said Sir David, smiling towards the Frenchman, who bowed slightly.

'Well, we have met, sir — I mean, Uncle David — but I'm at a disadvantage since I don't know the gentleman's name.'

'But, how terribly inconvenient for you — and how very neglectful of Arsène. Perhaps I should do the honours.' My uncle gestured to me, mock-formally, so that I almost laughed out loud. 'Arsène, allow me to introduce Monsieur Simon Lysaght, my nephew by marriage, and my dear wife Marion's nephew by direct line of blood. Simon, this is Arsène-René Prosper Charles Marie Theuriet-Brunetière, the Marquis de Remiremont, Légionnaire d'Honneur, member of the Académie Française, of the Académie des Inscriptions et Belles-Lettres, of the...'

'Sir David, please, not to embarrass me so much in front of my young friend. He will think I am such a fogey as to claim all these decorations and titles. We are not, alas, in France. Here I am simply Arsène Theuriet, a guest of your gracious self.'

The marquis simpered and stepped backwards, as though seeking to diminish himself. But I caught his self-admiring gaze and the slight tilt of his head as he sought and captured his own reflection in a gilded mirror behind Marion's head.

'The marquis has been with us for over a year now,' said Marion, and I detected a slight note of tiredness in her voice. 'His estate in France was swept up in the war. At present, the Germans are using his very fine château in the Argonne as a hospital for their troops.'

'One hears such terrible stories,' the marquis added, a look of pain crossing his face. 'That atrocities have been committed upon my staff. That the building has been sacked entirely — *je le jure par le bon Dieu* — and its finest works of art taken away by the Boche.' He paused. 'But let's talk no more of me or my pretty things. We have a tired young man to entertain. I think you said it was time for tea, Marion.'

Not 'Lady Marion', I noticed; just plain 'Marion'.

'Just so,' she said, a little frostily, I thought. 'I'll ring for Wilkinson.'

She took a step to the fireplace, a stepped angle chimney on which blue Delftware jars and Chinese vases were arranged in tiers. A little lever was set into the wall beside it, and this she now twisted. Turning back to the room, her attention focused on me.

'But, of course, Simon, you have not yet set eyes on your cousins, Thomas and Alice. They will be at tea — I told Alice's governess to be sure she was there. Tom — we call him Tom, you know. We stand on few formalities in this house — Tom has lessons with Mr Fitzgerald. I so much hope you and he will become firm friends. You are almost exactly the same age, did you know that?'

I nodded. 'Yes, my mother said...'

'How kind of her to mention it. Tom is a sweet boy, you will find him very easy to get on with.'

At that moment, the door opened, and a tiny woman in white and black uniform announced that tea was being made ready in the Chinese drawing-room.

The room was on the same floor, about two corridors away. We formed a strange procession, all four of us dressed in mourning (though for what or for whom the marquis might be mourning, I could not guess), Lady Marion whispering to her husband, then looking back from time to time to fix her wide smile on me.

But I was not destined to have that tea after all. Just as we came within sight of the drawing-room, there was a sound of quick footsteps behind us. A very strange woman came hurrying up the corridor. I learned later that her name was Mrs Armitage, and that she was the Trevelyans' housekeeper. She was dressed, like everyone else above a certain level in that household, in black, with an enormous mob-cap on her head, dressed with pink silk ribbons and garnished with purple bows. She was not made for running, given that her girth almost matched her height, and gave her the impression of someone best suited to rolling.

'Sir David! Lady Marion!' she called out before ever reaching us. Her voice sounded hoarse and wheezy, and she was clearly agitated about something.

'Sir, you've got to come quickly. Something's happened, sir, something dreadful.'

'Calm yourself, Mrs Armitage. There's no need for this. What on earth can be the matter?'

Sir David was clearly prepared for anything, but I noticed Aunt Marion put a knuckle to her teeth as she anticipated the house-keeper's reply.

'There's been an accident, sir. A fall, sir. Dead, sir, that's the thing. Stone dead, sir. And alive five minutes ago, sir, same as you or I.'

'Oh, no!'

Marion's face went quite white, and I thought she was about to faint. Theuriet stepped up to her, taking her elbow with one hand and striking a pose of elaborate concern.

'It's none of the family, ma'am — no need to fret on that score. It's one of the scullery maids, Rose Hood, ma'am. She's fallen out of a bedroom window onto the back courtyard. It's a smashed skull, I reckon, sir. There was blood everywhere.'

'Yes, well, we'd be obliged if you didn't regale us with the details,' said Sir David. 'I'd better go down and see to the matter. Mrs Armitage, would you please telephone to Dr. Quilty and ask him to come at once?'

Mrs Armitage scurried away like a large ball on legs. I knew at once who the girl had been, I could see her face as though she stood before me. Her frightened eyes blinked as she looked at me. Suddenly, my mind went blank. I lost all trace of where I was. I could fell my knees buckling. And inside, deeper inside than I had ever gone before, something came out of the darkness, and for several moments I felt nothing but the most utter desolation, a vast, all-embracing loneliness mixed with fear.

'Are you all right, Simon?' Aunt Marion asked anxiously,

catching me as though I'd been about to topple.

I barely heard her voice. All my senses were focused on what I might see coming from the darkness, or — which seemed for some reason much worse — what I might hear.

'Simon, what's the matter?'

She spoke more loudly this time, and more sharply. It served to bring me out of whatever stupor I had fallen into.

'Aunt Marion? What happened?'

'I think you fainted, my dear. Are you all right? Here, sit down on this chair.'

I complied without a murmur. My legs still felt weak and on the verge of collapsing under me.

'But, of course,' Marion exclaimed. 'You've just had a tremendously long journey, and you haven't eaten in some time. And on top of that there has been this most unpleasant business. I think we should get you to your room and let you lie down, and I'll see the kitchen sends you up something to eat. It's a while yet until dinner's served.'

'Marion, dear,' my uncle broke in, 'would you mind very much taking Simon to his room, as you say? I'm afraid tea would be in bad taste. He must be anxious to see that his things have been unpacked and put away properly. No doubt you can help him do that, or ask one of the chambermaids.'

'Perhaps not just now, David. What with this… unfortunate business.'

He nodded. 'You're perfectly right, my dear. Most thoughtful of you. Doubtless we'll have a few days of sighs and tears. I'd better get down and see to all that. Arsène, perhaps you wouldn't mind accompanying me?'

The little Frenchman nodded and bowed very slightly. Then my uncle turned to me, bending down.

'Simon, dear boy — I hope you'll soon be feeling better. I'm dreadfully sorry this had to happen so soon after your arrival. I assure you, servants don't fall out of the windows here every day. Try to get some rest. We dine at eight prompt. I hope to see you again then.'

I wanted to tell him what had taken place, for I was sure the girl who had killed herself was the maid the marquis had slapped and threatened with dismissal. But when I looked past my uncle, I saw the marquis looking in my direction, his face very formal and cold, and all I could do was nod my head and agree to Sir David's proposals.

When they had gone, Marion smiled weakly at me. I thought she wanted to take me in her arms but felt constrained by the formalities of life in such a place, or by the freshness of our acquaintance, for she and I, strange as it may seem, had not met before that day.

She took me to my room, which was on the floor above.

The walls were hung with green silk damask, against which dozens of badly-framed mezzotints had been hung. An oar of more recent manufacture hung on one wall, together with a range of school photographs and tasselled rugby caps. I wasn't much of a sportsman myself, and I hoped these objects hadn't been put there to make me feel at home.

'Will you be comfortable here, do you think?' she asked.

My bags had already been placed on the floor, and most of my clothes unpacked and stowed in the wardrobe. I looked around the room like someone on a house-hunting expedition. Except that I had no choice in the matter.

'It's very fine,' I said. 'I'm sure I shall be just right.'

'This was your cousin James's room, Simon. I hope you don't mind that. David thought you might like it. Of course, James never spent much time in it after he left home. He worked in the City. Did you know that?'

I shook my head. Trevelyan family life was a closed book to me.

'Well, I'm sure David will explain all about that when he has time. You may want to make a career for yourself there as well. And in not very many years' time. Anyway, I'll leave you now,' she said. 'Try to get some rest, you've had a long day. I'll ask one of the servants to bring you a plate of sandwiches. Would that be enough? Sandwiches and ginger beer? Or perhaps you're already an ale-drinking man? No? I thought not.'

She smiled at her own pleasantry, and shut the door behind

her.

For a moment again, I formed the impression that she had wished to rumple my hair, or kiss me, but that she could not bring herself to do so.

I sat on the edge of the bed for a while, staring at my muddy boots. He had as good as killed her, I knew that. I'd seen him strike her, and seen that scared, violated look on her face. The law of cause and effect said that the marquis had sent her to her death. But there was nothing I could do or say. They'd have taken her body away by now, there'd be no chance of my identifying her, and I knew in any case that my word against his would weigh very light indeed.

And I had my mother to think of. I knew I could hardly start my new life here at Trevelyan Priors by issuing accusations against a man I had only met, a man who was evidently a favoured guest of my aunt and uncle. And, worse than all that, a man whose home had been stolen by the Boche, forcing him into exile from his own country.

I felt wretched. If I'd known Marion better, I think I would have spoken to her and told her what I'd seen. But even then, I reasoned, it would have led to very little. He'd only struck her after all, not pushed her.

I crossed to the window and looked out. The view that greeted me was bleak in the extreme. The structure of Trevelyan Priors was more complex than I had guessed. Much of the old priory had been left standing at the rear, and incorporated somehow into the house whose facade dominated the gardens from the front. One of the consequences of this arrangement was the creation of a high-walled courtyard at the back, onto which my window looked.

The grey walls of the priory seemed very old indeed. They were much eroded by the elements, so that their fabric seemed eaten away. I wondered if that portion of the house was still used, but the windows I could see gave no sign of habitation.

It was starting to grow dark outside. I looked down into the well of the courtyard. A dark shape was moving there. I strained to make it out and saw that it was a servant scrubbing hard on the flagstones. She did not look up, and slowly darkness swallowed her.

A knock on the door announced the arrival of my sandwiches and ginger beer. The young girl who brought them looked a little like the one I had seen earlier, and for a moment I wondered if it might not be her after all. She curtsied and set the tray down on a little table near the middle of the room. I watched her as she did so, and decided she was not the girl the marquis had insulted.

I noticed that she wore a pendant on her breast, shaped like a medal, with the word 'Sacrifice' inscribed above, and a gold-plated heart hanging from a ribbon. I had seen such pendants several times before. It meant she had a sweetheart at the front, risking his life for England. I almost asked her about him, but a sense of decorum held me back. She was very young, and quite pretty, I thought, and no doubt she was waiting day by day for him to return and marry her. And one day a telegram would arrive at his parents' house, and they would summon her, and send her back to Trevelyan Priors crushed and dreaming of death.

I settled down to eat, discovering that I was really quite ravenous. It had been a long journey, and now it was over I felt let down, hundreds of miles from home, without any sense yet of a second home to take its place. Suddenly, feelings of loneliness and abandonment swept over me, and my keen appetite left me in an instant.

Just then, I heard footsteps in the corridor outside. On this floor, there were only bare boards in the passages, and I'd already noticed that passing feet sounded louder. Suddenly, my door opened and a boy of my own age hurried in, slamming the door behind him.

He took one look at me, raised his hand to his temple, cried out 'Private Trevelyan Oh One Nine Three Seven Four Oh, reporting for duty. Sir!', grinned hugely, and then, seeing my plate heaped high with bacon and tomato sandwiches, made a run at them.

'God, I'm starving,' he said, grabbing a sandwich and ramming it into his mouth. For about half a minute, he continued to do so, until the entire sandwich had vanished. He then reached out a hand for another.

'You don't mind, do you?' he asked. I shook my head, rather feebly I thought. 'It's just that something went wrong with tea today. Alice and I were all set for a scrumptious feast on account of your turning up, next thing old Armitage says it's been cancelled. She looked a bit odd. Mother's keeping out of the way, father's disappeared, the toad ditto — so I thought I'd see if you were here. And here you are. Dashed good sandwiches, these, eh?'

He threw himself into a much-battered armchair, both hands bursting with bread and vegetables. A piece of bacon fell on the floor, which he kicked under another chair opposite.

'Ages since I was last in here. Almost forgotten it existed. This used to be old James's place. You all right about that, are you?'

And so Tom Trevelyan and I got to know one another, talking like this, without introductions or formalities, while chomping our way through sandwiches and gulping down ginger beer. My appetite recovered almost the moment I set eyes on him. He was a force of nature, and from that first moment he knew he could do with me whatever he wished.

Tom was taller than me by about three inches. He had close-cropped hair, a ruddy complexion, and hands that could crush a turnip. With my wire spectacles and cramped breathing, I felt a weedy thing in comparison. Tom gave no heed to that. He wanted us to be friends, he was desperate for an ally, and so within minutes we were friends, best friends, inseparable and age-old friends.

We talked of everything that afternoon, while the darkness deepened outside my window and the wind broke loose of its daytime restraints and took to howling about the house and its high towers.

'I wouldn't much want to be out on a boat tonight,' Tom said. We could hear the high waves crashing against the cliffs like shells exploding against a salient.

'The sea's full of rocks along this coast,' Tom declared. 'Wrecks too, there's plenty of them.'

'Were there ever smugglers down here in the old days?' I asked, hungry for adventure.

''Course there were. I'll show you one day when the weather improves. We'll go in the *Demelza* — that's my boat. I'll take you round the caves.'

Our conversation never flagged. Though I was tired, it never fell to me to keep the pace going. Tom did most of the talking, while I acted as his sounding-board. I don't mean he was indifferent to me — quite the opposite. But I didn't mind in the least that there was such an imbalance. In a way, I think I'd always wanted something very like it. I had a friend for the first time in my life, that was all that mattered.

We talked about the war, and the circumstances of my father's death, though I tried to get free of this latter subject as soon as possible. In return, he told me what he could about James's death. He'd embellished it a little, even I could see that; but the horror and mystery were still there, and I shivered, thinking of James and my father together in a strange place, where we could not reach them, not even with our prayers.

'His fiancée killed herself, you know,' he told me, half in a whisper. I looked at him, wondering if he'd heard about the death earlier that afternoon. 'Threw herself off Bedruthan cliffs the day she heard of it. Mother told her. About James, I mean. She went over to Arch Zawn herself. Beastly thing to have to do. They say the fiancée was stark naked when they found her.'

'Was she very beautiful?'

'I suppose so. She had a long neck, and she kept her hair tied up. I've heard some men like that. She had very white shoulders.'

'Did you see much of her?'

'She used to come up here every Sunday. I thought she was a bit pitiful.'

'She must have loved him a lot, all the same,' I said, in instinctive defence of this pale, swan-necked woman whom I'd never met.

'She fancied herself in love with him, that's for certain. All the women are like that now, if they've got someone at the Front. Look at the maids: more than half of them are wearing those stupid pendants so everybody knows what a big sacrifice they're making.'

I was a little shocked by his bluntness, which seemed a little unpatriotic to me. But this was quickly forgotten, since mention of the maids gave me a chance to introduce a subject already on my lips.

'Hasn't anyone told you about the maid?' I asked.

'What maid?'

'I don't know,' I said. 'At least, I can't remember her name. But I saw her. I'm sure it was her.'

'Her?'

'The maid who killed herself this afternoon. It's the reason we didn't have tea together.'

I told him all that had happened. For the first time, I did the talking. He was rapt, eager for every detail of the tragedy, frustrated that it had escaped him so narrowly. Something drew me on and on until I told him about the marquis and the cruel blow he had struck the girl.

'It doesn't surprise me,' said Tom, a look of satisfaction settling on his face.

'Why's that?'

'It's typical of the man. He treats everybody he meets like a bloody servant, as though he's some sort of superior being.'

'You don't like him, then?'

'Of course not. Do you? No, I can see not. He's a sort of snake, don't you think? A viper, something hideous like that. I call him The Toad. I've made good friends among some of the frogs in the back pond, and I wouldn't insult them by calling him one.'

'What is he? What's he doing here?'

'You'd have to ask my father. But I doubt you'd get a straight answer. You'll find the Old Man a bit stiff. He's been a lot worse since James copped it.'

'But how long has the marquis been here?'

'Seems like for ever. Must be about two years. Arrived as a house guest just before Christmas, and he's been here ever since. Shows no signs of leaving. He has a suite of rooms to himself at the front of the house.'

'And that's it?'

'He disappears every month or so. Says he goes up to London, but I'm not sure. He could go anywhere. Sometimes he stays away for days at a time.'

'Does he never have any visitors?'

'A few times, yes. French, I think. They never stay to dinner.'

I looked at the little clock that I'd put on my bedside table.

'Crumbs!' I said. 'I'm glad you mentioned dinner. We don't have much time.'

He looked at the clock and groaned.

'We're meant to dress. Have you got the proper togs?'

I nodded.

'Right,' he said, scrambling to his feet. 'We'll meet there, then.'

'I... I'm afraid I don't know the way to the dining room.'

'What a bother. Well, they're bound to send someone up. I expect they'll be here any minute. I'd better get a move on. There'll be hell to pay if I'm late or turn up in mufti.'

He was through the door and down the corridor before I could stop him. Disconsolately, I dug out my dinner things, not forgetting the mother-of pearl cuff-links my father had given me the previous Christmas. Everything was abominably crushed by having been shoved into the smaller of my suitcases, but I had neither the time nor the equipment to do anything about it.

I dressed as neatly as I could, and brushed my hair, which my mother had encouraged me to wear long. As I stood in front of the cheval glass, straightening my bow tie and waiting for someone to come knocking on the door, I could hear the wind run among the half-broken walls outside.

My little clock cranked out eight strokes, and still no one had arrived to show me down. I went to the door and looked out. To both left and right a dimly lit corridor ran away into deep shadows.

Tom had told me that Trevelyan Priors was too remote to enjoy the full benefits of either gas or electricity, so we had to make do with a combination of candles and oil lamps upstairs. A small generator had been installed in the cellar, however, in order that the main rooms — the kitchens, the library, dining room, billiards room, and the central drawing-room — could have some extra light in the evenings.

I closed the door behind me and headed uncertainly to the left. I reasoned that there was certain to be a flight of stairs sooner or later, and that they'd be sure to lead me to the ground floor. Once I got that far, I'd as likely as not bump into someone able to show me to the dining room. I was resigned to the fact that I'd be horribly late, and that I would in all likelihood have to endure Sir David's wrath, but at least I would be there to give some account of myself.

I must have taken a wrong turning, letting myself be drawn back into the maze of rooms that huddled together in the rear of the house. I found myself in another corridor, one that ended in a plain door.

Realizing that I could go no further, I doubled back along the corridor. Here, away from any windows, the silence was seamless. I almost wanted to hear the wind, however violent, merely to know that an outer world existed, that I had not become trapped in a winding place of half-dark corridors and locked doors. I thought of the face I had seen looking down on me as I arrived, and wondered who it had been. If they were still up there, I thought, they might be able to send me in the right direction. But I could find no way to get past the floor I was on.

It was then that I noticed that not every door was locked. One lay half open, and when I stepped near to it I noticed that a faint light came from within. I made to hurry on, pretending I had noticed nothing, not knowing who might be asleep or watchful behind that door. But as I passed, a voice spoke from inside, a man's voice, trembling a little.

'Who's there? Is someone there?'

I stopped in my tracks, not knowing what to do. He called out again, and still I had no idea who he might be. It was that tremble in the voice, that faint exhibition of anxiety that encouraged me to put out one hand and push the door open.

The only light came from an oil-lamp set on a bedside table. On the bed itself, tucked under white starched sheets, a man lay propped up against a mound of spotless pillows. He gestured to me with the fingers of his right hand, beckoning me inside.

'Don't close the door,' he said. 'I prefer it open. There's a seat next to me, you can have that.'

I thought at first that he was an old man, for the hair that lay against the stark white pillows was itself white. But I saw my mistake within seconds. The face that looked back at me was a young man's, and the voice, when he spoke again, was undeniably that of someone in his mid-twenties.

'Who the hell are you? You're obviously not a servant, but I've never set eyes on you before. Well?'

My throat was dry. I felt reluctant to answer at first, then it dawned on me who this must be.

'I'm... your cousin Simon,' I said. 'Simon Lysaght, that is. I... I mean, you must be William, mustn't you, sir?'

'Must I? Come over here and let me see you. I don't know if I've the least idea what you should look like. Did you say you were Lysaght's boy?'

I felt a horror of drawing too close to the bed. Close up, I could make out the shape of his body underneath the covers, and I saw with renewed horror that he had no legs, just stumps that terminated at the point where the knee should have been. I'd seen enough soldiers in my time, crippled, hobbling by on sticks, legless, armless, grossly disfigured. But they'd always been at a distance, and they'd laid no claims on me.

I swallowed hard and nodded.

'Speak up, boy, I won't chew your head off. Here, sit down on the chair. You may as well get yourself comfortable.'

I set on the edge of the chair, still frightened of this strange figure.

'Did you say you were Charles Lysaght's boy? Uncle Charles's offspring?'

I nodded, though I wasn't too sure that 'offspring' exactly suited me.

'Lord Almighty! What can you possibly be doing here? I think I last saw your father when I was about five. Are your parents here with you?'

I shook my head.

'My... No, sir, they're not. My mother's at home in York. I left there early this morning.'

'And your father?'

I bent my head, as though embarrassed to mention death in his presence. Then I realised that it would be no stranger.

'He's dead. He died at Goose Alley two months ago.'

There was silence, then he swore. I'd never heard a man swear like that before. And when it was done and he'd got it out of his system, he just looked at me, and I noticed there were tears in his eyes. I had to struggle not to give way myself.

'I'm sorry if I was abrupt,' he said. 'Sit up in the chair, make yourself comfortable. I'm afraid it's not great in here. Still, it was my room in the old days. Don't expect I'll see many others.'

He reached out a hand and we shook. There were scars on his fingers, and several on his face.

'What age are you, Simon?'

'Fifteen, sir.'

'Oh, bugger the "sir". I'm your big cousin, and very pleased to meet you. Which bunch was your father with?'

'Prince of Wales' Own West Yorkshire.'

'Good men. I heard they'd had heavy losses. They were just down the line from us at one point. Oh, I'm so sorry your father's dead. Poor man. I'd always wanted to meet him. Properly, I mean, man to man. I never understood why he stayed away from this place. You've no idea, have you?'

I shook my head.

'He never said. It wasn't something he ever talked about.'

'Well, my father isn't the easiest of men. Maybe they had some falling out. I expect it was that. You must have known about us, though. He didn't keep you in total ignorance, did he?'

'No, I knew about you. I always wanted to come down and get to know you. I just wish...'

'Well, whatever the reason, you are here. Did you say your mother was still in Yorkshire?'

I explained.

'So you'll be staying with us? I'm very pleased. You'll be company for young Tom. Father wanted him to go to boarding school, but after James and I joined up Mother put her foot down. No Rugby for Tom, thank God. To tell you the truth, I think he had a lucky escape. Beastly place. You'll be far better off with Conor Fitzgerald.'

'Fitzgerald?'

'Surely Mother's mentioned him to you. She brought him in not long ago as a tutor for the young thug. I expect he'll have you to instruct as well. You'll have to...'

Suddenly, he arched his back and began coughing in the most fiendish fashion. I had no idea what to do. Then I saw that he was struggling to right himself against the pillows, being unable to lever himself with his legs. I leaned over and pulled him upright with a great deal of difficulty. I've already said that I'm somewhat weak-bodied and find heavy exercise hard. William nodded several times at the table beside him, and I saw that a round tin bowl stood on it. This I brought beneath his chin, and as I did so, he heaved up a great wash of phlegm mixed with copious amounts of blood.

He sank back against the pillows, and I returned the bowl to its place, covering it with a white cloth left there for that purpose. I watched him strain to recover his breath, and during all that time he was as unaware of me as of a fly or a mouse. Slowly, his face regained its old colour and his breathing grew smooth once more. He looked at me sideways, and with an effort smiled his apologies.

'I'm sorry about that,' he said. 'I usually manage myself, but sometimes it gets the better of me. Thanks for helping out. Would you mind awfully...? Over there, on that shelf, you'll see a thing with a rubber ball on the end of it. You wouldn't mind fetching it over, would you?'

I found it at once and handed it to him. He put some sort of mask over his mouth and squeezed on the rubber ball.

'What was it?' I asked when he'd finished. 'Gas?'

He nodded, handing the instrument back to me.

'Chlorine,' he said. 'Couple of days before I got this.' He indicated his missing legs.

I got up again and returned the instrument to its shelf. As I did so, there was a knock on the door, and next moment my Aunt Marion stepped into the room.

'William,' she said, 'I'm sorry to disturb you, bu...'

Just then she caught sight of me.

'Simon! Good heavens, I've been looking for you everywhere. Where on earth have you been? How did you get here?'

I struggled to answer, but William got in first.

'Oh, Lord. You don't mean to say young Simmy here was expected at dinner? Of course he was. How stupid of me not to have noticed what he was wearing, or the time. Marion, dear, he's been a staunch help in time of need.'

She caught his eye glancing towards the basin, and I noticed her cheeks lose their colour.

'Tell Father it's entirely my fault,' William continued. 'I held on to this unfortunate lad for the most selfish reasons. You may have him back now, but see he comes here for regular chats. I'm starved of intelligent conversation here, Simon. You must promise to pay me frequent visits.'

I promised, and crossed to the bed to shake his hand. Aunt Marion went to the door, then stepped into the corridor, as though impatient for us to be on our way. I was about to follow her when William beckoned me back to his bedside.

'Simon,' he hissed, his voice low and swift, his tone conspiratorial. 'Whatever you do, old boy, don't wander round this place after dark. Not on this floor, at any rate, and certainly not the floor above. Keep the door of your room locked, and stay inside.'

'But, why should I...?'

'You must swear,' he said. ' I mean it. On my blood.'

It was a terrible oath. I shivered, hearing it. He looked very hard and earnestly at me, and I swore, without really understanding what it was I had agreed to.

'Hurry along now,' he said. 'You can't keep your Aunt Marion waiting.'

It was only then I realised that he himself had addressed her as 'Marion', not 'Mother'. Then I remembered that William was Marion's stepson.

Marion popped her head round the door.

'What on earth is keeping you, Simon?' she said impatiently.

'I'm just coming,' I said, and stepped out into the corridor.

Dinner went off rather tensely. Sir David, though pressed by Marion to consider that I had been with his invalid son, and that they had been remiss in not sending a servant to guide me down, nevertheless insisted that this must be the last time I appeared at the evening meal so much as one minute late.

'I insist on punctuality in all things, Mr Lysaght. You must understand that if you are to live here. I do not tolerate the impertinence of someone turning up at any time they choose. Anyone here will tell you that.'

Aunt Marion tried to pacify him, saying it had not been my fault, and that it was only proper to be indulgent to a house guest on his first day. He subsided into a silence that set the tone for the rest of the evening. I developed a great fear of him during that meal, and I wonder how long I will be able to stand this dangerous world to which an indifferent fate had brought me.

A Letter from Marion Trevelyan to Harriet Lysaght

Mrs Harriet Lysaght
Minster Lodgings
Gilleygate
York

My Dearest Harriet,

I hope you will forgive me if I presume an intimacy which you may consider an imposition, and which neither kinship nor mutual grief may render entirely acceptable. However, now that your son — whom I have quickly come to regard as a dear nephew and a most dutiful ward — has taken up residence here, I cannot but be certain that his presence will serve to sew up whatever breach there may have been between our houses until now. And I do in some measure hope that you and I may come to regard one another as the sisters we have been all along.

Simon will, I am quite sure, have written to you by now, in order to inform you of his safe arrival and his rapid application to his studies under the supervision of Mr Fitzgerald. Fitzgerald is a good man, an MA of Trinity College, Dublin — but not, I assure you, a rebel in any sense. His family are respectable in an Irish way, and own property in a county called Wicklow, but the last few years have seen them come down in the world. In case you may be worried that young Simon is being taught by someone who has not gone to the Front, let me reassure you that our Mr Fitzgerald is not that sort of man.

He served briefly near Ypres last year and was gassed. They declared him unfit for combat and sent him back to this country, where he has been obliged to remain. I've told Simon of this, but not Tom, for fear he may glorify it out of all proportions, as he is wont to do.

We took him on in order to give him a chance in life, and in the hope that he may in due course, after the boys have grown and the war has ended, regain a proper position as a teacher in one of our public schools: so many teachers — as you know only too well, my dear, — have been killed or disabled in the fighting, and good schools will surely be in need of men like Fitzgerald.

Well, I shan't dwell on Mr Fitzgerald or his Irish ways. Perhaps Simon has told you something of the rest of our household. You must not think because we occupy such a splendid house and have so many acres at our disposal, that we are at all grand. A little formal, perhaps, and a little set in our ways, but nothing that should cause problems for your son.

He has already made firm friends with my boy, Tom. The two boys are, as I think you know, almost of an age, with Tom the elder by some two months only. Naturally, they find much in common, and when they are not at lessons with Mr Fitzgerald, I see them exploring the house together or, if the weather is fine, embarking on all sorts of mad escapades in the gardens and woods. We are fortunate here in Trevelyan Priors to have some of the finest gardens in England — something I think I can say without blushing or fear of refutation. Certainly, they are next to perfect as a playground for two healthy young men.

If I may say so, I think young Simon's health shows visible signs of improvement since he has been with us. The air seems to suit him most wonderfully — that, I think, and having so much pleasant company about him.

He displays quite another side of his personality when he is with my youngest, little Alice. Alice, as I'm sure you know, is ten, and already quite a beauty. For all that, she has rather more brains than anything, and a pensive temperament to go along with them. Where she got her brains from, I'm at a loss to say, for neither David nor I are at all clever, nor can I think of anyone on either side of the family — except, of course, for your poor departed Charles.

I don't suppose any of us — widows, mothers, sisters — who have lost dear ones in this terrible war will ever come to terms with our loss. Of course, your suffering must be so much greater than mine, for you have sacrificed a darling husband, whereas I have lost only a stepson. For all that, I was deeply fond of James, and would give anything to have him back.

My one consolation is his poor brother William, who is fated to spend the rest of his days here, shut up in his bedroom. The doctor has made some suggestions about lodging him downstairs, so he can make use of a chair and get outside into the garden. We mean to see to that once he is a little more himself and feels strong enough to contemplate the move. I visit him regularly in an effort to relieve as best I may the dreadful sufferings he endures. Under instruction, I am become the handiest little nurse you can imagine. I administer his morphia as necessary, I change his dressings — which is a most unpleasant task, I assure you — and I chat with him to keep his spirits up.

He never had a sweetheart as did James — or, if he did, she must have been the darkest secret of all time. That saddens me, for a true and faithful companion might have proved his best cicerone through the valley of pain and despair he daily walks.

Your boy Simon has become a firm favourite of William's. Simon found his way to his room on his first night here, as though some force had guided him there. He goes there now at least once a day, though I chide him for passing his time indoors when he might be out walking. Of course, I am privately pleased, since the days are very long for poor William, and very dull. He was never a reader, which makes it hard for him to pass the time well. Days on end he'll lie in bed just staring through the window at the sky. The most he sees are clouds in the distance, and seabirds coming in to pass some time ashore. Perhaps it will be best to have him downstairs after all. Not only that, but he needlessly distresses himself, fancying strange noises above his head, where no one lives. The doctor says his ears must have been deranged by the heavy shelling he was so often subjected to. But nothing either Dr Quilty or I can say will disabuse him of his notion that something is walking through the attics. He'll recover when he's downstairs, I'm sure.

It is strange to think where we might all be without this war. To think how many would still be alive who are even now interred in some nameless field in Flanders. Your husband would be with you today, teaching at St. Peter's and writing his books. James would still be alive, and perhaps married to Miss Fitzallan, perhaps they might even have a child by now, who knows? And poor William, poor, poor William might again have the use of his legs and go running across the lawns and down the long paths of our gardens to the sea's edge.

But it is no use dreaming. If the war has brought us dreadful grief, it has also brought hidden blessings, of which we must all be conscious. It has brought young Simon here to live, and it has given me a chance to write to you after all these years of silence.

My dear Harriet, there is something I would wish you to reconsider. You know well enough what it is, and I know that your first reaction will be to turn my suggestion down. Nevertheless, I mean to persist until you weaken, however long it may take. My dear sister — for I do consider you my sister now — don't you think it would be best for everyone if you were to come here to live as well? I know that Simon would be overjoyed to have you here, and to see his little sister again. For our part, we can truthfully say that whatever was in the past has been consigned to oblivion, and that nothing would give us greater pleasure than to welcome you here.

If you have reason still to hesitate, then at least consider making a short visit. It will give you a chance to meet us all, to see how Simon is situated, and to make a tour of the house and gardens. The latter are truly beautiful in spring, which is not so very far away. Perhaps a date towards the end of March would suit — but rest assured that, whenever you choose, you shall be made to feel heartily welcome.

If you come, you will find our Reverend Bains a most incomparable man. His sermons give me heart to struggle on, and I believe a talk or two with him would well settle your mind that is, I know, so troubled after your dreadful loss. You must also meet Dr. Quilty, who is the new man at Porth Buryan. There is talk of his being a homoeopath, whatever that may be; but in his treatment of William he has been nothing but punctilious. He has a kind voice, soft hands, and charming manner — what more could one ask for in a physician?

Simon sends you his love, and asks me to remind you that he left his galoshes behind (though I shouldn't worry, we have plenty here). David asks me to convey to you his very highest regards. For my own part, I wish you, dear sister, sweet dreams, peaceful awakenings, and an untroubled mind throughout the day.

Your devoted sister-in-law,

Marion Trevelyan

From the Ongoing Account in the hand of Simon Lysaght, dated 5 February 1917.

Tom is awfully rude about his father, whom he calls the 'old f—t' and 'Black Davey'. And I have to admit that my uncle is a dry old stick. He looks older than he is — he was some five years older than my father — and he behaves as though he's ninety. I don't know how Marion ever came to marry him, or how she goes on putting up with him after all these years.

I asked Tom about William and who his real mother had been. She was, of course, James's mother as well. Tom said she had been called Lady Alicia, and died twenty-odd years ago. She was a Price-Devereux or something, which I am given to understand meant a great deal, and she brought a vast fortune to Sir David when she married him.

I'm still not really sure what it is Sir David does. Of course, because of his own inheritance and what Lady Alicia brought, he has bags of money, so I suppose he doesn't actually have to work or anything. But I thought it must get terribly boring just sitting round in a place like this waiting to get old and die. He spends a lot of time in the library, and when he's in there, nobody else is allowed in, with the exception of the marquis, which is a fearful nuisance. Mr Fitzgerald, who often likes to go there in order to check things, or to prepare materials for our lessons, always has to ask permission, which must make him mad at times.

There are lots of rules and regulations here, and it is all I can do at times to keep up with all of them. Punctuality at meal-times is one of them, of course. No running on the stairs, that's another. No singing outside the music room. No dogs upstairs, no red wallpaper (a particular aversion of Sir David's), no curtains to be closed until one hour after sunset. There are rules about gates and locks and windows, about the winding of clocks, about grooms and horses and dogs.

We are not expected to attend church on Sundays — though the servants attend the parish church at Zelah. It's confusing, and every time you settle down, thinking you've got the hang of it, another rule crops up where you'd least have expected it.

'I imagine it's what you have to put up with to live in a house this size,' I said to Tom about a week after my arrival.

'Nonsense,' he said, ' there's nothing wrong with the house; it's my blessed father, that's all. When I come into my inheritance, I'll make quite a few changes round here. You'll see.'

'But you won't... You won't be given the house, will you?'

'Why shouldn't I be?'

'But I thought...' I was terribly unsure about these matters. 'I thought the house would pass to William. As the eldest son.'

'Oh, piffle. Father's never going to leave the estate and all the rest to a man without legs, a man who can't have children. William can have what he likes, but the house is mine, and the gardens, and the rest of the estate.'

'You mean there's more to the estate than just the gardens?'

He laughed at me openly for the greatest booby he'd ever seen.

'You'll see it all in due course, Lysaght. I'll show you the lot. We own practically everything round here. All the houses in Porthmullion, all the boats. Every fish that's caught out at sea, every crab, every lobster — a bit of that comes back to us. That's why it has to be mine, you see. If it goes to William and he doesn't have an heir, then anything could happen. Do you see?'

I nodded and said no more. But I've thought often since then of my cousin and his inheritance, and the changes he will make when he comes into his own.

It was that day or the next that the marquis made an appearance in the schoolroom, where Tom and I were doing our prep. He had been sent to ask if I would mind accompanying him to Sir David. Tom glanced at me, raising his eyebrows and squeezing his lips together. Summonses to his father's presence were, evidently, matter for comment.

My uncle was waiting for me in the library, his back to the elaborate Rysbrack chimney-piece, his hands behind his back, a perfect caricature of a country gentleman. The marquis smirked his way out, leaving Uncle David and myself alone. I was visibly nervous, I think, given what had happened that first night at dinner, and I feared a reprimand or worse. Like every schoolboy, I was frantically wracking my brains for some clue as to what petty rule I might have violated.

'Sit down, boy,' he rattled at me, like a staff officer faced with a new recruit whose very presence is a puzzle. He indicated a low seat a good six feet away from him, forcing me to look upwards to catch his gaze. 'And do try not to look like a sheep. You're old enough by now to know perfectly well how to put a face on things. Or did they teach you nothing at that school of yours? No, I don't suppose they did. Well, just remember that there are plenty of lads not much older than you out there in France being slaughtered at this moment. I daresay they know how to handle themselves.'

I was tempted to say that if they had real guts they'd hardly let themselves be slaughtered quite so passively, but I held it back, having a good idea what such a response might spark off.

'I'll put it all down to your provincial upbringing. I don't wish to suggest for one moment that your parents did anything but confer on you the most proper attention, within their means. But I daresay it's wrong to expect more from a schoolmaster's son, even if he has the right blood.'

I could not suppress the desperate urge I had to leap to my father's defence.

'I'd as soon you didn't speak ill of my father,' I protested. 'He did all in his power to give me a good upbringing. And he gave his life for King and country as willingly as the next man. As willingly as my cousin James. Or William, if it had come to it.'

He looked down at me with an expression I was at a loss to fathom.

'I daresay,' he said. 'But if I may add, you haven't turned out to be much of a specimen, have you? You're weak and spindly — if you were a dog, I'd have you shot. You barely know how to hold a knife and fork, you can't ride, you can't shoot, and you don't know a baronet from a duke. I have to say, it's not what I expect to find in a Trevelyan.'

'But I'm not a Trevelyan,' I argued, not entirely sure of my ground. 'My name is Lysaght.'

'My dear boy, you are such a simpleton. Surely you don't really think your father's name is the whole story. Whatever his reasons for choosing Lysaght, he started life as I did, a Trevelyan. Lysaght is merely an Irish branch of the family, to which our mother belonged. That's why I brought you here. I wanted to tell you that you are to regard yourself as if you were my own son. I intend to speak to your mother about it. I shall recommend to her that it will be in your very best interest if Marion and I were to become your legal guardians. Not stepmother and stepfather exactly, but in loco parentis, shall we say?'

I was speechless. Coming so quickly on the heels of my arrival at my uncle's house, this intimation of some deeper claim on my identity made me feel exposed, though to what I could not have said.

'Simon, I regret to have to tell you this, but the fact is that your father left very little money to you or your mother. Your mother has the house in York and a small annuity. You will inherit a piffling sum on coming of age, which is quite six years ahead. A matter of one or two thousand pounds, no more.'

'But I'll be working by then, I can...'

'No, listen to me. I have lost one son entirely to this war, and another has been so badly afflicted that he will never marry now or have a family. Tom will carry on my line, of course, I cannot doubt that. But I do not feel safe. If something were to happen to him, or should he marry a woman incapable of having children... You are my brother's boy, and you have a right to inherit some of the Trevelyan fortune and to carry on the name. I intend to alter my will so that you will become one of my heirs. And I shall ask my solicitors to make provision for you to come into a substantial sum when you reach the age of twenty-five. Do you have any objection to that?'

I didn't know what to say. I just looked up at him. He seemed grotesque to me, towering above my head and throwing down promises of lineage and inheritance.

'My mother and I... It was never our idea to ask for money. You offered me a place to live and a good education. That's all I ever wanted from you.'

'You're much too young to decide such things for yourself. I shall speak with your mother when she visits, and I'm sure she will talk to you directly about it all. Now, I think it's time you got back to your studies. Don't say anything about this to Tom. I don't want him to know just yet. His mother and I shall speak with him, explain everything to him in detail. But not quite yet. I trust you will be discreet.'

'Yes... yes, sir,' I stumbled, nodding briskly. I just wanted to be out of there.

And that was that. He dismissed me with a simple gesture, and I ran flustered from the library, closing the door tightly behind me. As I did so, I thought I caught sight, ever so faintly, of a door closing opposite. I almost fancied I saw the marquis disappear behind it just before it closed.

As promised, I said nothing about my conversation with Sir David to anyone, not even Tom. I was tempted to mention it in the letters I wrote almost daily to my mother, but each time something brought me up hard. Ever since my father's death, I have sensed that my life is no longer my own. It is more than simply being young in a society where youth has few privileges. After all, as Sir David said, young men almost my age are stumbling through heavy machine-gun fire, as if choosing a destiny.

My destiny had suddenly been thrown into hands I scarcely recognised. With the stroke of a pen, I could become another man's son. Perhaps my mother could, with a second stroke, be made my aunt or written out of my life entirely. How could I raise my fears with her, when she had acted solely for my interest, as she understood it? I knew that the prospect of a large inheritance would sway her, not because she was mercenary — for I knew her to be quite impervious to the lure of money — but because she wanted me to survive and flourish in a world that had become quite pitiless to its young men.

The Shot Tower

In the first weeks after my arrival, when I was wrestling with problems like this, Tom took me under his wing. At every available opportunity, he would arrange an expedition, now bicycling down to Porthmullion, the little harbour about a mile away, now exploring the vast expanse of the gardens, now marching me along corridors and up and down stairs in the house itself. And one day about two weeks ago, we went together through the gardens and all the way down to the Shot Tower.

I'd heard the tower mentioned several times, but it had never been clear to me what it was. Once or twice, passing through the gardens with Tom, I'd seen it rise up over the trees, a good eighty feet high, a narrow tower of brick that might easily have passed for a factory chimney in another part of the country. In Cornwall, it might have been taken for a tin mine chimney grown beyond all proportion.

'That's the Shot Tower,' Tom had said the first time I set eyes on it. 'We'll pop along some day to see how it's going.'

'What's it doing there?' I asked. 'It seems out of place.'

'Our grandfather Joshua had it built in 1858. It's been going ever since. They say it's the only one in the county. Did they have any where you come from?'

'Not that I know of. I could ask my mother.'

'Oh, it's not a women's thing.'

'What is it then? What's it for?'

He laughed and ran off, leaving me to hurry after him as best I could.

It was a few days afterwards that he decided the time had come for me to visit the tower. He could be a little imperious at times, or perhaps simply proprietorial. And since I knew so little and could never quite find my depth in anything, I found it easiest to acquiesce in his attempts to guide my life.

We made our way to the tower past the lower lake, then up through the Italian Garden and onto a path that skirted the cliff for a bit, before turning back inland to the tower.

If the tower had looked imposing from a distance, close up it seemed out of all proportion to the world it belonged to. It soared out of the ground, going up and up as though intent on piercing the sky.

It was a hushed, amber-coloured day. A faint gauze had attached itself to the sun. There was no wind, yet it was bitterly cold. Accustomed to more northerly expectations, I thought of snow, and for a moment I could see the gardens draped in white.

'What do we do?' I asked. I noticed that there was a little door in the side of the structure, bearing the message: 'Danger. Keep Out!' The warning had been painted in red against a white background, but the passage of who could say how many years had rendered the lettering faint and the card it was written on cracked and thin. Perhaps the admonition no longer applied. I saw moss on the bricks, and weeds higher up. Perhaps the shot tower was derelict.

'Can we go inside?' I asked, gesturing to the notice.

'Depends on what old Matthew's up to,' said Tom. 'He doesn't really like boys getting in the way.'

'In the way of what?'

'Don't you know anything? Making shot, of course. That's all old Matthew does from morning to night. It's what a shot tower's for.'

'Just one man?'

'Sometimes there's two, one up and one down, but Job Carker — that's old Matthew's assistant — likes the taste of liquor too much to be altogether reliable. When he's not here, old Matthew handles both ends of the operation himself.'

Saying that, he took hold of the handle and pulled the door towards him.

I had expected some sort of noise, perhaps a hum of machinery or a rattle of moving belts — something that would betray the presence of productive labour, the 'making shot' to which Tom had just referred.

Instead, the door opened on to silence. Not mere silence, for this had a presence in it, like the silence in a church that you know is vibrant with holiness or some such thing. This was like opening a church door and finding both less and more inside than you'd bargained for.

I caught my breath as my eyes, drawn by the light that streamed into the tower from high above, lifted upwards, scraping along the bare brick walls, drawn remorselessly to the uppermost reaches of the great edifice.

I saw two details at once. A wooden staircase, green-painted and flaking, ran its spindly way steeply up from the bottom along the inner wall. It came to a halt just beneath what appeared to be a wide platform, probably also wooden, that must have been the floor to some sort of chamber above, except that it had a hole of some sort in the centre, through which the light was streaming. It was fixed to the walls around it by heavy struts.

It was the light I noticed next. It was not a single stream, but hundreds of separate beams, as though it was falling through a network of leaves and branches. Even where the separate beams coalesced, the light did not altogether lose its sense of fragmentation, but rather seemed to ripple, as though something moved in it or passed through it.

Apart from this, a little grey light crept through the few glazed windows that had been set lower down the shaft of the tower.

Most of the floor at the bottom was taken up with a large circular bath or basin filled with what I took to be plain water. There were no pipes or hoses attached to this basin, yet as I watched, the surface of the water seemed to be disturbed. I looked hard, but could not see what was shaking it.

Tom cupped his hands round his mouth and shouted up towards the high platform.

'Matthew!' he shouted. 'Are you up there?'

He shouted several times, then I noticed a tiny change in the silence, as though it had acquired a new depth. A tiny figure appeared in the opening that connected the platform to the stairs, and started the slow spiral descent to the bottom. When he got about half way, he paused and called down. The tall space of the tower played tricks with his voice, thinning it and making it echo against the walls. We heard enough to know that he was asking us up, and that he wanted us to carry something for him.

On the other side of the basin, against the wall lay some sacks and several demijohns. Tom, who had done this before and knew what was expected, told me to fish in one of the sacks and to take out one of the packets it contained. I did as he said, but almost dropped the parcel, which was ten times as heavy as it had looked.

'Solid lead,' said Tom, laughing at my discomfiture. 'I'll take this.'

He picked up a demijohn, and I could see he was struggling with it.

'What's that?'

'Arsenic.'

He laughed and pointed to a smaller packet of lead. It wasn't light, but I was able to carry it.

We struggled up the winding stairs as best we could, hauling our loads up with us and wondering how old Matthew managed to make this journey possibly a few times a day. He had gone back up to his crow's nest above, and we could hear the sound of him moving about up there as we climbed.

The staircase was as narrow as it could be fashioned, and very steep. The wall pressing in from my left side seemed almost to want to push me over the flimsy balustrade and down to the floor below. I had to use both hands to carry the slab of lead, and the constant twisting and turning made me fear I was about to un balance any moment.

We made it in the end, and I found myself stepping directly from the top of the stairs into a strange, circular room. I'd scarcely entered it when a little man dressed entirely in black came up to me and wrenched the lead from my hands. He carried it a short way and dropped it on a bench. He was a hunchback, stooped by his deformity into what seemed like a defensive posture. Yet he moved as nimbly as Tom or myself, and walked on the bent floor of his little chamber with the confidence of a high-wire walker in a canvas tent.

Tom handed over his demijohn, puffing a little from his exertions.

'This is my cousin Simon,' he announced. 'Simon, this is Matthew Oram.'

The old man and I shook hands. I guessed him to be about eighty, but Tom told me later that he could not be much older than his father.

My eyes strayed round the little room in which we stood, taking in a host of small details. There was a little chair whose back had been fashioned to fit Matthew's deformity. Next to it stood a table on which he kept his lunch, and on it a primus stove on which he boiled water for his tea. A rope ran through a square hole about two feet by two, and I remembered having seen the bottom end of some sort of hoist downstairs.

Above our heads, a circle of unglazed windows ran round the tower. Up here, there was a stiff breeze, and I shivered, thinking how high we were. Matthew noticed my involuntary movement and capered over to me.

'Higher here even than the big house, eh? You can see everything from up here, you know — even the house. I see everything that goes on. Here, you take a look, see what you can see.'

'I don't think...'

The wind frightened me. It seemed almost to rock the tower. I felt a little seasick.

Matthew brought a set of steps and set them just underneath one of the windows.

'Don't worry,' he said, 'it's always windy up here. Never mind what old wind gets up to, you've got your feet firmly on the ground, 'aven't you?'

I wasn't so sure, but I wasn't going to say so in front of Tom and old Matthew. I climbed the steps a little unsteadily, and got my face above the window ledge. The wind blew straight at me, and I closed my eyes at first, until I was sure of my footing. Then I opened them.

I caught my breath. I had never seen the world like this before, never guessed that it could be seen in this way. The window I was looking through gave onto the sea. At first, there was only sea and sky, white waves travelling fast towards the shore, seabirds dancing in currents of warm air. Then I changed my position and looked down to see mile after mile of coastline in either direction, and Porthmullion tucked among great cliffs, and great woods to the north, and little narrow roads carving an imperilled existence out of the countryside. I thought I could climb into the window and throw myself out to land intact on top of the cliffs immediately below. Then I took another look and felt giddy, and had to step down.

'Takes getting used to,' murmured old Matthew. 'You gets the hang of it in the end.'

Tom stepped up after me and looked out, his head as far through the opening as he dared, and he let out a great shout that was carried away by the mounting wind.

Old Matthew looked admiringly at him, then glanced at me.

'Simon's my cousin,' repeated Tom, who wanted to get his message across. 'He used to live up north, but now he's at the house with the rest of us.'

Old Matthew did not take his eyes from me.

'Your father was shot, was he? Is that what brought you here?'

'How... how did you guess that?'

'No guessing, sir, just knowing. Old Matthew knows more than they gives him credit for. Ask old Matthew if there's anything you ever want to know.'

'Don't believe a word of it,' Tom sniffed. He'd acquired some of his father's mannerisms. He was not gentle. 'He's as ignorant as the next peasant. Aren't you, Matthew?'

'Daresay I am, sir, daresay I am. Now, sir,' he went on, looking at me once more, 'your cousin says you want to see a shot tower at work. Have you never seen one before? I hear there are plenty up north.'

'Not where I lived. I'd never even heard of one till I came here.'

'That's as may be. Has Master Tom told you what it is we make here?'

'He said you make shot. I suppose that's birdshot and the other sort you use for fishing.'

He shook his head.

'Used to,' he mumbled, 'used to. Mostly we made number nine shot. Number nine's the lad for pigeons and that sort. Tiny, but takes 'em down a treat. Nowadays we just makes number one shot. Sounds smaller, but he's not. A cartridge full of number one can kill a man. Blow his head off. It's what we makes him for, to kill men. A bullet's more accurate, but at close range shot is deadlier.'

'Is your shot used in France?' I asked.

'Course he is. A shotgun's a friend in the trenches. A soldier sleeps with him beside him, like he might sleep with his wife or a French woman of bad reputation.'

I blushed, knowing next to nothing of such matters. He saw me and smiled to himself, but said nothing more of the kind.

'Over here,' he said, drawing me to the large zinc sieve that filled the centre of the floor. I felt uneasy approaching it, sensing that the floor might give way and send me dropping to the ground below.

'This is what we call the shot holes,' he said. 'These are number one holes, for making number one shot. What we do is melt the lead down over here in the melting tray.' He indicated a blackened tray that stood on a tripod over another primus.

'We have a batch of lead,' he said, 'from old East Wheal Rose mine over by St Newlyn. They closed down 'bout thirty year back, 'long all the other mines. But we kept enough to be getting by.'

He ran one hand along the packet I'd brought up and nodded to himself.

'Once lead is melted down we adds some arsenic and mixes him about a bit, all the while keeping him hot. When he's fit and ready, we pours him across the shot holes.'

He straightened himself and walked across to the melting tray. In his monkey-like movements he appalled me. He might have been a magician or a witch-doctor. A ray of sunlight added a bronze tinge suddenly to his features. His eyes were wide and sparkling, and might have entranced me had I looked any deeper into them.

Back at the tray, he turned the blue flame up full, and before long the lead was bubbling like toffee, liquid and dangerously hot. He fetched arsenic tincture in a small glass that he'd filled from a fractured demijohn, and added it to the molten lead.

Using thick gloves, he carried this mixture from the stove and poured it across the zinc sieve. The metallic liquid pooled out suddenly, then tightened all across its surface, and for a moment it lay perfectly still, stretching towards its limits. Then it quivered as the molten liquid started to fall through the fine holes.

'Hurry,' said Old Matthew. 'Both of you, now. To the stairs, about half way.'

We ran out and down the staircase as fast as our legs and the narrow spiralling would allow, then stopped to watch the molten lead come streaming through the holes and embark on its long descent. And as it came towards us, we saw it pass from spirit to flesh. At least, that is how I pictured it. It was a grey shimmering that rushed past us, as though impatient to take on a more solid form. I took a boy's fancy that the souls of those who had died in the trenches were hovering just up there, each one ready to take on the shape of a deadly leaden sphere. I saw nothing in the war but revenge, and in the strange transformation of liquid into perfect spheres I could see nothing but German death.

Throughout those days, there grew in me a sense of hatred for 'the enemy'. Part of me, influenced by my mother and, to some extent, my father, wanted the war to end, and to end quickly, for the longer it went on, the more of our lads would be maimed or killed at the front. Another part, the part that spoke with Tom and visited William every day, wanted nothing of the sort. The longer the war went on, this part of me reasoned, the greater my chances of joining up and heading overseas to avenge the wrongs done to my nearest and dearest, to my father and James and William, to James's fiancée, whose name and face remained for me phantoms slightly out of reach.

I don't suppose I am very different to a battalion of boys my age up and down the country. But we feel it more keenly, Tom and I, perhaps on account of being cut off from that invisible battalion and left to our own devices.

When I was not studying or out with Tom, I would make an effort to visit my bed-bound cousin William, and, as far as I could, to entertain him. It caused me incalculable anguish to think of him trapped so miserably in that small, airless bedroom, with no one to talk to for most of the day, and no real recreation other than the constant whirl of his own thoughts.

I was once struck down with chickenpox, and was, as a result, forced to spend weeks in bed. My memory of the misery of those days served to reinforce my conviction that William needed to be distracted from his condition. There are things we cannot expect to understand at fifteen, and so we walk quite without intending into places we should never have entered.

William did not readily lend himself to distraction. For a start, he would neither read nor be read to, and he listened to the wireless very seldom. Sometimes, if he was in a particularly dark mood, I would spend an hour or more with him, neither of us speaking a word. I would bring a book up with me, or a magazine, and read to myself; or I'd go to the window and stare out into the dark courtyard below.

Of course, he was not always so vexed or turned in on himself. We played games — dominoes, draughts, or chess most of the time — and he taught me to play cards. That relaxed him more than anything. We played Bézique, Baccarat, Two-player Pinochle, Beggar My Neighbour, and something called Trumps — all the two-player games we could think of. We used a Belgian pack William had picked up in Amiens from a refugee: it showed General Haig as the Ace of Spades, and other heroes of the war as the other court cards. We played for matchsticks or pennies; but there were times I could see he was used to something else, to games played for high stakes. He told me some soldiers became obsessed with gambling. It was understandable: they were risking their lives every day, they knew there was nothing but luck to award them life or death.

William is my best source of information about the family. Sir David is too remote and forbidding for me even to think about asking; Marion is more indulgent, but she always seems to steer clear of the real issues; and Tom, as often as not, seems to know no more than I do.

The starting-point for everything is James. William's thoughts are fixed on him in an almost unhealthy fashion. Marion, who knows I spend many hours with him, urges me to follow her example in saying nothing about James on those occasions, and in fending off any enquiries that might take us onto difficult ground.

'He is still tormented by what he saw in the trenches,' she said. 'He and James were together almost to the last. They shared the same dugouts at the front, they occupied the same billets in the rear, they drank at the same estaminets when on leave. They were quite inseparable. That means that almost any memory of the war brings James back to mind, and thinking about James just makes him morbid and depressed. Try to make him think of other things, dear. Happy things. Things to lift his spirits. Do you know much about hunting? William was awfully fond of the hunt. He had a splendid cob called Alexander. Why not get him to tell you his hunting stories?'

I tried, but it was no use. He'd lost all interest in horses, hounds, or foxes. Alexander passed his days in the stables, taken out for exercise by one of the grooms. As William said, what earthly good was a horse to him now?

'Have you ever hunted?' he asked.

I shook my head.

'I think hunting's been suspended,' I said. 'Since you got back.' I almost added, 'Since James was killed.'

'I didn't know. What a silly thing. I'll have to speak to Father about it. What about you? Are you disappointed?'

I shook my head vigorously. Hunting and shooting had never held any fascination for me. In William's presence, I felt I could be honest about my feelings. He never laughed at me or tried to make me feel awkward.

A fire burned in his room all day and part of the night. Three of the maids had it as their special duty to keep it well-stoked. That meant several trips from the outhouse where the wood was kept all the way up to William's bedroom every day. None of the girls complained: William was a great favourite with them.

Sometimes he asks me to put a record on the gramophone. He has a little machine that stands on a table near the window, a Decca portable that he'd taken to the Front with him. Beside it stands a small collection of recordings, popular songs and dance music all of them. I put on whatever comes first to hand, cranking the little brass handle in between songs.

I can remember a day quite early on, when I'd put on *If You Were the Only Girl In the World*. I'd opened the window at his request, in order to freshen the air. I looked out onto the courtyard. The broad stone slabs that paved it were slick with rain, though the last drops had fallen over an hour earlier. The song escaped from the room, running away in every direction, colliding with old stone walls and grey mullioned windows.

I turned back to face William and, without thinking, said, 'You must have danced to this one a lot when you were on leave. Maybe you had a special girl, someone you always danced with.'

It was only then that I realised what I'd said. He didn't say anything at once, but the record kept on turning, and at my back a cold draught came in through the open window.

'Turn it off, will you, Simon?' he said finally. 'I don't think I want any more today. And will you be a good lad and close the window? It's getting chilly in here.'

I hurried to lift the gramophone arm and set it back on its rest. The music stopped instantly. I made to shut the window, only to find that the casement had fallen back to the wall, and I was forced to lean out and round in order to catch the handle.

As I did so, I caught sight of someone standing in the courtyard below, a woman dressed in a black cape, the hood lifted over her head. She was staring up at William's window, very keenly; but when she saw me, she drew back into the shadows. There was something about her movements I did not quite like. And her face, though glimpsed so briefly, reminded me sharply of Rose Hood, the maid who'd killed herself on the day of my arrival. I remembered her name this time, but I said nothing.

That night, I got up several times from my bed and crossed to the window. From there I looked down into the courtyard. It crawled with shadows as it always did. A patch of sky was just visible before a line of crumbling battlements shut off any further view of the outside world. I don't know what I was looking for. The woman perhaps. Some sort of confirmation that she had really been there.

On my second trip to the window, the scene I looked out on had not changed, except that when I looked at a sharp angle to my right, I could see that light was streaming from a window on a level with my own. Guided by an inexplicable instinct, I hurried to extinguish my own lamp, then crept back to my window and looked out again.

It was William's window, I was almost immediately certain of that. The light seemed to come from a single oil-lamp, in all likelihood the one on his bedside table, that he normally kept lit in the evenings. I don't know why I continued to crouch there as I did. For one thing, I considered William my friend, and yet there I was spying on him. For another, it was bitterly cold, and I was not properly dressed to sit in the open air.

I have an idea that I'd just started weakening, and was thinking of closing my window to return to my warm bed, when I heard a creaking sound and saw a casement of William's window swing open most of the way.

A minute or more passed before it occurred to me to ask who could be in William's room. It was past midnight already, and I wondered stupidly whether he had not found some means of manoeuvring himself out of bed to open the window and look out. The next moment my attention was caught by a low sound that appeared to come directly through William's window. It was at first barely distinguishable, then it rose in volume abruptly, and I recognised the strains of *The End of a Perfect Day*, a song that William often played.

I shivered and sat back numbly, unable to make sense of this peculiar behaviour. Then, just as abruptly as it had started, the music was broken off. I heard a woman's voice, very indistinct, then the window was pulled back with a bang. Moments later, the light went out, and I found myself alone in the darkness.

Snow and a Lost Garden

I woke up yesterday to find myself between warm blankets while bright late winter sunshine washed my room with colour. It took a few seconds longer to realise that Tom was in my room, and that he had been shaking me awake.

'Come on, Lysaght,' he said, 'rise and shine!'

I asked him what was up, and for answer he dragged me out of bed and across to the window. He pointed straight down at the ground. Snow had fallen in the night. It lay across the courtyard like a sudden coat of paint, and all the way down the walls had picked up small mounds of the stuff, wherever there were projections.

'Come on, will you? You never know how long this stuff's going to lie.'

'Come on where?'

'Oh, you are dim. Fitzgerald, if you haven't forgotten, is still up in Truro buying painting materials. He's not expected back till late this afternoon, and if the snow doesn't lift, he could be badly delayed on the train. Which gives us at least one day to ourselves. You don't have a toboggan, so I've asked Povey to fetch you one up from the cellars. I take it you know how to toboggan...'

I felt myself turn crimson. Sometimes I thought there was nothing Tom hadn't done, and nothing I hadn't still to do. Fortunately, tobogganing sounded within my capabilities.

'I don't, but I'd like to learn.'

'Put on something warm, then. And mittens or gloves if you've got them.'

Like a becalmed ocean liner, Trevelyan Priors was surrounded on all sides by a sea of snow. As we started out, muffled in thick, hampering layers of clothing that Marion had insisted we wear, and dragging our toboggans behind us, fresh snow began to fall. I pulled my scarf tight round my neck and pushed on into the swirling whiteness, walking six feet behind Tom and trusting to his sense of the place to find my way.

We walked through the main gardens, passing the lake, which had frozen over, leaving a handful of distraught ducks sliding and quacking across the surface as though life had played an ugly trick on them.

'There it is,' said Tom, stopping and pointing to a medium-sized hill right ahead of us. It must have been fifty or sixty feet high, with a long slope that made it perfect for gliding. 'We calls it 'obbs 'ill 'ere'bouts,' he said, in his poor impersonation of a local accent.

Luckily, the snow stopped falling as we climbed to the top of the hill. The sky above remained leaden for an hour or two more, but by noon it was showing large patches of blue that seemed to belong to another world entirely.

To my surprise, I found that toboganning came to me quite naturally. I was not a sportsman by temperament, and had made a bit of a fool of myself on more than one playing field; but after a few spills on my first descents of Hobb's Hill, I quickly found my seat, and soon Tom and I were racing neck and neck to the very bottom, down to the long sweep of snow-covered lawn that led to a frozen pool surrounded by a stand of tall firs.

At lunch-time, we were all set to walk back to the house for refreshments, when some figures appeared in the distance. My cousin Alice had been given leave to abandon her lessons for an hour or two. She was wrapped in thick furs and accompanied by Miss Cumberbatch, the whey-faced governess who had charge of her education, and by one of the scullery maids, who brought us huge flasks of beef tea and half a loaf of Mrs Burridge's wheaten bread, together with a slab of cheese fresh from Docking Farm.

I'd never before eaten with so much appetite. And when I crammed the last crumb into my mouth and rubbed the back of my hand across my lips, I realised something that had so far escaped me that day: in spite of the intense cold, I was not wheezing.

We played with Alice for over an hour, while Miss Cumberbatch looked on affably, her perpetual worried expression almost giving way to amusement as we hared up and down the great hill. And then the anxious expression returned, and Miss Cumberbatch said she'd promised to have Alice back at the house by two. Alice showed signs of tiring anyway, and Tom and I were eager to have the place to ourselves again, so we let them go, watching them walk away over the whiteness of the snow like shadows over a swan's back.

Within half an hour, Tom and I had reached our limit. We had played hard and eaten more than was wise, and I knew the mysterious improvement in my breathing would not bear up if I stayed on.

The patches of blue had gradually overtaken the entire sky about the time we sat down to eat, and so we walked back in bright sunshine that was still too weak to melt the tight-packed snow. It poured in from the West and warmed our backs a little. We walked slowly, well pleased with ourselves and the day we had spent so far.

Tom said he was eager to have some boys up from the village, so we could have proper races, and maybe some snowball fights. I resented the thought of boys I'd never so much as set eyes on bursting into my little paradise and driving away its magic with their rough cries. I think, too, that I feared rough-and-tumbles, and jeers, and the loss of Tom's friendship. I thought that, if I threatened to become an encumbrance, he would drop me like a brick.

Several times during that long walk back, I thought for some reason about the solitary woman whom I'd sighted in the courtyard. I considered telling Tom about her, but all the time something held me back. Pity, perhaps; or fear.

Soon after starting back, I noticed a large Gothic gate set in a long holly hedge, both rendered completely white by the snow.

'What's in there?' I asked.

Tom glanced round casually.

'Oh, that's the old garden,' he said. 'Nobody goes in there any longer. I've never been inside.'

I gave him a puzzled look, and he gave me an odd look back.

'Why not?' I asked, thinking it strange that an adventurous character like Tom had not ventured into this mysterious enclave.

'It's been let go,' he said. 'The gardeners haven't set foot in the place in twenty years or more. I've been in once or twice. The place is grown over. It's more like a jungle than a garden. You'd like it, I suppose.'

'Can I go in? It sounds very mysterious. And wrapped up in snow.'

'Yes, I expect you'd like that, young Lysaght. You've an eye for the picturesque.'

He'd a way of calling me 'young Simon' or 'young Lysaght' that I resented, for he was a mere two months older than myself and just an inch or so taller. For the rest, it was true that I was given more to contemplation than to action, and he the reverse.

'I'd like to see inside, ' I said.

'I'm not sure...' he answered.

'Why on earth not?'

He seemed lost for words for a moment, and I saw something cross his eyes that I did not recognise. I had never seen Tom flounder before.

'I think...' he began, 'that is, I don't think my father would approve.'

'Not approve?' I said. 'But it's just a garden.'

'All the same. He doesn't like anyone coming down here.'

'Has he ever given a reason?'

Tom shook his head.

'Then it can't be that important. Otherwise he'd have said.'

'Simon... I think something happened down here.'

'Happened? What sort of thing?'

He shrugged.

'I don't know,' he said.

'A murder? A serious accident?'

'I really don't know. I just sensed... when my father told me to steer clear.'

'But he isn't here. He isn't with us. Why don't we go in?'

I could hardly believe myself. I was arguing with Tom, encouraging him to break one of his father's iron rules. For I knew my uncle by then, and I could not imagine his laying down a vague and indifferent ruling about anything. At the same time, I was burning with curiosity just to see behind that tall hedge.

'All right,' said Tom, 'let's go in.'

We dragged apart the gate with no little difficulty, and when it did finally creak open on its ancient rusted hinges, it had to push back a good head of snow until I could slip through the narrow gap. I cleared more snow out of the way and Tom squeezed in after me.

I had expected a small place hemmed in on every side by the hedge. Instead, we set foot in a great expanse that rose up ahead of us and seemed to have no end.

'It's a good fifty acres,' Tom said.

'That means nothing to me,' I said, ever-conscious of my status as a town boy.

'What it means is it's too much land just to let go to waste. I mean to speak with my father about it one day. If he'd only stir his stumps, he could make something really nice out of it. They say there's a ravine and some sort of jungle with tropical trees. If we got it back in shape we could have tigers and — what are the things with spots?'

'Leopards.'

'Mind you, I wouldn't be surprised to find there were still some wandering about in here. What do you think?'

'I think we should have a look around.'

The moment I set foot inside the old garden I felt something. To begin with it seemed no more than a crawling sensation along the back of my neck. I shrugged it off, putting it down to the cold. But in my heart, I think I knew even then it was more than that.

'Do we have to?' Tom tried to pull me back to the gate and out to the open gardens again. I thought he was just worried about his father finding out, but when I insisted, I could sense in his reaction more than ordinary worry. He didn't like the place. Something in it had shocked or frightened him when he was a child, and left a lasting mark. Or so I imagined.

The combination of thick snow on the ground and unbounded undergrowth made it impossible to go any great distance. But none of this stopped the rush of excitement I felt every time I looked round. Even encased in snow, the garden seemed an island among the well-tended acres of the land around it. It seemed a place cut away, fit for adventure and mystery. Mentally, I melted the snow away from its trees and bushes, and in my mind I could see an enchanted world rise out of the whiteness. I longed for the cold weather to break, so that I could make my way back there.

We stayed just long enough to penetrate a little way into my lost domain. The gate through which we had entered led straight on to what must have been a main path, its outlines only apparent by reason of the trees and bushes that grew on either side. We walked along it, our cold feet carving out a double line through the heavy snow. Far in front of us and a little elevated, I could just make out the contours of some building, a summer-house, perhaps, or a pavilion, its windows cracked, or white with snow and ice and clinging frost.

I could see that Tom's aversion to the place had not lessened in intensity. Quite the contrary. His spirits, usually high as a skylark, had spiralled earthwards. I didn't ask him what was wrong: it would have been bad form, and in any case I knew I wouldn't get a straight answer.

I noticed the openings to what appeared to be half a dozen side paths running off the central avenue. It was tempting to follow one of them, but the shortest glimpse was enough to show me that none of them would be easily passable, not at least while the snow lay so thickly on everything.

We turned a corner to find ourselves on the edge of a roughly circular clearing, in the middle of which stood a fountain in the centre of a large stone basin, the whole structure blurred and simplified by the white sculptural hand of the snow.

'I think we should be getting back,' said Tom. 'Please, there's nothing here.'

His voice betrayed real fear, and for the second time I was tempted to ask what could be wrong. But something in his stance, some prickliness in his whole manner made me back off.

As I was about to turn away and head off down the avenue to the gate again, my eye was caught by some dark marks around the rim of the fountain, where it jutted out about six inches above the level of the snow. A closer look revealed something that made my heart seize up with fear. I wondered if Tom had seen it.

'Did you see...?' I asked.

He shook his head before I'd finished speaking.

'I've seen nothing,' he said. 'Seen no one. I just don't like this place, that's all.'

'But there are...'

I cut myself short. What I had seen had put the wind up me, and I thought it unfair to say more about it to Tom.

'Let's get out of here before it turns dark,' he said.

I said not a word more, and followed him down the long avenue to the gate. Tom went ahead, but I paused to close the gate. It pulled back easily, and I found a latch to hold it firm. I looked back up the avenue, where shadows were already gathering. I could still see in my mind's eye the track of footprints circling the fountain. Not heavy footprints, and certainly not mine nor Tom's, but small ones, as though a young woman had passed through the snow. But, as far as I had been able to establish, there had been no beginning to them, and no end.

I pondered on this puzzle all the way back to the house. My father had always encouraged me to seek for rational explanations for things, and I obeyed the rules he'd taught me. Whoever had caused those footprints, I argued, they hadn't been a phantom. Tom had told me the gardens were deserted, that whole acres had been thrown back to nature. But I had seen the roof of the little house — if house it was — and I wondered if someone didn't live there after all. An abandoned summer-house might have been a priceless gift to a poor family.

Alice

From the Ongoing Account in the hand of Simon Lysaght

We arrived at the Priors soon afterwards, our noses hideously scarlet, our hair rimed with frost. Tom had recovered from his upset already, and was warming up to afternoon tea with crumpets, toasted muffins, and Mrs Burridge's best fruit scones. Rationing hadn't made much of an impression down here, least of all on an estate the size of the Trevelyans'.

But the moment we set foot inside the house, something felt wrong. Any servants we passed seemed very subdued, and hurried past before we could tackle them. We dashed about, trying to find someone, but every room we looked in was empty. Tom's father was not in his study, nor Marion in the ground-floor drawing room. Normally about this time, tea would have been laid, but the little table from which Marion served was bare.

'Let's go up and see if William knows anything,' I suggested. Tom nodded, and off we hared to William's room, our feet loud in the silence that had gripped the house. My thoughts were running as fast as my feet, speculating on what might have caused this suspension of normality. Had the war ended? Or, horror of horrors, had the Germans conquered? But again and again the simple thought pressed on my mind, that someone in the house had died.

William was in bed as usual. He was dressed in full uniform, which was less normal. We dashed in, still in our outdoor clothes, our faces flushed, snow clinging to our boots, disorder apparent in everything we said and did.

'Hold on, hold on!' said William. 'Now, just what the hell are you two up to?'

We told him, and he returned our puzzled looks with a blank one of his own.

'All right, calm down. I'll ring for one of the servants. Perhaps they'll know.'

The bell was answered after more than one ring by a girl called Mary O'Connor, who spoke — to everyone's surprise — with a heavy Glaswegian accent. She'd come south to work in a munitions factory, but after a year or so she'd grown tired of the long hours and the constant din, and, in spite of the first-class pay, had gone in search of lighter domestic work.

'They all went out aboot half an hour ago, sir. A few of us wis told tae stay behind. They're oot looking for young Miss Trevelyan. There's an awfy fuss aboot it.'

It soon became clear that Alice had run on ahead of her governess and the kitchenmaid, saying she would race them to the house. They watched her past the lake, then, as her powerful little legs took her out of sight, they fell back, chatting, unaware of any danger lurking in the gardens. When they eventually got to the house — which would have been around the time Tom and I were exploring the hidden domain — Alice was nowhere to be found.

A search was quickly instigated, but there was still no sign. From the house, the search made its way outside, to the snow-covered gardens, drawing with it every member of the household, except those engaged in essential tasks. Everyone's worry was that she'd got lost in the strange, snowbound landscape, and that, if they did not find her before dark, she'd spend the night outside and as likely as not freeze to death.

Tom and I hurried outside, leaving William in bed cursing his disability. From the number of footsteps we saw, it was clear that the area immediately round the house had been scoured thoroughly. We had no idea which way the others had gone, or what might be a profitable route for us to pursue. In the end, Tom decided we should split up. He headed down to the Chinese pavilion, saying that Alice used to love going there in order to watch the grey ducks on the lake, and that she might have gone there now.

I wasn't sure where to go at first. Coming outside again after my brief spell indoors, I felt the cold twice as hard as ever. Not only that, but it seemed to be growing dark early, and a strong wind was whipping up from somewhere, lowering the temperature further.

I don't know why, but I was prompted to head for the Shot Tower. Several sets of footprints led in that direction, some going straight, others veering off to left or right. In the end, I could make out only two sets of footprints small enough to belong to

Alice. Where could the second set have come from? I wondered. Some of our neighbours had children of about Alice's age, and they came from time to time to pay little visits and play. But surely one of her friends would have accompanied her when she brought the food to Tom and myself.

I almost turned back, thinking that someone else must have found her. But simple reason told me that, unless they'd vanished into thin air again, Alice and her companion must still be down at the tower.

I was half right. Alice was there, sure enough, lying flat on the ground near the demijohns of arsenic. My first thought was that she must be dead. But when I knelt to touch her, she stirred and rolled over in her sleep. I feared to wake her, so tired and helpless did she appear.

I looked round the tower, wondering where Alice's friend could have got to. The place was silent. I guessed that old Matthew had taken the day off: it would have been foul up there at the top of the tower, with that ice-cold wind. I imagined icicles hanging at the windows, and snow being blown in.

'Hello!' I shouted. 'Is anybody here? Matthew? Are you up there?'

Nothing. Alice stirred in her sleep. Faint sounds of cracking came from all sides as the tower settled to the coming night and the movement of the wind. A delicious light fell into the tower's hollow interior, and hovered there, less like light than a breath of the coming storm. I looked high up, growing dizzy as I tried to take in the height and arrogance of the tower, imagining the light suddenly full of lead, like a curtain, or a waterfall falling.

If someone had been there, they were long gone. I picked Alice up, and she opened her eyes, yawning.

'It's all right, Alice,' I said. 'It's Simon.'

She half-smiled and went back to sleep. For the first time, I noticed that her skin was pale, and that frost had gathered on her dark hair.

An Account of Alice Trevelyan's Disappearance in the Hand of Lady Marion Trevelyan

Major Hazel has prompted me to set down a few lines about last week's bother with Alice. I've no particular wish to do so, but he seems to think it will do good to have a record, in case of any bother later. God, I shall be sure there is no bother. But a record may have its purpose for all that. As for Hazel, he can take his celebrated pipes (Meerschaums, as if that didn't sum him up) and smoke them. He's a tedious, interfering old bore, all tweeds and 'when I hunted with the Quorn', and if he weren't Chief Constable I wouldn't even invite him to tea.

I don't suppose she was missing very long, though by the time Simon appeared with her in his arms she was already suffering the first stages of hypothermia, and given her age and size, there was very good reason to feel alarmed.

Everything was made ten times worse by the fact the family and staff alike had scattered over the grounds. Nobody seemed to know where anybody else was. I found the house virtually empty and went outside again. It was just as I was crossing the front lawn that I saw Simon coming up from the gardens with Alice bundled against him. He was white-cheeked and gasping for breath, but he held on to Alice for all he was worth. I took her from him and got her inside, making her comfortable in the drawing-room. But when I looked round for someone to help me, there was only a gaggle of kitchen girls and the like.

I was on the verge of panic, for Alice was showing no signs of coming round. I needed advice, and I needed help. Simon was no further use: he was bent over the fireplace, wheezing and clutching his chest. One of the maids suggested that I sound the dinner gong outside. She was right, too: it brought everyone back to the house within ten minutes.

Mrs Armitage helped me get Alice upstairs to her room, where we undressed and bathed her before putting her to bed. One of the maids had had the foresight to start a fire in the room long before we arrived there. By this time, Alice had developed a temperature. I didn't know what best to do: let her sleep or try to keep her awake.

A stable-boy was sent to Porth Buryan to fetch Quilty, the doctor. The storm was making a fine nuisance of itself by then, raging in from the sea like a troop of banshees, and bringing yet more snow with it. I worried that Quilty might not get through, and I believe he had a hard enough time of it and was nearly trapped in the snow himself.

It was about nine o'clock when he finally made his appearance. David offered him brandy and a spell at the hall fire, but he just gulped the brandy down and insisted on going straight up to the child. She was still asleep. He gave her a thorough examination, pronounced himself satisfied, and made up a compound for her on the spot.

'Give it to her when she wakes,' he said.

'When do you think that should be?'

'In an hour or two, not more. If she hasn't wakened by then, just wake her gently. If she feels hungry, just give her some light soup. My one concern is that she doesn't develop pneumonia. Otherwise, she's come through her ordeal with flying colours.'

He said he had to get back to Porth Buryan, but when we looked outside it was clear he'd never make it even so far as the road.

'I'll have a bed made up for you in one of the guest rooms. And do say you'll dine with us. We've hardly had a chance to get to know you since you came here.'

'And a good thing too. People who get to know their doctors well usually turn out to be valetudinarians.'

'I've never known a day's illness in my life, but I think I should get to know you better. My husband is not a healthy man. And we have a young relative living here, Simon Lysaght, whose health gives great cause for concern. In fact, I'd appreciate it if you'd give him a once-over after dinner.'

I showed him down to the library, where the marquis took him under his wing. I then went upstairs to the Chinese drawing-room and summoned Mrs Armitage.

'Could you ask one of the girls to make a bed up in the yellow bedroom? And a fire, of course. It's for Dr. Quilty.'

'Yes, ma'am. Anything else, ma'am?'

'Have Miss Cumberbatch and the girl who was with her this afternoon come up to me.'

'Very well, ma'am. They're both in a bit of a state, though.'

'I should certainly hope they are. They'll be in a worse state by the time I've spoken to them.'

'Do you want them both at once, ma'am, or one at a time?'

'Oh, I've no time for that. Both together, and double quick.'

I dealt with them as fast as might be deemed proper under the circumstances. They came into the room blubbering, little wet handkerchiefs pressed to red eyes and noses, and I was almost tempted to pity them and send them down to a late tea. But when I thought of how their foolishness had very nearly cost my daughter's life, I had no doubts as to what I must do.

Quilty turned out to be admirable company. Self-made, of course, and somewhat unpolished, but rather witty for all that, and solicitous. I could see David didn't take to him at all, but then he has an aversion to doctors and anyone with an air of learning about them. The boys made the most of him, starved as they often are of dinner-table guests. Simon was recovering from his attack, but still wheezed audibly; I saw Quilty glance over at him several times with an appraising look.

Tom, who never knows when to leave things alone, rather put his foot in it when he asked the doctor why he wasn't at the front. He got a rather curious response when Quilty seemed on the verge of getting up and hitting him, then subsided all at once and murmured that Tom was right and that perhaps he should make enquiries about medical work in France.

I tackled Tom afterwards and told him he should have known by now my attitude towards baiting men with the front.

'I don't want you going round like those stupid girls one sees, handing out white feathers to any man they catch sight of in civilian clothes. Half the time, it's soldiers on leave that get handed them, or men who have vital work here at home and have been refused permission to join up. You were very rude to Dr. Quilty. I think you should apologise if you get a chance tomorrow.'

I don't know why I was suddenly so defensive of the doctor. But I was grateful to him for having come out in such a gale to see to Alice.

The cold spell took its toll. Poor little Alice remained in bed with a fluctuating temperature, and was visited every day by Dr. Quilty, for whom the long daily journey between Porth Buryan and Trevelyan Priors must have posed a sore trial. Nor was she the only one in the house to have succumbed. The good doctor was at least guaranteed a full complement of patients at the end of his journey. Several of the staff had caught influenzas and colds, and Sir David went down with the grippe. Dr. Quilty asked permission to try some of his homoeopathy on us. In a few days, he had some wonderful results. He says he wants to treat me over several months, and that he can do a great deal for my asthma. That would make a huge difference to me.

I got over my own outing better than I might have expected. I didn't mention it in my letter to Mother, of course, knowing what a fuss she would have made, and how unnecessarily worried she would have been. Quilty examined me several times and gave me some little white pills that made me feel much better. He seemed a little surprised by what I'd been given before, by Dr. Knightly up in York.

Tom wasn't as lucky. He caught influenza, a pretty bad case of it, and had to have a nurse brought in from Porthmullion, a Mrs Spreadborough. I visited him a few times, but he was in no state to entertain visitors, not in the early days anyway. And old Spreadborough turned out to be a fierce type. Every time I went up, it was 'No visitors today, thank you', and 'He wants no excitement this morning, young man'. I found her very off-putting, but I daresay she was right. You have to be careful with something like influenza, haven't you? Marion was very worried about him, and spent a lot of time with Dr. Quilty, discussing his case.

As for Mr Fitzgerald, he must have caught the same 'flu as Tom, for it struck him down as heavily and very nearly killed him. Mrs Spreadborough kept him in absolute quarantine, and I was strictly banned from going anywhere near his room, and wasn't even allowed to exchange messages with him.

Bereft of friend and tutor alike, I spent twenty-four hours

without direction, now reading, now staring out of a variety of windows, now writing to my mother and stacking each letter in the hall alongside several others that were later handed to Dr. Quilty to post in Porth Buryan. I heard that influenza had broken out in the village, and that one man and one woman had died.

When first apprised of my rapid recovery, Aunt Marion had quite abandoned me in favour of her swelling household of invalids. But when a few days had gone by and I seemed more and more inclined to sit in silence with William, or to take over the conservatory in order to listen to the wireless, or just hang around kicking my heels, she decided that a firmer hand was in order. Hence it was that she engaged the services of the marquis.

Although he and I had met daily since my arrival at the house, chiefly over dinner, the marquis and I were, in reality, strangers to one another. Apart from one or two inconsequential remarks by Tom, I had never succeeded in learning much about the Frenchman, nor had anyone else volunteered anything to me. Now that he was to be my doyen, however, I wished wholeheartedly that I did know more of him and his background. He frightened me, if I'm to tell the truth, and I thought that greater knowledge might make him seem less menacing.

I learned quickly that the marquis himself was not disposed to enlighten me. He skilfully deflected any question I put to him in an effort to find out what he was doing at Trevelyan Priors, or how he knew the Trevelyans, or what he had done in France before the war. For some reason, I thought William might know something, but he confessed he knew as little as I, and said he'd scarcely spoken two words to the marquis since the foreigner showed up. When had that been, I asked. 'God knows,' was William's reply. 'He was installed here long before I got smashed up.'

I was a little confused a to what Monsieur le Marquis and I were to do together. On the first day, he marched me off to the classroom, where he embarked on a lengthy discourse on French literary techniques of the seventeenth and early eighteenth centuries. He tossed around names and concepts as though they were as familiar to me as *je suis* and *il y a*. From the great themes of Molière, La Fontaine, or Racine, he would trip with the lightest of steps to Saint-Evremond or Bayle or Fontenelle, dazzling me with long passages of poetry or prose read in a mournful, declamatory voice that left me far behind.

Lunch was spent in a sort of light-handed inquisition about myself, in which he returned often to the topic of my parents and grandparents on both sides. He said he was an amateur genealogist, and that he hoped one day to produce an annotated tree for my family, by which he meant the Trevelyans. I wondered if Sir David had said anything to him about his plan to adopt me, but nothing he said led me to believe so.

In the afternoon, we made our way back to the classroom, where I was subjected to another lecture, this time on the great eighteenth-century porcelain ateliers, with particular attention to the work of Johann Kandler in Meissen and Franz Bustelli in Nymphenburg. I must have fallen asleep, for I remember finding myself in my chair, a little chilly, and all alone.

He said nothing about my lapse, but that evening after dinner (which was attended only by ourselves and Marion) he apologised for having chosen a subject so far lacking in interest to a young man of my years. I confessed that I had found both his lectures considerably out of my depth, and apologised for having fallen asleep in one.

'Tell me, then, what makes most your imagination to be awake? Is it the sport? No, I did not think so. Well, then, the history of your great country, per'aps? Not so much? The thoughts of the great *philosophes*?'

Awkwardly, among his suggestions, I blurted out that I would like to know more about art and architecture.

'*Parfait*. Say not another word. All will be so arranged. And no more lectures for you to fall asleep in.'

So it was indeed arranged that, rather than sit in the schoolroom while the marquis imparted his knowledge of books I had never read in a language I knew only imperfectly, he should take me on a gradual tour of the house, using its fine collection of paintings and objets d'art as the basis for my first proper education in matters art historical.

The following days passed, quite to my amazement, in sheer delight. The marquis' erudition was all-encompassing, but, in this instance, lightly enough worn. Though he made no attempt to bend to my level of understanding, I seldom found myself out of depth.

On that first day, I had taken in nothing — just vague impressions of rooms stuffed with old furniture and artworks of different kinds. I had noticed the colour of wallpaper, but not the paper itself, I'd taken note of the innumerable gilded picture frames on every wall, but not of the pictures; I'd even been overwhelmed by the grand scale of the fireplaces without paying heed to the magnificent carvings that gave them life.

That all changed overnight. There was nothing the marquis did not notice, no painting whose identity he did not know, no portrait whose sitter he could not name, no artist about whom he could not relate anecdotes from Vasari or Cellini, no style or technique he could not trace in Alberti or Cennini. In a matter of days, I learned to distinguish between an aquatint and a mezzotint, to tell a Hals from a Rembrandt, and to know there were three Bellinis and that there were three paintings, one by each of them, at Trevelyan Priors — rarities all of them, like so much else in that place.

Delighted to have found an audience for his extemporisings, the marquis accompanied me from room to room as though I was a prize pupil admitted to adult mysteries, the three arcana of painting, sculpting and engraving. Trevelyan Priors did, as a matter of fact, possess one of the finest collections of engravings in England, if not in Europe, and it was there that I first learned my love of Piranesi's etchings. Someone had gone to a lot of trouble both to collect and to display this collection, which had works dating back to Finiquerra, Pollaiuolo, and Mantegna, and which ended sometime around Rowlandson, fifty of whose aquatints graced a small, wood-panelled room on the ground floor.

The sacred truths of taste and discernment were, unfortunately, the only ones imparted to me that March. About himself and his origins, the marquis retained his Buddha-like posture of silence and impassivity.

But there were moments when he let his guard drop slightly. He mentioned once that his father had played a leading role in the bloody suppression of the commune in 1871, and had later sat in the Assembly as an Orleanist. Of, course, I didn't know then what an Orleanist was, but it did sound very grand. I confess that I managed to get mixed up in my head Joan of Arc, the Huguenots, and the American city of New Orleans, all forming a delicious romantic vagueness within me.

In the 1890s, his elder sister, the Comtesse de Gontaut-Biron, had hosted a Wednesday salon that was spoken of in the same breath as those of the Duchesse de Maille, the Duchesse de Polignac, or even the dreaded Comtesse de Lévis-Mirepoix. His mother, now many years deceased, had once publicly snubbed the Princesse Mathilde as an upstart and an orange-seller. Why, he himself had once fought a duel by the sword in defence of the honour of a certain General Boulanger. He showed me the long scar he had suffered on the back of his right hand, and forbade me to speak to anyone of the matter.

My marquis was all mystery and allusions and, I now realise, affectation. Though he did not win me to him — in my heart I continue to mistrust and fear him — his love of beauty and his unfeigned erudition, which was perfectly genuine, disposed me well enough to him through the course of each day we spent together.

Once only did we have a set-to. It had been a drab day, with clouds heavy enough to crush the soul, and I had suggested that we take the opportunity to walk round the house, studying the architectural features of its various stages. This appealed to him greatly. Trevelyan Priors, he said, was not merely a shell, like a museum or gallery, but deserved to be viewed as a work of art in its own right, a work of many hands and many periods.

Yet, as we made our way from wing to wing, I became aware that Monsieur le Marquis's pretty explanations lacked the whole-hearted enthusiasm he had shown when speaking of a Holbein or a Mantegna. I detected soon enough a different devotion. At some point or other, he would falter in his description of a window, or pause in his praise of an arch, only to take second wind and launch into a recitation of the wonders of this or that part of his own dear home, the Château de Vitry-la-Ferté.

On the second day, he embarked on a description of the extensions and refurbishments made to the château seventy years earlier. Feeling no little irritation, I decided to chivvy him into paying better attention to the task in hand. We were indoors at the time, and had come into an open area off which several doors radiated. I had not been there before, and thought I could turn this to my advantage by making the whole thing into a sort of riddle. You know the sort of thing: the hero is face to face with three doors, monsters lie behind two, a beautiful maiden behind the third — how should he choose?

There was a particularly old door three or four paces in front of me. It seemed quite different to the others, either here, or in other parts of the house, and I persuaded myself that it might prove a gateway to adventure or intrigue.

'Where does this door lead? Do you know?' I asked, stepping towards it and grasping the large metal handle.

No sooner had I spoken than I felt a hard hand on my shoulder, twisting me about and pulling me firmly away from the door.

'I'm sorry,' he said. 'I did not mean to pull you so hard.'

'Why on earth did you pull me at all?'

'I merely wanted to advise you that the door you wished to enter through, it is not... advisable. Not permitted, perhaps I should say. *Interdit*.'

'Not permitted? What nonsense.'

He shook his head briskly.

'No, no, no — not nonsense. This is the bottom entrance to the old attic storey. Per'aps no one has mentioned to you. But the attics are — what you say? — out of bounds. They are unsafe. So the door is kept locked, and the key is in a locked box. Only your uncle David may go there.'

I said nothing to my uncle of the matter, fearing what he might say, but I did mention it to Marion that evening after dinner. Her response surprised me, so strong was it, as though I had touched on a sore spot or referred to something faintly indecent. She too made it clear that the attics were closed indefinitely and that under no circumstances should I — or Tom and I — attempt to enter them.

'They are extremely dangerous,' she said, accepting my undertaking not to venture in there. 'I think I should speak to David about it, ask him to hurry up with the repairs. They've been put off on account of the war.'

By then, I'd remembered the face I'd seen on the day of my arrival, staring down at me from a high window in the attics, a pale face whose blurred features I could not readily identify with those of anyone living at Trevelyan Priors.

From the Ongoing Account in the hand of Simon Lysaght, dated 15 April 1917.

The following day was so good that, instead of spending the next hour or so with William as I had promised, I headed out into the gardens. The snow had melted wholly away, leaving behind a glistening expanse of grass, leaves and freshly-opened flowers of every imaginable colour.

Ever since the day when I first set foot there, I had been determined to visit my lost domain and to explore it properly. The mystery of the footprints I'd seen on the snow about the fountain still bothered me, but I said not a word about it, not even to William, in whom I confided most things.

On the way there, I made a long diversion to the Shot Tower. Old Matthew was there, high up in his eyrie, mixing lead and arsenic and sending it spiralling down through the dusty air as though light and dust alone were being spun finely into tiny fractions of death. I stood underneath, watching the fine adjustments of the air, listening to the sea slip and foam on the rocks below. And all the while, the bath filled with shot, dense and cold and unlike any other substance I had ever seen or touched. I stood, and I thought of William alone in his cold room, and I imagined how he must have lost his legs, hot lead tearing them apart, blood running in all directions and growing cold.

I had acquired a romantic view of death, even an elevated concept of pain. In part, it was the war. I was growing up in a culture of death, where men were little more than seeds planted in bloody soil, from whom nothing had yet grown, but in whom we invested endless and inordinate hopes. At fifteen, I would gladly now march off to the Front, willingly scrambled over the Top in a clutching sort of rush to glory. Death and disfigurement play equal parts in that.

The shower of hot lead suddenly halted, and moments later I heard feet on the wooden steps far above. I thought Matthew might let me go up again, perhaps even show me how to mix the base materials and throw them on the sieve. I waited patiently for him to appear, watching his foreshortened body descend the narrow staircase, making the cracked wooden treads creak and groan, as if in sympathy with the pains of his own limbs.

The figure had reached a point about twenty feet above the floor when I realised with a shock that it was not Old Matthew after all. Moments later, the man stepped off the stairway and looked at me. He was a much younger man. I noticed that he had a hare lip, and that one of his hands was deformed, having only two or three fingers, the rest knitted together somehow, as though by some oddity of birth. His hair hung down almost to his shoulders, lank and knotted.

'Who are you?' he asked.

'I'm Simon Lysaght,' I explained, thinking he might have heard my name somehow. But he went on looking blankly at me.

'I've never heard tell of you,' he said.

'I'm a friend of Old Matthew's,' I said, exaggerating the extent and nature of my brief acquaintance with the old shot-maker. 'I live at Trevelyan Prior's. Sir David's my uncle. I...'

But he cut me off, unimpressed by all this talk of kinship and connectedness. Names and houses meant nothing to him.

'Old Matthew's not 'ere,' he said. 'Not been for days. I been sent down to keep old tower going.'

'Is Old Matthew ill? Does he need help? I can send Dr Quilty over to take a look at him.'

He looked blankly at me. He'd probably never set eyes on a doctor in his life.

'Old Matthew ill? Don't reckon so,' he said. 'Him just never turned up for work, and 'im 'aven't been seen since then.'

'How long has that been?'

This seemed too much for his limited mental resources.

'Look,' I said, 'think hard. Did anything happen before he left? Was he given the sack, or perhaps he had a fight with someone?'

He shook his head slowly.

'There were no fight,' he said, 'and he weren't given sack.' He stopped and seemed to be considering something.

'There was something,' he said, 'but you musn't say aught to anyone.'

'What was this?'

'They found a girl in here. In they shot tower. Young girl from they big house. Did you hear of that?'

'I was the one who found her,' I said. 'But Matthew wasn't here, not when I arrived, at least.'

'He never come home that night, and not since.'

'Has there been any kind of a search for him?'

'He'll turn up by and by, don't you go frettin' after him.'

'I'll do what I can,' I said. 'Perhaps I'll speak with my uncle. Up in the big house. Perhaps he can get the police to help.'

He looked at me quickly, with a combination of alarm and anger.

'No need for police,' he said in a loud voice. 'No need for big 'ouse. Us can look after oursel'.'

'I'm only trying to help,' I said. 'If I... should hear anything of Matthew, I'll let you know.'

He looked sternly at me.

'What brought you to here?' he asked.

'I told you. I came to see Old Matthew.'

'Well, Old Matthew ain't here.'

'I know that now.'

'Well, you've come and snooped round. Now, I'd like you out of 'ere, please. I got plenty of work to do.'

His brusque manner and quick dismissal dismayed me greatly. I don't suppose anyone has ever spoken to me like that before. Parents or schoolmasters, of course, can be stern or angry or sarcastic. But for a member of the working classes to speak in such terms is not the expected thing.

However, I quickly threw off the unpleasant feeling that the man had left in me. I worried about Old Matthew, not knowing what to make of his disappearance. Did Marion and the others up at the house know? I wondered. If so, why hadn't I been told?

I almost lost my way after that, having visited the lost garden only that one time, when trees and shrubs and grass had been covered in dense snow. But by careful use of those few landmarks I could find, I came again to the little gate that led beneath tangled branches onto a weed-choked path and so into the hidden spaces of that enchanted world.

I don't know how long I spent in the garden on that first day.

When I got back to the house, tea had finished, and I was given a dressing-down for having missed it. I didn't say where I'd been, having a fine instinct that Marion would tell me that the lost garden was out of bounds. Already, the thought of not returning there made me feel as though I might suffocate.

In there, the time did not pass like time outside. Just as the garden seemed to have its own climate and its own light, so it had its own time that hung on every leaf and every branch and every flower. In the days that followed, I discovered places where time stood still. I found a glade filled with bluebells, torrents of blue flowers that grew thick among uncut grass and the roots of ancient trees. Sitting there gripped by a blurred silence for which I could find no explanation, I let whole days pass, thinking and dreaming. And I found a deep valley filled with palms and tree ferns and other jungle plants, a lush, warm place that seemed, of all the places I set foot in, the most timeless.

Not everywhere was accessible: over the years, trees had fallen, blocking paths, while in places others had seeded themselves and grown up, shutting off whole areas from their surroundings. I could see among ivy and high-growing weeds what seemed to be greenhouses and potting sheds and a small summer-house nestling among a stand of tall bamboo that had run wild all about it.

Each time I visited, I was drawn to the pavilion with its pointed roof and strange, empty windows. There were two rooms and a cramped scullery downstairs and four smaller ones above, and they were all still furnished as though someone had suddenly abandoned them, without waiting to finish their meal or the chapter of the book they'd been engrossed in, or the sampler they'd been working. A patina of age and weather lay across the entire place. Anything soft, like chair seats or books or clothing had long since rotted, while wood had warped and varnish blistered as it peeled away.

In drawers and cupboards I found stacks of crockery and cutlery, the latter dull and showing signs of rust. Downstairs, one narrow cupboard held a child's toys, most of them rusted and tarnished. Among them I found a wooden music-box that miraculously still worked. A small clown danced on top of it as it turned slowly round, playing a sad song out of tune.

I came to regard the pavilion house as my retreat, almost as my own property. I said nothing of it or the garden to anyone, not even Tom, who said nothing more of it to me, whether out of forgetfulness or design I don't know. As things slowly returned to normal at the house, I had increasingly less time to myself. Tom was soon out of bed, and although he was not allowed out of doors for some little time, he could move about indoors. Mr Fitzgerald remained bed-bound for the duration, although the services of Mrs Spreadborough were no longer required on a twenty-four hour basis.

I spent a lot of time now indoors with Tom. We were supposed to have lessons with the marquis, but Tom often extricated us from these by pleading a return of ill health. Not even he, however, could keep up the pretence indefinitely. Dr. Quilty, while indulgent for a week or so, soon took his measure and pronounced him quite teachable. A Mr Ellis, a retired schoolmaster who lived in Porth Buryan, was engaged to come up to the house once a day in order to provide Tom and myself with regular lessons. Dull lessons they were, worthy lessons fit for policemen's sons that usually ended with a short homily about 'Our Boys at the Front'.

We endured these for a while, until Fitzgerald regained his strength. While in the house, I mostly divided my time between Tom and William. But every day I'd look for an hour or two to go down to my hidden garden. I discovered a small lake fringed with reeds, complete with a rotting landing stage, but no boat; and I began to work at it, clearing weeds and other vegetation from the sides, and skimming a bright green coating from the surface. I came to imagine it with lily pads and white lilies opening to the light. I thought that when summer came Tom and I might go there on hot days to bathe.

Wherever I went in the garden, I was from time to time aware of being watched, and nowhere more so than when I sat by my little weed-choked lake, tossing pebbles into the water, or watching birds come to bathe there. It was as though some presence sur-

100

rounded the whole area. However hard I looked, I could never succeed in seeing anyone. Nothing, not so much as a branch moving or a bird crying out betrayed watching eyes. And yet I was certain they were there.

The shot tower was visible from the upper storey of the pavilion, and each time I climbed up there I would catch sight of it. I wondered how long I could comfortably let pass before venturing back inside.

As soon as I got back to the house on the day of my visit to the shot tower, I told Aunt Marion about the business of Old Matthew's disappearance. I didn't let on I'd been to the Shot Tower, of course, since it remained out of bounds, but I did say one of the gardeners had told me.

'What was his name, this gardener?' she quizzed me.

'I don't know. I didn't ask.'

She sniffed.

'Well, no doubt you can pick him out if necessary.'

I said I was sure I could. She smiled and stroked my head indulgently.

As I was about to leave her drawing room, she called me back.

'Simon, there's something I must know. Tell me honestly, now. What brought you to go to the Shot Tower in order to look for Alice?'

I had feared this question ever since returning with Alice to the house that day. Fortunately, my illness, not to mention both Tom's and Alice's, had served to distract everyone from me and my doings. But now, a foolish reference to the subject had brought it up again.

'I... I don't know. I used to see the tower over the trees. She could have passed it on her way back. I thought so, anyway.'

'Perhaps you'd visited it before? Is that it? Did you go there with Tom? The thing is, we discovered that Tom had been going there for some time, that he'd struck up an unsuitable friendship with Matthew Ellis. He's been forbidden to go there, but I don't entirely trust my son. Has he taken to going there with you?'

I found myself speechless. I was still too young or too naïve to be able to guess how much she knew or could find out.

'Come on, boy. You know you can't hide the truth from me.'

'What will you do to Tom?'

'He'll be grounded for a few weeks, I expect. I take it it's true? You and Tom have been visiting the tower?'

I shook my head.

'Not visiting,' I said. 'We went there once. He wanted to show me how it worked.'

'I see.' I noticed her lips grow taut, and was glad Tom wasn't there. 'Was Matthew there when you went?'

I nodded.

'Very well,' she said. 'You may be excused. You were clearly an innocent participant in this affair. Tom will have egged you on. I'll have words with him on that account. His father may want to punish him more severely. After all, this escapade was in direct defiance of our clear instructions.'

'Please don't let him be hurt. I should feel awful if he had a beating on my account. I wouldn't have told on him…'

'Simon!' my aunt snapped, revealing a side of herself I had not seen before then. 'It is not a matter of betrayal on your part. My son betrayed his trust with myself and his father, and therefore forfeited any right he might have had to immunity. This is a domestic matter, I know; but you and Tom live here at our good will. If you cover up a minor infraction like this, perhaps tomorrow you will cover up a theft or something worse, and perhaps when you are fully grown you will become a criminal yourself. Please give me your assurance that nothing like that will happen. For if either Tom or you were to fall into corrupt ways, it would break my heart.'

I assured her that nothing could be further from my mind, though in truth I simply hoped to avoid a beating at my uncle's hands. Tom had told me of some of the punishments he'd endured in Sir David's study, and I heartily hoped never to be on the receiving end of his strap myself. My own father had never so much as hit me, even when provoked, and I dreaded physical chastisement more than most boys my age.

I made to leave, but as I came near the door, Aunt Marion called me back.

'Simon, you say you are being honest with me. I hope that is so. For I wish to ask you something to which it is most important you give a candid answer. If not, you may place yourself in very great peril. Do you understand?'

I nodded, not understanding at all.

'Tell me, Simon, have you ever set foot inside the old garden? I'm sure you know the one I mean. You'll find it not far from Hobbs Hill, where you and Tom went tobogganing on that dreadful day.'

'Yes,' I said, trying to preserve a look of innocence on my face, desperately frightened lest she discover my secret and I be barred for ever from my private place. 'I remember we passed it on our way back here. But it was deep in snow, and there seemed no way in. Tom told me it had been a garden, but he said it was overgrown and unwelcoming.'

'And you did not venture inside?'

'No, Aunt. Not then or ever.'

This was the greatest lie I had ever told, the first serious breach of faith with another person I had dared commit. But the garden had come to matter much to me. I felt as though it called me to itself, or as if weak voices drifted from it to me. Had I been laid beneath an old spell? Whatever... I smiled at my aunt and I lied, and I knew I had committed a great sin that might never be undone.

'Now, listen, Simon, my dear, and listen closely. You are at your liberty to explore the house, except for certain parts that our good marquis will have mentioned. And you have free access to all parts of the estate. Dr Quilty says you should have as much fresh air and sunlight as possible, and I'm sure he is entirely right. Later, when this dreadful war is over, I hope we can all go abroad together, to the south of France or Italy. Would you like that?'

'Could my mother come as well?'

She laughed.

'Of course. She would be very welcome. Let's talk about this another time. The war still drags on. It may last another year or more, but once it's over and done with, we shall make plans for a long spell in the Mediterranean.'

'I'll look forward to that.'

I started to move away, but she called me back again.

'I hadn't quite finished, Simon. What I wanted to say to you was this. You are free to go where you wish, except for the tower and the cliffs near it… and the garden I just mentioned. You are never to go inside it.'

'Is it so dangerous?'

She stepped closer to me, and I detected in her face something unexpected — a look of apprehension. I thought then it was meant for me, that she was merely considering my welfare. Now, I am sure she was thinking of nothing but herself. And William, perhaps. But William was already safe.

'Simon, I don't really know how to put this in words without frightening you. But you really must understand that the garden is not out of bounds for a trivial reason. You are still too young to be told more than this. But I tell you now that if you set foot in there, you will come to regret it sooner or later. There is something… wrong about the place. Something not right.'

I almost blurted out that I had never sensed anything amiss in all the times I'd been in there, but caught myself just in time.

'Not right?' I asked.

'There is something out of place. Things are not as they should be. It was a garden once, but now it's grown to weeds and shadows. There's nothing in there for you, Simon, take my word.'

'Is it dangerous?'

'Not in the ordinary sense, at least, not so much. It's your soul I fear for, Simon. Yours and Tom's. You would be at great peril once inside that place. Now, I think we've said more than enough about it. There's no afternoon tea today, but if you ask Mrs Armitage she'll ask Cook to get something ready for you. Why don't you ask for sandwiches in Tom's room?'

'He'll only steal mine.'

She laughed, recovering the light manner I associated with her.

'Then tell Cook to make more. You weren't brought here to starve.'

I told both Tom and William about Old Matthew's disappearance. Tom and I took our tea and sandwiches along to William's room, where we all tucked in. My appetite had grown considerably since my arrival at Trevelyan Priors, and I took the bulk of the sandwiches for myself.

'You'll grow fat, young Simon,' William said, laughing and swiping a sandwich for himself.

We speculated about where Old Matthew might have gone, or whether he might have done away with himself.

'That's the first place the police will look, of course,' Tom said. 'He could have jumped from the top of the tower. Or over the cliffs like Miss Fitzallan.'

He stopped dead, realizing that he'd overstepped the mark. Geraldine Fitzallan's death touched on the honour of his dead brother James. William directed an angry look at him, but said nothing.

I jumped in to tell them about the hare-lipped man who had told me about Old Matthew.

'His name's George, you ninny. I thought you knew that.' Tom seemed peeved that I had not known such an elementary fact about his world. He'd grown very impatient during his illness, and a bit tetchy. His father was growing in him, and I guessed that, in time, my friend Tom would become a man of wealth and stature, and in the process lose the honesty and freshness I had come to admire him for. I grieved for him, thinking I would never grow like that myself.

'He's Old Matthew's assistant,' William put in. 'He's been a feature over there for years. I think he started as a hand on Petherwin Farm. Probably never set foot in a school. When he was eighteen or so, he fell in with some bad sorts down in Porthmullion. They got to drinking and fell into all sorts of trouble. Stealing, mostly. He was arrested and sent to prison for several years. When he came out, Petherwin wouldn't have him back. Old Matthew offered him a job, and he's been there since. He gets drunk from time to time, though God knows where he gets the money from — Old Matthew can't pay him much. Anyway, he's welcome to it so long as he stays out of trouble.'

I bit into a ham and mustard sandwich. The bread had been baked early that morning by Mrs Douch, the cook, and was as fresh as bread can be.

'Where does he live?' I asked, barely squeezing the words out through the wodge of bread and ham in my mouth. 'George, that is.'

'I think he lives with Old Matthew,' Tom said, helping himself to another sandwich. He still seemed pale, and he'd lost a great deal of weight since falling ill. Maybe he'd start pulling round, I thought. I was lonely without him to share my days.

'That's right,' said William.

'Doesn't Old Matthew have a wife and children?' I asked.

'I've never heard of any,' Tom answered.

'Well, I'm afraid you're wrong,' William said, cuffing him gently across the ear. 'I believe there was a wife once, and a couple of kids. They aren't with him now, that's for sure.'

'What happened?' I felt consumed by sudden curiosity.

'Reckon he done murdered 'em,' drawled William, adopting his version of a Cornish accent.

'Did he really?' Tom was wide-eyed at the possibility.

William shrugged.

'I doubt it. But they could well have run away. Old Matthew has a reputation for a foul temper. I've been on the receiving end of it more than once.'

'Who owns the tower?' I asked.

'We do, of course. We own everything. But Matthew Ellis rents it from us for a peppercorn. His father did the same before him. In return, he keeps the work going and produces lead shot from one year's end to the next. He takes most of the profit, and the rest goes to us. It's all grist to the mill.'

'Maybe he thought he'd be blamed when he heard Alice had been found at the tower and was ill as a result. That could be why he ran away.'

'You could be right, Simon,' William agreed. 'But maybe we'll never know the truth.'

From the Ongoing Account in the hand of Simon Lysaght, dated 24 April 1917.

Tom's last week of convalescence was allowed to run concurrently with his week of being grounded on account of the shot tower visits. To our delight, it rained all that week, so that staying indoors seemed wholly preferable to getting soaked in the gardens. Tom still grumbled, as though it was his duty to do so, saying he'd developed cabin fever and would go absolutely mad if he stayed at home another minute.

'I haven't taken you sailing yet,' he said. 'Now the weather's a lot better, a trip along the coast is in order.'

I looked at him with a schoolboy's wonder, forgetting he was scarcely older than myself.

'Does Sir David... Sorry, Uncle David — does he let you go sailing?'

'As long as I go out with Peter Tregaskis. Pete's a fisherman, a few years older than me. He's a rough sort, like all the fishermen down there, but you'll get on with him well enough. Pa bought me a smashing boat called the *Demelza Ebrel*. That's a Cornish name: I think it means Daisy or something of the sort. She's a seventeen-foot crabber painted yellow and white, with red sails. Sometimes Peter takes her out for crab-fishing on his own, but in turn he has to see the boat's well looked after, and take me out and teach me the ropes. I've been sailing since I was twelve. Pa says it's too soon for me to go out on my own, but I know I could handle it.'

'Why don't you?' I was mistrustful by now of Tom's lack of control.

I looked through the window, at the constantly falling rain. It didn't seem as though it could ever stop. Like arsenic and lead, it fell straight down. I'd been promised sunshine in Cornwall, but this was much the same as Yorkshire.

Tom guessed what I was thinking.

'It'll pass,' he said. 'We're not that far from summer. Give it a few days more, then I'll send a message down to Peter. We'll be out on the ocean wave by next week: you wait and see.'

I didn't always spend my time with Tom. For one thing, I'd promised Fitzgerald that I'd continue with my studies. In fact, we'd both promised, but Tom, being nothing of a scholar, simply ignored it. Thus, I spent a few hours a day in the schoolroom, reading all I could, for I have hopes of going on to Oxford or

Cambridge. My father read Classics at King's College, Cambridge, and I hope to follow in his footsteps.

When I wasn't so preoccupied, I went upstairs to have a chat with William, who languished most of the time without company, at least while the foul weather kept neighbours at bay.

'I hear you've been seeing a lot of the Frog,' he said one afternoon, while we were playing backgammon, a game he had recently taught himself, and which he was now teaching me. We played for matches as always, but I could sense as before that real stakes would have given the game a sharper edge for him.

'Not so much since Fitz got back on his…' — I had to bite back the word 'feet'— 'since his recovery. The marquis gave me lessons in art. He knows more than you'd think.'

'Oh, I expect our marquis knows more than most of us would like. If I knew half as much about him — well… Did he show you the Old Man's collection of nudes? No? I didn't think he would.'

He'd said it deliberately, of course, and I rose to his bait, giggling and asking what nudes he meant.

'I'm not sure,' he said. 'But I've heard something about sketches by different artists. Nothing dirty-minded, you understand, I'm talking about real art. The squire keeps them in folders in his study. Prints mostly. I've heard they're worth a bloody fortune.'

'But what's the good of them if you can't put them on display?'

'Simon, old boy — did they teach you anything at that school of yours? The thing about pictures like these is that you don't put them on display. Heavens, there'd be an uproar if you did.'

'Have you seen your father's collection?'

'God, no. There'd be hell to pay if he thought I had. I think he and the marquis have mutual interests. Stay strictly out of it yourself, if you know what's good for you. My father would have you thrown out of here if he thought you'd tampered with any of his things.'

On other days, our conversations grow duller. There are times when simple pain or the reality of his position force William to become introspective. I've learned to accommodate his darker moods by now, and I fancy I could help steer him through them — not that he cares to know that.

A few days ago, I managed to get him into a conversation about his suffering.

'Do they hurt much now?' I asked. There was no need to say more, he understood. He lay silent for a while, not really thinking his answer over, but conjuring up more of the pain, so he would not give me a false picture.

'The stumps? They're giving me hell,' he said. 'It's like daggers carving you up, all over the wounds, then up higher till your thighs are a mass of little knives. I can't help shouting when it gets like that, no one could put up with it in silence. Have you ever heard me?'

'No,' I said, but it was a lie, and I think he knew it. Sometimes, late at night, I've heard his cries. The walls are thinner on this floor.

'Most of the time, the morphine keeps it down. But the doc only lets me have so much at a time.'

Quilty is seeing him regularly now, at Aunt Marion's request.

'The wounds haven't healed, of course,' he went on. 'I expect it'll take years. Marion does for me most of the time. Takes the old bandages off, washes the wounds, does it all up again. You'd be surprised at how good she is at it. Quilty says he'll make a nurse of her, and they joke about turning the Priors into a hospital for the war wounded. I can't see my father agreeing to that, though.

'There was a nurse used to turn up once a fortnight. An old bat. She used to give me a bad time, she'd be very rough. In the end I gave her hell and told her Marion would take care of the legs full-time in future. Quilty's got rid of her entirely. He says Marion knows what she's doing without her help.'

He talked on through that spring afternoon, about the unendurability of deep pain, and the difference between day-time pain and night-time pain, and the unstoppable ache of a phantom leg, and its impossible itching.

The light changed and faded. I thought I heard guns in the far distance, rolling and rolling.

'Do you ever hear guns?' I asked.

He shook his head, and I could see that my foolish question had troubled him. There'd been a time when barrages had continued for a day or more at a time. He'd acquired the rhythm of them.

'Two days after we arrived in France, we got sent straight up the line. Place called Delville Wood. It was as if the Bosch were waiting for us. Their big guns started up and kept right on for forty-eight hours. It just ploughed up some of the trenches. Ploughed them until there was nothing left but a mash of mud and bodies. There was nothing left to bury. You just got on with it, you and the dead, sharing quarters, sharing what sunlight there was. That was my introduction. But you don't want to know about it.'

'I want to go out there when I'm old enough,' I said. 'I will be soon. It's better for me if I know what it's like.'

'Is it?' He looked at me oddly. 'If I told you the whole truth, Simon, you'd cut an arm off sooner than go to France. I've seen men rigid with fear, good men, men I'd trust my life to. And I've seen our own men shot because they hadn't the guts to walk out into the machine guns when our guns had missed their targets and left the Bosch untouched.

'What's going on in France is senseless. It's slaughter with no purpose — believe me, there's no love in it, and no hatred. It's just men and their blood against machines. I lost my legs to a machine gun, and I never even saw the face of the man who fired it. Stay in England. Do some good with your life. At your age you should be thinking about girls, not how to get yourself killed. And you have your studies to attend to.'

I left him soon after that, frightened by his words. He was my hero, my flesh-and-blood Galahad, and he was talking treason. Everyone else I knew praised the war and the heroism of our troops, and any adult who heard of my wish to enlist at the earliest possible moment would gravely hold out their hand and congratulate me on my loyalty and spunk. Now, here was the one person I knew who'd been there, and far from shaking my hand, he was trying his best to dissuade me from going.

I was pensive all through dinner, which elicited a whispered enquiry from Aunt Marion, who saw all deviations from everyday behaviour as the first clouds of illness. I reassured her that I was well, but that I was thinking about my Cicero text in preparation for tomorrow's lesson.

After dinner, I retired early. There had been a letter from my mother the day before, saying that she had made up her mind to visit Cornwall once the weather was more dependable. No date had been given, but Aunt Marion reckoned some time in June would be the first choice, and undertook to write back to my mother suggesting the fifteenth.

Buoyed up by thoughts of this impending visit, I fell asleep. My dreams were confused, but I remember vividly that I woke with images of battle in my mind. It must have been a little after midnight. I at once became aware of a light wind that had come up since I slept. I'd left my window open, since the night had seemed warmer than usual; now it was banging gently against the frame.

As I closed it, my eyes swept across the courtyard. It was empty, but I know I had expected something else. Looking up again, I noticed, as before, that a light still burned in what I took to be William's window. At the thought of him lying alone in bed reading or simply thinking, I returned to the upsetting conversation he and I had had earlier. I had not spoken to him since then, but I wanted to get things right. Surely he hadn't meant all that about the pointlessness of the war. To think that would mean that James had died for nothing, that my father had given his life for absolutely nothing, that William's lesser sacrifice had been for nothing. However embittered, he couldn't believe that, surely...

I resolved to talk it over with him. He'd said more than once that he stayed awake into the early hours, and that I should feel free to visit him whenever I wished. I'd never taken advantage of the invitation — I was always well asleep by that time — but I decided that this was as good a moment as any.

Outside my room, only a couple of flames had been left burning. With my dressing-gown tightly wrapped about me — it was still very chilly — I hurried down to William's room, my slippered feet silent on the lightly carpeted floor.

As I drew close to the door, I hesitated, wondering if, after all, I might not be disturbing him. Perhaps he preferred his own company at this time of night, perhaps he kept his light on to avoid waking into darkness out of a fitful sleep. I hesitated, with my knuckles poised to knock, and as I did so I heard a soft voice behind the door. Not William's voice, but a woman's. I thought it must be one of the maids, bringing coal for the fire, perhaps. Then she spoke again, and I realised it was Marion.

My first thought was that something must be wrong for her to be visiting him so late. I knew she generally looked in on him last thing, to make sure his bandages were in place, that his morphia was to hand, and that he had anything else he might need for the night ahead. He'd told me that he sometimes experienced some sort of crisis. Perhaps she'd stayed on to see him through it. It occurred to me that I might be able to relieve her, and let her get back to bed.

I was on the point of opening the door, when I thought twice. If Marion was dressing William's wounds, he might find it awkward to have someone bursting in. I paused for several minutes, uncertain what to do.

Torn between retreating back down the passage and the potential embarrassment of invading William's privacy, I committed a terrible breach of propriety. I remembered that William had once commented on the way that a draught forced its way through the original keyhole half-way down the door. It was an old door, and the key had long ago been lost, as had most of those on that floor; ten or twenty years earlier, new locks had been fitted higher up, but the originals had been left as they were, and no one had ever got round to blocking them up.

I bent down and put my eye to the hole. It took a little while before my pupil adjusted to the light, and a little longer to make out what I could see.

I found myself so situated that I could see most of the upper part of the bed, which faced sideways on to me. William was lying with his back propped up against some pillows, as he often was. He was entirely naked, except for the bandages that reached from just above his knee down to the tip of his severed stumps. My Aunt Marion was also on the bed, kneeling above William, and facing him. His legs — or what was left of them — were pressed hard against her waist, while she stretched forward, stroking his chest and belly. For a moment this seemed quite natural to me, since I imagined William required regular massage to keep his upper body in shape.

But moments later that misconception was dramatically dispelled. Marion took her hands from William's body and reached them to her throat, and so began to unbutton her blouse. Another garment followed, then she pulled them both back and over her shoulders, to reveal her upper body entirely naked. I crouched, watching in a kind of disbelief, for I only guessed at what was happening, and at what it meant.

Then I saw her reach between William's legs and begin a slow, rhythmic movement whose purpose I could not even start to guess at, though in William's posture and the soft groans he let utter there was perhaps sufficient suggestion.

I could watch no more. The overwhelming intimacy of the scene I had stumbled upon, combined with my very real ignorance of such matters, made me wish the earth would swallow me up. In my frightened embarrassment, I almost made my presence known. Can you imagine what might have happened if I had?

I made my way back to my room and slipped inside, shivering. I did not sleep for the rest of that night. And for the first time in my life, I did not pray.

Letter from Harriet Lysaght to Lady Marion Trevelyan, from the original kept in Trevelyan Priors

1 May 1917

My dear Marion,

Thank you so much for your last letter.

I was most distressed to hear further of the ailments that continue to dog your household, though naturally relieved, as well you might think I was, to hear that my own dear boy is thus far safe. He has never been a robust child, and his asthma has given me much cause for alarm in the past. And yet, like many frail children, he seems less prone to infection than many others. They say they grow out of it in the end — do you think that's true? Or perhaps it's the country air. I'm told his father was much the same as a boy, though he went on to make a full recovery. Anything less and they would not have passed him as fit to fight for King and Country. Sir David will, of course, know all there is to know about Jonathan's childhood. I so regret that I never got to know either his father or his mother well, after that awful breach. I wonder did they ever say anything to you about his early years?

I am looking forward greatly to my stay with you, now that I have made up my mind to the journey.

I shall take the same train as Simon, as you suggested, though the day of departure being a Saturday and not a Monday, I shall arrive at Porthmullion a little later, at five o'clock. Do you think it will be possible for you to provide transport to the house? Otherwise, I shall be happy to make what arrangements I can at the station, where I am sure there are plenty of vehicles for hire.

Perhaps, dear Marion, it will be best if I clarify certain issues before my arrival, rather than see them hang over us like a cloud during my visit. The first is, of course, your kind proposal that I stay on at Trevelyan Priors and make it my home. I truly cannot contemplate at this juncture such a major change for myself. As you say, my natural predisposition is to be wherever my darling son is, and I admit freely that I am sorely tempted. But I think you know that it is for the wider interest I must decline.

What can I say to your second proposition? You seem to have made up your minds as to what is best for Simon. He will, you say, become your son, in name at least, and this, you say, will ensure his future and afford him the means to carry on his father's name. He will at length share in the Trevelyan fortune, and before that will be well provided for.

Marion, dear Marion, this is one thing that I cannot countenance. Do not press it with me, I beg of you. Simon is my son, my only son, and a precious reminder to me of his dead father. Without him, I should hate to live another day. Whatever the good such an arrangement might contrive to bring about, only think how it would break my heart to know that all meaningful relations between my sweet child and myself had been terminated. I might not openly call him son, nor he again address me as Mother. Think how little time it is since I bade his dear father a last farewell, and you may guess what feelings agitate my heart when I read of what you propose, knowing how little power I have to countermand you.

Please, let no more be said on this subject. I have made my mind up and shall not be swayed. And I pray you, do not let this become a cause for division between us. Our families have known more than their share of estrangement, and I could not bear to be the cause of yet another generation knowing the disharmony ours has known, however innocently. Do reassure me of this, my dear Marion: let me know that all is well between us and shall continue so.

I don't think I've told you yet about Reverend Thaddeus Upham Pope, one of the lesser clergy attached to the Minster here — you would call it the cathedral. You are all so far away, I cannot guess if you have cathedrals at all. Durham, which is about an hour from us by train, is by far the finest: the Venerable Bede is buried there, and Cuthbert. I'm sorry, I digress. The Reverend Upham Pope is a very pious man and a treasured member of the chapter, and though devoid of ecclesiastical honour, he does have a small reputation in the town as the author of religious tracts, which he has published at his own expense by a small press in Petergate. His most recent composition is a meditation on the War, entitled *The Great Crucifixion*. It is fifty pages of the most edifying reading I have known. I told him in person of your dreadful loss just last week, and he at once handed me a copy of his booklet, which I enclose. I draw your special attention to pages 7, 17, and 39 to 41. He did not ask for payment, but I know that contributions are most welcome, since they furnish the means for his next ventures.

He asks me to say that he was once in the confidence of the Baron and Baronness of Stourcaster, and that he still harbours a deep affection for your family. He tells me that he attended your christening, my dear: that was in the days before circumstances obliged him to seek for a living in the York diocese.

I live a narrow life here now, between Upham Pope and my church activities. We dispense charity to widows and orphans of the War — believe me, there are so many fresh each week, it is hard to keep pace. Some of the women suffer greatly, having depended so utterly on their husbands' incomes. I am very sorry for the youngest ones, many of whom married while their husbands were on leave and now find themselves widows days or weeks later. And then find they are expecting a mouth to feed. I sometimes think that if they were sent to the front they would tear the ground from beneath the guns and silence this thing forever.

May God keep you and all that are dear to you until we meet.

Believe me your loving sister-in-law,

Harriet

Extract from the medical records of Dr Samuel Quilty FRCP, MRCS, MD, then practising in Porth Buryan in the county of Cornwall

12 May 1917

I am concerned about a little girl in my care, Alice Trevelyan. This child was brought to me following prolonged exposure to inclement weather, having been found unconscious some distance from her home. She had been there for several hours, as near as can be determined, and when I first examined her, she seemed to me to be beyond help. I was also concerned that she might have been the object of an attack, an attempted abduction, or a rape, though further examination satisfied me that she was still virgo intacta. There were no scratches or bruises on her body (though some few on her hands and wrists, which were consistent with her having spent some time outdoors playing).

For all that, I thought her unconscious state might have owed more to some sort of shock than to prolonged exposure to severe conditions. Her previous history, as recounted to me by the mother, gave no indication of previous episodes of this or any related type. When I made my first examination, I found her temperature seriously low at 89.3°F (this was established by the use of a French rectal thermometer, admitting calibrations below 91.4°F). Her skin was pallid and chill to the touch, even though she had been warmed by fires and blankets for some time. I was especially worried by this, for some time had already elapsed between her discovery and first warming and my eventual arrival at the house just after 9.00 p.m.

I had the maids prepare a bath in her room, heated to a temperature of 113°F, which slowly brought her back to a core temperature of 91°F, without waking her or effecting any change in her appearance. From there she was placed in an armchair and wrapped once more in a blanket. I did not allow her to be placed back in bed, for fear she become heated too quickly. To the same end, I made sure the room itself did not become heated above 84°F.

My chief concern was that too rapid re-heating might result in a more marked episode of the usual vasodilatation and hypovolaemia, which would mean a serious decrease in the volume of the blood in her veins. At the same time, I took note of the fact that, as long as my patient remained hypothermic, the greater the risk of death. Brandy was administered in small sips, and the nurse who had come up from the village, Mrs Spreadborough, was left with strict instructions to regulate the intake of alcohol and to make half-hourly checks on the child's temperature, using an oral thermometer. I planned to keep a vigil by the child's bedside for as long as I could hold out. Before that, however, I had other patients waiting.

Given the possibility that the little girl had been, at the very least, subjected to some shock, and that its after-effects might be interfering with her recovery, I administered a homoeopathic preparation of aconitum in the 30th potency, in the form of a small sugar pill, which I left to dissolve beneath her tongue. I then left to see to my other charges.

I was then almost certain that she would slip away that first night, though I held out hope to the parents that she might pull through and wake in the morning. Pull through she did, but she did not wake that day or the next.

When I examined her properly that first morning, I discovered that, although her core temperature was coming close to normal, her appearance was still waxen, her flesh cold (except where covered by clothing and blankets), and her skin unnaturally white. The whites of her eyes were quite abnormal, being bright red, and the pupils much contracted. It seemed that the tiny capillaries in her eye had filled with blood. What was stranger still was that I was sure that she — or someone — was looking directly at me, with clear intelligence and full consciousness. Nevertheless, my little patient was clearly still in a hypothermic coma, and seemed unlikely to come out of it.

I persisted in my treatment, giving her Aconite in the same potency and at the same frequency as before, sitting her in the window so that as much sunshine as possible could reach her. Her mother came to sit with her, as did her father, though he remained but briefly.

By the afternoon, I was faced with a strange dilemma. Her core temperature, as measured by the rectal thermometer, was returned to normal. Yet she was still profoundly unconscious, and could not be reached by any means. Not only that, but her skin retained its death-like hue, and the eyes that bloodshot appearance.

I agreed to stay on at the house, in view of the number of members of the family and staff who had come down with colds and influenzas. There was also the matter of young William Trevelyan, an amputee whose stumps are causing him unusual pain at present.

On the third day, the Aconite began to do its work, cure progressing from inwards outwards, and from bottom to top. This in respect of the touch and appearance of the skin, which slowly regained its former hue and became warm. The eyes lost their bloodiness, and, last of all, the child's hair recovered its pristine sheen.

But the child herself remained in her coma. Her father and mother came at regular intervals to speak to her, as did her brother, Tom and her cousin, Simon Lysaght. Children, friends of hers, were brought in from the surrounding countryside, for the snow had passed away quickly. They all talked to her in familiar voices, in the hope of re-awakening memories that might draw her back to us. But never a flicker of recognition did she give. My fear now was not that she might die, but that she might remain in this state indefinitely, sustained by capable nursing. I went down to Porthmullion that afternoon and spent some hours consulting Kent's *Repertory*. After that, I attended to several of my patients in the village, some of whom had desperate need of me.

By the time I returned to Trevelyan Priors, it was almost midnight. I hurried to the child's room, hoping against hope that she might be a little improved.

Lady Marion met me in the great entrance hall. She told me there had been no change, and I grew more than ever convinced that little Alice was beyond my grasp. I had already resolved to bring in a second doctor, James Witherspoon from London, but, to be honest, I thought it might well prove a waste of time.

Lady Marion indicated that I should go upstairs at once, and that she would join me there later. I knew my way well by now, and went up, proceeding quietly so as not to wake others sleeping along the same corridor.

When I opened the door I knew right away that something was wrong. I had given strict instructions that as many lamps or candles were to be left burning as possible: instead I found but a single oil-lamp giving out a curious smell. In a chair next the bed, the nurse had fallen asleep. Alice lay propped bolt upright on the bed. She was staring straight towards something that lay in the shadows just beyond the foot of the bed.

I followed her line of sight and to my horror saw something crouching in the space between the bed's end and the tall wardrobe that stood near against it. I could not tell if this shadow was an animal or a small human being, but it seemed as though it was about to leap for the bed.

The door closed behind me. I took half a step back and tried to open it, but it was stuck, the handle would not even turn.

I faced the bed again. This time, Alice had turned her head towards me and was staring hard. Without warning, she screamed, a single loud, piercing scream that went right through me.

When I got to her, she was wide awake and shivering. The screaming had woken the nurse: I shouted at her to bring some lights and to fetch my bag, which I had dropped in the corridor. She hurried out, leaving me with the child and whatever the thing was crouching near her bed. Once, I looked in that direction and made out the same shape as before, but in the act of rising on its hind legs, or so it seemed. The room seemed cold, and I could detect a curious smell, as though some sort of incense had been burned there, an incense that had left an odour that reminded me of rotting vegetation.

Suppressing my own fears, I looked back at the girl, then took her in my arms and whispered to her.

'Don't worry, Alice, everything's fine. Mrs Spreadborough is coming with a light. I'm Doctor Quilty: I've been looking after you. You've been very ill, but you've come round now, and we'll have you up and out of bed in no time.'

'I'm frightened,' she said, whimpering and pushing her face into my chest.

'There's nothing to be frightened of,' I said, at the same moment looking back towards the foot of the bed. The crouching thing was standing now, tall and very, very thin. It moved, and I thought I saw long hair trail down its back as far as its feet.

In almost that same moment, Mrs Spreadborough came running in carrying a well-lit lamp she'd taken from the kitchen. The light brought everything into focus. The thin shadow passed in moments from grey to nothing. One moment, there was a distinct presence, the next nothing. The foul smell vanished with it.

Moments later, the door was crowded by members of the family and staff, who had come running on hearing Alice scream.

I looked up at them.

'Alice is out of danger,' I said. 'She has come out of her coma and is fully conscious, as far as I can tell at present. It's best we don't crowd her. Lady Marion, if you will step inside. It will help reassure her. But if the rest of you don't mind going back to your beds, I think it will prove best for the child.'

'Why did she scream? asked a woman at the back.

'She came awake suddenly,' I said. 'The shock will have frightened her. But she seems quite recovered now. I'll be able to tell you all more tomorrow, after I've given her a thorough examination. Put your minds at rest. The crisis is over.'

Inwardly, I thought it had only begun, and that it might prove a crisis of quite a different order than any I had been trained to handle.

'What happened?' Alice asked me. Her mother was still in the corridor, giving instructions to the staff and reassuring family members. 'How did I get here?'

'You were found a few days ago,' I said. 'At the Shot Tower. It was the day of the big snowfall. Do you remember?'

She nodded.

'I remember,' she said. 'I brought some sandwiches for Tom and Simon. I was in the Shot Tower, at the bottom.'

'That's right. That's where Simon found you. Can you remember how you got there? Were you by yourself or with someone else? Did someone take you there?'

She nodded.

'I met her while I was walking back,' she said.

'A lady?'

She smiled for the first time.

'Yes, a lady. She had on such lovely clothes, but she wasn't dressed for the snow. I expect her mummy told her off.'

'Was it someone you knew?'

Another nod. I could hear them murmuring out in the corridor. The housekeeper came in and started lighting the lamps.

'Oh, yes. She's an old friend. She was engaged to my brother James. That's before he was killed in the War. Her name is Geraldine. Pa calls her Miss Fitzallan, but Pa is thought very stiff. Have you met her?'

'No,' I said, very quietly, fighting down a desire to get myself away from there as fast as possible. 'I'm afraid I never had that privilege.'

'I can introduce you if you like,' she said, and I felt a chill spread through me.

'That would be a lot of trouble,' I said. 'Maybe another day.'

'But it's no trouble at all,' she persisted, sitting up straighter against her pillows and pointing. 'She's standing just there in the corridor, next to Mummy.'

The weather remained unsettled for the rest of April, and is still unpredictable. As a result, Peter the Fisherman (as Tom likes to call our young boatman) turned down all Tom's requests to take the *Demelza* to sea. The weather was still unsettled, and sudden squalls were rushing in across the Channel and hitting the Cornish coast almost every day. The fishermen went out much as usual and rode out the storms, each little fleet sticking close together. Tom and I would go down to Porthmullion as often as our other activities allowed, and stand on the harbour wall in the hope of catching a glimpse of them heading out past the Lizard into Mount's Bay, or sometimes south to the Bay of Biscay or the great Biscay Plain. Deep in the Channel, they'd outsmart the little French smacks and catch sole and plaice and red gurnard from under their very noses. In the cool evenings, we would sit in Peter's little cottage and watch our heroes come home from a hard day's fishing.

Tom showed off the *Demelza* at every opportunity, on days when Peter had joined another boat and left her behind. She was never an ocean-going vessel anyway, and if he did go out in her, it was always within the confines of the Channel's western reaches, and never far off our own coast. He'd take her out for crabbing mostly, and sometimes to tend his strings of lobster pots and his shrimp pots. We'd wait for his return, and fill a bucket with whatever he brought back. The contents would be rushed back to Trevelyan Priors, where we'd hand them over to Mrs Douch. That meant shrimps for breakfast or lobster for lunch, or crab sandwiches for afternoon tea. Our regular fish came from Mr Spargo, the village fishmonger. He always took the best of any catch and had it on his slab long before the rest made their way to Exeter or Bristol or London. He'd been a fisherman himself before a rotten accident mangled his left leg and grounded him for life.

I'm finding it very hard to pick up where I left off with William. Even all these weeks later, I find the whole thing stomach-churning. I think I understand very well how it must be for him, to have those feelings yet be unable to do a thing about them. But why can't my Aunt Marion just arrange for a woman, a girl of easy virtue, one of the servants, perhaps, to come at regular intervals to… see to him. It would be a lot more discreet, and even if the scheme was found out, well, who would kick up much of a fuss under the circumstances? But for his own step-mother….

I know that what I saw was pretty high on the list of things you don't talk about, and I'm sure that, if William or Marion were to learn what I know, I'd end up in fearful hot water. I once tried to think — very briefly — of my own mother doing something of the same to me, and the idea made me sick. So I intend to keep what I know to myself, even when — especially when I'm with Tom.

But I also know I can't leave poor old William in the lurch. He's become my friend, my ally, my older brother; however shocked I may feel, I know I could never so much as hint that I know about him and his step-mother. And I can't just cut him. He'd wonder why I wasn't calling in very often, and before long he'd say so to Marion and others, and they would be bound to pester me with questions.

So I go to him when I can, and play game after game of poker and chess, and try to behave normally, even though I know I'm not making a very good job of it.

I saw him just yesterday. His cheeks were red, and he was in one of his better moods.

'What's up with you, old boy?' he asked more than once. 'You don't seem yourself.'

'I'm perfectly all right,' I said. 'It's just… sometimes I miss my mother.'

That was perfectly true, but I'm not sure that I managed to convince William it was the real reason for my preoccupied mood.

'She'll be here before long,' he said. 'Then you can hug and kiss her all you like.'

'Not likely,' I said. 'I'll kiss my mother but I won't let her kiss me back.'

I realised too late how I'd put my foot in it, but there was no reaction to my remark. Instead, William changed the subject abruptly.

'Tell me, young Simon,' he said, and he moved his remaining

knight to take one of my rooks, 'do you still lock your bedroom door at night, as I advised you?'

I hesitated a moment or two before answering.

'I do what I can,' I said. 'I keep my door firmly closed, but the lock won't work.'

He grew very agitated when I said this.

'Damn it! Damn these stumps to hell! Damn this sepulchre of a house, damn it to hell!'

I was terrified by these outbursts, too frightened to speak, even in an attempt to calm him.

Just then the door opened and Aunt Marion came in. She did not see me at first, and burst into the room precipitously. William stared at her, his mouth half open in yet another obscenity. I looked away from him. My aunt's face was in movement between icy calm and what I took at first for anger, yet on reflection recognise as fear.

'Alice is sleeping,' were her first words. 'You may waken her. And anyone else that can hear you. Do you understand me, William? Anyone else.'

She caught sight of me then, and threw a dark look in my direction.

'You,' she said, quite unlike herself, 'what are you doing here?'

'He's visiting me,' said William, quite collected all of a sudden.

'I'd better go,' I said.

'I'd rather you stayed,' said my cousin.

He gave a lop-sided smile, a winning smile that he knew would keep me by his bedside come what may. He'd worked out long ago how desperate I was for his approval; and I knew that, whatever his sins, I would stand by him.

But I was unable to resist my aunt.

'William, I think it would be better if Simon left you alone for a while. I'm sure he has studies to catch up on. Mr Fitzgerald returns next week, and I'm sure it would disappoint him to find his two charges spending all their time playing chess or cheering on the local fishing fleet.'

'It's all right,' I said. But I looked at William, trying to convey to him my intention to return later that day.

I looked everywhere for Tom, but he was nowhere to be found — not in his room, not in the kitchen, and not in the schoolroom. I asked Alice, but she hadn't seen him all day. She had been conscious for several days now, but Dr. Quilty insisted on keeping her indoors and free from any excitement, which meant Tom and I were all but banned from her room. Nevertheless, I sneaked in from time to time, whenever her nurse — the same Mrs Spreadborough who'd been looking after Tom — was out of the room for lunch or tea, or for any other reason. I now went along to Alice's room and knocked, keeping an excuse up my sleeve should Spreadborough prove to be inside. But there was no reply, so I turned the knob and pushed the door open.

The curtains were drawn, even though there was bright summer sunshine outside, and the room was lit only by candles. As the door swung away from me, the first thing that drew my attention was a heady smell, or rather a complex mix of perfumes, some sweet and some bitter, others with rich scents of their own.

As I drew close to the bed, I noticed that Alice was asleep again, though she did not seem to be in the coma she'd been in previously. Nevertheless, I thought it better not to wake her. Above and around the bed were dozens and dozens of plants, some flowers, others garden herbs, yet others, I thought, taken from the woods. I had acquired a little knowledge of plants during long walks with my mother outside York, and I recognised some of those surrounding my cousin.

There was mugwort, betony, rue, St. John's Wort, all mixed in with bay leaves, burdock, and green holly without berries that I knew must have come from the bushes at the edge of the old wood. Glancing round the room, I saw yet more herbs and flowers, some in vases, others worked into circlets or chaplets or rough balls, and put to hang from pictures and ornaments. I made out white heather and jasmine, yarrow twigs and arbutus, dill and aconite and anise. Bowls had been filled with common tansy, which I'd seen one day passing near the kitchen garden.

My father, a year before he died, gave me *Dracula* to read, and I'd finished it in three or four long sittings, strictly by the light of day, and bored him for days afterwards, and my poor mother, who jumped if a spider came into the room, telling them how entertaining I'd found the story.

Now, I was swept back to the atmosphere of the tale, to the desperate, doomed efforts to save young Lucy Westanra from a vampire's fate, to the image of poor Mina, surrounded by wreaths of garlic, slowly wasting away as Dracula preyed on her mind and body. Was that happening to my dear little cousin? Was Alice dying before our eyes, her blood sucked, her soul ravished by some Cornish vampire?

My father had always insisted that there were no vampires outside the imagination of Bram Stoker, and I had believed him. Now, my convictions were turned upside down. I could see no garlic in the room, but that did not prevent me from interpreting the entire scene as if vampires were lurking behind every shadow.

Half in a fever of apprehension, I remembered that, in the story, the vampire count had hidden in his coffin by day and roved abroad by night, only to be brought down by shafts of sunlight entering his hideout. Was that why the curtains in Alice's room had been drawn so close, and candles lit, and herbs of all kinds tied around the room?

I hurried across to the window and pulled the heavy velvet drapery aside, opening a gap of about two feet in the centre. Right away, bright sunlight rushed into the room, dimming the candles and throwing the shadows into disarray. Turning back to the room, I saw that the sudden light had startled Alice, and that she had started to emerge from her sleep. I ran to her. She was paler than I had seen her, and when she opened her eyes, I saw something dark and ugly in them, and looked away, but when I looked again, she seemed her old self, except that her skin was still pale, and her eyelids dark and bruised, with purple shadows in them.

She opened her mouth to say something, but just then I heard something in the room behind me. I whirled round, but saw nothing out of the ordinary. It had been a crisp scurrying sound, and I wondered if one of the many house cats had strayed upstairs and slipped in. Satisfied, I went back to Alice.

'What are you doing here, Simon?' she asked. 'Nobody's supposed to visit me. Weren't you told?'

'I thought I'd just look in,' I said. 'Sorry I wakened you. What are all these flowers and things?'

'I'm not sure,' she said. 'Father put them there. And that nasty count came with him a couple of times, to lend him a hand. Father said they're to help me get well. I like the smell of them, don't you?'

I said I did, but, to be honest, the mixture of sweet and dark bothered me. The herbs did not seem entirely guarantees of health or vitality.

'I'm glad you came out of your coma,' I said.

'Is that what it was?'

I nodded.

'I think so. At least, that's what William said. And he told me to apologise for not being able to visit you.'

'Tell him I understand. But you must tell me how *he* is.'

I gave a full description of the time I had spent with William.

'I didn't know you played chess, Simon.'

'Well, I do, but not very well. Would you like me to fetch a set and play a game or two?'

She shook her head from side to side.

'Yuk!' she said. 'I hate chess. It's far too difficult. I don't know how you understand it.'

'I'll come and show you sometime, shall I?'

'I think I'm too young. I'll play with you when I'm grown up.'

'You're already grown up, Miss.' I liked teasing her, and she adored being treated as an adult.

'Not as grown up as you,' she said.

I laughed and shook my head.

'I've some way to go,' I said. 'But I wouldn't hold your breath. The minute I turn sixteen, I'll say I'm nineteen and join up. If I'm not quick, the war will be over before I get to do my bit. You'll think I'm grown up then, when I'm writing to you from the Front.'

I'd been looking away while I spoke, but now, returning my gaze to Alice, I realised how stupid I'd been. Tears had started down her face, and her eyes were wide open with fright.

'No, Simon, you're not going to the war. Not you. Not Tom.

You must never go there, do you hear me? You'll go and leave me alone, and when it gets cold in the winter, and it's dark, there'll be no one to chase them away.'

'Chase whom away?'

A voice sounded behind me.

'She think something looking for her. Maybe she get the hallucination after such an illness. But that is nothing to worry for. You must give her time, Master Simon.'

The count walked past me and sat on the edge of Alice's bed.

'Now, young lady,' he said, ignoring me. 'You are suppose to be asleep. What am I to do with you, *mon enfant*?'

She looked at him winningly, and I sensed a rapport between them that had not been there before. He must have formed a liaison with her while she was ill. He had his little ways, his connivances to lure and repel, his *bonbons fourrés*, his box of *bibelots*, his collection of eighteenth-century *brimborions* and *colifichets*, all perfectly designed to amuse and win over the heart of an eight-year-old girl. I'm still not sure what his motives are, but I do sense his duplicity and falseness.

My parents once took me to see a magician perform on stage in Harrogate. The magician — The Great Lombardo — had been a consummate actor, his words and gestures glistening across every moment of his performance, in order to mislead the audience and leave them astounded at every twist and turn. Now, watching the count with Alice, I saw again the minutiae of charm and misdirection that were done to dazzle my little cousin and myself.

'Simon woke me up,' Alice said, her voice pale and drained. 'I don't feel tired. I don't think I need any more sleep today. Simon and I are going to play Snakes and Ladders. I haven't asked him yet, but I'm sure he will.'

'Later, perhaps.' The count's tone was peremptory. 'You will have to allow Monsieur le Docteur and myself be judge of how long you are to sleep. You are still the invalid, *mademoiselle*, you cannot decide.'

He looked round suddenly. 'Who open the curtains?' he demanded.

'I did,' I said. I wondered what I could have possibly have

done wrong.

'*Mais, bien sûr*... But really, you should not have done so. Very bad to open curtains. The darkness, like everything else in this room, has his purpose.'

'What about the herbs? All these smells can't be healthy.'

He raised an eyebrow, and as he did so reached inside his jacket to bring out a packet of long French cigarettes. There was a gold crest on one side of the packet, which was a deep blue. It meant nothing to me, but as he turned the pack, I noticed a helmet above a five-pointed star, and wondered what they might signify. He looked round for a box of matches and found it next to a candle not far from the bed.

'Monsieur Simon,' he replied, 'you are a privileged guest in this house. It give you certain rights, *naturellement*. You are, as we say, *de la famille*. But you must be very careful, for you are not always so free at Trevelyan Priors. You cannot always choose. That is the price you pay for such privilege. It is the price of duty. If you go into the army as you plan, you will quickly learn what is the duty.'

He selected and struck a match, holding the flame gently to one end of the pale violet-coloured cigarette he held lightly between his lips. I could detect a faint odour of scented smoke rising among the other perfumes in the room.

'*Mon cher* Simon,' the Frenchman went on, 'sometimes you see things, and sometimes you hear some other things, *n'est-ce pas*? In an old house like this, many sounds, many thoughts, many echoes, but you must not think of them. Between day and night, the timbers groan. At dawn, the floorboards creak. In the daytime, the sun warm the house, at night it grow cold again. But here is nothing from the unusual. Is nothing wrong. Just this old house making the changes.

'Sometimes at night, when I cannot fall to sleep and I think everyone else in their beds sleeping, I leave my room and walk the corridors. No one knows I am there, no one. I pass silent like a ghost. I imagine everyone is so asleep, and I think to myself what dreams they have.'

He stopped suddenly and looked at me intently.

'Tell to me, *mon petit garçon*, what dreams visit you in the night?'

He was looking directly at me, and I did not know how to reply.

'Come, come, sir,' he said, 'we all have dreams. Even the dead have dreams. Didn't you know? Then what dreams must your dreams be.'

'I never dream,' I said, knowing by some instinct that I must shut him out of my mind. 'I sleep too deeply. Or, if I dream, I have no memory of it come morning.'

The count smiled cruelly at me.

'Then you are certain to dream those dreams again, now or in later life. Or perhaps when you are no longer among the livings. You should pray that the day of your death is far away. You do not want to dream those dreams when you can no longer wake.'

'Did Alice dream?' I asked when he paused. 'Did she dream when she was unconscious all that time?'

He put the cigarette to his lips and drew on it hard several times, and finally exhaled a tremendous cloud of smoke. A long ash appeared on the end, which he tapped off into a little porcelain bowl on the bedside table.

'It is the same thing, pretty nearly,' he said. 'The dead they do not wake, but the half-dead dream alongside them, their souls half here, half in the realm of the departed.'

'Are you saying Alice was half dead? I thought she was just....'

He shook his head.

'Perhaps she is still half in the world of the dead. But that is all I shall say. You are a healthy boy, you should not entertain thoughts of such things. You should go outside to play now. I have things to attend to here.'

I very nearly insisted on staying, but when I looked in his eyes, I knew he would not stand for such insubordination.

'Very well, monsieur le Marquis. But I may visit Alice later, perhaps?'

He gave me a long look, and I thought for a moment that he was on the verge of telling me something I did not know, making a revelation. But finally he decided against it and simply shook his head.

'*Écoute-moi*, Simon, your cousin, she is still ill. She needs the rest and quiet above all. You may see her from time to time when your Aunt Marion calls on her. But you must not persist in bursting in to her room and drawing aside the curtains. Now, we must say *à tout à l'heure*.'

"Bye, Alice,' I said, my eyes on her pale face.

'Bye, Simon,' she said. But her eyelids were growing heavy, and I knew she would soon be asleep again.

'Goodbye, Monsieur le Marquis,' I said, trying to remain polite. He was the first human being I ever detested. I could not stop myself thinking of him prowling in his silk evening gown through the corridors of the Priors by night. Was that all he did? I wondered. Prowl and listen? Or did he peep through keyholes, as I had done, to my great shame and confusion?

'*Au revoir, Simon. Fais le brave, eh? Et sois patient. Attends, donc, jusqu'au fin de cette sale affaire*.'

I went out, closing the door firmly behind me.

Aunt Marion was downstairs, writing letters in the green study, where she spent a good deal of her time. She was writing with a glass pen that she filled repeatedly from a pot of dark green ink. She did not look up at first, but went on writing, pausing only to dip the finely-tapered pen into the little well and bring it out again, its grooved and bulbous nib fat with ink.

A minute or more passed before she put down her pen and looked at me. She seemed tired. I could detect bags under her eyes, that had not been there previously. She got a smile together and displayed it for me.

'I'm sorry to keep you waiting, Simon. The thing is, I'm busy writing to your dear mother, and I wanted my thoughts in good order. Now, what can I do for you?'

'I can't find Tom,' I said. 'I've looked everywhere for him.'

She looked surprised.

'Why, didn't he tell you he went off shooting crows with his father? They're down in Cripplesease Woods. It's game-keeper work, really, but Sir David thinks it can do no harm for Tom to get in a little shooting practice ahead of the season in August.

'He'd have asked you to join them, of course, but he knows how you feel about wild animals and snares and all that. He told me he didn't want you along in case you'd have some sort of reaction when he shot the first crow. You're not a hunter by nature, are you?'

I shook my head. Tom's instinct had been right. But it still stung, that he'd left me out of his plan.

Aunt Marion continued, 'I don't think shooting birds is your thing at all, Simon. But I do hope you'll be able to join the hunt this autumn. We ride mostly with the South Cornwall, quite often from the Priors, though sometimes we go further afield to the Duke of Beaufort's or the Vale of the White Horse. That's pretty countryside. Good riding country. A bit of a journey to get there, though.'

She stopped and looked at me quizzically.

'Simon... you do ride, don't you?'

I reddened. Whatever I did, I was still going to seem the provincial hick.

'I'm afraid... I've never so much as sat on a horse, let alone ridden one,' I stumbled.

'A young man of your years, and you say you've never even had your feet in a pair of stirrups? Good heavens, what did your mother think she was doing? And your wretched father, how'd he keep his head up?'

I felt my cheeks redden further.

'He had no choice, Aunt. We had no money to spend on a horse. A horse was beyond our reach, especially a hunter.'

'But, dash it, how did you get about, the three of you?'

'We walked, mostly. We never minded, except in a downpour. And not even the finest stallion will stop you getting wet. But we're not so far behind the times in York as you might think. We have motor cars and omnibuses. If we wanted to go to Harrogate, say, an omnibus would take us there and back for sixpence apiece.'

My aunt looked shocked.

'It's one thing to get about,' she said, 'and quite another to ride to hounds. An omnibus will never replace a good hunter.

133

Unfortunately, there are no hunters left in this country. The war has just about done for hunting. First, lawn meets were cancelled. Then the War Office asks for every available hunter in order to supply the cavalry with mounts. And look what happened to the cavalry, and all those poor horses dying in the field. A disgrace. And, of course, nobody nowadays wears scarlet. Black coats and ratcatchers, not at all the same. Then, you'll be lucky to find as many as fifteen at a meet.'

'Wouldn't it be better…?' I began.

'No, it wouldn't. I wouldn't let all this get you down. I'll speak to Sir David, see what sort of horse we can come up with for you. Our man, O'Brien, has a good eye. There's a horse market up in Truro every week. You've got time enough to learn to sit a saddle. The autumn season won't start till the end of August. We'll make a hunter of you before then.'

The thought appalled me — Tom had regaled me with enough stories of foxes being torn apart by hounds — but I said nothing to contradict her.

'Thank you,' I said. 'Now, I think I should go outside. I'll speak to Tom later.'

'Don't forget to put something on your head, dear. The sun's directly above, and it's over eighty degrees today.'

'I'll be all right,' I said, and thanked her as I backed out of the little room. As I closed the door, I realised I'd forgotten to ask her what she was writing to my mother about.

From the Ongoing Account in the hand of Simon Lysaght, dated 20 May 1917.

The following day, I decided to find out what I could about the plants in Alice's room. Tom wouldn't come with me, so I headed out alone to visit the kitchen gardens. These were laid out at the rear of the house, in little walled plots that were seasonally adjusted. At the back stood a great apparatus of glasshouses, stretching away in two directions along the high rear garden wall. They grew grapes and melons down there, and pineapples in deep pits. Near the glasshouses stood a collection of sheds: both-ies, a large potting shed, tool sheds, and a dark house. This was where the head gardener, Dick Tregideon, had his headquarters. I headed there without pausing at any of the plots on the way.

Tregideon was a robust man in his early sixties. His appearance was striking. His long hair and abundant sideburns had been long bleached by life in the outdoors, and his skin had turned swarthy from a lifetime's exposure to the sun. To my surprise when I first made his acquaintance, he wore, not a gardener's apron, but a sailor's outfit all save the sou'wester, for he had been a fisherman in his early days and was still on the rota of volunteers to go out with the Porthmullion lifeboat when the great bell sounded down below.

He had not been fishing many years before he discovered his true vocation, which was gardening. Like many a sailor in those parts, he used to keep a garden patch behind his little cottage, and in it he grew vegetables and the like, to supplement his daily ration of fish and shellfish. He dined on lobster, as often as not, and in season he'd supplement it with potatoes, asparagus, or lettuce, or with samphire he gathered from the cliffs where Miss Fitzallan had fallen to her death.

Tregideon's garden was reckoned to be the finest along that stretch of coast, and he regularly won awards at all the village shows, exhibiting leeks and marrows no one in a hundred miles could match.

How he came to be there at all was, I'd been informed, a long story. The post of under-gardener at Trevelyan Priors fell vacant one year, and by coincidence Tregideon was then courting a girl from Porthmullion called Jane Menadue. Jane was never made to be a fisherman's wife, waiting for days at a time for his return, fearing for his life whenever a storm whipped the waves to a frenzy, selling his fish in the market, chasing the fish smell from her clothing and her home. She told him she would not marry him unless he took the gardening job, and before long he was proving to be the best gardener the Priors had ever known. He and Jane married and rented a small cottage on the estate, and nine months later a daughter was born.

I found him bending down by the strawberry patch, a section of the garden from which we children were particularly warned off.

'After some strawbs, Master Simon?' Tregideon called out as I approached, catching sight of me as he straightened himself.

'I wish I were,' I said, 'but I'm not.'

'Cain't get enough of these, though, can you? Tell truth.' As he spoke, he held up the large wicker basket into which he'd been dropping today's crop. It was a modified lobster creel, something else salvaged from Tregideon's days at sea. I almost expected a steely claw to reach out and pinch my sun-reddened fingers.

'This be my very own variety,' he said, picking a strawberry from the creel and placing it between my teeth. 'I call it Morwenna Trevelyan Pink. Very sweet, ain't it, my dear?'

I'd grown used to this Cornish term of affection by now, and merely smiled and said it was the sweetest strawberry I'd ever tasted — which it was.

I swallowed the last of the fruit, and nodded my approval to Tregideon.

'Mr Tregideon,' I asked, 'what does that mean — Morwenna?'

He looked at me with a sudden look of loss on his face.

'Has no one told you about my little girl, Morwenna?'

I shook my head.

'That was my private name for her. It's an old Cornish name. "Wave of the Sea" is what it means. I used to call her that whenever we were alone together. Her mother would call her Rose, for that was her public name.'

'How old is she?' I asked, and he looked away suddenly, as though she was there beside him, and he wanted to introduce her to me.

'She died when she was about your age,' he said, turning his face back to me. 'That was a good many years ago, before your time. Well, it's over and gone now, and we've all of us moved on. She was a lovely little thing, though. You might have fallen in love with her if you'd met her as she was then.'

He stopped, as though realizing such fantazising could hurt him. Next moment, he changed the subject entirely.

'Now, what brings you here, Master Simon?' he asked, while urging me to eat more strawberries with a wave of his hand.

On my way over, I'd worked out an elaborate story about Mrs Spreadborough and a list of herbs and plants she wanted, but which I had lost. Thinking it through now, I realised I'd be found out before long and arraigned before my aunt or uncle. It was easier just to tell the truth.

I told Tregideon I'd visited Alice in her bedroom, and that the count had found me there, and that he and I had talked at length about the garlands about the bed. However, I said, I still could not remember the names of the plants or what they were good for.

'Good heavens,' he replied, removing his straw hat and scratching his grizzled beard. He affected the outward appearance of a simple son of the soil, but I knew him for an intelligent and capable man, the superior of many supposedly clever men I'd met through my father.

'That be a hard question, and no mistake,' he said, humouring me by pretending to ruminate on my question. 'But I'll do my level best to help you. Let's you and me go up to the big glasshouses. That's where I picked most of plants I was asked for. I grows them in there in order to have them in different seasons as needed.'

The large glasshouses ran all along the back wall of the garden, and were generally out of bounds to the servants and us younger folk. But with Tregideon by my side, I stepped confidently into the largest of the series. I was at once assailed by smells far out of the ordinary, many of which seemed very close to those in Alice's room. She and Tregideon were old friends, and every so often, as we spoke, he would break off to ask about her health.

We walked together down the middle aisle, stopping at every plant Tregideon knew had been picked and taken up in a trug to the house at the Count's bidding.

'This is tansy,' he said. He spoke in English with me, as he did with everyone from the house, only lightly sprinkling his speech with dialect words and phrases. 'A very bitter taste it is, but ideal for the stomach. And this over here is St. John's Wort.'

He showed me a plant with little clusters of four or five yellow flowers.

'It's just coming into flower now, as thees can see. These will all

137

fall again by the day of St. John the Baptist, which is the day bold King Herod had his poor head chopped off for the love of Salome.'

'What's it for?'

'I've heard it called good for a great many of man's sufferings. There be rheumatics and shingles, and then burns it's a sovereign remedy for, and cold sores, and melancholy.'

'Surely Alice had none of those. She's a sight too young for rheumatics, isn't she?'

'That, my 'andsome, she is indeed. But old St. John is excellent for nerves in children, and is recommended for wetting the bed, which is a condition known in children and men in their middle age and beyond. Has passed me by so far, though, and I pray as it continues so.'

'I'm sure Alice doesn't wet the bed. Not at her age, surely.'

'No doubt, but I fancy how she may have done so while in her coma.'

'What's this over here?' I asked. So far, none of this fitted together very well. What did rheumatism and digestive problems have in common, for example. Or bedwetting, for that matter?

I pointed out a plant with green leaves shaped like arrows from which purple flowers emerged.

'Ah,' said Tregideon, 'that's burdock, that is. Reckoned good for diseases of a man's skin. Rheumatics too. And I've heard tell they use it when a man or woman is fallen into a sleep that's like a trance. That makes some sense, now, don't it?'

He paused and crossed to the other side.

'I sent some of this up too. Hyssop, that's its name. You'll find it with flowers toward the end of summer. The old folks laid it out to chase away whatever flies or bugs were about. My mother used to do that, and I've done so mysel'.'

We continued thus from plant to growing plant. Mullein, asafetida, vetivert, witch grass, bryony, galangal, black hellebore, toadflax, arbutus... on and on until my head spun and the names formed a tangle in my brain. I would ask questions, he would do his best to answer. But none of it came to more than a miasm of uses and illnesses.

'I think I'd better get back to the house, Mr Tregideon,' I said, in an attempt to extricate myself from this futile charade. 'And you'll need to be getting back to your work.'

'It's not so confusing as it seem, Master Simon,' he said, sensing my distress. 'God gave us poor humans herbs and plants for the relief of our bodily and mental ailments. Each plant has its own uses and its special virtues. They will serve to heal one man of gout and another of phlegm and yet another of the toothache. It do depend on what you picks and when you picks and where.'

'Perhaps we're missing something,' I said. 'Could the plants have other meanings? The way we use flowers to spell out messages, for instance. Like Acacia for Friendship, or Daisy to say "I share your feelings", or Mignonette for "Your qualities surpass your charms"? My grandmother used to love all those things. She taught me some before she died.'

He looked at me while I recited my little knowledge of flower lore, and I thought a shadow crossed his face. Pursing his lips, however, he shook his head.

'Tell me if you think of anything,' I said, and started to walk away. I'd reached the door when he called me back.

'Master Simon,' he said, 'don't thee take this amiss. But I want you to promise me you'll stay out of Miss Alice's room.'

I walked back to him.

'Why should I do that?' I asked.

'I'd rather not say, sir. I was told to say nothing. I'll lose my post if they find out I've spoken with you.'

'You needn't worry,' I replied, 'I shan't tell anyone. But I have to know just why I'm to stay out of there.'

He hesitated for a full minute or more, then succumbed.

'Very well, sir. The thing is this. What I told you about the plants is what a wise-woman or a travelling apothecary might tell you, how to boil the roots and infuse the leaves and crush the flowers to make remedies for all manner of illnesses. But there are others that use plants. Witches. Sorcerers. Folk of that sort.'

'Really? Do you know any of them?'

He laughed and shook his head.

'I have heard of some, but never set eyes on one to my knowledge to this day…'

'And what do they use them for?'

'Well, sir, the ones I helped set up in Miss Alice's chamber was all for one thing.'

'And what was that?'

'Why, sir, to protect her and to drive away.'

'Protect her? Against what? She had no enemies.'

He hesitated, then spat his answer out.

'Against evil spirits, sir. Evil spirits and evil ghosts. To protect her, and to drive them away. That's why we put them all round her bed, and will continue putting them until she be out of danger, if she ever be.'

He walked me to the garden entrance, out of politeness. We exchanged few words. His last remarks in the glasshouse had unsettled me, and I wanted to be on my own in order to think.

As I came to the gate, something quite unrelated occurred to me.

'Mr Tregideon, what do you know about the old garden? Was it used in your time?'

When I turned to look at him, his face had gone white.

'What old garden is this, sir?' Very formal, very stiff.

I described for him the location of the snow-bound garden Tom and I had run across that fateful day, which my cousin had told me was abandoned.

I had scarcely got the words out when he grabbed me by both shoulders and brought his face unpleasantly close to mine.

'Have you ever been inside that place?' he demanded.

'I… N… no,' I stammered. 'It was full of snow. No one could get inside.'

'Thank God for that,' he said fervently. I could not understand his agitation. 'But you must promise me faithfully never to set foot in it, come what may. Do you understand me?'

I nodded, though truly I did not.

'Not you,' he went on, 'not Master Tom. If I hear either of you has gone there, I shall be obliged to speak to your uncle. I'm sorry, for I know you do mean well, but I should be neglecting my responsibility as a servant in this house if I didn't. I don't like to speak so harsh, it's not in my nature; but there are circumstances that make that garden no fit place for a young man like yourself to enter.'

I could see it would be futile to ask just what those circumstances were. But I resolved to find out for myself.

I arrived back indoors with just enough time to spare to get dressed for dinner. On my way to my room, I passed Alice's door and noticed a sign pinned to it: 'Do not enter without permission'. I tried the handle, but the door had been locked. I asked myself where they had managed to find a key, and resigned myself to being locked out from now on unless I could find a second key of my own.

No one had particularly noticed my absence. My uncle and Tom had remained engrossed in their shooting until quite late, and when I spoke with Tom before we sat round the table, he showed no interest in where I had been, but spoke only of birds he had killed, and the fineness of his marksmanship. My great fear had been that the count would betray our confrontation in Alice's bedchamber, but not a word was said of it. He did speak briefly about her condition, reassuring all of us that she was making steady progress.

After dinner, we retired to the long reception room, with its Adam fireplace and Persian carpets. There, Aunt Marion sang for us, as she did on many evenings, accompanied by the count. I admired his playing, which was graceful and accomplished, his notes rising and falling to carry my aunt's voice better than it deserved. At the same time, I thought both piano and voice rather cold. My mother, I thought, could give feeling to any musical piece, whereas the count seemed to discard emotion in favour of precision and elegance.

At about nine o'clock, there was a sound of the front door being opened and slammed shut. Our old friend Mr Fitzgerald had arrived back from his convalescence. He looked somewhat haggard, and had, indeed, just made a tiring journey, but when questioned, he just laughed it all off, and said he was recovered and eager to start work.

Tom and I spoke with him just before it was time to retire. He seemed his old self, but something had gone out of him. I sensed that his bonhomie was forced, not a little overheated. His eyes were pink and staring and gave the impression of someone on the edge of a mental precipice. If he doesn't settle down quickly, I thought, he'll crack and we'll need a new tutor.

I lay awake for some time, thinking things over. I was desperately sleepy, due, perhaps, to the time I had spent in the garden; but my mind would not let me fall asleep at first. Everything I had heard and seen throughout the day played in front of my brain like a moving film whose characters could be heard as well as seen. Most of all, Alice's pale pretty face practically floated in space before me. She seemed to change each moment, now her old self, without a shadow to cloud her cheeks, now something barely human. In her eyes I could see raw fear, and I asked myself why that should be, for surely she was out of danger.

My aunt and uncle meant well, no doubt of that. But I suspected the count of sinister motives. Between sleep and waking, his face came before me like a small balloon, turning this way and that, altering hue and shape, but always smiling.

In the end, sleep rolled over me like heavy waves on a troubled sea, and I was no longer thinking but dreaming. It felt like the deepest sleep I had ever known, and it must have continued for two or three hours, for when I woke again the room was in pitch darkness, even though I had left the curtain open to let some fresh air enter.

I had pushed my bedclothes aside, for the night had grown warm and humid. My nightgown was soaking with sweat, and when I ran a hand over my hair, it came away with a film of sweat on the palm. I sat on the edge of the bed and fumbled with the box of matches that were always on my bedside table. I wanted to towel myself down before finding a fresh nightgown in the chest of drawers, for I knew I'd catch a chill if I kept the same one all night. Finally, I struck a match and put it to the wick of my candle. The flame burned badly at first, then lifted itself and gave out a little light, but not much.

At about that moment, I heard a sound. It was at first difficult to place and to identify, but I persisted and in the end decided it was coming from the door. It was a scratching sound, as though a cat or some such creature was sharpening its claws on the wood. But the movement was too regular for that.

Puzzled and a little frightened, I went to the door and put my hand hesitantly on the handle. Up close, the scratching sounded louder, and I could just make out a voice.

'Simon,' it said, 'please let me in. Just for a little while. I'm cold out here. Let me in, please.'

Suddenly, I realised it was Alice's voice. I turned the handle at once and drew the door towards me.

She was standing in front of me, her face half-hidden in the shadows, dressed in her nightgown, her feet bare, her long hair falling past her shoulders.

'Come in, Alice,' I said. 'You look as though you've been shivering.'

She said nothing, but stepped into the room. As she did so, I started shivering. The sweat on my nightgown had grown cold, and the chill was starting to enter my bones. But I could hardly change while Alice was there.

She stood for a moment in the centre of the room, then headed for the bed and lay down, drawing the bedclothes up round her neck. I could barely see her now, for she was well out of the range of the little candle's flickering, just a long white thing resting on my bed with her head propped up against my pillows.

I decided to get more light and crossed the room to where I kept an oil-lamp. Removing the glass, I used the candle to light the wick, then set down the candle in its holder, and replaced the glass.

Turning, I raised the lamp and extended it towards Alice. But what sat on my bed was not my cousin. It was something hideous beyond imagination, filthy rags on its body, flesh and bones exposed at every gap, matted hair on top like the nest of a giant bird, and a thin piping coming from its throat.

I screamed out loud and shutting my eyes tight, tried to pull myself away from this creature as far as possible. The lamp flew from my fingers and smashed on the floor. Opening my eyes, I saw flames everywhere, following the oil where it had splashed over the bedclothes and floor.

I screamed again. The moment I did so, I found myself in bed, starting out of sleep with my eyes wide open. It was pitch dark. 'Help me, God,' I said, 'help me, God.'

I reached out as before, my hand trembling, fearing at every moment a hand that would seize my wrist and drag me back to its embrace. But I found the match and lit the candle, and when I held it up, there were only shadows.

Nervously, I got out of bed and stood for several minutes, trying to re-anchor myself. I could still see the horrid face, still hear the piping sound it made.

In order to dispel the shadows more completely, I lifted my candle and, as before, headed for the table on which I kept my oil lamp. Half-way there, I looked down, and the small flame of my candle picked out shards of broken glass strewn across the floorboards. There were traces of oil among them, but no sign of flame.

In the morning, they were still there.

An Argument and a Departure, followed by a Meeting

The next day, Tom and I resumed our lessons with Mr Fitzgerald. He had left us ill, but in good spirits, and was now returned to us, a changed man, more melancholy than before, more given to stopping and staring in the middle of a lesson. Boys though we were, still we understood by instinct what a difficult life a man like Fitzgerald must lead. He was a kind and scholarly man who should by rights have been teaching in a university or, at the very least, a public school, but who had settled, for some reason beyond our ken, to live here in the country in order to teach two young scoundrels, only one of whom had any real attachment to learning, such as that was.

We guessed his age to be around thirty, which we thought terribly old. And we reasoned that, if this was indeed his age, he could not have been recently graduated from his college. He had no wife that any of us knew of, nor, as far as we could tell, much prospect of one, buried as he was here in the depths of the Cornish countryside, in a house with no women other than maids of a suitable age. That meant that he had little hope of children. Tom had discovered that his father paid the man a miserly sum on which to subsist, with next to nothing to put aside for his future needs. That meant that he never went out of the Priors much, whether to dance in Truro (as we both hoped to do before very much longer), or to the theatre, let alone to London to see the sights and visit the galleries (which, in our expectations, came immediately after the dances in Truro).

That morning, he taught us about the French Revolution. When he reached the end of the historical portion of the lesson, he read to us for a while from Thomas Carlyle's remarkable account of the event. I can still hear his voice, trembling as he read:

For Night and Orcus, as we say, as was long prophesied, have burst forth, here in this Paris, from their subterranean imprisonment: hideous, dim-confused; which it is painful to look on; and yet which cannot, and indeed which should not, be forgotten.

And when he'd done with Carlyle, he turned briefly to *A Tale of Two Cities*, and Sydney Carton's thoughts before he faced the guillotine.

It is a far, far better thing that I do, than I have ever done.

I listened to this latter part with the liveliest interest, for my father had read the first few chapters of the book to me not long before departing for the War, and I had identified him, ever since his death, as a modern-day Sydney Carton, sacrificing his life unselfishly for others.

After a short lunch, we returned to the same theme. Fitzgerald seemed as though he was burning from within, and I wondered whether he might not have returned too soon, before his health was properly restored. He talked with undisguised enthusiasm about the impact the Revolution had had around the world and, as might have been expected from a man with a fearsome Irish accent, its reception in Ireland. Wolf Tone, one of the great patriots, had got himself somehow or other to Paris, and in response to his representations the Revolutionary Government dispatched the first of several fleets to Ireland. That was in 1796. Two years later, a French army invaded Ireland and was joined by rebel forces in a great uprising.

'The French and Irish together,' Fitzgerald told us, 'were fighting for liberty, freedom, and equality. It's a struggle that is not yet over, for Ireland is not yet free.'

Tom, who had often confided in me his low opinion of the Irish, leapt to his feet and accused our teacher of being a traitor. He said he was in league with the rebels who'd risen in 1916 and attempted to stab the British Empire in the back in time of war.

I thought Fitz would go for him.

'You've no right to make such accusations at all,' he said. 'Almost two hundred thousand of my countrymen have served on the English side in this insane war. About thirty thousand of them have given their lives so the likes of you can live here in luxury. And you may like to know that around forty Irish soldiers, men of no rank or style, some dead and some alive, have been awarded the Victoria Cross.'

To which Tom's only answer was spiteful and petty.

'Then what about you, Fitzgerald, how come you're here in this house of luxury and not out in France with your mates and their

VCs taking the same risks my brothers took? Why aren't you in your grave like James?'

For a moment, I thought Fitzgerald might kill him. His face went a plum colour, and he had difficulty breathing.

'Don't... be so impert... inent, young man, as to ask... anyone such a thing. I'm... not answerable to you... or anyone else.'

'Then why don't you just head on back to Dublin?'

As the argument continued, I knew very well that, if Tom were to relay any of this to his father, Fitzgerald was done for. Not only would he lose his job at Trevelyan Priors, but he would receive no reference from either my uncle or my aunt, and would find it very hard to find a future position.

When I could stand it no longer, I got to my feet and asked them both to use more common sense. Mr Fitzgerald was no traitor, I declared, and it was wrong of Tom to suggest it. On the other hand, as our tutor, Mr Fitzgerald should not have introduced such a provocative subject into the classroom, especially in a house that had experienced the loss of one son and seen another brought home legless and purposeless.

The Irishman agreed that he'd spoken out of turn, and said lessons were over for the day. He packed his briefcase, a model very like the one my father had used, and left the room looking rather grey and discontented.

The poor man knew just what it was he had done. My father had always had a healthy respect for the Irish, whom he described as the most shabbily treated people in the Empire, and, as I watched Fitzgerald go, I prayed there would be no repercussions from this incident.

Tom could not have been more jubilant. Fitz's apology had awarded my cousin — not the most sensitive of boys — with a victory, and I sensed he was seeking to get what he could out of it.

We went outside, Tom eager to make the most of a fine late spring day. My plan had been to stay in the classroom in order to catch up on the reading we'd missed since Fitzgerald's departure some weeks earlier; but Tom would hear none of it.

'Where shall we go?' he demanded.

'Really, Tom, I don't think this is wise. We should stay indoors and get some reading done. I have a dozen Latin proverbs left to translate, let alone that speech of Cicero's to read through.'

'Bugger Cicero,' said Tom, rather preening himself on this use of profanity. 'Bugger Gildersleeve's *Latin Grammar* for all I care. Most people get by very well without Latin or Greek. I can't really see the point of languages anyway, can you? Unless you find yourself off in India sorting out the wogs. You'd need to learn Persian and Hindustani for that.'

'Look, Tom, I'll go with you, wherever you like. But I want you to promise something in return. The thing is, I know just what you're thinking, and I know you'll cause all sorts of trouble if you go ahead.'

'And just what is it I'm thinking, Lysaght? I suppose they taught you mind-reading at that awful school of yours.' There was a sneer on his lips that I'd never seen before. He knew perfectly well what I intended to say.

'You want to shop Fitzgerald to your pa. You want to tell him the man's a traitor, a rotter, and my uncle should give him his marching orders. Am I right or not?'

'They must have taught you better than I taught. But the thing is, I don't have much of a choice. Fitzgerald doesn't deserve better treatment. He comes here to England, gets himself a cushy number teaching a couple of country bumpkins like you and me, and waits for the day he can pick up a good reference from Pa so he can lurch off to Eton or Harrow to take the job some poor English teacher like your father should have had. If you ask me, I doubt he ever saw the inside of — what's the place called? — Trinity College. Anyway, that's in Cambridge, isn't it? I can't imagine they have colleges or schools or things like that in Ireland, can you? And did you notice he shut up pretty quickly when I asked about what he'd done in the war? No answer, not even a Paddy one.'

I put a hand up and turned on him, determined to stop this hysterical rant. I really could not understand why he was behaving like this.

'Don't go another step, Tom. Frankly, I've heard enough to

sicken me. What have you got against the Irish? They're very decent people on the whole — my mother will tell you that.'

I had an answer for him, but my conscience fought to prevent me revealing what had been told me in strict confidence.

'Your mother has never set foot in Ireland.'

'Nor have you, you ninny.'

'For all we know, Fitz was in that stupid business in the Post Office, reading out declarations of independence and God knows what other Paddy nonsense. That was just last year.'

My patience snapped. I'd tell him and be hanged.

'You're more of a fool than I thought, Tom. I won't have you brand a loyal man a traitor. If you must know, he wasn't anywhere near Dublin last year. He was in the thick of the fighting at Ypres. He was gassed and sent back to England, to a hospital near here, at St. Germans.'

He looked back at me, open-mouthed.

'Who...? Who told you all this?'

'Your mother — and don't for God's sake tell her I've told you. She wasn't supposed to pass it on to me, but she thought I'd respect him the better for knowing it. I was new here, she had to make it easier for me. William thinks he's a terrific sort, and has him in when he can. So I think you should play it a jolly sight smarter than you've been doing. He's been at the Front: the nearest you've been to a war is shooting crows in Cripplesease Wood.'

That brought him up cold sober, as though I'd splashed cold water in his face. He stared at me, radiating anger from every pore. I'd gone right up against his most sensitive spot, and pushed.

'You'll be sorry for this,' he said in a level voice. 'I'll show you what an Englishman is made of. A real Englishman, not a mummy's boy like you.'

With that, he stormed off in the direction of Trywardreath Farm, and was soon out of sight behind a ridge that dipped down towards one of the farm tracks. I watched him go, fearing I had lost a good friend, my only friend, wondering how we would manage to rub along together following such a dreadful row. I wondered whether Aunt Marion could sort it out, but I reasoned that now was not the time, while tempers were raw and passions hot. This evening, I thought, or perhaps tomorrow, if it seemed appropriate.

With the aim of cooling myself down, I went straight off in quite a different direction to the one taken by Tom. This was the path that had taken us to our tobogganing hill a few months earlier. Only a slight deviation took me down to my lost garden. This was my private place, I felt, somewhere I could mentally block out my hotheaded fool of a cousin and anyone or anything else that threatened to disturb my peace of mind.

I pushed open the gate, which had become blocked by weeds and grasses since my last visit. Spring and the first beginnings of summer had changed the face of my little domain completely. There were flowers in every nook and buds in every cranny. They peered out between rocks, grew wild on the pathways, on the guttering and roof of the building. Wildflowers in profusion, and the unbowed remnants of well-bred domestic flowers, roses of every hue, lilies, honeysuckle. It was all like a wild echo of Master Tregideon's flower gardens to the rear of the house.

From the gate I walked slowly down to the little pond, on whose weedy edges grew tall clumps of yellow irises. Ducks panicked as I approached, and took to the half-misted air on strong, blue- and grey-feathered wings, or swept their tiny broods under the curtain of gently hanging weeds. They would return, I thought, once I had shown myself to be no danger to them. But how was I to do that? I might be a hunter like Tom, come to shatter their lives. I turned my back on them, and sat down to contemplate the beauties of my long-neglected garden.

I wondered why Richard Tregideon had shied away from my question concerning this garden. Did this place hold a dark secret, I asked myself. Could Dick have worked here at one time; could he, perhaps, have lived in the pavilion?

The garden and its history were, however, the least of my worries. I'd gone there, after all, to think carefully on the events of less than an hour ago. I could see real dangers ahead for us all, though I had no idea how severe they might turn out to be.

I had developed a real affection and admiration for Conor

151

Fitzgerald. His lessons had in some degree reminded me of my father's, even his manner and the way he stood to the blackboard had brought my father back to mind. If Fitz had to leave on account of Tom's manipulative plotting, it would prove a severe blow, to me certainly, but perhaps even more than he could imagine, to Tom himself.

Tom, however, had become a real friend. The thought of a lasting breach between us chilled my spirits as nothing had done since my father's death. If we could not find a way of patching things up, I'd certainly have to leave Trevelyan Priors and forfeit my chances of an education and a place at King's College. My mother would be shocked and disappointed, my aunt and uncle haughty and glad to be rid of me.

Although Tom and I had often woven a fantasy about joining the army and serving King and country at the Front, I knew it would not now become more than an aspiration. My health would never have permitted me to get past basic training. The military were always on the *qui vive* for new recruits, but even they drew the line at lame ducks who would put the lives of other soldiers at risk. And I wondered if that mattered, considering the great number of men they had sent out to their certain death. Yet I knew too that, if Tom and I were to split, not even the fantasy of soldiering would remain.

The premature heatwave had gone, leaving the world cool and full of awakened promise. I lay back on a low, grass-covered bank and gazed skywards, where light clouds drifted sleepily across the sun, blurring and soothing it. Quite unaware of my intruding eye, birds wheeled above me in sweeping, triumphant arcs. Against the brightness, I could make out neither their colours nor their individual shapes, even if they came swooping in quite low. Some would be seagulls, for they regularly came in about this time of day, but I was too much of a landlubber and a town boy to be able to identify one species from another.

I closed my eyes and let my thoughts wander, accompanied by the strange cries of the circling birds, dipping and spinning in their private universe.

From time to time, red sunlight would flicker on my closed

152

eyelids, only for a cloud to pass and dim the day again. I did not fall asleep, of that I am certain, but lay suspended, rather, as if caught between two levels of consciousness, between the natural world around me and the darker realms of my confused thoughts. I made up my mind at last to leave the garden and return to the house in order to seek out Tom and talk him round.

A voice behind me brought me round with a start.

'I said, what are you doing in my garden?'

I blinked and half rose. It was a girl's voice, and none I recognised.

'I'm right behind you,' she said, and giggled.

I twisted and fell back, and this time I saw her, exactly where she had said she was.

From where I was sitting, she seemed quite tall, but I guessed she would be about my height, or perhaps an inch or two shorter. She seemed about my age as well, perhaps a year younger.

'You shouldn't laugh so much,' were my first words to her. 'You sneaked up behind me and caught me napping.'

'You weren't napping,' she said. 'Your thoughts were going round much too fast to let you. Anyway, you must have known I'd find you.'

A few days have passed since then, but however often I think about what she said, I realise she was right. I was half expecting someone, though I could not have said exactly whom.

Now that I stood opposite her and my eyes were clear and I could see her face clearly, it struck me that she was uncommonly pretty. Her hair was long and lustrously black, and someone — her mother, I supposed — must have brushed it out behind her, letting it dance around her slim white neck.

Until then, as you may well imagine, I had never paid more than passing notice to a girl's or a woman's neck, but at that moment her face and her neck held all my attention. At her throat, she wore a fine silver chain, from which there hung a lucky charm of some sort.

She looked at me as though she had always known me, and I racked my poor brains in an attempt to remember whether or not I had seen her before, and, if so, where and when.

She was dressed perfectly simply in a long, white dress with front pockets, with white stockings and bright red shoes.

'Hello,' I said, 'I'm called Simon.' And I extended my hand. She hesitated, then smiled the most beautiful smile I had ever seen, and took my hand in hers. Her skin was surprisingly cool. I did not know what to make of this until I remembered that my mother's skin was often cool to the touch, and that her doctor had said there was not enough blood in her veins. We always laughed about it, and now, though I had been made serious by the pangs of first love, nevertheless I regarded the coolness of my newly beloved's skin as yet another instance of her perfection.

'Pleased to meet you, Simon,' she said. 'You've been here before, haven't you?'

'How… how do you know that?'

'I've watched you,' was her answer, followed by fresh laughter. Suddenly, she began to draw me away from the pond, in the direction of the pavilion.

'Where are you taking me?' I asked.

'Where do you think? Just over there,' she said, pointing with her free hand off towards the roof of the little house, where it rose above the bushes.

It was only as we set off that I realised my new friend had not given me her name. I had already guessed that she must be one of the girls from the village. She spoke with the local accent, though without the dialect extremes common among the farm hands and other labourers I had met — and whom I found it almost impossible to understand.

'You haven't told me your name yet,' I said.

'And shan't either. You shall have to guess it, you shall. If'n you can do that, I'll give you a kiss, a proper kiss.'

This promise of a kiss, a 'proper kiss', sent me into a near tizzy.

'Come along through here,' she said, clearing the way to take us into a much-overgrown path bordered by lilies.

Catching sight of them, she called back to me.

'You can call me Lily, if you like,' she said. 'But just remember 'tisn't my real name, and I won't kiss you less you find out what that is.'

154

'You'll ruin your dress,' I said, seeing thistles and other gross weeds stabbing at her from every direction.

'No need to worry,' she said. 'It's strong cloth. My mother sewed it for me, by hand. She can set herself to anything, can she.'

Willy-nilly, I followed her down the path, where it took us round to the front door of the little habitation. As we reached it, I caught sight of the fountain and circular pool I'd taken close notice of when I first set foot in the garden. Had the mysterious feet I'd seen in the snow been Lily's'?

Scarcely had I asked myself the question than her voice came back to me.

'You're asking yourself if the footprints you saw in the snow that day were mine. The answer is "yes".'

I pulled up short. Surely it was not possible.

'You were here then?' I asked, my voice thick with disbelief.

She nodded gently and smiled.

'Of course I was. I was watching you from that first moment. The moment you set foot in this garden. You were drawn here. I could feel it.'

'Where...? Where were you? I couldn't see anyone.'

She laughed loudly.

'I didn't want to be seen. You'd only just arrived. I knew who you were, of course, but that was no help. I needed to see you, to form an opinion. I don't let just anyone in here, you know. Your cousin Tom, for example, he's not my sort. Far too rough. I think he has a bad temper, and lets it get the better of him at times. Now, come on, you have to come inside.'

Up close, the pavilion seemed less magical than it had been in the snow. There were cracks in the windows, and a film of fungus and grime over most surfaces. It was scarcely possible to see through the windows at all, and I noticed how their frames had warped and buckled over the years, unpainted and unvarnished, the wood beneath exposed to rain and ice in winter, and the heat of the sun in summer. The west wind and the south wind would bring salt from the sea, and everywhere I could see its effects, how it had eaten into any part of the building that had become exposed to it.

'Come this way,' my pretty 'Lily' ordered, pulling on my hand so that I was compelled either to break our grasp or do as she said.

We were right at the door in moments. She let go of my hand.

'Why don't you behave like a gentleman?' she said, 'and open the door for me. It's a little stiff to push.'

I bent my shoulder to it, but it would not budge.

'It must be locked,' I said, falling back. 'It feels locked. I've done my best to push it open.'

'No, you haven't,' she protested. 'If you don't put your mind to it, I shall be very disappointed, and I shan't give you that kiss you've been looking forward to.'

To be truthful, I was not altogether sure I liked the idea of a kiss, for though I was handsomely smitten by Lily, I had never kissed a woman on the lips, and found the thought of it unsettling. But I allowed her to boss me about — to be honest, I think I took some form of pleasure in it, in the submission to her will, for she made it seem like play, and I was earnest for her.

This time, I took my Barlow penknife from my pocket. It was a Wostenholm, a present from my father two birthdays ago. I had kept it immaculate till now, but my beloved was standing beside me, urging me on. I drew out the main blade and scraped it all the way down between door and jamb. It must have done something, for when I wiped the grime off on my handkerchief and returned to the door, it swung open smoothly as though a hidden hand had unlocked it from within.

We slipped inside. I went first and held my hand behind me for her to take hold of, and again the hand she placed in mine was cold. Inside the pavilion, the warmth of the day vanished. More than that, we were plunged into a semi-darkness to which it took my eyes half a minute or more to adjust.

Fortunately, the darkness was far from absolute. Clear patches remained where the weak afternoon sun found a way in to the interior of the summer-house. Lily let my hand fall from hers. I turned and saw her several steps away, watching me. For some reason, the muted light made her seem almost translucent. She smiled at me and whispered something I did not catch. I was more smitten with every glimpse I had of her face.

Everywhere around us was dead vegetation and, alongside it, cobwebs that had grown luxurious over many years. The flagged floor was covered in a thin coating of what I guessed was moss, and on it stood pieces of furniture made from cane. The fabric of the upholstery had rotted, and seeds had fallen on it from above, pushing up now in the form of weeds and wildflowers. I saw a sofa and three chairs with high spreading backs, and in the centre a low table on which lay cups and saucers and plates from an afternoon tea long ago abandoned.

'Why did they want to leave this?' I asked, supposing she might know.

'This summer house? I don't know. Perhaps they just grew tired of it.'

'And the gardens? Surely not. They must have been magnificent.'

'You can't have answers to everything you ask.'

I wondered if she meant that there were no answers, or that she had them but would not pass them on to me.

I remembered that I had been warned off the garden twice, once by Aunt Marion, once by Tregideon.

'Lily...' I said.

'That's not my name,' she replied, archly.

'If you won't give me your real one, Lily will have to do.'

'I suppose so. What were you going to ask?'

'Do your parents allow you to come here? To the garden, I mean, and this summer house.'

She took a quick step away, almost flouncing, turning her head, and stepping into a clump of green shadows. Trying to follow her, my eyes found it difficult to adjust to the dimness into which she had gone. Then her voice came to me.

'I'm here, aren't I?'

I took a step in her direction and found her standing untroubled by the sofa.

'Help me get these cushions off,' she said, making as if to pull one away from the cane seat. 'They're too damp to sit on.'

I put my hand on the nearest and drew it away. The rotted

thing was unpleasant to touch, and, I thought, probably infested with all sorts of creepy crawlies. I looked at her. She stood watching me, as though waiting on me to do the manly thing. I smiled back.

'Leave these to me,' I said. 'You could get your lovely white dress stained.'

She seemed to take this remark very seriously, biting her lip and frowning.

'Please,' she said, 'please don't let it get stained again.'

'Again? Has it been stained?'

'Yes. Badly stained. Not now. Before. When...'

'But it's all right now, isn't it? I can't see any stains.'

She shook her head gently.

'Not if you look up close. Some of the stains are still visible. Now, let's forget about all that. Why don't you and I sit down here and talk?'

I took hold of the cushion. Thoroughly rotted though it was, it remained intact enough for me to haul it off the sofa frame and hurl it off to one side. I hastily brushed my hands together, then tackled the second cushion, sending it the way of the first. The cane underneath was far from clean, but I took my handkerchief and wiped it as best I could.

We sat side by side, and again she placed her small hand in mine, and again it was cool, and I could feel the fine bones beneath the skin, and the way they moved. She seemed very like an angel to me, even if she had no wings and no name.

'Where do you live?' I asked, suddenly possessed of a need to pin her down somewhere in a real place, among real people.

'Why, in the village, of course,' she answered. 'In Porthmullion. I've seen you down there once or twice, with your friend.'

I had indeed been there a couple of times with Tom, and was due to make a third visit in order to speak with Peter Tregaskis, to arrange our first outing on the *Demelza Ebrel*.

'How come I've never set eyes on you before today?' I asked.

She laughed.

'I stay indoors most days, with my mother. I help her with her work. She fillets fish for my father. He's a fisherman, of course.'

'What's his name? I may know him.'

'Like as not. I'll tell you when I tell you my name. Will that suit?'

'It looks as though I've no choice.'

'That's right. You do not. Now, come tell me all about yourself. If we're to be lovers, I shall need to know everything about you. What's such a handsome boy as yourself doing up in that great pile?'

With no small hesitation, I began to explain who I was and how I had come to live at Trevelyan Priors.

We talked for what must have been two hours. Outside, though sunset was still some time away, the sky had grown overcast. I sensed that the air was damper than before, and feared it might come on to rain before I got home.

Getting up, I went to the nearest window and cleared a space to look through. I was right. Dark, rain-sodden clouds were lumbering across a slack sky, and I guessed they might at any moment disgorge heavy showers across the countryside.

I went back to the sofa in order to warn my companion of the coming deluge, but she was nowhere to be seen. Lily had gone as quietly and invisibly as she had come.

When I got back to the house, I headed straight for the schoolroom, in the fervent hope of finding Tom. He wasn't there. I looked round. The blackboard was still covered in Fitzgerald's careful handwriting, and there on his desk was the copy of *A Tale of Two Cities* from which he'd been reading. I conjectured that he had not been back to the room since our upset.

I picked up the book to close it and, as I did so, thought I could put it to good use.

I decided to look for Tom in his room, where I thought he might be sulking. Taking the book, I hurried upstairs. I knocked at his door and went in, but his room was empty too.

On my way back, I tried Alice's door, but, as before, I found it locked. Neither Mrs Spreadborough nor Tremain the butler, nor any of the maids were about so I could not ask them for the key, and, in any case, I realised that they might have been given instructions not to hand it over.

159

I stood in the corridor thinking what to do next. There was a profound stillness up there, as though no one alive could venture this far. Downstairs, there were always voices, above all below stairs, in the kitchen, which was the true hub of the house. Someone upstairs would tug on a bell-pull to summon a servant, or my uncle would bellow in that peremptory voice of his, or a door would slam some distance off. And always there was the sound of clocks, whirring or striking or simply ticking away, day in, day out, remorselessly. Very often, friends or relatives would call, and there would be the sound of eager voices over lunch or tea.

Up here, there were no clocks, no voices, not even whispers. Nothing moved, nothing breathed. And behind the silence lurked something I could put neither a name nor a face to. I had felt it first on that day in Alice's room, a darkening of the mind, as though something unholy, something vulgar and unblessed hung in the air like a miasm.

I looked through the window next to me and found I was gazing down into the old courtyard. A woman waited there, unrecognisable from above. Her head was uncovered, and her long hair drifted down her back like smoke; her face was turned away from me. She walked away a few paces, hesitated, and turned back. I could not tell who she might be, not even when she turned her face upwards and stared in my direction for a while. Finally, she abandoned her vigil and walked silently out of the courtyard.

I stood frozen to the spot until she was gone. Just as she turned the corner and disappeared, I calculated that she must have been looking up at one of the bedrooms on this floor, William's, perhaps. Or James's… What did she expect to see, I asked myself — or, rather, whom?

The thought of William prompted me to head for his room. I knocked gently, knowing he often slept through the day, but I was instantly greeted by a bellow of 'Come!'

I had stumbled on him in an outgoing mood.

'Simon, old boy! Come in and pull up a pew. Where the blazes have you been? Everyone's been out looking for you. Absolutely everybody. You're in deep trouble, my lad.'

'I can't see why. I didn't know anyone was looking for me. I went down to the lake. I wanted to find out if the swans had come back yet. No luck, I'm afraid. In any case, I've been looking all over for Tom.'

The benign expression on William's face turned serious.

'Tom? We thought he was with you. They've all been hunting for him as well. Do you have any idea where he could have got to?'

I shook my head.

'Of… of course not. Otherwise I wouldn't have been looking for him. Why have you all been looking for us? Has something happened?'

'I'm not really sure. I suppose something is going on, or they wouldn't be after you. Actually, Mother told me about your tutor, what's his name?'

'Fitz. I mean, Fitzgerald.'

'That's right. The Irish patriot. Well, the Paddy has handed in his notice and gone. Bet you're relieved.'

'Relieved? I most certainly am not. Why did he hand in his notice?'

But I knew, of course, I knew perfectly well why.

'I don't have a clue. You'd do better to ask Mother, or Father, come to that. It was Pa he spoke to.'

'Actually, I don't need to ask. I think I know what it was. I just didn't think he'd have taken it so much to heart.'

I told him what had happened. He listened sympathetically, as I'd known he would. Aunt Marion had once told me that the war and the loss of his legs had sucked the anger from William, an anger that had been with him since childhood.

I felt limp. Passing on the same information to my aunt and uncle was unlikely to be half as easy. They'd question me about every little detail, perhaps even charge me with making the whole thing up. And I would go to bed with a gnawing sense of guilt for having betrayed my cousin and gone without a thought into the forbidden garden.

'You're saying that Tom didn't know about Fitzgerald and his having been gassed?' William looked at me in astonishment.

I nodded.

'He can't have known. If he had, he wouldn't have said any of the cutting things he did.'

'No, I suppose he wouldn't. Not even Tom could be such a fat-head.' William said these last words without smiling.

'Nevertheless, he should have been told.'

'Of course he should,' said William, 'but let them work that out for themselves. You shouldn't be the one to point it out, it will only put their backs up. Look, Simon, I don't like to worry you or anything, but I do think it's time you found Mother and told her what you've just told me. Better get her on her own, if you can. This could be very important. If that fool Tom means to run away at a time like this, I don't know what will happen. Mother will be distraught. Before we know it, the old boy will be on a rampage after all and sundry.'

I said I'd do my best to prevent that, and made for the door. My hand had barely touched the handle when a voice called behind me.

'Just a tick, Simon. Have you seen the state of your clothes? What the hell have you been up to?'

'N... nothing. I just...'

'Can't have been nothing, old chum. The seat of your trousers is filthy. Looks like muck and slime of some sort. And your shoes are caked in the stuff. Now, what's been going on?'

For some reason, it didn't seem to matter to tell William the truth. He must have sneaked into the garden himself when he was younger. So I explained where I had been, how I had first stumbled across the garden dim in the snow, and what had brought me back there that day.

'You went into the pavilion?' William asked.

I nodded.

'And you sat down?'

'Of course I did. I was tired. I needed to sit down, I wanted to think about what had happened in the classroom, and I thought that would be the place, that I'd find some sort of seat. Which I did. There was some old garden furniture in there, and I was grateful to sit on it.'

'I see.' William's face was grave. 'Look, Simon, I, ah, think you'd do well to change out of those togs before going down. Just give them to your usual maid, or slip them down to the laundry, if you prefer. No one will ask questions.'

I thanked him. He just nodded and waved his hand, but as I reached the door again, he called me back.

'Tell me something, Simon,' he said. 'And I don't want any fibs. When you were in the garden, or perhaps later, when you went into the pavilion — did you see anyone? Meet anyone? Tell me, now. It's important.'

'No one of any significance,' I stammered.

'What does that mean?'

'I don't know, she...'

'You saw a girl?'

I nodded guiltily.

'What sort of girl?'

'A village girl. From Porthmullion.'

'What did she look like?'

William's questioning had turned suddenly into a proper interrogation.

I described Lily as best I could. It did not take long.

'Now, Simon, I want you to answer me carefully. Are you in love with this girl?'

'In love? How could you think so? She's just a village girl, I told you. A common girl. Why would you imagine I was in love with a girl like that?'

'Because I can see it in your eyes. Because I was once in love with her too,' he said, and at once fell quiet.

'But...' I stammered, 'surely... surely that's not possible. She can't be much older than I am.'

'Yes and no. Simon, listen to me. Don't close your mind to me, whatever you do. This is not a light matter. You've stumbled on something you should never have stumbled on. The girl you met today is Dick Tregideon's daughter, Morwenna. Morwenna died years ago, long before I met her.'

'She told me her name was Lily. They can't be the same person....'

'Lily is the name she uses to distract attention from who she really is. She never told me her real name. I had it once from Tregideon.'

'Morwenna,' I whispered. 'Yes, I remember. She said if I guessed it, she'd give me a kiss.'

'She offered me that same kiss. I was not much older than you are now. Simon, Morwenna is very beautiful and very beguiling, and I wanted that kiss quite as much as you do now. But you can't go back to the garden. I want you to promise me that you'll never set foot in that place again, however strong the temptation.'

I had seldom seen William so serious. But he had told me so little, and Morwenna was so beautiful. She had done me no harm that I could see, and I thought it unlikely she could do any. Though I had the profoundest respect for my cousin, I was not wholly convinced that what he had told me was the truth, or, at least, the entirety of it. No doubt he believed it all himself. But nothing could persuade me that the girl I had met that afternoon had been a ghost. She couldn't have been. Her hand had lain quite solid and alive in mine, her voice had been as audible as my own, her little breasts had risen and fallen with every breath she took.

'You think I would be in danger?' I asked.

'What do you think?'

'Very well, if that's your advice, I'll promise. I've no wish to be in that place with a ghost. You've well and truly frightened me off her. I'll steer clear of the garden from now on.'

The barefaced lie did not hurt me. Perhaps a little of my soul has already rotted like the furnishings in the pavilion. I meant none of my promises. Ghost or living woman, I had already determined to meet Morwenna again, to speak with her once more, and to discover whatever truth lay behind it all.

'I'll hold you to that, young Simon. Now, you'd better hurry and get changed. Speak to Mother as soon as you can, and when you've done, ask her to come up. My dressings need changing.'

All went as planned. I found Aunt Marion in the kitchen, going through some last-minute arrangements with the cook. I told her about everything I thought she had the right to know: the argument and Tom's hurrying off in a paddy.

'Damn it,' she said, the first time I had heard her swear. 'The boy is getting out of control. I shall certainly have words with him when he gets back.

'As for you, I'm extremely disappointed. What on earth were you thinking of, running about without a care in the world without coming to me directly to report what you've only now told me? I won't be able to keep this from Sir David. He may very well want to speak to you separately. And I shall have to send someone for Mr Fitzgerald. It was honourable of him to tender his resignation under the circumstances, but rather foolish at the same time. He was not wholly in the wrong, as he made himself out to be. You reckon him a good teacher, do you?'

I nodded enthusiastically.

'Very well. Now, go up and dress for dinner. You're already late. We may speak again later.'

But there was nothing further for us to speak of. Tom did not return for dinner, which was eaten without him. Just as we came to the end of the meal, however, the butler, Tremain, came in carrying a piece of folded paper on his tiny silver tray.

'I'm loath to disturb you, sir, ma'am, but I thought you should see this without delay. One of the maids found it when she was turning down Master Tom's bed for the night.'

It was Aunt Marion who took the sheet and read it before the rest of us. All eyes were fixed on her. The count sat with a glass of red wine to his lips, frozen.

'This is a note from Tom,' my aunt said. 'It must have been written sometime this afternoon. There's not much to it. Here, let me read.

'"Dear Mother and Father, dear William, dear Simon. I'm sorry to have caused such a hullabaloo today. But when old Fitz told me about the Irish at the front, it made me realise how rotten I'd been, and when Simon told me Fitz had been gassed at Ypres last year, I wished the earth would swallow me up. In can see no other way to retrieve my honour than to enlist. So I'm heading to London by the next train. Don't try to stop me, any of you: it just won't do. I'll make you proud of me. Once I'm in basic training, I'll write again to let you know how I'm getting on. All for now, your loving son and cousin. Tell Fritz I'm sorry, and say 'It is a far, far better thing that I do, than I have ever done.' Tom."'

Aunt Marion dropped the note with a sob. I noticed that Sir David had gone white as a sheet.

They sent one of the servants right away to the railway station at St Austell. Uncle David telephoned several people in London, and left instructions concerning Tom, all in the hope of heading 'the young idiot' off before he signed anything. Tom looked older than his years, and recruiting sergeants were not known to turn away many able-bodied lads for the sake of a year or two.

I was sent to bed, where I sat up until well past midnight, on tenterhooks lest word come of my cousin. But nothing happened. One after another, my aunt and uncle and the count came upstairs as well.

The house settled after the heat and rain of the day. In the corridors downstairs, the clocks ticked away the seconds and minutes of the night. The more I thought of Tom and his hot-headed decision to get to the Front, the more my heart froze within me. At fifteen, I was soul-weary. My father dead, and cousin James, whom I'd never known, his brother William trapped in his bed like a diseased ghost in a rotten summerhouse. I thought of Morwenna, of her pretty, elfin face, her green eyes, her fine-combed hair, her half-parted lips and their offer of a kiss. Outside, a wind had come up, and I thought of Tom tramping in it alone, knowing he had made a preposterous mistake, too proud to back down from his decision.

I dozed off for what must have been an hour or so. Suddenly, a gust of wind sent something crashing in the courtyard below. I woke with a start. My heart was already beating. I could hear nothing but the wind and the occasional rattling of the object it had knocked over; but I knew something was walking in the corridor outside, and it was not the count. It came to my door and stopped. And then it started to scratch. I got up and went to the door as if in a dream, though I knew I was wide awake. As I approached, the scratching grew more insistent. I reached the door, and from behind it I heard a voice, thin and appealing as before.

'It's Alice, Simon. Let me in.'

And as she spoke, the scratching continued.

Softly, I turned the key in the lock. Whatever it was, I felt more certain now than ever that the speaker in the corridor was not Alice. And I remembered the thing I had seen in the bed before.

A Letter in the hand of Harriet Lysaght, posted York, Lendal Post Office, 3.15 p.m., 1 June 1917

Lady Marion Trevelyan
Trevelyan Priors
Near Porthmullion
Cornwall

My Dear Marion,

I was so distressed to receive your latest letter. It left me shaking all day. Mrs Cunningham (who makes tea at the parish lunches) called at four, and I cried on her shoulder for a full hour. My nerves are not what they were, and without Simon by my side, I wonder I get by at all.

Tom gone for a soldier? Surely that cannot be. Little Tom, whom I used to dandle on my knee? Simon's little friend from all those years ago? Surely he can't be old enough to enlist, not even as a drummer-boy or whatever it is they have nowadays. They will turn him away the moment they set eyes on him, rely on it. Not even the army's lust for blood can be so all-devouring as to welcome children to the slaughter.

Or has the poor deluded boy grown out of proportion, as you suggest? When you write of him, I do wish you would not be so harsh. He is only a boy, after all, and boys have no common sense whatever, nor are expected to gain any, even when they become men, who are, as you must know, nothing more than little boys in big suits. If that were not so, what other use could men have for women?

Is Tom old enough to be wed, do you think? If you could find him the right girl, it might do him as well as fighting. My late husband was awfully keen on... that sort of thing; but he'd grown quite used to it after so many years together, so it was no longer a sufficient distraction from the war and duty and all that. Tom might get a taste for it if he found a keen sort of girl, and he might decide to give the pleasures of the marriage bed priority over getting himself shot. It's worth a try, don't you think?

I trust you and David will keep a steady eye on Simon. He is, perhaps, less impulsive than Tom, and his view of the war has darkened since his father died. But he is capable of great determination and has a fierce sense of loyalty, and I would not put it past him to take it into his head that Tom is in need of moral support. That could well lead him to adopt the same path as Tom. Part of him is well-disposed to such a course of action. Though he is temperamentally both shy and gentle like his father, I know from his letters that he longs to take revenge for his father's death. You say he will not hunt, but it's more complicated than that. Put a deer with big eyes in front of him, and he will hesitate to pull the trigger. Put a German in uniform in the same spot, and I warrant he will shoot him through the heart.

He writes to me often, as you know, and in many of his letters he discourses on his adventures with Tom. They really have become terrific friends, as you and I hoped they might. However, Tom is clearly the leader and the initiator of their mighty deeds: Simon follows behind like a faithful dog, and I have no doubt that, given the chance, he would go with Tom through hellfire and damnation.

Since that is precisely where Tom is now headed (I see no need to beat about any bushes), I fear Simon may end up there too, with none of Tom's outgoing spirit and martial courage. Simon could very well find himself facing a British firing squad, on a charge of desertion, when all that would have failed the boy would have been a lack of the necessary temperament.

Marion — do you have any young women you can interest him in? I know he is much too young for any serious attachment; but if he were to fancy himself in love, or even half in love, with some delicate little darling with bows in her hair and a tendency to blush, why, that alone might keep him back from taking the King's shilling.

He has written to me several times of Alice, as you yourself have done. What can be wrong with the poor child that she keeps so long to her sickbed? You speak of a Dr. Quilty and say he has been treating the whole household. Do you think he is sound? You say he is a 'homoeopath', but do not say what that is. My neighbour, Dr. Gibb, says it is a medical heresy and a form of quackery, and that I should not let my child be treated by one. However, I shall trust to your judgement: you would not employ the man if he were not capable, and I suppose you have little choice of medical men in your region. All the same, perhaps it might be time to bring in someone fresh for a second opinion.

Simon has told me, albeit with some misgivings, that Alice languishes in bed, and that the poor child is surrounded by herbs and flowers of all varieties. No doubt that is the work of this homoeopathist, who, I am sure, has fancy notions about the restorative powers of nature. My mother is a little inclined that way: she still believes in the concoctions of an old wise-woman who lives in the forest near her. Mushrooms and the like. But my late husband used to take her to task for this, saying that modern medicine has come a long way from leeches and hellebore. My dear, however much you may cherish this man, if he is harming your precious Alice, then you must give him his marching orders, and quickly.

Marion, I have made up my mind not to wait until Christmas before I venture down. Simon needs me close to hand. That is not to diminish in the least what you are to him now, or what you and your dear husband have done in his interest. But I am his mother, and my presence may do him good at this time. I should, in fact, like to make my journey to you in two weeks' time, let us say the Friday after next, which is the 15th. as you suggested. A simple telegram will suffice in reply. If it does not prove convenient, let us negotiate a later date.

Until then, my fondest wishes to you all,

Harriet

A Letter from Marion Trevelyan to Harriet Lysaght
Written at Trevelyan Priors

4 June 1917

Mrs Harriet Lysaght
Minster Lodgings
Gilleygate
York

Dearest Harriet,

What a delight to learn that you will soon make your long-await-
ed journey South. Simon, as you can surely guess, is over the
moon. It is the right thing to do in so many ways, I think. It would
have been hateful to venture on such a journey in the dead of
winter, even by train. Far better to come down now and to stay as
long as you possibly can. Perhaps we may finally persuade you
to remain at Trevelyan Priors for as long as you wish. There is
plenty of room, I assure you.

Bring with you what you need now, and if you decide to stay, we
will arrange for a carrier to transport the rest of your luggage in
due course.

We were grateful for your concern about Alice, but do not labour
under any misapprehensions about Dr Quilty. His homoeopathy
is a small matter of tiny pills and even tinier pillules the size of
poppy grains (I do assure you), tinctures, and long, absorbing
conversations. I myself have found it most efficacious.

And do not forget that it is widely used by royalty both on the
continent and here. The late King Edward used it, as do the present king and Queen Mary. Not to mention half the aristocrats in
England. I meet these people, my dear, and they assure me it is
the very best thing.

The herbs and flowers you mention are nothing to do with Dr
Quilty, but rather conceits of our head gardener, Mr Tregideon,

and the housekeeper, who, as you will soon find, is in other respects a most respectable and dependable person. We had her from the Allingdales five Christmases ago come this December.

Yes, we are mightily worried about Tom. After James's death and William's terrible injuries, we do not know what we should do if we receive word of his having been wounded or, dare I say it, killed. It would make a mockery of all I believe concerning God and His Universe. I do think the Trevelyans have given more than enough to the country and to the war.

As for the French and Belgians, they may all go to hell for all I care. David's language on the subject is rather more robust than mine. I wish for our victory, of course: do not have me set down as a pacifist or a dodger.

You need have no fears for Simon. He was brought up an English gentleman and plays the part very well, leaving aside the sort of indiscretions to which all Englishmen of his age are prone! He may long to join his cousin on the battlefield, but between ourselves and yourself, I think he can be made to see sense. All David and I ask is that the sacrifice we have already made be not in vain, that to ruin the lives of two fine young men be not counted a trivial matter, and that the government take more positive measures to defeat the enemy finally.

As for marrying Tom off, we should have to find the young devil first. He did not go to London as he wrote, but took a branch-line train to Truro, where he headed the next morning for the recruiting office in the town hall. Despite David's many contacts and influence, the Army is behaving most unhelpfully, refusing to hand out useful information.

Of course, they don't want to admit to a mistake, let alone a deliberate one, and they won't want to see a headline saying 'Baronet's son recruited at 15'. Of course, it is common knowledge that the recruiting sergeants are under orders to take any able-bodied youth who presents himself, and they'll connive at his age whether he give it or not.

We have been privately informed that he is in a base training camp somewhere in Essex, but that even if we could find the camp in question, we would not be allowed to visit Tom or take him out. They say it would damage morale. In fact, having gone for a soldier, he cannot just walk away without being declared a deserter and shot. The silly fool joined the army as a common soldier, not an officer, and he has no choice but to follow orders, left, right, left, right, wherever that takes him.

David plans to speak to some friends at the War Office at the beginning of next week, in the hope that we can have Tom transferred to a military unit in this country, or, failing that, at least somewhere behind the lines, perhaps a posting to General Command or whatever it's called. They can't have many men among the ranks who can read and write to his level, so I imagine they may be pleased to have him as a clerk or something.

As I said above, we intend to do everything in our power to ensure Simon makes no effort to follow in Tom's footsteps. Of course, we cannot lock him up, and I don't think he is yet ready to be married off, or even engaged! However, it may not be such a bad idea to get him to form some sort of youthful attachment. It would surely tie him to this locality, and perhaps be enough to see him through the war.

You seem to suggest a more physical attachment may be necessary. No doubt that could be arranged with discretion. Perhaps one of the chambermaids: there are two or three pretty ones. Or, if that does not appeal, there are other possibilities. Geraldine Fitzallan, James's ill-fated fiancée, had a younger sister called Helen, who is Simon's age. She's a pretty girl and, from what I remember, shapely enough, if we ignore a little puppy fat. Well, we shall see. I'll invite her and her rather boring mother over for tea while you're here, so you can judge for yourself.

I'm sure Simon has told you by now about our guest, the Marquis de Remiremont. He is with us in part because he is a refugee from the War: he owns a most beautiful château from the sixteenth century — or perhaps the thirteenth: I can never get these things straight — and acres enough to fight a war over. All of this has been appropriated by the Boche, who have stationed a school for aviators in the château proper and cut down half his forests. He calls it his lost domain, and has sworn to recover it and to seek full reparation from whatever government replaces that of the Kaiser in Berlin.

He has neither wife nor children, and is rich enough to devote his time to the study of art and architectural history. You will see for yourself that he has a most formidable brain, but you must not be at all nervous of him. He is most charming to the ladies, and I suspect him of forming liaisons in the French manner. Perhaps he will try to make love to you while you are here. Well, if he does, I shall only encourage him. When the war is over, you could be mistress of Château Remiremont. He, of course, would carry on affairs: but you would nonetheless find him an attentive lover.

He and David have certain things in common, which surprises me since they are in other respects like chalk and cheese. They spend time in the library practically every day. Sometimes they come out looking like men who have seen a ghost. These French, when they are not out forming liaisons, have such an inordinate love of philosophy it can be quite wearing on other people. Mind you, the library here is absolutely enormous. It's on two levels and contains centuries' worth of books, including some very rare Shakespeare folios, and even some of the earliest books printed by Caxton.

You will find Simon changed. The country air, mixed here with sea breezes, has done him great good. His breathing has become easier, for one thing. I'm hoping to buy a pony for him on which to learn to ride, after which he can join me (and Tom, should our prodigal son return to us) in the local hunt. You may come too, if you like. Or do you not ride as well? Do let me know.

I shall be there to meet you at Porthmullion station. Do take care.

Your loving sister-in-law,

Marion

Letter from Simon Lysaght to his mother, Harriet Lysaght, dated 4 June 1917, Trevelyan Priors

Mrs Harriet Lysaght
Minster Lodgings
Gilleygate
York

Dear Mother,

I'm writing this letter so it can go in the post along with Aunt Marion's. The boy will be along shortly to take the mail down to Porthmullion. Mrs Orchard runs the little post office there: you can buy postcards from her as well, and sometimes crabs, if the boats have come in. Old Westerby opposite sells sweets. I sometimes buy a toffee apple from him. He gets the apples from one of our orchards, from Tregideon the gardener. Tregideon's a good sort and a good friend. He lets me have apples whenever I want, or strawberries, or whatever's in season. Of course, I don't stuff myself — that would be greedy.

It's spiffing news that you're coming down next week. I'll be at the railway station with Aunt Marion to welcome you to Cornwall. Do you think you can stay for good? We could be together again. I miss you a lot, even if I don't say so to anyone here. I think Aunt Marion guesses, but Sir David is awfully grand and would think I was being a sissy.

Aunt Marion says there's plenty of room at the Priors, or there is a little dower house where you'd be comfortable. I could visit you there every afternoon for tea. And some days you could come up to the house, and we could have tea with my cousin William. I suppose he's really just a half-cousin, but he's a terrific sort, in spite of his injuries, and he knows everything that goes on here, because all the servants find reasons for visiting him and bringing him little treats, and having little gossiping chats, which he adores, and which he says are often much more fun than the conversations he has with the local nobs, when they bother to come to see him.

Tom has run off, as I expect you know by now, and I suppose you're coming down to make sure I don't hare off after him. To tell the truth, I've no intention of doing anything of the sort. War is a terrible thing, but sending more men in to fight will only end up making matters worse, let alone sending boys my age or Tom's age. We can only pray he gets out safe and sound. I think he should be here, because I don't think all is well at the Priors, and he might be able to help.

We shall have to think of lots of ways to amuse you during your visit (though you will stay on after all, won't you?). We could go to Fowey (which you pronounce Foy, by the way); it has a lovely harbour, or so I'm told — I haven't been there yet myself. Or you might go to see the beautiful gardens at a place called Heligan Manor — the Trevelyans know the people there, the Tremaynes. Like all the families around here, they've lost most of their gardeners to the war.

William suggested you might like to go for a sail one day. The weather has been exceptionally clement, with smooth seas and easy winds. Some days the winds have dropped entirely, forcing the fishing boats to stay in harbour.

Tom owns a little sailboat called the *Demelza Ebrel*. It's a crabber, whatever that is. He used to go out in it with a sailorman called Peter Tregaskis. I've not been out in the *Demelza Ebrel*, but Will says there'll be no problem about my getting permission to take her out as long as Peter comes along. We could sail round the bay, maybe even bring a picnic. Perhaps Aunt Marion would like to come too. And the marquis, if he can be spared. Uncle David is a bit proper, as you probably know, and I don't think he'd be very keen on boating or picnicking. It would be nice if Alice could come along, though. She's been in bed far too long, and needs some sea air. If I see Dr Quilty, I'll ask if he approves.

I've added a list of some old books I'd like you to bring down. I left all my Hentys behind, but you only need to bring *Beric the Briton*, *The Young Carthaginians*, and *St. George for England*. You should ask the porter to carry them at both ends of your journey. We have a library here, of course, but it's not much for story-books, though I did find a very fine copy of Mallory's *Morte d'Arthur*, with about forty good illustrations, all of them engravings. I spent an afternoon last week reading it. One illustration disturbed me a lot. It showed a beautiful woman who had turned into a fierce fiend. The caption read 'That gentlewoman was the master fiend of hell,' which was taken from the story.

Mother, tell me truly when you come here — do you believe in ghosts? I'm not saying I've seen one, but William seems to think this house is haunted. You mustn't say a word to either Aunt Marion or Uncle David — they'd probably be quite angry with him for frightening me. There's a lady who comes into the rear courtyard sometimes, and looks up at James's window, or so I think. She may be one of the servants, but she could just as easily be Geraldine Fitzallan, the girl he was engaged to.

I don't really see how there can be ghosts, though. I know Father didn't believe in them. He said that maybe people who are dead don't go anywhere, they just lie in their graves and go back to the earth after years and years. So, how could they be ghosts as well? But suppose they do go somewhere, like heaven or hell, then why would any of them want to leave heaven, and why would Satan let any of his lot out of hell? I talk to the marquis sometimes about these things, and he can be very helpful.

Time to finish if this is to be in the hall when the boy calls.

Your loving son, Simon

From a Private Journal kept by Lady Marion Trevelyan, discovered at Trevelyan Priors some years after the death of Sir William Trevelyan. The entries date from 1917.

5 June 1917

I am very near despair. Things are not working out as they should have done. It all started to go wrong when David's boys were killed and injured. But for that, things might have worked out differently. For one thing, I should have found it easier to remain faithful to my marriage vows.

Poor William was in such a very bad state, troubled by urges that most men of his age find awkward, but which they assuage by visiting the nearest brothel or by marrying the first half-decent debutante willing to open her legs for him twice a week and to put up with the brats she gives birth to. There's none of that for William now, of course, nor ever likely to be, not unless I can find him some distracted little thing who wants to marry a baronet and is willing to spend her life with a cripple who needs an occasional spilling of his seed.

It would, of course, be demeaning to the family if we were to bring a prostitute into the house, or even to pay a girl from the village to relieve his passions now and then. Mark you, there are one or two of the maidservants who may be happy to do it for a suitable fee: he's a great favourite with them, and I don't expect a woman of that class will put up much of a fuss. I'll look into it once things have calmed down a little. Though not, I think, while my sister-in-law is here.

For the moment, then, it falls to me to spare him that sort of humiliation. He was ill at ease with me when I first suggested it. But I am his step-mother, not his natural mother, and I convinced him that there would be nothing amiss in our having relations of a limited and charitable sort. He put me off for a while, but I finally overcame his reluctance late one night by entering his room naked apart from a loose gown, which I let fall as soon as I had closed and locked the door.

His natural impulses did the rest. Some weeks later, when he had grown comfortable with this arrangement, I taught him that

I had needs of my own, and showed him how to fulfill them. Dear God, he gives me more pleasure now than David ever did, with his hissing and panting and coming quick.

So much is hidden here in the Priors. Fear, for one thing. I had a childhood blissfully free of unhappy feelings, and I never knew fear, not true fear, until I set foot in this dreadful house. To this day, I am confident that David conceals from me more than he has ever revealed. I think that has always been the way with the Trevelyan men.

When I was first living here, a mere week or two into my marriage, isolated, far from friends and family, a young bride whose body had been used every night without tenderness — when I was first here, I ventured to the attic chambers in search of abandoned furniture I might put to use in my morning room or in the separate bedroom I was already planning. My parents had brought me up to be thrifty. My father was a lord, but a very impoverished one, and in those early days I had not yet acquired an understanding of the benefits real wealth can bring. So I climbed the stairs without asking anyone's permission (for they would have dissuaded me had they known), and I went on climbing until I reached the upper floor.

The fear started even before I set foot on the top landing, before I entered the corridor that led through the upper storey, connecting rooms and stairwells. As I came up, I felt my breathing grow more difficult, and within minutes my heart was beating unnaturally fast, as though I'd been running a race. Of course, I had been climbing several flights of stairs, so I thought little of it, apart from the discomfort. But when I had been standing for above five minutes on the landing and the same symptoms persisted, I was sure something must be wrong.

I felt afraid. Not over-exerted, not agitated, not even merely anxious. Afraid. My mouth felt dry, my hair, which I wore up, was tingling where it grew out from my neck, I was sweating for all it was a cold day. My instincts told me to run, but I checked myself. I was held by a different fear. What would happen, I asked myself, if I gave way to unfounded jitters brought on by over-exertion — for surely, I reasoned with myself, that was all it

179

could be — and ran downstairs again, all the way to the bottom, screaming and shaking?

What would happen? Why, the servants would see and remark on it all. And David — a man who brooks no foolishness, who tolerates no weakness — would be sure to come from his study at a steady pace and take my wrists as though to break them, and tell me I was a stupid little fool. He might even slap me, and order Mrs Armitage to bring me a calming potion. But from that day forth, I knew he would use my fear, he would make it his tool for working me. He would deny me pleasures, he would place parts of the house and gardens out of bounds, he might even send his dear boys away, to be safe from my surrogate influence.

I stood there for a long time, shaking, my heart and soul and body invaded by a sense of evil darker than my darkest fears. Nothing moved, there were no sounds, there was nothing to be seen. All I felt was a sensation of growing cold. But the sense of dread did not change.

I did not run down the stairs screaming after all. I simply retraced my steps and went to my morning room and sobbed until I was dry. I have never lost my fear of this house. Since that first encounter with the evil that inhabits Trevelyan Priors, I have seen and heard much to confirm me in my certainty that the house retains an evil that may, for all I know, have been born along with it.

What am I to do with Harriet?

Help is Sought

Extract from the medical records of Dr Samuel Quilty FRCP, MRCS, MD, then practising in Porth Buryan in the county of Cornwall, this extract dated 7 June 1917

I have just returned from London. The problem at Trevelyan Priors has been giving me cause for thought, especially the child Alice, whose case appears to be developing in a frightening direction.

As I have previously described, the child has not yet recovered properly from her adventure a month or so ago, when she disappeared and was later found freezing and dangerously close to death. My earlier report describes certain matters that gave me cause almost to doubt my own sanity. But I am a rationalist, and I refused to give in to such bugaboos.

At first I thought we had found her in time and that she would make a full recovery, but she took an inordinately long time to emerge fully from her coma. She returned to deep slumber again and again, as though in the grip of some powerful force that refused to let go of her. Once she woke more regularly, however, I fully expected her to progress at the normal rate. I gave instructions myself to the cook that she was to have plenty of beef tea with red wine, eggs twice a day, however prepared, and a little stout, whether she was partial to it or not (she was not).

Aside from this I repertorised her case as fully as I could, which meant detailed attention to her physical symptoms, since I could elicit very little verbally, and could only hazard educated guesses as to the mental and emotional symptoms. I used Ringer's *Handbook of Therapeutics* to provide an allopathic basis for treatment, followed by Kent's Repertory together with Philips's two *Materia Medica*, especially the volume on inorganic substances, as well as Clarke's more recent *Dictionary of Practical Materia Medica*.

From all this, I prescribed opium, a small tablet to be dissolved twice a day in water. Bearing in mind the patient's extreme loss of vitality, I administered the remedy in the 30th potency. It was given to her every day for six days.

During that period, Alice seemed to deteriorate rapidly. In order to determine whether or not the medicine had in some way harmed her, I discontinued it, but went on with the diet, ensuring that she drank plenty of fresh milk from Docking Farm. A week later, and she still had not pulled round.

I decided to make more strenuous efforts to speak with Alice, in an effort to extract more about her inner feelings and thoughts, which might be holding back her recovery in some way. Indeed, I have often seen it to be the case that, once a patient's mental state has been addressed, his physical ailments clear up like magic.

Feeling I had no time to waste, I dismissed the nurse, who fussed and fretted about the child, causing a distraction that I considered unhelpful. With her gone, the room was completely quiet. Alice herself was awake, though from time to time she drifted off into a drowsy state.

'Alice,' I said, 'I want to talk to you about what happened when you went to the shot tower. Or if there are other things you'd like to talk about, we could do that instead. Can you understand what I'm saying?'

She looked at me and burst out in a peal of laughter that had no sense of humour in it. Moments later she stopped laughing. I shivered and pressed her.

'It's all right, Alice. I'm just asking some questions so I can help you. You seem to be in a bit of a fog, ever since that day you were found half-frozen in the shot tower. Do you remember that day at all?'

Her eyes shook rapidly, then closed. My fingers were on her wrist all the time. Her pulse had been low; now it sank further, as though she were back in her coma. I watched her carefully. Suddenly, her tongue started to push out between her closed lips, and when it was fully extended, her eyes opened and she looked at me without looking at me. I moved my free hand in front of her face, but she did not respond. I took her tongue between finger and thumb to examine it. As I did so, it turned black. It felt as though covered in some kind of mucus or slime. I took my hand away and her tongue moved back inside her mouth, as though removing my fingers had been a cue.

Suddenly she spoke.

'Dark... I can see them in spite of the dark... Little children, can you see? All around us now, can you see? You saw some of them before, you can see them now, if you look. You only have to scrape away the blood… Little hands, little eyes, little teeth… They say they are my friends… Can you hear their voices? I hear them all the time.'

Then, without warning, her voice deepened.

'Tell the doctor there is no God… Aren't you afraid, doctor? That you will die, now or later, maybe asleep, maybe in pain… There is no soul. There is only death. Tell the doctor to leave… No cure… Can you see the dead? Look, doctor, can you see the dead? Open your eyes.'

I looked round the room. I could see nothing.

'There's nothing,' I said, but my heart was beating hard.

She spoke again after that, but only childish things. Eventually her eyes closed and she fell into one of her deep sleeps. When I checked her pulse this time, it had returned to its earlier state.

I could see that the child was going to die if she continued in this inconstant condition. I told as much to the parents, who were, understandably, much distressed. They expressed a wish for a second opinion, and, to be frank, I was greatly relieved, since the responsibility of the case was weighing unduly heavily on my shoulders. The next day, I sent a telegram to my old teacher, Sir Reginald Hall, who is presently President of the Royal College of Physicians. Having both studied under him and worked under his supervision for a full year before setting up in practice here in Cornwall, I knew him to be sound, honest, and sober, in addition to which he is a remarkable man of medicine.

He came down the following day and found me in Alice's room, poring over my *Materia Medica*. We greeted one another with much shaking of hands and talked of trivia for a good fifteen minutes in an attempt to stave off the inevitable confrontation with mortality. I had warned him that he might find himself close to more than death.

He examined Alice from head to foot, internally and externally. She answered his questions, but without the dark allusions she had made previously, and in her normal voice.

He spent half an hour with her, perhaps more. When he had finished, he folded his instruments back into his bag and closed it

184

with a sharp click. He had been grave throughout, but now he smiled widely at Alice and bent down to kiss her on the forehead. I noticed, however, that he did not let his lips touch her. The moment he left her and returned with me to the corridor, his face exhibited the same gravity I had seen earlier.

'My dear Quilty, why did you bring me here on a wild goose chase?'

'I'm sorry,' I said. 'I don't understand.'

'Well, tell me what you think has been happening here.'

I shrugged.

'No more than you do, I expect.'

'Medically speaking, no doubt you're right. Her physical symptoms are only too obvious, but they're not what is killing her. I think you knew that long before you sent for me. But I suppose you had little choice in the matter. The parents insisted on a second opinion, no doubt?'

I nodded.

'Well, let me be blunt. From the moment I set eyes on her, I could not quite get it out of my head that she was already dead. Pondering all you have told me, I'm now perfectly certain she died before she was found by her step-brother in the shot tower. She's dead, Quilty. Forget her body — that's already lost. It's time to save her soul.'

'I... If you recall, sir, I don't believe in the soul.'

'Then, perhaps it's time you did. At least this poor creature must be saved. Her soul is caught in some sort of limbo. You must find someone to free it.'

He spoke at length with the parents, and left them with the same advice he had given to me. Sir David had me to his study, where he told me he wished to suspend Alice's medical treatment. I could not argue with him.

We parted with talk of a new cottage hospital he planned to build for Porthmullion and the surrounding countryside. He even offered me the post of medical director. I could not then tell his motives in this, but I knew he wanted me on his side. God knows what I truly suspected.

A few days later, I called to treat William Trevelyan. I had for some time known he had something he wanted to tell me, something he wanted to get off his chest, and I hoped that, if I had more time to spend with him, he might get up the courage. But instead our talk fell to Alice. As always, I told him there was hope. He asked if the flowers did any good: he had recently acquired a wheelchair, and had been able to visit the child. I said it would help me to know what the plants were, and asked if he could obtain for me a list of their names.

This he did, through one of the maids, who was on intimate terms with one of the under-gardeners. Once I received this list, I made a copy and sent it to a friend of mine who lives in Oxford. Dr Robert Makepiece is a don, a Senior Fellow of Magdalen, and a Reader in the Department of Classics.

Dr Makepiece is not — and I ask you to treat this with all due seriousness — a medical man, nor is he a botanist or a natural historian. But he has a worldwide reputation as an expert on the magical traditions of the Greeks and Romans and Neoplatonic theurgy. In addition, he has an unrivalled knowledge of medieval and Renaissance magic and alchemy, including the work of the Hermetics, and has written monologues on Paracelsus, Cornelius Agrippa, and Raymon Lull.

Someone in the house had been playing at magic, I was now sure of that, and I hoped that Robert, if he would travel down this far, would understand the language of Alice's flowers better than any herbalist in the country.

He replied by telegram the following day.
IF POSSIBLE DO NOT GO TO HOUSE STOP DO NOT VENTURE NEAR CHILD STOP REPEAT DO NOT SET FOOT IN CHILD'S ROOM STOP QUERY IN EXAMINATION OF GIRL DID YOU NOTICE ANYTHING UNUSUAL HOWEVER MINOR THAT YOU HAVE NOT MENTIONED STOP IF NECESSARY DECLARE CHILD HIGHLY INFECTIOUS AND KEEP ALL BUT ESSENTIAL PERSONS AWAY STOP

I felt it best to conceal this communication from Sir David and his wife, but I could not in conscience neglect Robert's final injunction, which was to protect the rest of the household by keeping them at a distance from Alice's contagion. I knew perfectly well, of course, that there had never been the least reason to suppose the child actually infected or infectious with any known disease, however uncommon. Nor had there been anything in my original letter to Robert which might have misled him into drawing that conclusion. Indeed, I know him very well, and never have I detected in him any ambition to play the amateur physician. In medical matters, he has always deferred to me or to one or another of our medical acquaintances.

I was, indeed, quite certain that, when Robert spoke of infection, he intended a double meaning. The child is dangerous in some way I cannot yet understand, and may be capable, deliberately or not, of passing on her spiritual contagion. This I understood — but I was at a loss how to convey it to the child's parents.

That same day, I had a long conversation with William. I had reached the conclusion that he was ready for prosthetic legs to be fitted, and I wanted to see how he might cope with the new Belgian leg. A prosthetist was waiting for him at the military hospital in Falmouth, the one converted from the old Pendennis Hotel at the start of the war. I planned to drive him there in one of the family cars.

I found him in poor spirits. He said he was perfectly happy to remain as he was, and that he wanted no artificial leg.

'I'm perfectly happy in this room. I'm privileged, don't you see. If I want the fire lit, a servant drops what she's doing and lights it. If I want drinks brought up, the butler takes care of it. If I want a woman, there are discreet ways of bringing one in: some of the maids do very well.'

I pretended not to be shocked; but I could hardly let him drown in his own misery. We argued back and forth for an hour or more, and, in the end, he agreed to let me bring Alan Trefusis, the prosthetist, to the house. I'm told this is fairly common, where amputees seek to avoid contact with the outside world, preferring to nurse their injuries and disappointments in private. And, need I say it, Captain Trevelyan had been born to a life of privilege.

When our talk was over, I asked him what he knew about his little step-sister. His reply was evasive, and I did not press the matter. But I conveyed Robert's message without divulging

187

anything about him or his studies.

'Will you pass this on to your parents for me?' I asked.

'Why don't you speak to them directly?'

'I think it may come better from you. They must not grow alarmed.'

'If you want to avoid that, just keep your mouth shut. My father is doing what he can to bring Alice back to us. The Marquis likewise. No doubt your learned friend is right, and we all run great risks. But this is a family matter, Quilty, and I'd urge you not to go poking your nose any further into it.'

I had never seen him this indignant.

'William, I am still Alice's doctor, at least until your father finds a substitute for me. I was brought in to save her life, and that is what I intend to do.'

He shook his head.

'Better just drop it, Doc. Let the family take care of it. We've dealt with things like this for centuries. This is an old house, and it keeps a lot of secrets. You're an outsider, you don't belong here. I'm sure you don't mind my saying that.'

'You make me feel unwelcome, and I don't believe that's really what you mean. You forget that I'm bound by oaths of confidentiality as much as a priest in his confessional. Any secrets will be safe with me.'

'No, thanks, old man. These aren't the sorts of secrets you tattle out to the nearest medic. I'll pass your message on, but don't expect an answer. Now, if you'll kindly pull that bell cord, I'll have the kitchen send up something. You'd best be off.'

That night, a telegram was delivered to me at my house in Porth Buryan. It was from Robert.

MEET ME TOMORROW AT PORTHMULLION HALT STOP ARRIVING 12.17 STOP INFORMING TREVELYANS SEPARATELY OF MY ARRIVAL STOP NEED UNUSUAL SYMPTOMS STOP

The boy took back my reply.

WILL MEET AS REQUESTED STOP HAS CALLOUSES IN SEVERAL UNEXPECTED PLACES STOP THESE INCLUDE TOP AND REAR OF SHOULDERS BACK OF NECK AND TEMPLES

His train was on time. I watched him step down from the carriage, immaculately dressed as always, and attentive to the porters and the station master. As he came towards me, however, I thought he looked tired, as though he had gone without sleep all night. And that, of course, is exactly what he had done.

I had hired a little motor from Bill James at the village garage. Robert, always unsettled by cars, put up a fight at first, but I finally persuaded him to get in. With him half-frozen in the front seat beside me, I drove out of the halt and onto the road that led to my house.

'You look ghastly,' I said.

'Can't be helped.'

'Well, it can be improved. Have you eaten breakfast yet?'

'I had something in the college kitchens before leaving.'

'Not good enough. You're to come to my place for a spot of lunch. I'm sure the Trevelyans won't mind a short wait.'

'On the contrary. They may not even welcome us. I asked James Ruddock to send them a telegram. He's an old friend of theirs. I asked him to introduce me, make me seem rather important, convince them they'd be fools to turn my visit down. He's good at that sort of thing is old Jimmy. Pity you don't know him.'

'Actually, I do. I was at High Table a few times as his guest. Now, pay attention — my cottage is just round that bend.'

But he wouldn't wear it.

'There's little time to waste,' he said. And he insisted so loudly that I had no choice but to turn the car right round and head up the hill in the direction of Trevelyan Priors.

I'd noticed that he was carrying a large leather briefcase, and guessed he'd brought down some books to refer to.

'Suppose you tell me quickly what's going on,' I said.

'It's very complicated,' he answered. 'The list of flowers and plants you sent me pointed me in the right direction. I could see right away that they hadn't been put there just to decorate the room or to rectify the girl's physical symptoms. Anthony, they answer precisely to formulae set down in ritual magic. You will find the correspondences in Paracelsus and elsewhere. Wormwood guards against bewitchment, for example. Mugwort will counteract charms and spells. Ash, blackthorn and elder will help you pronounce a curse.

'Someone has known exactly what to do in respect of botanical defences. They are shields against evil, Anthony, you can be sure of that. But they are of very little use on their own. Well, let's see what else there may be when we get there. Drive a bit faster, will you, old boy? I don't wish to waste time.'

The long drive to the house had been tarmacadamed the previous summer, and I was able to make rapid progress. We arrived at the front entrance in not many minutes and left our car to be taken to the rear by one of the servants.

We were expected, and were shown directly to the print room, where Lady Marion was waiting. She stood as we were shown in, and invited us to sit.

'Gentlemen, I'm afraid your timing is most unfortunate,' she said, sitting down herself. 'My husband makes his apologies, but he and the Marquis de Remiremont have had to travel to Truro today. It's this wretched business of my son Tom. You know all about it, of course, doctor. I take it this is the same Dr. Makepiece that James Ruddick wrote to us about.'

I made the introductions, stressing Robert's scholarly reputation and the fact that he had been a recipient of the new honour, the OBE. Lady Marion seemed suitably impressed, but also a little puzzled as to what he was doing there.

She explained to him all about young Tom's impulse and their efforts so far to find him and have him returned home. Robert sympathised and said he'd make enquiries with some people he knew in the War Department.

'But for the moment,' he said, 'I've come here to see your daughter Alice. I must see her without delay.'

Lady Marion frowned.

'Really?' she said. 'Well, I'm not sure that will be either possible or desirable. Only my husband and the marquis enter her room now. And the nurse, of course, who keeps her clean and tidy. Even Dr Quilty here has been asked to avoid her for the present. I don't think my husband would like anyone seeing her in his absence. Not even a medical man like yourself, Dr Makepiece.'

I was about to correct her as to Robert's status, but he nudged me hard, and I could see what he was getting at. If she thought he was no more than a don, and a non-medical one at that, she would be sure to deny him access. Better to let her think he had earned the title Doctor slaving over *Gray's Anatomy*.

'Lady Marion,' I said, 'My colleague can provide a more varied second opinion than Sir Reginald. He has one of the best minds in England, I assure you. However, he has an important engagement tomorrow at the Palace, where he is often called in to advise on difficult issues. If he does not see Alice today, he may not be able to see her again for a month or two, by which time it may be too late. I fear you must make up your mind quickly.'

She looked at Robert.

'Dr Makepiece,' she said, 'do you think there is any hope for my daughter?'

'Based on what Dr Quilty has told me, yes, I think there may be a slim hope, ma'am. But I have serious doubts about the present regime of flowers and plants. I don't believe they will be of real use to her, indeed, I fear they may harm her in some way. Let me examine her first, then I will see what can be done.'

'You say it must be today?'

He nodded.

'Very well,' she said. She reached into her pocket and took out a key. 'You'll need this to get into her room. I can't come with you. I find it too painful to see my poor darling lying there half-dead.'

She stopped, and I noticed tears trickling down her cheeks. And then she wiped them away with the back of her left hand, and straightened her back, and was herself again, or at least a facsimile of herself. 'I think Dr Quilty can show you the way. He has...'

Robert interrupted her.

'I'm sorry, your Ladyship,' he said, 'but before I see the child, I need to refer to a number of books. I have them in my own library at college, of course, but they were simply too bulky and heavy for a lone traveller. I understand you have a library here at Trevelyan Priors. Do you think...?'

She looked for a moment as though she would refuse his request. But a few moments' reflection changed her mind, already softened by tender thoughts of her daughter.

'Yes, of course,' she said. 'I'm afraid the library isn't my province. But we have a schoolmaster here who uses it from time to time. He may even be there now. I'll have him sent for.'

Conor Fitzgerald appeared about five minutes later. He had indeed been in the library, working on lessons for the coming week. We knew one another from the brief period he was my patient. He shook my hand as previously, but I could tell he was no longer the easy-going fellow I had known then, and was now in low spirits.

Lady Marion had already absented herself, saying she had to go to the kitchen, in order to give instructions to the cook. She offered to have lunch sent to us in the library, but Robert said we would be better to concentrate on our books, since he would have to return late that afternoon and he wanted to make best use of his time.

We followed Fitzgerald to the library. Before we entered, Robert took him aside.

'Mr Fitzgerald, I think it unlikely you will be familiar with the volumes I wish to consult. Is there, by any chance, a good handlist?'

'Better than that, there's a printed catalogue. If you'd care to step inside, I'll fetch it for you.'

The library at Trevelyan Priors is one of the finest in the country, though it has never been open to the public. As we entered, Fitzgerald explained that it takes up six substantial, high-ceilinged rooms in the centre of the house. Generations of Trevelyans had bought, borrowed, and, I'm told, stolen enough books to make up a priceless collection. Most of them are in fine leather bindings, together with a separate archive of manuscripts from around the world. There are specialist holdings in law, theology, philosophy, French poetry, Arabic and Persian calligraphy, Mughal miniature painting, and editions of epic poetry from Dante to the *Shahnama* and the *Lusiads*. The Trevelyan baronets clearly enjoyed a wide range of interests down the centuries.

It was a dizzying sight to behold so many books in one place. Fitzgerald did his best to orient us, then went off to fetch the ten volumes that made up the principal catalogue. When he had placed the last on a table, he summoned us to join him.

'What was it you were after?' he asked.

'We might start with one of the books of Paracelsus,' said Robert.

'I've never come across any, but that means nothing. He lived when?'

'From 1494 to 1541. His real name was Theophrastus Philippus Aureolus Bombastus, if that's any help.'

'Let's take a look...' He opened the volume containing the letters P to S. 'Yes, there are several here. What were you looking for?'

'One is the *Volumen medicinae Paramirum*. And take a look for two others, the *Liber Azoth* and the *Archidoxis magica*.'

Fitzgerald bent over the catalogue again.

'Yes...' he said. 'And yes again. And yes. They're all in here. Unfortunately...'

He looked at us, puzzlement on his face.

'Is something wrong?' I asked.

'It looks as though they haven't been placed on open shelves. This is something I've come across once or twice before. Take a look. You can see that most books in the main library carry a shelf reference, which makes it easy to locate them. The library is arranged both thematically and alphabetically. But certain volumes bear the annotation "RA". Since these items can't be found on open shelves, I have to assume the letters stand for Restricted Access. We had something similar in the Main Library at Trinity College.'

Robert nodded.

'We have something of the same at my college, except we use the letters PP. I'm told it stands for poofs and pederasts. I believe it's where they store the papers of former members away from prying eyes. It's tempting to think that Paracelsus comes under a similar rubric, but I hardly think so. I think the reason for this separate shelving is obvious.'

'Are they particularly valuable?' Fitzgerald asked.

'Only to certain people. I venture you have many more titles of monetary value on the shelves around us. No, it's not their value that needs protection. Nor any suspected obscenity. It's their content. Have you not formed some idea of where books like these may be kept?'

The schoolmaster closed the catalogue. I could see he knew something, but that he was wrestling with his conscience.

'Mr Fitzgerald,' I said, 'I think I understand your dilemma. You owe your loyalty to your employer, whereas you and I are practically strangers. But you must believe that we've come here today in a last attempt to save Alice Trevelyan's life, and perhaps more than just her life. We mean the Trevelyans only good.'

'I'm sure you mean well,' Fitzgerald said, 'but that may not be enough. I meant only good, but I argued with Tom and forced him to enlist in the army. He may die on the Front. Youth is no barrier to German shells. I can't compound my guilt by betraying my master's secrets.'

'In that case,' said Robert, 'you may count yourself in part responsible for letting the child die as well. You don't want that on your miserable conscience as well, do you?'

The Irishman reeled. He hadn't expected to be spoken to in such tones. I was shocked too, and made to speak, but Robert spoke again.

'Gentlemen, a life is at stake. A young life. Judging from what I have heard, I hold out very little hope. But I do intend to rescue her immortal soul. Mr Fitzgerald, the books I seek may help me do that. Now, are you prepared to help us or not?'

He took a few moments, then nodded.

'This is guesswork, you understand. Right at the end of the library, there's a section of panelling that has been left bare. No bookshelves, no paintings, just linen-fold panelling. There's a table in front of the panelling, and on it a bronze bust of someone called Agrippa. Not Herod Agrippa... something else.'

'Cornelius.'

'Yes, that's it. I've sometimes wondered whether there might be some sort of space behind that panelling. A room, perhaps. If there is, it's the logical place to put any forbidden books.'

We soon had the bust and table away from the wall. It had to be assumed that the panelling slid aside or even downwards or upwards in order to provide access to whatever lay behind. Accordingly, we pressed, now on this section of the panelling, now on that, always trying to trigger a cunningly concealed lock or some other fiendish mechanism, in the manner of characters in *The Mysteries of Udolpho*.

Though we tried for a good half hour, nothing moved, nothing gave way, not by so much as the tiniest fraction of an inch. We stepped back and stood staring at the panelling as if it would throw up the answer to its own question. But it did not. We found chairs and sat on them, and quietly reflected on the wall in front of us.

Robert was the first to break our silence.

'Tell me, Mr Fitzgerald — in that catalogue of yours, have you found a systematic layout of the collection? You said it is thematically arranged. How is that done? By letters of the alphabet?'

Fitzgerald fetched the final volume of the catalogue and set it down on the table from which the bust had been removed.

It was then that I noticed that the temperature in the library had dropped dramatically. I said nothing, nor did either of my companions. Fitzgerald opened the book towards the rear, at a group of pages between the main text and the index. He thrust it towards Robert, who consulted it for several minutes.

Robert then went down on his knees and examined the books on the bottom shelf to the left of the panelling. This done, he took one of the little step-ladders that were set against the walls, and went up to look closely at the books on the top shelf on the other side. This done, he stepped down and turned to us.

'Gentlemen, I think we should ignore other possibilities for the moment. There is a distinct break in the sequence of books between here' — he pointed to the left — 'and here' — and he pointed to the top right.

'Now,' he said, 'try to take a closer look. Can you see how this book, the last one on the left, is markedly darker on its top portion than it is below. None of the other books on that shelf suffer that discoloration — d'you see? But look again at the first book on the other side. The same thing, yes? Over time, the pressure of human hands has darkened the leather. Someone has been pressing these books in. Samuel, would you mind going up that ladder and pressing on the book I showed you? I'll kneel here and do the same.'

I did as he asked, while he followed suit below. Seconds later, the central panelling moved and slid behind the wall on its right.

I'd expected to see a room waiting for us to enter, but instead we saw ahead of us a spiral staircase inside a dark stairwell. As I looked at it, the temperature dropped yet again. This was followed by a second, more inner sensation: that encroaching sense of evil I had first encountered in Alice Trevelyan's sick-room.

'Don't worry, Samuel,' Robert said. 'You're not the only one to feel it. If we're to achieve anything here today, we must resist it as best we can. Mr Fitzgerald, I take it you can sense it as well?'

Fitzgerald nodded.

'I do, so help me, Mother of God. What the hell is it?'

'The Darkness,' Robert said, and immediately I thought of the darkness we could make out waiting for us in the stairwell. But then he raised his lamp and indicated letters carved into what must have been a wall of the original priory. In a quiet voice, he read what was there, a few words in Latin.

'"*Non credit quod reverti possit de tenebris.*"'

'It's a verse from the Latin Bible,' said Fitzgerald. I had not recognised it, but I am neither a Catholic nor a Latinist.

'Job chapter fifteen, verse twenty-two,' said Robert. '"He despairs of escaping the darkness." Evil pushes through the fabric of things, and wherever it appears, it brings darkness with it. It is not a darkness you can see, unlike this darkness above our heads. But one may sense it and sometimes even smell it. And if you let too much of it creep within you, you will grow dark and dead inside. Now, gentlemen, we have no choice but to climb these stairs. There may be little time to waste before Sir David and his instructor return.'

'Instructor?' I asked, not guessing what he meant.

'Yes, indeed. His teacher, his guide, his Mage. That is why the marquis is here. They live off one another. They drink from one another's poison. They inhabit the same darkness. Now, let us go higher.'

Fitzgerald went to fetch candles and an oil lamp from the schoolroom, where they were left to guard against the frequent failures of the house's new electrical generator, which had been installed in one of the outbuildings.

We went up slowly, and at every moment of our ascent I expected to hear or see something frightful. But there was nothing but the twisting staircase, a construction of stone and mortar that spiralled upwards between stone walls. For some reason, it must have been left standing when the priory was ruined under Henry, and subsequently incorporated in the grand house the Trevelyans constructed on the site. Judging by the stone, it had evidently been built in the thirteenth or fourteenth century, when the building was still an active priory. This, then, must have been the oldest part of the house by far.

The stair ended at a low wooden door, pointed at the top and fastened on one side by long metal bands that supported the hinges. It seemed of an age with the stairwell. I thought it would not open, but to my surprise it gave way with but little pressure.

Robert grasped the handle — a simple iron ring — and pushed forwards. As he did so, I noticed out of the corner of my eye that Fitzgerald was crossing himself. I am not even a churchgoer, but my hand followed his across my breast. The sense of underlying evil grew stronger the moment the door opened. Here we were, three university-educated men, fearing for our souls from something we could neither name nor see, which we knew only as 'the darkness'. If anyone reading this report should imagine that reason had been dethroned in us, then I can honestly answer, yes, it had. But I will challenge any mocker to climb that staircase himself, and enter that room, and not tremble or cry out or faint.

'Gentlemen,' said Robert, 'I do not think we should stay here very long.'

No one contradicted him. My own instincts were telling me to turn tail and run, never to approach that foul nest again, so long as I might live. And every morning and every night since entering that room, and since the events that followed close upon that day, has found me on my knees in fervent prayer. Reason has indeed been toppled from the throne of my heart. I do not believe in God or Jesus Christ, nor in something called the innate goodness of humankind, I believe in evil and I believe in hell and its daily intimacies, and I dread the eternal life a damned soul might live there, in its tiny, squalid rooms, where little Alice Trevelyan sits on a chair smiling at nothing, with eyes that see nothing.

Robert led us, one by one, into the room. In size and shape it was commensurate with a side chapel in a large or medium cathedral. I now think it really had been a chapel at some time, for reasons I shall give in a moment.

Once inside, we found that it was yet colder here than elsewhere in the house, even on the stairs. Our candles were too weak to dispel the all-encompassing darkness. Fitzgerald lit the oil lamp and adjusted the wick until it shone out brightly. I noticed that his hand shook as he trimmed the wick, and when I reached out to steady the glass, I found that my hand shook as badly as his.

In this increase of light, we looked around the room. On the longer walls to our right and left, shelves had been put in to take a prodigious collection of old books. Some still bore the chains that had secured them to desks in some monastic or early university library. Robert took the lamp and went directly to one end of the shelves.

After a few moments, he turned back to us.

'My dear friends, the arrangement could not be simpler. The books begin here at "A" and end near where you are both standing with "Z" or some other letter. I will start with Paracelsus, and if you, Dr Quilty, would please locate a book called *Picatrix*, and you, Mr Fitzgerald, Cornelius Agrippa.'

He set off to find his author, taking the oil lamp with him on the grounds that his eyes were older, while poor Fitzgerald and I had to make do with our candles. We had just started when we heard Robert give a stifled cry. He was standing, lamp in hand, at the room's far end.

We joined him and saw at once what had driven him to cry out. The far wall where, I imagine, the statue of a saint or the Virgin might have stood when the room was first consecrated as a chapel, was instead covered by a wall painting that appeared to date from the thirteenth century. I had seen several like it in parish churches in several counties.

It was this painting that had caused my friend to utter his cry. The light from the lamp allowed me to see his face, on which was fastened an expression of the keenest fear.

I took the lamp from his shaking hands, for fear it might fall and smash, and stepped closer to the object of his terror.

The painting, which was done with pigments directly on a backing of thin plaster, had flaked and faded; but what remained was unmistakable.

A tall figure stood in the centre of everything. He wore the black outer garment of a Dominican monk, the hood of which came over his head so that his face could not be seen, just blackness cloaked in blackness. There were no eyes, but even after so many centuries, I could feel them there, invisible yet intense, burning into me, mocking and insolent.

Some of the painting had crumbled away around the edges, but the great hooded figure still stood, somehow immune to the ravages of time. In the background, castles and towers, houses and forests burned with flames that had become muted to ochre and terracotta.

On the other side, and much nearer the foreground, stood a low building that had a Roman character and seemed to be a tomb. Its door was open, and from it issued a line of people in shrouds. They were led by a man in a shroud, carrying a staff. When I looked more closely, I realised that this leading figure was an adult, and that the shrouded dead who came behind were children.

In the air above the figure, a painted scroll stretched from one side of the painting to the other. On it was another Biblical verse.

Obscurent eum tenebrae et umbra mortis

'It's from the Book of Job again,' Robert said. '"May darkness and the shadow of death claim it once more".'

'"It"?' I asked.

'The day of his birth. Job wishes he'd never been born. He curses the day he entered this world. But I don't think *"eum"* is intended to mean that here. It may stand for "him".'

We looked at one another, wondering who had been cursed in this way. For myself, I was most disturbed by the image of so many dead children led from the tomb into further darkness.

'We shall have to move quickly,' said Robert. 'Try not to look at the painting, as far as you can turn your eyes elsewhere. He unsettles me greatly, and I'm sure neither of you wishes to prolong your acquaintance with him.

Robert quickly found his Paracelsus, and Fitzgerald and I the books he had asked us to locate. But for some reason, Robert was not content. Lamp in hand, he made a rapid survey of the titles on show. As the light moved from shelf to shelf, it flickered on old bindings and washed back and forth across the painted monk, making him seem to move, giving life to the shadows that surrounded him.

When he had done, Robert turned to us and, in a voice that shook palpably, said we should have to leave as soon as he had examined two of the books he'd identified.

'Gentlemen,' he said, 'I do not feel easy up here. This small library contains the most frightening collection of texts on the black arts that I have seen anywhere. There are volumes here that no sane mind would ever think to read, let alone offer to others to read. I have seen for the first time certain titles that are known only to a few scholars, others whose contents are designed to lead the unsuspecting reader to eternal damnation.

'There is a book made up of papyri taken from the Nekyomauteion of the Acheron in ancient Greece, all taken in antiquity from the oracle of the dead. There are several grimoires from the sixteenth century, texts of ritual magic. Two copies of the *Clavicula Salomonis*, the *Lemegeton*, and the *Goetia*. Worse than any of those is a book on the shelves to my right. I have never seen a copy before. It is the *Matrix Aeternitatis*, a translation from an Arabic original by Avimetus Africanus. There are those who say it is the most evil book ever written. Only three other copies are known to be in existence. Most have been destroyed.'

He looked back towards the painting.

'Have you seen?'

I strained my eyes and took several paces towards the far wall. And then I saw. Beneath the deep cowl, where there had been only darkness, there now were visible two red lozenges where the figure's eyes would have been. We were being watched.

'Keep your eyes open,' Robert directed. 'I'll do what I have to as fast as possible. Then we must get out of here.'

He opened the first of his books and began to read. I shivered in the deepening cold, like Fitzgerald beside me. At first the room was plunged into a deep silence. But as time passed, I could make out a sound. As it grew in volume — though it was still faint — I could make out scratching. Rats, I thought with relief, it must be rats. But I knew in my heart that it was not rats.

I kept looking round to see where the scratching was coming from, and as I did so noticed what seemed to be a gap between the shelves near me. I got up and went to it, finding a narrow opening that seemed to lead into an inner chamber of some sort. Holding my candle high, and with my heart thudding hard in my chest, I squeezed through.

There was indeed a narrow room. My eyes took a little time to re-adjust, having nothing in here but my candle for illumination. When my pupils had dilated sufficiently, I saw something quite unexpected. On the walls of this little recess, someone had hung pictures, making it like some sort of gallery. But the art that hung there disquieted me greatly.

The pictures, it quickly became clear to me, were all of children of different ages. Some were in frames, others painted directly onto a flat surface, like icons, and some on the wall itself. The portraits were in a variety of styles and often showed clothing from differing periods. A few were medieval, many others seemed to belong to the fifteenth or sixteenth centuries, and so right up to the nineteenth. And then I saw a little group set apart. These were framed photographs, some from perhaps five decades ago, the rest appearing quite up to date. One showed little Alice Trevelyan. I took all the modern portraits from the wall and slipped them into my inside pocket in the hope that others might show familiar individuals.

'I've finished here, gentlemen,' said Robert. Rising, he lifted the books he'd been consulting and gathered them together. With a collective shudder, we hurried back to the head of the stairway.

We retraced our steps as far as the library, where we replaced the panelling and made all as it had been.

When we had done this, Robert put his hand on my shoulder.

'My dear Samuel,' he said, 'I think it is time we ventured up to the child's room. Perhaps you will lead me there.'

He then turned to Fitzgerald.

'Mr Fitzgerald, thank you for helping us find that den of misery, and for having the strength of will to remain there with us. I would invite you to join us with young Alice, but I think the fewer involved the better. Apart from that, I would like you to stay with your mistress. She may hear things likely to alarm her. She may even wish to come up to see her daughter. Can I rely on you to hold her back by force if necessary? She must not come to the bedroom under any circumstances.'

'Do you mean to exorcise the poor thing, is that it?'

Robert nodded.

'Perhaps not as the Church would do it. But it is something very like that I intend.'

'Very well. I'll stay with Lady Marion. But before anyone takes a step, I think we could all benefit from a glass or two of something strong.'

He spoke like a true Irishman, but I applauded the thought. I could have downed a bottle of spirits without pausing. Fitzgerald went off to find the butler, and ten minutes later rejoined us in the library with a bottle of brandy and three glasses.

'What the doctor ordered, eh?' I said. We all smiled weakly, but no one had the strength to laugh.

We finished half the bottle, and I for one felt much the better for it. In spite of the brandy, I had never felt more sober in my life.

I shook hands with Fitzgerald, and so we parted. Robert and I headed for the back stairs, which I knew from my previous visits. Before heading up, I made a slight detour to the table where the household oil lamps were kept. I took one for myself and another as a back-up.

The room was as I remembered it. Inside, the light scent of fresh flowers was almost overwhelmed by the odour of decaying ones. And the odour of decay was itself interwoven with a perfume that was stale and sweet, and strong enough to make me sick. I took out my handkerchief and held it over my mouth. Robert had already done the same.

'Let's open the curtain,' I said.

To my surprise, Robert shook his head.

'That may be unwise. Her father and the French dabbler have done all this in an attempt to save her. Something must have gone wrong, perhaps as a direct result of their attempts at conjuring. The marquis has an unsavoury reputation, but…'

'You know of him? You didn't say.'

'No. I'm in the habit of keeping things to myself. The truth is that I did not think of his identity until I heard his name mentioned by Lady Marion. He is the most evil man in Europe, some say. I know nothing of Trevelyan: he has no reputation whatever, and I think his amateurish bungling may be what led to Alice's sad condition. And now they are both trying to wriggle out of it.

'Samuel, I think they may have awakened something. I think this house holds many secrets, and I think they brought one too many out of the shadows.

'You know, of course, that medieval scholars believed in a system of spheres rotating around the earth: the lunar sphere, the solar, the sphere of Mars, of Venus, and so on. Beyond the spheres, according to the Christian writers like Albertus Magnus, is the dwelling-place of God and His angels. But others believe that there is a dark quarter, a place where things that should never have come into being breed and from that great distance descend to the spheres beneath. Some arrive in the sphere of Saturn, say, some in that of Venus; and yet others reach Earth. It is said that there are unspeakable things that have inhabited the earth for millions of years. Some are dormant. Some stumble about in their own darkness. But others sleep and dream. One of them is dreaming about this house and those who dwell in it, and is dreaming about those who lived here down the centuries.'

'Do they ever wake, these dreamers?'

'Oh, yes,' Robert said. 'That is when I fear them most. I think that whatever dreams in this house is about to wake up. We may not have very long to wait.'

'Can't we just take Alice away from here, to a place of safety somewhere? I'm sure we could find a priest willing to testify she was in spiritual danger.'

Robert nodded, then shook his head.

'We might very well find such a priest. I can think of several myself who would serve that purpose well and perfectly sincerely. But it would not help Alice to be at any distance from Trevelyan Priors. She is tied to the ghosts of this place, and if she tries to break from them I can scarcely think what might happen.'

'You think this house is haunted?'

'Haven't you thought so yourself?'

I looked down at the carpet, a large silk Shiraz woven with brilliant colours.

'Yes,' I said, 'I had suspected it. Especially in this room.'

'Yes. I would guess they are in this room even now. Don't worry: they won't show themselves. That is... unless Alice calls them to. Come now, let's set to work. First of all, I think you should examine Alice.'

The child lay with her eyes closed, neither sleeping nor waking. I called her name several times, but she gave no sign of hearing me. I pinched her nose, to see if this would waken her, but she went on sleeping without a murmur.

With Robert's help, I rolled down the bedclothes, which were, I observed, rather heavy. I removed her nightgown, but still she did not come awake. In spite of the heavy blankets, the child's body was very cold. I checked everything I could within reason, noting all I could in my journal: a copy of my observations is enclosed with this report.

Her skin was remarkably pale, almost transparent in parts. When I lifted her eyelids to examine her eyes, they seemed cloudy and grey rather than white. The pupils neither dilated nor contracted.

What struck me most were two symmetrical marks placed on either side of her navel. They seemed red and angry, and when I examined them closely, I could have sworn they were bites, the work of a small animal perhaps.

The only other matter worthy of remark is that she was no longer a virgin. I refused to think what this implied or whom it implicated.

'If you have finished,' said Robert, 'I would like to examine the flowers round her bed.'

Slowly, he went from flower to flower, plant to plant. After satisfying himself that all was as he had expected, he called me to his side.

'These are all in one way or another defensive plants. It is what they defend against that perturbs me. Take this piece of cinnamon, for example. It is used to banish negative and unwanted spirits.'

He stepped back and lifted a twig.

'Or this juniper, it is a specific to guard against evil. And look here, this is mandrake and beside it periwinkle. They are prescribed for the removal of demonic possession. Periwinkle also serves to cure what the ancients called devil-sickness.'

'And, just look, this is tansy. Tansy serves to keep evil ghosts out of the house. And here's some hawthorn, a specific against the same evil ghosts, as is the sandalwood on the other side of the bed. Can you see the arbutus on the bedpost? That will serve to exorcise malevolent ghosts. The burdock next to it is more prosaic — it will protect from sleep like a trance. Now, what else have we got?'

He went from one side of Alice's bed to the other with me, pointing out the plants to me and explaining them. Most of them were designed to ward off evil ghosts. But there was no way of telling what those ghosts might look like or be capable of doing.

On Robert's instructions, we placed two lamps on tables either side of the bed and turned them as high as possible. Robert found a chair free of plants and emptied his satchel of books onto it. From a tin box he took out a variety of objects: a crucifix, a long knife with a silver blade and an ivory handle with letters engraved all along the blade, a small silver chalice, a vial of holy water, a bottle containing consecrated oil, a bottle of salt, a sheet of what looked like vellum on which someone had drawn a pentacle in red and black ink, and several blocks of incense.

'Myrrh,' said Robert, placing the stick in a little holder he'd been keeping in his pocket. 'It's used in ritual magic for ceremonies of healing and protection. The ancient Egyptians used it for rituals of Healing and Passing. Some say it was brought to the baby Jesus to protect him from demonic forces.'

He lit the first stick, and almost immediately the air was permeated with myrrh. I remembered the powerful scent from days spent in church as a child, and later in College Chapel at Evensong.

'Samuel, if you would be so good, could you take a few spoonfuls of her blood and put them in this silver cup?'

Robert handed me the chalice. It was a matter of moments to take the blood as requested.

'It seems unusually dark in colour,' I said, handing the cup back.

'Yes,' he said, 'I had expected that. Now, take some of mine and add it to what's already there.'

His was much redder, but as the two bloods slowly mingled, they seemed to darken even more.

He took the silver knife and began to stir the two bloods more thickly together, adding some of the consecrated oil, and as he did so, he recited lines from the Canon Missae:

Agnus Dei, qui tollis peccata mundi: miserere nobis
Agnus Dei, qui tollis peccata mundi: miserere nobis
Agnus Dei, qui tollis peccata mundi: dona nobis pacem.

He half-read, half-chanted the words, his voice rising and falling steadily, without a trace of fear. While he did this, I kept a close eye on Alice. On the third line, her eyes opened.

The room was growing colder all the time, but, in spite of this, both Robert and I were sweating profusely. Beads of moisture had gathered on his forehead, but he did not pause even to wipe them away. I took out my handkerchief and drew it across his brow, then over my own. I looked at Alice and noticed that she too was sweating. I put the back of my hand on her forehead and cheeks, and found that her skin was burning, even though it remained as white as paper.

Next, he read — to my surprise — from the Mass for the Dead:

Agnus Dei, qui tollis peccata mundi: dona eis requiem
Agnus Dei, qui tollis peccata mundi: dona eis requiem
Agnus Dei, qui tollis peccata mundi: dona eis requiem sempiter-
nam.

With the first lines he had prayed for himself and myself, now he was praying for Alice's soul. I am not myself a Catholic, indeed not a religious man at all, but somehow this intoning of prayers seemed appropriate to the setting.

Things continued thus for some time, and as I watched the child, eager to observe the slightest change in her, I saw her eyes grow less vacant, her expression less agonised. And the sweat had vanished wholly from her skin. I bent down and put my hand on her forehead. She had cooled down considerably. As my hand rested on her, she looked up at me and smiled. I began to have hope that Robert's prayers, though said without a priest, might prove effectual.

Robert continued his recitation.

De profundis clamavi ad te, Domine: Domine, exaudi vocem
meam.

Without once taking my eyes off Alice, I listened to my friend's voice.

When he came to the end of the Mass, he turned to me.

'How is she?' he asked.

'Much improved, I think.'

'The evil is leaving her. When I am done, she will be herself again.'

'Robert, why did you read the rite for the Dead?' I asked.

'To bury the evil in her. To bid farewell to the demonic sickness suffocating her. To expunge whatever was dead in her, whatever in her belonged to death rather than life.'

'You're not a priest, Robert! How can you arrogate…?'

'Arrogate? You're very mistaken. I was ordained an Anglican priest long before we met. I use neither the title nor the office. Today I read the Roman rite because this is an ancient evil and, if it understands anything, it will not be the Book of Common Prayer.'

'How can you be sure what it understands? How can you know what the evil is, or where it comes from?'

Robert grew flushed and angry.

'How do I have to put this so that you will understand? There is something in this house. It has neither name nor flesh, but I assure you it is as real as you or I. Do you understand what we're dealing with, or are you an utter fool?'

'I know there's something, yes, but surely...'

'Your scepticism's unwelcome, especially after all you've seen. There is something terrible among us. Perhaps it has been awake all this time, perhaps Sir David and his marquis have awoken it, I really can't tell. Now, we must get on.'

He reached for the pentacle, which he placed on the floor, and in its centre he set the chalice containing Alice's blood and his own. Fishing in his pocket, he drew out a small packet of communion wafers.

'These were consecrated yesterday,' he said, 'by our college chaplain.'

He proceeded to crumble two of the wafers into the chalice, then set the rest aside. As he did so, Alice sat bolt upright on the bed. From her throat came a soft moaning sound that troubled me, for it seemed scarcely human, scarcely capable of being placed on any scale of normality. It might have been the sound of a woman in the throes of passion, or an animal crying aloud in its sleep.

'Dear friend,' said Robert, picking up a small book bound in black leather, with a small golden clasp on one side, 'I'm sorry if I seemed harsh some moments ago. I merely wish you to understand that I have not come to exorcise this child. That was indeed my intention when I first arrived here, but everything I have seen since then convinces me that much greater forces are involved in this case than I realised. I may need to come back more than once.

The house needs to be cleansed. The evil threatens everyone who lives here. You say there's a boy, a cousin or something?'

I nodded.

'His name is Simon Lysaght. His father was David Trevelyan's brother, though for some reason he chose to call himself by his mother's maiden name. There was a split between the brothers, I believe; but I understand young Simon's coming here indicates an end to all that. The boy's father died last year in France. Simon arrived here several months ago. The Trevelyans have another boy of about the same age who has run away to join the armed forces.'

'That's very sad. He'll die for an inch or two of soil in Northern France. Another terrible waste. But the boy Simon — I think he may be at greatest risk. I would like to meet him later, if at all possible. But now we have little time to waste.'

He opened the clasp and the book fell apart almost exactly at the page he wanted. He began to read in a level voice, without affectation or contrivance, making the sign of the cross wherever it was indicated.

Exorcizo te, immundíssime spíritus, omnis incúrsio adversárii, omne phantasmaa, omnis légio, in nómine Dómini nostri Jesu+Christi eradicáre, et effugáre ab hoc plásmate Dei+....

As he spoke, Alice grew very still. I looked at her for several moments, then turned my gaze to Robert. Just beyond him, in a shadowy corner of the room, stood a little girl. She wore a blue silk dress in the Regency style, and her long blonde hair was tied up high on her head in a very adult fashion. Her skin was disturbingly pale, almost transparent. I could see that Robert had noticed her, but he did not pause in his recitation.

Recéde ergo in nómine Pa+tris, et Fí+lii, et Spíritus+Sancti

When I looked again, the little girl had been joined by two others, both taller than her, two boys of about twelve who appeared by their clothes and appearance to be identical twins. It was hard to be sure, for their faces were frighteningly pale, and their clothing stained in places with blood. I guessed that their outfits belonged to the early part of the last century.

Da locum Spirítui Sancto, per hoc signum sanctae+Crucis Jesu

Christi Dómini nostri....

A boy of about fifteen appeared. His hair and clothes were more modern in style, similar to the togs worn by young fishermen in Porthmullion. Both his eyes were missing.

The children, joined silently by others, gathered about Robert and began to encircle him. Their faces were white and their eye-sockets dark and their lips as dark as the blackest blood.

Robert's voice began to falter. I made to go to him, but my feet felt as though they had been nailed to the floor.

'Robert!' I shouted, but I could scarcely hear my own voice. What came out of my mouth underwent some strange transformation, sounding in my ears faint and muffled. Robert did not turn his head. I heard him mutter more lines from the exorcism, but his voice too was muffled.

There was a movement to the rear of the room. Shadow seemed to move upon shadow, like a wave upon a wave at night when the sea is slow and the water dark and deep. The layers of light and darkness within the room were deeply confusing. I tried to call, but by now my mouth would not even open. As I watched, a figure moved slowly out of the darkness. It was tall, thin like a skeleton, yet not a skeleton, for there was flesh on it, and skin, and above that a shimmering that might have been gold dust or blood. Its face was covered with a veil of some sort, an old, tattered, cobwebby veil through which I could see nothing of the face, save for the eyes, which peered above the veil and were terrifying beyond measure.

Robert dropped his book. It fell to the floor with a muffled thump. I watched him as he stepped back, his hands outstretched wide, as though in the grip of some ghastly inner terror. But he went back only one step, and now I heard the thin man call out using words from the rite of exorcism, spoken in a voice like death.

Robert arched his back and, as he did so, turned his head and looked at me, and his face was a mask of grief and fear. He called out, and still I could hear nothing.

Then the deep beating sound began to fill the room, and this time I could hear it properly, and it was a thudding like wings, not a bird's wings, but vast leathery wings beating through vast spaces as it headed our way. I could see that Robert heard it as well and that it increased his sense of fear enormously.

Then the wingbeats — if that's what they really were — fell silent. A moment later, the thin man stopped chanting. The children broke ranks and moved away from Robert, and there was no telling how many of them there were. I could hear my heart beating. Thump, thump, thump. I looked down. There was something on the floor, something with long dishevelled hair and hands like claws.

It crept towards Robert, and I saw him recoil. When I looked at Alice... When I looked at Alice... When I... Dear God, I cannot bring myself to set down here what I saw.

I tore my eyes from her and stared at Robert. I saw him stagger and fall, then reach out helplessly towards the fallen book; but his fingers could not reach it, and so fell away and were still, and his entire frame, from head to foot, grew motionless as well.

The next thing, I could feel whatever held me to my place lose its hold. I broke free and rushed to where Robert lay inert upon the floor. A moment's examination told me the worst. There was no visible cause of death, no bruise, no wound, no laceration. But in the years during which I have studied and practised medicine, I have never seen a dead man look so inhuman or so much in torment.

There was a rustling sound to my left. I stood frozen, wondering what fresh hell was about to appear. But at that very moment, the door burst open, and I turned on my heels to see Sir David Trevelyan and the Marquis de Remiremont come headlong into the room.

'What the hell are you up to?' Sir David bellowed at me, as if I were a servant or a child. 'Damn you, who gave you permission to come here?'

I looked at him stunned, thinking there were more weighty matters to hand than that of who had given me permission to be there.

'I asked you a question, man,' he snapped. 'Out with it!'

My temper snapped.

'Damn you, Trevelyan. You may be Alice's father, but I've been her doctor, and I demand an explanation for all this. You've put your own daughter's life at risk with your conjuring. Robert and I were trying to put things right.'

He glared at me, and for a moment I thought he would strike me or worse. I looked at the marquis, and in return he stared at me with such a cold look, a look of contempt mingled with the most disengaged *froideur*. I expected some sort of reply from Sir David, but it came instead from the Frenchman.

'"To put things right"? What would you or your friend know of that? If he had even guessed what was wrong, he would not be lying there now and his spirit would not be undergoing torments more frightful than anything you can imagine. You speak of Alice Trevelyan's life. Don't you realise Alice is dead, has been dead for weeks? Whatever lies on that bed, it's not David Trevelyan's daughter, and nothing you can do will bring her back to life.'

I looked at the bed. 'Alice' was sitting upright as before, but whatever seeming improvement I had professed to notice earlier had left her. Her skin had turned light grey, some of her hair had fallen out, but her eyes still stared at me malignly, without blinking.

There was a voice behind me.

'Sir David?'

The marquis had got down on one knee beside Robert's body. Further back, the children had retreated into the shadows. But the tall figure hovered just between shadow and light.

'This man is dead, Sir David. There's nothing to be done.'

Trevelyan threw a glance at him.

'What's that book lying next to him?'

The marquis reached over Robert to where his book had fallen, and picked it up.

'*Ritus Exorcizandi Obessos a Daemonio*,' he read. 'And there's a bag here with others. Let me see. He's stolen books from your library. Books that put us all in great danger. Leave now, Sir David, and take *ce pauvre diable* with you. I'll do what I can to put down whatever it is his friend so stupidly raised up.'

Outside, Sir David turned the full force of his anger on me. I can scarcely remember now the many things he accused me of. He ended by dragging me by the arm all the way downstairs and getting his butler to throw me out. The last thing I heard in Trevelyan Priors was Sir David's raucous voice calling for his wife. His mood had not in the least abated.

Gentlemen, I do understand how little these pages bear resemblance to a conventional medical report; but I have had matters to bring before you that would not fit within the normal categories of medicine or medical science. I have related in honest words what I believe I saw and heard during my visit to Trevelyan Priors in the company of the late Reverend Doctor Makepiece.

As a man of science, I find myself totally out of my depth. I have seen things I had no right to see, and heard things I should have shut out from my hearing. But I have survived to tell a tale — or part of one — that goes to the heart of our dilemma, whether or not our patients have souls or astral bodies, and whether there is an afterlife or not. I leave the final judgement in these matters to you all, gentlemen.

Before closing, may I add that I have noticed strange scraping sounds in my chimney late at night. I fully expect to wake out of sleep one night and to see something standing there at the foot of my bed, to find myself face to face with something blind and speechless, a pale, flapping thing sniffing its way across my room in urgent quest of me. I know I should expect it, for I have seen it clearly in my dreams every night since Robert Makepiece died.

From the Ongoing Account in the hand of Simon Lysaght, dated 8 June 1917.

I saw Morwenna again yesterday. She was more beautiful than ever, and I loved her with all my heart, far more than I did that first time. I think she loves me truly in return, though she is naturally more inhibited in matters of the heart than I. She says she could never mention me to her parents, for they would never approve of her becoming involved with a young man from the big house. Perhaps we should elope together, I don't know. It might be difficult for me, coming so close on Tom's running away. We'd have to head for Scotland, come what may, and here we are, at the very opposite end of the country. But if I was able to make my way down here from York, then a little further north can't be so difficult. When the time's right, I'll suggest it to Morwenna.

I said my cousin William had called her a ghost.

'What?' she replied, laughing. 'What'll he say next? He's nearer dead than I am. Expect he's not hardly warm, lying up in that room of his all day and night. Touch one of his hands sometime and you'll see what I mean.'

As if by illustration, she stretched out her own hand towards me.

'Here,' she urged me, 'feel that. That's warm flesh. It goes all the way up. If you were ever to see me naked, what you'd see would be a woman's flesh. And if you touched me, you'd be drowning in it. Oh, Simon, you've gone quite red.'

When I recovered, I told her her true name, of course, and in return she gave me a kiss. Not just a peck on the cheek, or our lips touching, but a proper kiss that made me quite dizzy with a strange kind of excitement. If being married means lots of kissing just like that, I fancy I may like it very much.

'How did you hear my name was Morwenna?' she asked, when her lips had pulled back from mine at last.

Still reeling from the kiss, I told her the plain truth. On finishing, I could see she was upset and disbelieving.

'What did he say I was?'

'I told you, a ghost,' I said, seeing the absurdity now I was here with her. In the twilight of the summerhouse, it was hard to gauge her reaction. I was worried she might just turn on her heel and run, thinking my cousin insane and myself no doubt on the verge of the family madness.

Instead, she doubled up laughing, and continued like that for a few minutes, struggling all the time to catch her breath and regain her composure.

'Kiss me again,' she said, 'and feel how ghostly my mouth is, how stale my breath is, how dead my tongue is.'

I kissed her harder this time, and as I did so, she lifted my hand to her breast, and I realised this time that she was warm, not cold, and that her flesh was just like my own, and that I wanted her as a man wants a woman, flesh and blood, body, heart, and soul.

I'd gone down to the garden in order to clear my head of its confusion. Aunt Marion had told me that morning that my cousin Alice had died in the night and would be taken to the family plot to be buried in four days from now, the moment my mother is due to arrive.

Aunt Marion has sent a telegram to York, to advise my mother to postpone her visit for some weeks at least, perhaps for several months. I've no doubt she is devastated, both by news of Alice's death and by the suggestion that she should cancel her journey south. It could be Christmas after all before I see her dear face again. I shall write her a letter explaining as best I can the circumstances of poor Alice's death, and how the funeral went, and how we were all handling it.

My poor aunt is, of course, by far the worst hit of any of us, for Alice's loss comes hard on the heels of Tom's disappearance. William has taken it badly too, for he was most fond of his little step-sister. It's harder on him too, since he cannot hope to attend the funeral unless carried and wheeled there. I hope he will try: I think it will do him good to find a reason for going downstairs at last and venturing out of the house for the first time since he was brought back here with his injuries. My uncle shows little emotion, as ever, and the marquis, though preoccupied, does not preoccupy himself with Alice and her fate.

They've been trying desperately to get in touch with Tom, to give him the news, partly, I think, in the hope of encouraging his return, if that's possible. When I say 'they', I really mean Aunt Marion, who has written letters everywhere, to Tom and to people she thinks might know of his whereabouts. Some of these letters were sent soon after he disappeared, and the latest the day after Alice's death. With me, William does not hold out much hope of making contact, though he will never say this to his stepmother's face. He says that this is typical of the army, that mail often goes astray, and that letters will as often as not reach a man's billet long after he is dead or sent home wounded.

I don't speak to William of Morwenna, nor does he broach the topic with me. He must have met her before he left for France, and perhaps he still carries a torch for her and is trying to turn me against her.

Today has seen further incidents at the Priors. Mr Fitzgerald has been given his marching orders after all, without any explanation. And it seems that none of us is to be treated by Dr. Quilty ever again. As before, no explanation. When I am fully grown, I shall expect people to explain things to me properly.

A Visitor from the North

Extract from the daily journal of Mrs Harriet Lysaght, during the period of her stay at Trevelyan Priors.

15 June 1917

What a dreadful day, one of the most dreadful since dear Charles's death or the day I bade farewell to Simon. Today was ghastly and wholly unexpected.

As arranged, I arrived in Porthmullion by the five fifteen train, and got down from my carriage, the only passenger to do so. As the porters hurried to take my luggage down, I scanned the platform for my sister-in-law. She was nowhere to be seen, and I assumed that she must have sent Simon or even just the chauffeur to pick me and my bags up, and to drive me to Trevelyan Priors. But look as I might, I could see no one but the station-master.

Once the train had gone, huffing and puffing its way out of the station, I hurried over to this gentleman and asked if anyone from the big house had come to fetch me. He frowned and, lifting his cap, scratched his head.

'Not unless they be late, ma'am. They know you're coming down, do they?'

'Yes,' I snapped, for I was not a little put out and considerably worried. 'Yes, of course they know. It wouldn't be like Lady Marion just to leave me to fend for myself. I was assured someone would be here.'

He had no answer for me beyond the scratching of his grey head, so I went to the waiting room and waited. I remained there for a full half hour, and still no one came. Seeing my predicament — for it was clearly out of the question for me to walk to the hall with so many bags and boxes — the station-master sent to the local garage, and before long the owner, a Mr Jobson, turned up driving a very fine Lea Francis motor and offered his services to take me to the Priors.

We set off, my bags secured by leather straps to the rear of the motorcar. Ten minutes of driving through the most circuitous roads I have ever seen, through charming countryside, brought me to the front of the house. I had never seen it before, except in photographs: the feud between Charles and his brother had ruled out visits until now.

I made to pay Mr Jobson, but he refused, saying he would be content if I mentioned his name to the Trevelyans.

Moments after he drove off, a butler came running down the front steps to enquire what my business was at the house. He looked at my bags with great misgiving. I told him my name and identified myself as the Trevelyans' sister-in-law, and instructed him to go straight to his mistress and announce my arrival.

He looked a little agitated, and opened his mouth as though he had something of importance to communicate; but he thought better of it, and instead propelled himself back up the steps and through the doors.

Half a minute later, Marion came running out, staring at me as though I were a ghost.

'Gracious heavens, Harriet — how do you come to be here? Didn't you... didn't you receive my telegram?'

I looked at her blankly.

'Telegram? No, I didn't get a telegram. When did you send it?'

'Five days ago. On the tenth.'

'Oh, my dear Marion... I didn't mention to you that I set out before then, in order to spend a few days with my sister Alicia and her family in Bristol. Alicia has been ill — not seriously — and I wanted to spend a few days with her.'

Marion's hand went to her mouth. It was only then that I noticed her eyes were red with crying.

'Oh, my dear!' she said, the anguish in her voice suddenly vibrant. 'Then, of course, you can't have heard.'

Even before she could speak, I saw what was wrong. Marion was dressed in mourning. Black ribbons adorned her hair, and her dress was black. I had taken note of it all, of course, but at first my thoughts had gone to her son James.

'Not Tom?' I asked fearfully.

She shook her head.

'No, my dear. Alice. Our little Alice died. We buried her this morning. In the family tomb. I telegraphed to tell you and to ask you not to come down. This is not a suitable house for you at present. We cannot be as welcoming as we would have liked.

Everybody loved her, Harriet, simply everyone. Even the maids and the gardeners and those of our friends who met her whenever they paid a visit, they are all in mourning. It's a black day for Trevelyan Priors. And with my darling Tom gone to a stupid war...'

I reached out to embrace her, and she fell into my arms like someone desperate for solace. From what little Simon had told me in letters, I guessed Sir David would be but a weak support at most times, how much more at this.

We stood like that for a very long time, and when it was finished, I sensed that a bond had been forged between us.

'I think it's for the best that I came down after all,' I said. She nodded silently.

As I pulled back from her, I saw a blur in the corner of my eye, and next minute a black-clad figure rushed into my arms. Simon embraced me, kissed me, and was, in short, so mightily pleased to see me that it exceeded anything for which I might have hoped earlier. Then, sensing the mood between Marion and myself, and being himself still dressed in official mourning, he stepped back and apologised to Marion for having been so exuberant in her presence. She brushed off his apology with great tact, and ruffled his mop of hair with her hand.

'But how you've grown, Simon,' I exclaimed. 'Hasn't he grown, Marion?'

She nodded thoughtfully, as though the thought meant more to her than the obvious.

'Yes,' she said, 'I'm sure he has. I see him every day, of course, and so do not notice. But he's at an age when boys grow, is he not? He'll be a man soon, won't you, Simon?'

He blushed and muttered something I could not make out. I noticed how much he resembled his father, and something tightened in my heart. I recalled vividly the emotions of my own bereavement, and my love for Charles, my love for Simon, and my desperate fear that he might decide to follow his cousin Tom to bloody Flanders and there fall prey to a German sniper.

'Simon,' I said, 'you and I have a lot to talk about. But in view of what has happened, would you mind very much if I spent some time now with your aunt?'

He was disappointed, but did his best not to show it.

'I understand,' he said. He pulled my head down to kiss my forehead, for I am still a little taller than he, then ran off on some secret errand or other. I was sad for him that he had lost his playmate, that he might never see him again.

The next moment, staff started to appear, and before I knew it, went off carrying my luggage into the house.

'I'm sorry to have seemed so unwelcoming, Harriet,' Marion said as soon as the last of the servants was out of hearing. 'Don't form the wrong impression, please. If there is a cloud over me, it's not on your account, believe me. I think you may be right: your visit may prove a blessing in disguise. We have all been looking forward to your visit for weeks, Simon more than anyone. And now you're here, we intend to make your stay as enjoyable as it can be under these exceptional circumstances. Your room has been ready for you ever since we had your charming letter proposing the visit. But perhaps you'd like to have some freshly-brewed tea to refresh you after your long journey.'

'Oh... Oh, that would be far too much trouble for you, so long after tea-time. And you must have had a very tiring day.'

'Today hasn't been normal for anyone. We all ate lunch much later than usual, not that anyone had much appetite for it. Fortunately, the funeral was restricted to family members, so we did not have greater numbers than usual. But dinner has, in consequence, been set back to nine this evening. So, please do come and have tea with me, then you can go up to your room and rest a little before getting ready for dinner. I'm afraid David is rather a stickler for the formalities. But I'm sure you can cope with that.'

She stepped back and looked me up and down.

'Oh, dear,' she said.

I nodded.

'I was going to say you really should wear something black. He won't look at you in that.'

For all that the rules of mourning were growing less severe, I knew I had come quite unprepared to appear in public.

Seeing my expression, Marion smiled.

'Of course, my dear, you were hardly expecting a death to occur. How very rude of me. You needn't worry, though — you and I are much of a size. I'll have my maid lay something of mine out for you while we're having tea.'

'You mentioned Sir David. How is he taking this?'

'With his usual sang-froid. But I know he was terribly fond of Alice and must be deeply upset. Unfortunately, he's not a man to express his emotions. Of course, none of them are. It's the result of sending them away to these beastly public schools.'

'I dare say it is; but I think you're being very sweeping. Charles was a very emotional man. The French and Italians are positively ruled by their feelings. This hardness most Englishmen practise is something Charles never could understand. He said what he thought, what he felt, and he encouraged his pupils to do the same. Of course, very few of them ever listened, they had been told so often by other masters that emotions are the province of women, and that men should celebrate their manliness and cultivate virtues like duty, resolve, courage, and enterprise. And always, of course, not giving way to feelings.'

'I feel that if Charles had had the chance, he might have made a poet or a painter.'

This was a sensitive point, and I knew it as I said it, but she took it well.

'You can't be sure,' she said. 'David was his brother, and he had every chance, but poetry and art never held the slightest attraction for him.'

'How terribly sad. What does he do for distraction, then?'

We were walking along a corridor painted light blue and white, with paintings of seascapes on the wall. I could tell at once that this was Marion's part of the house.

She came to the fourth or fifth door and beckoned me inside the little room she had set aside for tea. She rang for the maid, and we sat down and made ourselves comfortable.

'What does David do?' she repeated. 'And, by the way, you really shouldn't call him "Sir David" while you're here. He is your brother-in-law, which makes familiarity perfectly reasonable. We're in the twentieth century, after all. Of course, David has no idea what century we're in, or, if he does, he thinks it's the fifteenth or sixteenth. You and I, however, are still young enough to consider ourselves women of the new era. I am absolutely a suffragette, and I'm sure you are too, in your heart.'

'Well, yes,' I said, 'I suppose I am. I mean, I do think we should have the vote.'

'Exactly. But I'm digressing. You asked what David does for distraction. To be frank, it's all quite boring — the usual country stuff. He hunts, he shoots, he sails, he orders the staff about, he organises a Christmas ball every year without fail. That's to say, he orders Giles Lewisham, the estate manager, to see it's taken care of. David doesn't lift a finger. It's not that he's lazy, it's just that he was brought up to have different priorities to most people.

'I shouldn't forget old books: he has an excessive interest in them, passes an inordinate amount of time in the library, and spends a disgraceful amount of money on antiquarian purchases. In fact, he's in there now with his bosom companion and viper, the Marquis de Remiremont, whom you will meet later, and against whom I warn you most keenly.

'He and David have common interests. Ever since the marquis arrived here, they have become inseparable, and the pair spend many hours a day locked up together in that blessed library like monks.'

'I believe Mr Fitzgerald also uses the library. I'd very much like to see him. I do want to know how Simon's education is progressing.'

I saw at once that I'd spoken out of turn.

'Harriet,' Marion said, 'I'm afraid you're too late for that. David dismissed Fitzgerald a few days ago, and the poor man has packed his bags and gone without even a reference. I fear he may never work as a schoolteacher again. I don't know where he is, or I'd send him a reference myself. It was rather cruel of David to let him go without one.'

Tea arrived. As we drank it and nibbled little pastries, we talked of children and death, of dead husbands and old husbands. We discovered that we were both aged thirty-nine, and we complained of a world in which women had so little say in things, and wondered if our sons would grow to be men and, if they did, whether they might prove less hard on their future wives. Charles had never treated me harshly, but I relented from what I had said earlier and let Marion believe he had been less than kind at times.

She confided in me that David had never cared for the physical side of marriage, and I said that the memory of Charles's caresses was still so vivid to me I could scarcely breathe at times.

It was after seven when Marion suggested I go up to my room to bathe and change. One of the maids would fill the bath for me. She told me I would find a black dress and some pieces of Whitby jet for my neck and ears. I smiled feebly and thanked her. Whitby had been a popular destination with Simon, and his father and I had taken him there often. I wondered if Marion even knew where Whitby was.

A fire had been lit, making the room over-hot. The maid, a handsome young woman who introduced herself to me as Lily, came to help me bathe and dress. The bath had already been half-filled with warm water. Lily helped scrub my legs and back, dried me with a large towel, and fixed my hair, which I had avoided getting wet. She unpacked for me and offered me fresh undergarments. I was thoroughly ashamed of these ancient bits and pieces, with their torn lace and signs of devoted mending. Lily, unlike other lady's maids I'd met, showed no concern whatever about it.

I asked her the usual questions — for I have never been one to treat servants as though they scarcely exist — and she told me she had lived in Porthmullion before taking this job, and that she now slept downstairs in the servants' quarters. She told me she sometimes bumped into Simon in the course of her duties, and that she thought very highly of him. Indeed, she said laughing, he was quite a favourite among the female members of staff.

'They do think him very handsome, ma'am, and very well-mannered and polite to everyone. He's a real gentleman. As you must know, who brought him up. Ma'am, do you think he intends to run off to war like his cousin, Master Tom?'

It seemed such an innocent question.

'Not if I can help it,' I said. 'But this is really none of your busi ness, Lily. Why, you're not even my maid, you're employed by Lady Marion.'

She gave me an odd look, as though I'd said something wrong, then went back to work, fastening the many buttons on the rear of my dress, which had been left on my bed by another servant.

This continued for several minutes, during which neither of us said a word. In order to break this silence, I decided to continue our conversation.

'Tell me, Lily, you say you see my son from time to time. Would you say he strikes you as happy here? Would you describe him as content?'

'Why, of course I would, ma'am. He always has a smile for us servants, and a kindly word. But he do be a bit low since his cousin left, and now in lower spirits since little Alice died. He was always very fond of her. But I'm certain sure it won't be long before he finds a young woman of his own to concern him. That'll cheer him up no end.'

The thought of Simon, all grown up as he seemed to me to be, cavorting with the parlourmaids was not one I cared to entertain for long.

'Concentrate on your work, Lily,' I said. 'I'd like time to rest before I go down. Will there be a gong?'

'Ten minutes before, ma'am. You can't miss it. The sound will travel up here.'

'Very good. Thank you. And, oh, Lily, do you know which room is my son's?'

She took me to the door and pointed to another opposite, across the landing.

'That's Master Simon's room, ma'am. I'm sure he'll be there now, if you want to visit him. Or would you prefer him to come here? I'll fetch him for you, if you like.'

"No, it's all right. You must have other duties to attend to.'

'I'd be happy to help, ma'am.'

'Another time, perhaps. Now, I'd like to sit in that armchair and doze off for a few minutes.'

I closed the door and went to the armchair, where I fell fast asleep in moments. The next thing I knew, the sound of a gong was ringing in my ears.

Letter from Private Thomas Trevelyan, Second Army, near Messines, 18 June, 1917

To Master William Trevelyan
Trevelyan Priors
Porthmullion
Cornwall
England

Dear Will,

I know you must be angry with me, and I expect everyone else is absolutely boiling mad. I don't blame them, not much anyway. But it's you I'm writing to, because I know you'll understand what it's like here. I can't tell you anything operational, of course, but I expect you'll know all about this outing by tomorrow or the day after. They've just started a massive bombardment of the German lines, which will probably go on for weeks, just to soften old Jerry up. It can't be much of a secret any longer, since I expect you can hear it over in England. Once it's over, no doubt we'll go in for a hell of a push, and as likely as not most of the lads I'm with will be dead minutes after we set off.

I probably won't be in that offensive, since my regiment's going over the top tomorrow. The barrage will be suspended for half an hour, during which time we've been ordered out to test the enemy positions. If we can get past the wire, we'll probably be mown down by their heavy machine-guns. There's no point in my trying to hide that, not with you of all people. You know the odds in these situations as well as I do.

I feel as though I've let everyone down. Mother, Father, you Simon, even old Fitz. It's not glorious out here, not glorious at all and none of the acres of mud or the stench, the rotting corpses the wires, the trenches, the shelling, the whistles, or the sad sol diers make it any more glorious. Our officers, some of whom ar nearly as young as myself, talk of King and country, but the me here couldn't give a damn, especially the older ones who've bee in France a long time and seen several battles, and lived to tell the tale.

The man beside me is a miner from the North-East. He's been down tunnelling in one of the mines they're digging in order to place high explosives under Jerry's backside. It was work he was used to, but he started to have trouble with his lungs, so they sent him up here instead.

I can hardly understand a word he says. He must be twenty or thereabouts, and he's been out here about three months, which makes him an old hand. The things he tells me in his barely comprehensible way of talking remind me of the things you used to tell me when we chatted in your room. This man has a sweetheart waiting for him back home, and he tells me he intends to marry her when he next gets a bit of leave. That's all any of us have to look forward to — a bit of leave. But I expect you know that. And you must know I can't go back to the Priors, even if the war should end tomorrow.

What you won't know is how hard these men's lives were before they even put on khaki. Billy — that's this miner's name — first went down a coal pit when he was ten. He'd get up every morning at four, walk a mile or more to the pit with his father and an older brother, and then it was down into the darkness for the rest of the working day. In winter, they'd rise in darkness and go home in darkness, and never see the sun. They had meat in a stew once a week, if they were lucky. A loaf of bread would often have to last the whole family for days. Over half the babies his mother gave birth to died as they were born. And the ones that lived suffered from all kinds of illnesses, because they never had fresh food.

William, I know you're a bit of an old stodge, but if I die tomorrow, I want it to be for a better world, one in which Billy and his family will never go hungry or have to work all day in darkness or be forced to walk into the German guns.

If we can't improve things when this bloody war is over, then my getting peppered by a machine-gun means nothing. If nothing is done, men like my father will still run things they way they always have done. God, Will, how I wish you had proper legs and

227

could take over from the old devil while there's still time. You know what I'm talking about. Whatever you do, tell Simon everything. He needs to know, and he needs to get as far away from Trevelyan Priors as possible.

I'm enclosing a short note for Simon and another for Mother. I want to make my apologies in case things go badly tomorrow. The thing is, Will, I'm scared witless, waiting here, waiting for first light and the whistle that will send me and hundreds of others hurtling out of our trenches and on to the Messines Ridge.

Please don't let on to them I was scared, though. Say I was in good spirits, that I was looking forward to going over and having a crack at Jerry. If I die, as I expect I will, make sure to get hold of my CO here, a man called Coombes-Lazenby, and make sure he praises me to high heaven when he writes to them. He's a terrible snob, so be sure to tell him I was a baronet's son blah blah blah. He'll lap it up and spew out something beyond the statutory 'died bravely'. I'll die a coward, as will most of the men here, but I'll push on for the ridge first because Coombes-Lazenby or some other officer will shoot me if I turn and run, or I'll be captured and put before a firing-squad, for my own side will kill me if the Germans don't. What a farce, eh? What a bleeding, cruel farce. Why don't we just take out, say, a thousand men on our side and shoot them, then get Jerry to do the same, and call it quits?

Willy, old boy, I'm scared to death. I won't even see the face of the man who shoots me, not unless he gets up close with a bayonet — and that's not what will happen tomorrow. The Germans have Maxim machine-guns all across the ridge, and Plumer wants to send us in there in the hope that sheer numbers will run their positions over. He thinks Jerry's getting weak on this front and may be ready to pull back, but he wants to test it tomorrow morning, and we're the blood and flesh he needs. One of the old hands in my troop says he thought that last year as well and was horribly wrong.

Will, old boy, there's something I need to ask you. When you and James were out here, did you see any children? You must know the sort of children I mean. The sort that aren't dead and aren't alive. I can see them now, sitting or standing in the trenches, staring out into the darkness as though waiting for something

228

or someone.

There's a living boy out on the wire somewhere. I guess he must be about my age. He's been there for hours. He cries out for a while, then goes silent, then screams. Each time he calls out, they look in that direction, even though it's dark and there's nothing to be seen. Nothing but the mud and broken trees in No-Man's-Land, when a flare goes up to turn night into day. Some of us have tried to shoot the boy, to put him out of his misery, but he's too well hidden. Or maybe it's just Jerry winding us up.

Once in a while, one of the dead children will turn his or her head and look at me. I've seen Alice among them. She's dead like the others, but she doesn't seem to know it.

Sometimes at night, when the shelling starts and the sky is filled with flarelight, they go over the top together and head out into No-Man's-Land, all of them in a little string, singing silly songs like the ones they used to sing. Nobody sees them go, nobody sees them return in the early dawn. Nobody but me. When the boy stops screaming, that's when they'll go tonight.

If I look up, I imagine I can see the Shot Tower. It's as high and as heavy and as black as ever it was when you and I used to go there to watch the lead shot form out of nothing. And as bloody as the days when the children visited and went up and were never seen again. You never told me what was in there, did you? You said it could wait till I was grown up. Well, I'm as grown up tonight as I'll ever be. I was a child when I left Trevelyan Priors, but I'm an adult now, and what they bury tomorrow will be a man, make no mistake of that, and be sure they remember it at home, all of them, but my father most of all, may he drown in my blood, may he climb the tower and never be seen again.

None of the men with me can see the children, of course. We Trevelyans are a happy breed, don't you think? We see death everywhere. The children are trying to tell me I won't be going home, and I'm sure they're right. Do you think Simon will do the right thing? Will you tell him that, if he goes against his will, my father will have him done to death or worse? This business Father and the marquis want him for, would you advise me to write to him about it, try to warn him? I don't suppose I'll have time. If I don't, will you take that on yourself? Have I thrown a spanner in the works? Or do you have plans of your own?

Someone's playing a harmonica just down the line. He's good, whoever he is, and some of the lads are joining in, singing like a Welsh choir. It's a futile gesture, but it lifts our poor spirits nevertheless. Kiss Mother for me. That shouldn't be too hard, should it? Shake Father's hand and, if you have a moment or two alone with the vile marquis, why don't you tell him on my behalf to go to hell? Or should that be 'back to hell'?

Tell Simon to stay clear of the war, please, and to get as far from the Priors as he can. He may be poor, but surely he won't be stupid enough to think of staying there a day longer than necessary.

As for yourself, I have no grievances. If I bump into James, I'll tell him how you ended up, though I suppose he already knows.

The sergeant-major's telling us to turn in for the night, so I'll stop here and get this into an envelope. Take care. Pray for me. Pray I never go back there.

Your brother,

Tom

A Visit to the Attic

Letter from Harriet Trevelyan to her sister Alicia Nesbitt, St Nicholas Street, Bristol. 19 June 1917

My dear Alicia,

I implore you to destroy this letter after you have read it, lest it should bring any shadow of suspicion on you or your family. But when you have destroyed it, I beseech you to write to me speedily, as if to say that something terrible has happened, that you have fallen ill again or that Henry is ill, and that you need me with you at once, and that I must bring Simon with me lest the worst befall, in anticipation of which sad event his presence is greatly desired in Bristol, etc. etc. Send by telegram in order to save time, for I think that even one day more spent in this accursed house may prove fatal to Simon and myself.

No doubt you are wondering what can have happened to bring me to this. The truth is — and, believe me, every word you read here is true, as God is my witness, even though it may at times seem hard or impossible to credit. Yesterday, I spent a leisurely morning taking tea with Marion and Simon. He was excused classes for, as it happened, there were none. For reasons best known to himself, my brother-in-law had dismissed the former schoolmaster, Fitzgerald, and had not as yet engaged a successor. From my point of view, of course, this was better than I could have hoped for. It meant I could see Simon almost as often as I wished to.

Marion was called away soon after we finished tea, so I asked Tom if he'd care to show me round the house. It astonished me to find him so eloquent and knowledgeable about the architecture and the many paintings and other works of art that were displayed in every room and corridor. Sumptuous chamber followed sumptuous chamber, though I was for the moment denied access to the library, since Sir David and his pet Frenchman were in there, doing whatever it is they do.

From the house, we went on outside. Simon was more at ease with me now, and I with him. You know how awkward it can be even between ourselves, dear sister, after long absence. And Simon, of course, had changed.

I needed to talk to him about the alterations I had noticed in his frame and character, how he was coping with his father's death (which, as you well know, is still an open wound in my own soul), with his separation from me, and with the new relationships he has been forming with his aunt and uncle and cousins. Most of all, I need to speak to him about Tom and his hasty decision to enlist for France.

The weather being mild, he suggested we walk down to the little stretch of water they call the Swan Lake, which had once been a familiar habitat for the creatures, but has so far this summer been bereft of them. We walked there over green swards, and everywhere wild flowers in abundance. It seemed to me such an idyllic place, and I believed I had done the right thing to send my son down here.

We talked intermittently of Tom, and of how he'd come to run off. Simon reassured me that he would not follow his cousin. All thoughts of vengeance on the Germans had been expunged by the horrors of which William had told him.

I was due to see William that afternoon for the first time in many, many years, and I already felt my heart warm to him, for his compassion in having taken the scales from Simon's eyes. Charles would have approved, I know.

I counselled Simon as best I could on how to cope with Tom's flight, and tried to buffer him against the almost certain news that his friend was dead.

'We could pray together that he return safe,' I said. 'Is there a chapel in the Priors?'

He shook his head.

'Just the parish church over at Zelah.'

'I see.' I was puzzled that this should be the case. 'How very strange that there should be no chapel in a house of that size. But I suppose you go with the family to… what is the church called?'

'St Just,' he said. 'I'm afraid no one goes there but the staff. Uncle David and Aunt Marion last set foot in the place for James's memorial service. But they only felt obliged to do that because it would have looked extremely bad in view of his having died for his country and all that. There's a plaque on the church wall now, but I don't think anyone goes to look at it. Well, perhaps they go when I don't know, or maybe Aunt Marion on her own; but I've never been told of it and never been asked to go with them.'

'But, my darling, this is terrible. I shall have to speak about it with your aunt at the earliest opportunity. Have you never thought of going there yourself, or along with the staff?'

'I did think of that, yes, but Tom wouldn't hear of it, and said it wouldn't go down well with his parents. I think there's some sort of dispute between them and the vicar.'

'Well, at this rate they'll be turning you into an atheist. I shouldn't like that, love. I'll do my best to get to the bottom of it with Marion. She's a good sort. Her heart's in the right place.'

I thought it best to drop the topic, but I have to admit that Simon's confession troubled me greatly. I resolved to go over to St Just's myself tomorrow, along with the staff, and I'll try to persuade Simon to come with me. I cannot imagine what the Reverend Upham Pope would make of all this.

'How do you entertain yourself in the evenings, Simon?' I asked to change the subject. 'Is there much music? I don't think I've seen a single piano in the house.'

He nodded.

'You're right: there isn't one. We play cards or read. Uncle David is usually off somewhere with the marquis. Aunt Marion often embroiders: she does counted cross-stitch, and makes cushions and firescreens. When Tom was here, he and I would play billiards or backgammon all evening. Or we'd go up to William's room and play there. Tom's a good sort. He knows practically every game you can think of. Alice always went to bed early, straight after dinner, so she didn't count.'

'Poor Alice,' I exclaimed. I'd never known her, but the death of a child so young is a most terrible thing.

'Mother,' Simon said, looking earnestly at me. 'There's something I want to tell you. But I want you to promise you'll not spill a bean to anyone else. It has to be a secret between us.'

'Well, of course, my dear. You know you can tell me anything you like. I won't breathe a word to anyone, unless you say you've committed murder or some other great crime. But I fancy you want to confide in me something about Tom.'

'No. It has nothing to do with Tom. And nothing to do with murder. The thing is this — now, you must listen carefully and not interrupt — well, Mother, not very long ago I went exploring in a little garden out that way, an old garden, a place nobody from the house ever sets foot in, a private place I sometimes visit to be on my own. Only, this time I met someone. A young woman the same age as myself. She's called Morwenna. It's a Cornish name. She comes from Porthmullion, the little fishing village that belongs to the estate. Where you arrived on the train.'

He pointed, and I followed his finger to the brow of a low hill, beyond which I could see the blue sea merge with a soft summer sky. My son is in love, I thought. My son at fifteen, infatuated by some trollop of a fisherman's daughter, her hair no doubt filled with the stink of the latest catch, her hands reeking of crab and lobster and seagulls' wings.

'Yes, I see,' I said, though I didn't see at all. I left it to him to tell me his secret. I prayed that he not be in love with her. What, after all, could he hope for at such an early stage of his manhood? And would this young fisherwoman give him what he wanted from a woman, a pretty face and a kindly manner? For marriage, I knew, was intimate and cunning and full of pitfalls for the rash, the unwary, and the inexperienced. I dreaded the truth, and feared he might say she was pregnant, or that he intended to run away with her, just as his hero Tom had run away, never to return. A war is on, I thought, a war that has already killed my husband and a nephew, that may soon claim another nephew's life, yet there I was, wondering what consequences Simon's confession might come to have for his personal and social future.

'We talked the first time we met,' he said, 'and we became very close in a matter of hours, but you must know, Mother, or you must try to imagine how beautiful she is, and how tender, how like an angel. I wanted to kiss her when I first set eyes on her.'

'And have you kissed, the two of you? Is that what you want to tell me in secret? You must tell me. I won't rest otherwise, wondering what has passed between you.'

'We have kissed, yes...'

235

'And more than kissed?'

He looked blankly at me.

'More?' he queried. 'What more could…?'

'You're much too young to know. Oh, Simon, why are young men always so easily won over in matters of the heart? You scarcely know this village girl, yet…'

He looked up — for he had all the time been staring in embarrassment at the floor — and gazed at me with such an expression of mingled hope and pain in his eyes, that I realised how seldom I had ever refused him anything until now.

'I know her better than you think,' he said. 'We've not met often, it's true, but it feels as if we've known one another years. Mother, I've told her all about you, and your visit to the Priors, and she says she wants to meet you. Would you like that? Would it help if you met her? You would see right away what a dear, sweet girl she is.'

'I'm sure she is all you say she is, my darling, though had she been brought up properly, she might not have permitted such an impertinence on your part. But you surely know that you're both too young even to think of a liaison. You're both still children in the world's eyes. Adorable children, I do not doubt, if a little troublesome.'

'My cousin Tom is practically the same age as me, and they took him into the army and sent him off to fight like a man twice his age or more.'

'Yes, I know that, dear,' I sighed. 'But surely you do not admire him for it? It was the act of a child, to go so hastily and on such a flimsy pretext, and it was the act of an utter fool to have allowed him to enlist. Besides, you must consider other people's feelings for a change. Mine, for one. And your aunt and uncle. They've done so much to have you here with them. Don't you think it might cause difficulties for them if you were known to have a common girl like that for a sweetheart? You could never marry, you must know that. David and Marion cannot risk any hint of a scandal — it would lower them in the esteem of all their neighbours.'

'Does that matter?' he asked, as he was bound to. My heart

might have sympathised with his predicament, but it was my duty as his mother to prepare him for inevitable disappointment.

'In this world, Simon, a good name is worth more than you yet realise. And you have no right to besmirch the good name of others, especially close relations who have gone to such lengths in order to make you one of their own. I don't wish to hear more on this subject.'

'What about love?'

'Love is a luxury, like chocolate. It's not enough in itself to build a life on. With love should go intellect and refinement, in all ways matching each partner's station in life, and with true piety on both sides, as the Reverend Upham Pope often reminds us. If you let it, love will destroy you both in the end. Many who welcomed it to begin with have come to regret it in the end.'

'Did you love my father?'

'How can you ask such a thing? Of course I did.'

'I asked because I thought it might have helped you understand.'

'Oh, it's not because I don't understand, dear,' I said. 'It's because I do. Let's not talk about this any more today. If you really do insist, I'll meet your Morwenna later. But not now.'

Lunch was — ironically — freshly caught seafood, with lobster and shrimp and the white meat of a dozen crabs, which we ate with salad from the garden and washed down with the local ale, which is called cider. It was brewed at Docking Farm. Marion told me it's made from apples and that it can be quite strong, like the stronger beers. But some of the farm cider is brewed less strongly for the house, and even Simon was allowed to have some.

We had planned to make a little tour of the grounds in order to walk off our banquet, but a note was sent in for Marion just as we were taking some strawberries for dessert. Having read it, she asked Tom to find Parkin, the chauffeur, then turned to me apologetically.

'Harriet, my dear, I do hope you won't mind, but something unexpected has come up. I think we have to call off this afternoon's walk.'

'That's perfectly all right,' I answered, though, to tell the truth,

I had been looking forward to another stroll through the gardens. I think Marion heard the disappointment in my voice.

'The thing is,' she said, 'I shall have to take Simon off with me. He probably hasn't had a chance to tell you that I've promised him a pony for Bob Miller to teach him to ride on. It's something all we country dwellers simply have to do.'

'You're not planning on taking him hunting, are you?' I said, alarmed.

'He has already told me he doesn't much relish the thought. But when the season begins... We hope Tom will be safely back well before then. He sits a hunter very well, and goes off to hunt any chance he gets. It's all very limited at the moment, but the government is bound to relax the current restrictions. Simon may decide he wants to join in. Or...' — she had just caught sight of Simon's face as she made the suggestion — 'or he may like to try his hand at lepping.'

I had no idea what she was talking about.

'Lepping?

'Perhaps I should call it horse-jumping. It's getting to be quite the fashion at some of the county shows.'

'Yes, I see. Well, no doubt that is fairly safe.'

'Oh, we don't mean to coddle him. I know you're anxious for the boy, but Simon is tougher than you think. When you see him next, he'll be well on his way to being a man. He'll look good on a horse, you'll see. But you can be assured, I won't let him go to war, not for King or country or his own ego. Men, as you well know, are very silly creatures, and they don't seem to mind much if millions of them get blown to pieces for a scrap or two of land. But the widows and the orphans and the mothers mind very much, and it's our job to resist this war fever and bring a quick end to all this bloodshed.

'Well, enough of my ranting. The man who has a pony to sell will be over at St Keverne this afternoon, so I think it's wise for us to go over in the car and see if this piece of horseflesh matches our expectations. I'd love you to come with us, but I think you could unsettle Simon a little. He needs to feel entirely confident if he's to feel right with the pony, but he knows you aren't entirely happy with this.

'I know you planned to spend some time upstairs with my dear William. He's been asking for you. I'll see one of the chambermaids takes you there once Simon and I have gone. By the way, David is up at Petherwin Farm, and the marquis... Heaven knows where he has got to. I don't encourage you to seek him out as a companion. He's not an easy man to know, and even now I do not feel at ease with him. I could tell yesterday evening over dinner that you're not his cup of tea, nor he yours.'

I said nothing, but inward I felt myself agreeing with everything she said. The marquis had struck me as somewhat sinister, and I found it hard to comprehend his motives in staying so long with the Trevelyans.

The car came, a maid ran and fetched a hat with veil for Marion (in which she looked more intimidating than ever), Simon came in to kiss me farewell, and they set off down the drive, bouncing gently on the car's suspension.

Another little maid appeared — they all seemed to be dreadfully young, but I've had very little experience of such creatures. This one was called Martha. She took me upstairs to the bedroom floor and led me through its corridors until we came to William's bedroom.

I found him in good spirits, and we spent the best part of two hours chatting like old friends. We spoke of anything but the war or death or amputation. I could see he was in great pain at times. He regretted the loss of Dr Quilty, who had done wonders for him. He'd heard that half the American doctors with the troops in France were homoeopaths like Quilty, and that they'd not needed to perform a single amputation at their hospital in Paris. He had no idea why Quilty had left, or whether he'd gone of his own accord or on someone's orders, by which he probably meant his father.

In the end, he began to show signs of tiredness, so I said goodbye, promising to return the next day, if I could. I rang for Martha, and she arrived within a few minutes.

'I don't know if he needs any help,' I said to her, for I was at a loss in such matters.

239

'It's all right, ma'am,' she replied. 'I know exactly what to do. I was a nurse in France. I'll take care of him, don't you worry.'

'Then, I'll go to my room to lie down for a bit,' I said. 'I'm tired after yesterday. I had a long journey down. Will you please wake me when Lady Marion and my son come back?'

She said she would and curtsied, then led me to my room. I thanked her and, when she had gone, I lay down on the bed fully dressed.

Sleep came over me quickly, and within less than a minute, as I suppose, I was dreaming. I dreamed I was in a room surrounded by books, and that on one wall there was depicted a monk with a deep cowl thrown back to expose his face, a leering, lustful face with eyes set deeply in their sockets, eyes that were as cold as the coldest threat. I tried to tear myself away from him, but all the time felt myself being brought closer.

Suddenly, I awoke. I lay awake, feeling my entire body perspire with fear. Then there came a knock on the door, and I guessed from its urgency that someone must have knocked more than once.

I opened the door to find Lily about to knock again.

'Where's... Where's Martha?' I asked, still blurry-headed after my dream. Or had it been dreams?

'Martha has other duties, ma'am. I was sent to wake you up.'

'Has your mistress returned with my son?'

'Yes, ma'am.'

She held her hand towards me, and I saw she carried a sheet of paper.

'I've brought a note, ma'am, from Master Simon. Please to read it, ma'am.'

I took the note and unfolded it. It was brief.

"Dear Mother,

Morwenna and I are waiting for you. Please come to meet her. We're in the attic upstairs from you. Don't be long."

'Is he up there now?' I asked. 'In the attic?'

'Of course, ma'am. His young woman is there as well. He said I was to take you up. I'm ready now, if you'd like to come along.'

She was a remarkably pretty girl, I thought, like some of the girls I'd envied when I was that age. Long dark hair, full red lips, and green eyes like the darkest jade.

'It's Lily, isn't it?' I asked.

'That's right,' she said. 'You can call me Lily.'

She led me up a steep flight of stairs, which was illuminated by an oil-lamp that Lily had brought for the purpose. For it was dark in the stairwell, and cold, and everywhere old dust and cobwebs covered the walls. The stairs creaked and sighed as I went up them, and I was sure I could hear sounds further up, like foot-steps and muted cries.

As my unsuspecting foot reached the top landing, I felt the first pricklings of an obscure and all-pervading fear. I stood there, half-paralysed, then behind me Lily spoke in a reassuring sort of voice, telling me to open the door ahead of me. I hesitated in front of it.

My breathing had become more difficult, and when I paused I noticed that my heart was beating unnaturally fast, as though I'd been running a race. Of course, I had been climbing stairs, so I thought no more of it. But when I had been standing for above five minutes in front of the door, and these symptoms persisted, I was sure something must be wrong.

I felt afraid. Not over-exerted, not agitated, not even simply anxious. Afraid. My mouth felt dry, my hair, which I was wearing up, was tingling at the roots, I was sweating for all it was a cold day. My instincts told me to run, but I checked myself, goaded by another fear: what would happen if I were to give way to unfounded jitters brought on by over-exertion — for, surely, I thought, that is all it could be — but nevertheless, what if I gave way and ran back down the stairs, all the way to the bottom, screaming, perhaps, and shaking? I'd be a laughing stock throughout the house, from the servants to Marion and David — and even the hateful little marquis.

When I turned, intending to go back down, I saw Lily still standing behind me. The light from her lamp gave her face a weird, ghostly appearance, and I quite started at the sight of her. But she smiled and gestured at the door.

'You won't need this,' she said, holding up the lamp. 'It's light in there. You'll see. There's no need to feel afraid.'

'I don't think I want to go through,' I riposted. 'I can feel something.'

'That's just your imagination, is all, ma'am. I never pay attention to such things. Anyway, Simon's already in there, waiting for you, ma'am. Morwenna too. They'd like to talk with you.'

Seeing her hold back, I asked if she was planning to accompany me after all.

'I'm sorry, ma'am,' she said, her accent very thick, 'but there are duties I can't avoid downstairs. You'll be all right, you'll see. I'll leave the lamp for you to help you back down these stairs.'

I stood on the landing for several minutes longer, letting it all wash over me: my own fear, and the sense of an evil that I knew must lie behind the attic door. I would have turned and fled, but she had told me Simon was in there, and I dared not run and leave him there alone. A moment longer, and my fear for Simon overcame any fears I harboured for myself.

I reached out with a shaking hand and turned the half-rusted knob and pushed the door fully open.

What little light there was came from a skylight in the ceiling, long encrusted with filth by passing seabirds. The entire attic was filled with a musty smell. Dust hung in the pale air, old dust, a dust of centuries that had never left this corridor or these empty, lonely rooms. Wherever a shaft of sunlight stabbed down, there would be ten thousand motes of dust to be captured and lifted by it.

I closed the door behind me. Simon was not waiting in the corridor. I wondered who else might be waiting. Someone I knew? Someone I might not like to know?

The terror was a constant agony in me. Any moment now, I thought, something will happen, and I listened intently for the slightest sound. I shall see something, I thought, and my nerves, already jangling, would snap together, leaving me here insane and drooling.

Sometimes I heartily wish that that is what had happened, that I was up there still, oblivious to everything. James's death, William's injuries, Alice's illness, Tom's going (as we supposed) to the Front, even the danger now encircling my beloved Simon, would all be the problems of another woman.

Someone laughed. My pulse raced even faster. It was a young girl's laugh, no, I was wrong, a little girl's. It came from further down the corridor. On either side of me, brown-painted doors, their paint peeling away from the wood in places, stretched down to the first corner.

These rooms had been lived in by the female house servants from the mid-eighteenth century until about twenty years ago. I've heard it said (I had this from Mrs Armitage, the housekeeper) that it grew hard to keep servants from the time of David's grandfather, Sir Henry Trevelyan.

Apparently, there were rumours of whispering when there should have been no whispering, and of things said that should not have been said, of Bibles opened to show black pages, of a tall, thin figure, a man who entered the girls' rooms late at night. Two maids died, from fright, it is said. And in the end, David's father ordered the old storage rooms in the basement to be rebuilt as bedrooms. New storage sheds were built outside, and the old attic rooms were shut up for good. This was just before he died. It must have been around the time David and Marion were married, a few years before Charles and myself.

I don't know how long I forced myself to remain there, listening to that unholy chuckle. I knew there were no children anywhere in the house, but wondered if one of the servants was concealing one up here. What if one of the maids had been put in the family way by one of the footmen? It seemed the merest craziness to think of such a child being brought up in such unspeakable conditions; but better a living child, I thought, than some dead thing I could hear but neither see nor touch.

I opened up Simon's note again, to see if he'd left any information about where to find him, but, to my astonishment, the sheet on which the message had been written was now entirely blank on both sides.

Dredging up what little courage I had left, I made my way steadily down the corridor. The floorboards beneath my feet creaked and groaned. When I reached the corner where the corridor turned at right angles, I saw a pedestal and, on top of it still, an old vase that might at one time have held spring and summer flowers. It was covered in cobwebs, whose long strands connected it to the floor and walls and ceiling. The thought of spiders weaving webs and walking on their long, uncanny legs made me shiver.

I continued along the next passage without arrest until I reached a point about halfway along. On my right stood a door much like all the others, except that it had a label pasted to it at eye level. On this label was all that remained of a name, written in ink many years before, and now faded and illegible to my tired eyes.

I cannot describe adequately what happened next. Oh God, let me never go through that again. All I did was stand in front of the door, trying to read the inscription. It did not open, and I did not try to open it. There was no sound but the laughing of the child. I saw nothing, least of all a phantom or an ectoplasm. I just stood and stared at the door, with its faded ink and peeling paint, I stared at the door and, as I did so, I felt as though my soul was being raped, violated by something unspeakably foul. It was as if my entire insides had filled up with despair, as if the blackest despair ran through my body, down as deep as my veins and arteries. I wanted to die. And at the same moment I experienced fear of death like no fear I have ever felt before.

The laughter must have stopped some time before. From somewhere I could not identify, I smelled a powerful perfume of flowers, dozens of different flowers all mixed together, their scents mingling indiscriminately. I looked up and down the corridor. Nothing. But I heard something. I heard footsteps on the bare floorboards to my left. They — whoever they may be — were still a little distance away. I decided it was just one set of footsteps after all. A child's. Coming my way. Was it Simon, I wondered?

Suddenly, my limbs felt loose again. I still sensed the evil presence behind the door, but I kept my eyes fixed on the corridor up ahead. I waited, heart in mouth. There is no one up here, I tried to tell myself, not even Simon. If you have been hearing footsteps, they must be in your own head.

She appeared at the second corner, and I fell for her at once, even though I knew she could not possibly be real. I knew right away that she was not Simon's girl, for she did not meet her description in any way. For one thing, she was too young by perhaps three years. She had long blonde hair tied up in pink ribbons, and she wore a quaint grey dress of silk that must have dated from perhaps fifty years earlier. She walked towards me steadily, a smile on her face, and when she reached me she slipped one hand inside mine, though I felt nothing, and said, 'Very pleased to meet you. My name is Agnes. You'd best come with me.'

She led me away from the door and back down the corridor, right to the door that led onto the landing. I tried to speak with her, to question her, but all she would do was look up at me and smile. She smiled very prettily, and I tried to smile back, but I knew she should not be there, and still I could not feel her hand in mine, and in the right light I could see straight through her.

I came to my senses again, to find myself shivering in the morning room. Mrs Armitage found me there, for one of the maids had been concerned when I had not been in my bedroom, and a search had been instituted.

The housekeeper asked where I had been, and how I had come to be in the state she found me in. I told her, and she looked at me as though I had died, and finally ordered me never to set foot up there again, for any reason whatsoever. My sister-in-law's housekeeper, ordering me where I might and might not go in Marion's house. But I think she knew nothing of substance, and knows nothing still. 'I was taken there by a maid,' I said. 'Perhaps you would summon her, find out if she knows anything about this mysterious note. Her name is Lily.'

Mrs Armitage just looked at me and shook her head.

'You must be mistaken,' she said. 'There's no one in this house called Lily. Not one of the maids, certainly.'

As for myself, I carry it within me for ever now. The child is beside me in every room, and I can feel her hand in mine.

A Picnic by the Sea

Letter from Simon Lysaght, 20 June 1917

To Pte. Thomas Trevelyan, The Duke of Cornwall's Light Infantry, Messines, France

Never Posted

My Dear Fool Tom,

I saw you last night, in my bedroom, just before getting into bed. You were in your uniform, and looked very handsome in it, except that half your face had been blown away. I shouldn't think it hurts, though, not now.

You just stood in the corner, staring at me. I might have screamed, if it hadn't been for my state of mind that night. I think you understood. You were smiling, as far as it was possible to tell, and I knew it was you, once I had got up the courage to look properly.

I don't know whether you appeared to anyone else that night, or only to myself; but I won't ask the others, they may not have seen you after all and might wonder why you chose to show yourself to me. Or they might think I'd made it up, that I was lying to them.

No doubt there'll be a knock on the door in a day or two, and a boy from the Post Office holding a telegram, perhaps not his first of the day. They'll let us know if you've been buried or not. That's what happened with my father. Tom, if you ever want to visit me again, would you try to do it with your head in one piece, please?

You never had a chance to see my new horse, Aladdin. He has Arab blood and was liberated by our forces during the capture of Baghdad last March. He saw some action at Falluja soon after that, but he got badly spooked by the bombs and was sent back here on a troopship and sold. You'd like him, I'm sure you would. He's glossy black without any markings, and thirteen hands, and he's very gentle with me, though he still starts at sudden noises. But I'm afraid I won't be able to ride him.

Tom, I've just been putting off what I have to say. Something

247

has happened here. Maybe you know already, maybe you ghosts are aware of things we mortals aren't.

Aunt Marion and I got back with Aladdin shortly after five o'clock, rather later than she had anticipated. That was two days ago. A stable boy rode him back and saw him settled in his new quarters. We found my mother in a small room that caught the late afternoon sun. She'd been served tea there on the advice of Mrs Armitage, but the first thing I noticed when I entered was that she seemed not to have touched any of the breads or cakes that had been placed before her.

When Aunt Marion and I sat down beside her and started to talk, we found her moody and withdrawn, an emotional state quite alien to her usual placid temperament. I thought this must either be on account of her having been left behind while your mother and I went to fetch Aladdin, or as a result of what I'd told her concerning Morwenna and myself earlier that day.

Thinking she needed cheering up, I asked your mother if she would mind if I took your little boat out the following morning. I assured her I'd borrow Peter Tregaskis to sail us to some beauty spot, where we might have a small picnic. Your mother was smashing and consented right away, though she apologised and said she could not accompany us. She gave me stern instructions not to lark about, and pointed out that I'm not the strongest swimmer she had ever seen. My mother confessed that she couldn't swim at all, but she said she'd look forward to the trip, that it might get her out of the house.

'There should be good weather, at least,' Aunt Marion reassured us. Outside, bright sunshine fell in patches on the lawn. There were no clouds in the sky, and no hint of any to come. Aunt Marion made a phone call to the Post Office, and asked Mrs Orchard to send her son to Peter's and ask if he could make himself and the *Demelza Ebrel* available in the morning. Mrs Orchard said she'd speak to Peter when the boats came home that evening.

Dinner turned out to be a gloomy affair, for Mother remained drawn down inside herself and responded only feebly to our attempts to jolly her along. Of course, your father and that hateful marquis of his were as much help as a pair of pallbearers. The marquis kept looking at me throughout the meal, as though he suspected me of something.

We got through all five courses somehow, and then it was the three of us again — your mother, my mother, and I — while Sir David and the blessed marquis went off to smoke fat cigars or something — they never say, do they? I desperately wished for you to be there, but you weren't.

Your father has been looking a bit grey round the gills in the past week or so, and his marquis isn't looking much better. You'd think they'd seen a ghost, but I don't think it was you! Maybe they're just worried about you. More likely, they're worried about themselves.

Mother and I set off yesterday morning at eight o'clock, being driven to Porthmullion by the chauffeur. The good weather seemed set to stay, though it was colder than it had been, and I noticed a few clouds in the sky. It was a short drive down to the village, and we arrived with some time to spare. I was tempted to ask if I could see Dr. Quilty, however briefly, but for some reason my mother seemed unhappy at the suggestion.

'What's wrong, Mother?' I asked, hoping to find a way into that other mood of hers, the dark mood of yesterday evening, which still hung around.

'I think you should speak to your Aunt Marion,' she said. 'Dr Quilty has not been welcome at Trevelyan Priors since your cousin Alice died. Marion tells me he is a medical heretic of some sort — in short, a quack. I earnestly plead with you not to see him again. I don't want to see you putting your health at risk.'

'But he's done absolute wonders for my asthma, Mother. He told me he could cure me completely.'

'You will grow out of it in due course. I don't wish this man Quilty to claim the credit when that happens, as he is bound to do. Now, which is Peter Tregaskis's cottage?'

Peter lived in a small house in a terrace, whose rear windows faced on to the harbour and the sea beyond. His father opened the door and asked us in. We found Peter standing in the kitchen, drinking from a mug of hot tea and eating a buttered split. He seemed embarrassed that we'd piled in on him and hastily put down his mug and bread, but we assured him we weren't the sort to stand on our dignity, and told him to finish his breakfast. He didn't take long to swallow the last crumb, and was soon ready for his guests.

I introduced myself and Mother, and he followed suit.

'I'd like to get moving early,' he said. 'I thought we might go over to Nancledre Sands, just a few miles down coast. Nobody goes there much, for you can only get at the beach by way of the sea. The sands are sheltered from behind by tall cliffs, and there's no way up or down, not unless you're both Alpinists. Main thing is, it's your own beach for as long as you're on it. As private as they come.'

His manner was most reassuring — well, you'd know that better than most — and even my mother's apprehension over the looming boat trip was laid to rest for the moment at least. He did surprise her, however, by expressing disapproval of her clothing.

She had turned up wearing an everyday sort of dress of cotton and silk, the sort of thing one might wear in a place like the Priors, but hardly suitable for a day out boating.

'You'll regret wearing that dress, ma'am,' Peter said. 'It'll get soaked with sea-spray, and if there's a wind, it'll blow right through.'

'I dressed for a picnic, not a sea cruise,' she answered. 'And surely you don't expect there to be a wind. Just look at it.'

'My mother isn't fond of winds,' I explained. 'Out on the moors where she lives, it gets fearfully cold in winter, when the high winds come in from Russia and blow right across. Isn't that right, Mother?'

She struck me playfully with the yellow parasol she'd brought to keep the sun off her head.

'Well, I shan't mind if I get a little wet,' she said. 'This is an old dress, and it does me well enough. It's respectable enough to have on when guests call without prior warning, and it's comfortable enough to wear around the house on my own. A few drops of water won't do it or me any harm.'

'Very well, ma'am. It's your dress and you must live in it. I'll say no more on that count. But tell me, can you swim?'

'I'm afraid not. But I have no intention of bathing.'

'I wasn't thinking of you bathing, ma'am. I was thinking what would happen if you should fall in. You must just be sure you hold on tightly all the time we're at sea, and pay special attention if we have to change tack: I'll call out before I touch the tiller. I don't want you in the water, ma'am, for then I should have to jump in right after you, and that's something I'd rather not do, for I no more likes getting wet than you do.'

With that, he flashed a great smile at her and bent at the waist in order to kiss her hand, and thus raised her out of her chair and onto her feet.

'The *Demelza Ebrel* is this way, ma'am, if you'd care to follow me,' and so saying, Peter led us out of his kitchen and through his front door.

The *Demelza* was moored in the spot where it lay when you first showed her to me. Mother wanted to know why she was painted yellow and white, and I explained what her name meant. Your little Trevelyan flag was fluttering briskly in the breeze and, catching sight of it, Peter asked if there was any news of you.

'Still nothing,' I said. 'All we know of a certainty is that he's somewhere in northern France.'

'Can't think how he got such thick ideas in his noddle,' Peter said. I could tell my mother was fascinated by his Cornish accent. I remember she used to talk to working men and women in York, just for the pleasure of hearing them speak in dialect. I'm sure she thinks I'm well on the way to becoming an out-and-out Cornishman, and it's no use telling her I can scarcely understand Peter myself, or most of the staff at the house, and that my attempts at speaking 'local' are pretty weak.

Peter got us on board, stepping in first, then helping Mother down with a firm hand, while I tried to hold her straight from behind. Once he had us and our picnic hamper safely stowed and distributed, he cast off, then set about trimming the sails. Suddenly, a stiff wind caught us out of nowhere, and the *Demelza* darted forward into the harbour. Peter sat unruffled by the tiller, and steered us very neatly out past the buoys and through the harbour mouth.

As we entered open waters, the sea grew a little choppy and the boat started up and down as you can imagine. Mother kept her hand firmly on her hat, and however much I urged her to stow it safely somewhere, she refused to pay heed.

'Now, my dears,' cried Peter, 'what is it to be? If we head on out that way' — he pointed more or less due south — 'we shall come in time to the Azores. I've not been there, but my old father went once, and according to what he told me, the people there is mostly Portugals and such, and Catholics to boot. But if we were to head out west, we should come to Ireland by and by, where they speak an uncouth language of their own and are fearful Catholics too, of the worst sort.

'But we may not choose to go ashore in Ireland, and if not, why, in time we should come to the Amerikies, where 'tis said they put chicken feathers on their heads and go half naked all day and night, women and men both, and are known to eat one another hungrily at their feasts.'

'That's quite enough, Peter my lad,' said Mother, who was trying her hardest not to laugh and not to be sick at the same time. 'You must not tease us poor landlubbers. I have relatives in Ireland, Protestants to a man, and as clean a people as ourselves. As for the Americans, they sent us troops to help win the war, men who are out in France still, fighting side by side with our brave English lads.'

Peter continued to find ways of diverting us until we'd grown used to the boat and its constant motion. Though we rocked, our course held steady, and Peter steered the *Demelza* ever out from the shore, so we could see the full expanse of coastline stretch out behind us as he tacked westwards. On one stretch, as we looked back once more, Peter pointed out the different towns and fishing villages along the coast, and, most prominent, our own Shot Tower, high above the highest trees. Mother rummaged in her black bag for a pair of binoculars she'd borrowed from William — his old military glasses — and trained them here and there, for all the world like an artilleryman finding the range for a big gun. But you'd know about that better than I do.

At last Nanstallon Cove came in sight, and in its sweep,

Nancledre Sands, stretching like gold leaf from one side to the other. Peter pushed the tiller, the sails came round, and we headed in towards the coast. When I looked up at the sky, I could see dark clouds making their way in from the South.

'Looks like we'll have rain after all,' I said.

'It could well be, Master Simon,' Peter said. 'It's starting to turn squally. This weather's coming in sooner than I thought. There's somat funny going on.'

Dipping and rising through the wind-lashed waves, we ploughed on towards the beach in the hope of securing an anchorage for the *Demelza* and a shelter of some sort for ourselves. I stayed down by the tiller, working the sail on Peter's instructions, learning in minutes what might have taken hours under softer conditions. You'd have had a great time.

We were making way, and the beach was at last in clear sight, when my mother half stood up, pointing towards the beach and calling out.

'There are some people on the beach! Look! Can you see them, Simon?'

I took the glasses from her and, with some difficulty, focused on the beach. I could make out three figures at the western end: a man and a woman with their child, as far as I could tell.

Suddenly, the binoculars were almost thrown out of my hands, as the *Demelza* was caught by the leading edge of a mighty squall, fierce gusts of rain-soaked wind beating her sides, now across the bows, now from the stern. The waves rose higher, and the little boat started to take in water, fortunately not in serious quantities. Making good use of the gusts in our rear, we sailed forward quickly, Peter adjusting the tiller the whole time. I barely held the sail to his liking.

This preoccupied us until we were very close to shore. I kept the sail full of wind — most of the time — while Mother got down on her knees to invoke the Deity and, when Peter shouted instructions to her, to bale out the water.

Her labours brought her near the stern at one point, and, on seeing her there, Peter called out.

'Do they have a boat?' he asked, shouting above the wind.

'Who?' Mother shouted back.

'The folk on the beach,' he cried. 'Did you see a boat moored or anchored anywhere near them?'

'I don't remember one. I know I looked from one end of the cove to the other, in case there were others, but I saw no boat.'

He looked at her with manifest puzzlement.

'Then tell me how they got there,' he said. 'I told you earlier that no one gets onto Nancledre Sands without they come by boat or balloon, and I'm sure they aren't balloonists. The cliffs are too high, there are no paths down, there are no staircases cut in the cliff face, and I know of no tunnels or smugglers' holes. You gets in by boat or not at all.'

'What about an aeroplane?' I suggested. 'Maybe they're not a family, as we think, but bold German spies flown in this morning by a Hun pilot.'

'Now, don't you go frightening us,' Mother said. 'Why would the Germans send their spies to some old cove they can't even get out of? But I do wonder if they could have been left here by a hired boat and are now waiting for it to return. Maybe they think we're that same boat on its way back.'

'Which, of course, it can't do, ma'am, on account of all these great winds and high waves.'

We returned to the task of getting to the beach in one piece. I didn't feel afraid, oddly enough, though I can't say I much liked the leaping up and down of the boat. I thought hard of you, and hoped we wouldn't sink your *Demelza*.

It was Peter who inspired me, for he sat at the tiller as calm as you please. By then, we were perhaps twenty yards from the shore. That's when I heard my mother scream. When I looked, she had one hand to her mouth, and was pointing at the cove.

I followed her finger, and in a few seconds made out what had terrified her. You were there in your muddy bloody uniform, and half of your head was missing, just like I saw it last night. I expect you know you were there. Next to you was Alice, dressed only in her nightgown, and bone dry, despite the rain. And her hair was straight and unruffled, despite the wind. Holding her hand was my Morwenna, the girl I was going to tell you about. She was dressed much as I had seen her in the summer-house, but today she was almost unrecognisable, for someone had cut her throat from side to side, and blood had spilled all down her front. Her beautiful hair was bloody too, her eyes were wide open, and she was smiling. At me.

My mother was leaning over the gunwale, being sick.

I turned to Peter. His hand seemed frozen to the tiller, and he was praying, reciting the Lord's Prayer over and over again. He had recognised you, I think, or guessed who you must be, and he must have known Alice as well, not to mention Morwenna, who may have lived only doors away from him.

My mother had spent an hour or more the night before examining Aunt Marion's family photographs, in which both you and Alice figured prominently. But I think it was Morwenna she most feared.

I pulled the tiller from Peter's hand, but jerked it the wrong way, for I'd never steered a boat before, and the yard swung round heavily, the sail emptying and filling again, throwing my mother backwards into the sea.

I screamed after her and dashed to the side. She was in the water several yards away, and she could not swim because of the waves and her long dress that was filling with water and hampering her increasingly desperate attempts to keep her head above the surface. Even as I watched, the dress filled with yet more water and an enormous wave pulled her under.

I was stripping off my heavy jacket ready to go in after her, when I felt a hand on my shoulder.

'Stay in the boat, lad. You don't know these waters as I do, and you haven't swum in waves like these, which I have. Stay here and try to bring in the sail. Once you get it tied, hold the tiller in one position. I'll have your mother back on board in no time.'

He shook my hand once, then kicked off his shoes and dived over the side and started swimming towards the spot where he'd seen my mother go down.

Over the crash of waves falling ashore, and the blowing of the wind, I could make out Morwenna's voice, calling my name aloud like a seal woman calling for her lover across the northern seas.

It took me a minute or two to work out which sheets to pull on in order to bring the sail down, and another minute to do the thing. Once it was down, I rushed to the side to see Peter thirty feet away, struggling to keep my mother's inert body buoyant in the hard-running waves. How was I to get the boat to them? I looked down and found a pair of oars in the chine, but there were no thwarts aboard that I could use for a seat, and the gunwales had no rowlocks. On reflection, the *Demelza* was too large to be easily steered, and it's likely the oars were for a little skiff trailed in the stern. You would know.

I hurried astern and found a length of rope that I used to tie the tiller fast. I lacked a sailor's skill with fancy knots, but when I finally got the rope fast, the tiller stayed in place. I stood and looked back to where I remembered having last seen Peter and Mother.

They had vanished. My heart was in my mouth as I scoured the sea in all directions, desperate for even a glimpse of either one. And all the while Morwenna called my name, *Simon, Simon, come to me, come to me, my love.* And I closed my ears with my hands and watched helplessly as the waves tossed me about. At last, afraid of being thrown overboard myself, I crouched down in the bottom of the boat, while the *Demelza* lifted and dropped like a ball kicked hard in a rugger match.

I let five minutes pass, to my estimation, and another five after that. And the hard grey sea did not part. There was no hand of God. There was no staff of Moses. Just the cold sea. I knew they were both dead by now, no one could have survived for long in waters like that. I just waited for the waves to take me as well. Could I have made it to the beach alone? Perhaps. Certainly, I was within reach of it. And now that I looked, I saw that you had gone and taken Alice with you, and that Morwenna alone had been left by the water's edge, and that her wound and the blood that had been spilled had both gone, leaving her as beautiful as the time I'd first set eyes on her. I would have gone willingly to her, but not with my mother's body still being tossed beneath me by the deep currents of the swirling sea.

As fate had it, the *Demelza* was dragged by currents away from the coast, and on into yet a stronger current. Under this impulse, I was pulled out towards the open sea, where the waves were increasingly heavy.

I went haplessly out like that, the weather deteriorating all the while, and the sea running high and angrier by the minute. I was doomed, if ever a man was doomed, and I knew it. I weighed up in my mind the deaths and the dead, and I asked myself what curse lay on Trevelyan Priors.

There came a point when, if I looked back, I could no longer see the land, yet still the inexorable current took me away from any hope of safety. All the time, I shivered, not from cold — though I was bitterly chilled — but from the fear that you or Morwenna might appear in the boat and drive me off it into the bitter sea.

Then something happened. I kept looking across the gunwale, to see if the current might take me back within sight of land. Suddenly, I caught sight of something in the distance, but when I looked properly, it had gone. Then, moments later, it appeared again, one hundred yards to starboard and moving like the *Demelza*. It disappeared again, but this time I knew where to look for it. Once more, it came up from the trough, and I saw there were others behind it, and felt my heart lift, that I had never hoped to feel again. They were fishing smacks, and they were heading towards me.

Old Father Tregaskis was waiting in his cottage. He watched the men bring me up from the harbour, my slow feet slipping on the cobbles, and he went to his door and opened it. I couldn't look at him, but he put an arm round my shoulders and led me inside. I let him take me to the little parlour looking out across the harbour to the rain-drenched sea. One by one, the little boats, heavy with fish, were easing themselves to their mooring-places, for the water was almost calm within the harbour walls.

I stood looking out while he went to fetch me some of Peter's dry clothes. When I was dressed, he gave me a cup of whiskey to drink, and ordered me to swallow it in sips, like medicine. When was about halfway down, I collapsed onto a chair and began to ob. In spite of his own grief, he held me and soothed me with ind words spoken over and over.

When the worst of it had cleared from me, I sat back from him a little.

'He died trying to save my mother,' I said. 'He wouldn't let me go in after her, but risked his own life. She dragged him down, her and the silly dress I'd told her not to wear.'

'Don't fret so, my dear,' he said. 'We're used to men drowning in these parts. Not many fishermen die in warm beds. But I'm pleased he died as you say he did, and I'm sorry for you that your mother drowned in spite of his efforts.'

He continued to comfort me in this fashion, and to press the whiskey on me until word could be sent up to the house, and a car sent to fetch me.

I'm sure you can guess how grief-stricken your mother was to hear the news. But she rallied when she saw the miserable state I was in and heard my story, though I left out the details concerning the figures on the beach. She sent me to bed to sleep, and that's when I saw you for the second time, smiling in the corner of my room.

When I woke this morning Aunt Marion was sitting by my bed, watching me. I looked up at her and could see at once that she too had been crying. Her eyes were red and her cheeks almost as white as plaster.

'I'm so sorry about what happened to Mother,' I said. 'Peter did all he could, but her dress pulled them both down.'

'I'm sorry, Simon, but I have more bad news for you. While you were out at sea, a telegram was sent up from the Post Office. From the Ministry of War. Tom is dead, killed in a sortie at a place called Messines. The marquis says it's not far from his château.' She hesitated and took my hand. 'Simon? You don't seem surprised.'

I explained that I'd seen you last night and on the beach. She in her turn, didn't seem at all surprised.

'Simon,' she said, 'now that Tom is dead, your uncle wants to proceed with his plan to make you his son and heir. Ordinarily, would like nothing more, but I think David has more in mind for you than simple inheritance. I'll be frank: I don't trust him or his friend the marquis, and I don't want you to spend another night under this roof. I know this will be difficult, particularly in the wake of has happened. But you must leave this house once night falls.

'I've packed a bag for you, with food and extra clothes. You'll find an envelope containing a generous amount of money. I'll send more later, once you're away and safe. Parkin will drive you to Porthmullion halt, where you'll catch the last London train. Tomorrow morning, get the first train back down to Bristol, and seek out your relations there: I've put their address in the bag for you. I'll write to them and arrange to have you stay with them until you can go to university.'

She has gone now, leaving me to myself. I've spent the time since then writing this, even though I know I shall never send it. I may leave it for Aunt Marion, to let her know just what took place. I'm going to suggest she settle a pension on Peter's father. If the bodies are ever found, I want them buried at sea, not in the graveyard here. If you see Morwenna, tell her I still love her very much.

Your unfortunate cousin,

Simon

Death and a New Beginning

4 May 1925

Mr Simon Lysaght
10 Gillygate
York

My dear Simon,

I have dreadful news to communicate to you. My beloved William is dying. He says he would like nothing better than to see you before he dies. Though he and I are very close, he has said nothing to me about why he feels this need, and I suspect it may be that he cannot bear to depart this earth without seeing his only relative and friend.

The doctors are pessimistic, and give him only weeks. His injuries have left his heart weak, and in himself he is as low as could be. I have tried everything, but I cannot help him further, and he does not want me to. He is resigned, even cheered by the prospect of extinction. This life has not treated him well, and living here at Trevelyan Priors has been an agony.

For myself, I am devastated. He was not my son, but I loved him in ways not everyone would understand. I don't know what I shall do without him, and without you, my dear.

Simon, you must not forget the warnings I gave you when you left here. Make your visit a short one, and leave before nightfall. I will try to keep David away from you. But no doubt you're man enough now to handle him should he lose his temper or threaten you with anything. He has never forgiven you for 'breaking your bond' to become his son legally.

I think of you often, and of your late mother. If only I had sailed with you that day, I might have warned young Peter about Nancledre Sands, and so two unnecessary tragedies might have

261

been averted.

Come soon: I cannot say how long William may last. His appetite has fallen off dramatically, he has lost a great deal of weight, and his eyes stare out from hollow sockets. It will prove a shock to you; but at least you will come forewarned.

Yours in haste,

Marion

From the Ongoing Account in the hand of Simon Lysaght for the Month of May 1925.

Being unmarried and without dependents when I received my summons to go back down to Trevelyan Priors, it proved no insurmountable problem to ask for leave and pack my bags.

Before my departure, however, I received a second letter from Cornwall. This was from William, and in it he told me how things were with him. I cried as I read it, for it pained me to think of my old friend suffering so much. There was a second purpose behind his writing, however, and this pained me more. In short, he asked me to bring certain items down to Cornwall, things he could not easily obtain for himself, whose purpose he would explain to me when I arrived, though I had a perfectly good idea what he meant by them.

I bought a ticket for the first train my duties at Guy's allowed me to take. Our Great War may be seven years away now, but no one complains if time is taken from work to visit a war hero. My department chief, the illustrious Professor Brocklehurst, had a policy of denying leave to staff except in cases of acute personal emergency. But once I explained the situation and who William was, he grew affable and said I could take as much time as the situation required. But he did remind me that I was due to assist him in an operation four days later.

Marion opened the door to me in person, and over a lunch of cold meats and salad, told me of William and his sudden decline. The local doctors had decided there was nothing to be done for my cousin beyond palliation. It was, they said, his mind that ailed him more than his body. One of them had recommended an Austrian physician working in Vienna, but it was highly unlikely that this Dr. Freund or Freud would make the journey to Trevelyan Priors, and impossible to think of William travelling in the opposite direction.

She pointed out that Sir David had gone hunting with the Vale of the White Horse and wasn't expected back for two or three days.

'So we won't have any fuss,' she said, smiling at me. 'Now, I think you should go up. You know the way.'

He was waiting for me, propped up in bed as so often before, a stiff smile on his face, his eyes dead. Marion left me alone with him.

'What's all this, William?' I said. 'You don't write for years, then you tell me you want to die.'

'Sit down, Simon, and try not to sound so smug. It's something you learn about in my position, how smug other people can get. Marion's grown smug, all the doctors she wheels in have had a dose of it, and now it's got hold of you as well.'

'You were never so critical, William, old man. Here, I'll let myself down here, on the bed.'

'It crept in with all the rest. How can you even wonder at it, knowing what you do? That's why I wrote to you — because you know what this place I live in is. I can never leave it physically, so I must leave it in the only other way possible.'

'What makes you think you'd be leaving it?'

He hesitated for the first time. The deadness of his eyes was momentarily replaced by a look of raw panic. He'd been locked in here with them all these years, but the thought that he might actually become one of them...

'I don't belong with them, I should be out there in France with James and Tom.'

'I saw Tom the night he died. Right in the corner of my bedroom,' I said. 'And I saw him before my mother drowned.'

'I've seen him many times too. I've even spoken with him. But I have to take the risk. That there's a way out.'

263

'It's all right, William. You asked me to help, and I will. But there are some things I want to ask you. You said once you'd fallen for that girl Morwenna. She turned up on Nancledre Sands along with Tom. But someone had cut her throat.'

William told me that he knew she had been killed in the Shot Tower, but that no one had ever discovered who had done it.

'Have you seen her since then?' I asked.

He shook his head.

'No,' he said. 'I lost interest, you might say. What about you?'

'Once or twice. Once in London, in the operating theatre: I think she wanted to offer some competition. And once on a spring hike round the Scottish lochs. She's still as beautiful as she ever was.'

'And you're as smitten.'

I laughed, but when I looked again, he was not laughing, and his thin smile had grown more tense.

'I think it may be time, William. Are you sure you don't want Marion with you?'

'I don't want to give her that pain.'

'Perhaps she has a right.'

'A right?'

'To your pain. To share it.'

'She'd never let you do it.'

'I think you'd be surprised what she would let me do. Let me fetch her.'

A smile flickered across his mouth, one of the old game smiles I'd always associated with him.

'You're the real thing, Simon, aren't you? Quite the bedside manner. Harley Street before long, eh? All right, then, you're the one to judge. Go and fetch her. And thank you for the risk you're taking. None of the other doctors would have understood.'

'Quilty would.'

'Father would never have let him near the house. Quilty knows too much. No, things are fine as they are. Let Marion come in.'

She was in the corridor outside. For some reason, she had taken off her dress, and was dressed in a long white shift on which there were what looked like red wine stains. She was leaning with her

264

back against the wall, and her long hair streaked with grey fell past her shoulders. I had never seen her smoke before: between her fingers she held a short Brazilian holder in which a well-smoked cigarette rested.

I told her what I'd come for, and after a couple of minutes she nodded, knocked the cigarette onto the carpet and stubbed it with her toe, then went to William's door ahead of me.

I gave them a few minutes together. They were like a loving couple of many years' standing, well past the first flush of youth. I turned my eyes aside, for their last embrace was too close to emotions of my own. To carry this off, for both their sakes, I had to carry this off as a professional.

While Marion held his right hand in hers, I took out my hypodermic syringe and made a solution that I reckoned would do the job without unnecessary distress either way. Beyond the act of injecting him, I simply did not know what to do. Marion helped me. She looked at me and nodded.

'It's time,' she said. 'Don't keep him waiting.'

A minute later, he was dead.

I left her with him for as long as she needed. When half an hour had passed, she came out again.

'He's at peace,' she said.

'Do you think he has escaped?' I asked her.

She shrugged.

'Who knows? Time alone will tell.'

'You should get dressed,' I said. 'You look a mess. Beautiful as always, of course; but a mess. I'll stay till you're more yourself. Then I must go. Perhaps Sir David will be back by then.'

'I certainly hope not. I don't suppose this will make much difference to him anyway. He lost interest in William once he knew he couldn't have children.'

'That's not entirely true, surely... Just because he lost his legs. You don't need...'

'Oh, for goodness' sake, Simon, stop being such an old maid. You're a doctor now. You know practically as much about William's private parts as I do.'

She persuaded me to stay for another day at least. I was to

explain William's death to my uncle. And to take part in the funeral the day after tomorrow.

'There'll be no trouble about the death,' she said. 'I'll take care of that. No one will ask impertinent questions, you can be sure of it.'

She took a bath while I found a suitable dress for her to put on. To my astonishment, she had more black dresses than I'd seen regular ones in a clothes shop. It impressed me no end to find that she had her own private bathroom. Her bedroom — I should call it her boudoir, really — was the last word in sophistication and what I suppose is decadence.

She came out in a silk turban and a very large towel, and for several minutes I had the distinct impression she was offering to seduce. But the mood passed, and in the end I think she was only playing with me.

I managed to get her downstairs, where I found some servants, all of them at a loss. I explained what had happened and left Marion with them while I telephoned Dr Scobie in Falmouth, who had last attended my poor cousin in person.

If Scobie guessed, he said nothing. He put it down to his heart, the very thing he'd expected to do the job before long. I did not feel guilt on account of the deception, my first independent action as a physician. I am at the bottom of a rigid hierarchy, and I find no difficulty in letting responsibility linger with those above me.

Scobie was not asked to dine that evening, indeed it would have appeared odd in the extreme, given the circumstances and given that Sir David had still not returned from the Vale of the White Horse.

We took one look at the dining table, with its two places at one end, and decided neither of us could face it. We ate in her private room, cold cuts again, more than we had appetite, and we talked about the ghosts of Trevelyan Priors. She asked me to write about it all, but later, much later. I've made a mental note to do so, but only when my medical duties leave me enough time.

We went to bed about ten that night. I gave Marion a sedative (to be precise, Dr Scobie left a small packet, for me to administer as prescribed by him), and her maid took her to her room. By the

266

time she'd been undressed, her feet were giving under her, and it took two maids to get her into bed.

I did not sleep at all. There was the natural guilt attendant on the action I had performed that afternoon. Moreover, it was the first night I'd passed at Trevelyan Priors since my mother's death. I was in my old room again, and the passage of time had only served to fill its shadows, nooks and crannies with bogies no amount of rationality or adulthood could dispel. I found my Hentys on the shelf where I'd put them the evening Mother arrived. Children's tales, but I wasn't in the mood for anything more demanding. To my surprise, I found the author's jingoism jarring. Tom's death had left me without any further taste for King and country, and William's passing that afternoon had seemed to bring the War and my small connection to it to an end.

I must have fallen asleep about fifty pages into The Young Carthaginians, for it was lying across my stomach, spine up, when I awoke. I felt groggy, and cursed myself for having taken so many glasses of wine to drink on such a light stomach.

Something had wakened me. A host of fears flooded back, but I had only to turn my lamp up full to see that the room was empty. So far as it seemed. I listened hard and became aware that a fierce storm was moving round the house. At that moment, a prolonged flash of sheet lightning lit up the sky outside and penetrated my bedroom through the wide gap where I had left my curtains to hang apart.

Darkness resumed, broken only by my lamp. I was sure thunder must have woken me earlier, and waited for the next clap. But before it came, I heard something indoors, voices in the corridor outside, or perhaps a little further. I listened and heard the first voice again, a man's voice, deep and muffled, shouting — I could not tell what about.

His cries were suddenly drowned by a massive racket of thunder that shook the whole house. It was followed not many seconds later by another flash of brilliance. In between, heavy rain was pouring down with unlimited ferocity. I got out of bed and put my feet in my slippers before draping my dressing-gown round my shoulders.

As I had more than half expected, David Trevelyan had returned home in the middle of the night. He was at the top of the grand staircase, bellowing, and Marion was trying to calm him down. The thunder and lightning merely lent drama to an otherwise tedious situation. I resolved to help her put him to bed, and to stay longer the next day so I could speak to her about her best course of action for the future.

I moved forward into the broad polished area that divided the top of the stairs from the corridor that leads on into the bedroom floor. It's a wide area, almost like an apron stage, and I remembered how Tom and I used to play there with toy swords, and how we would take turns to be stabbed to death and roll lifeless to the floor

The light from my lamp gave little illumination to the place. But I could tell right away that it was here this latest little drama was being played out.

'You killed him,' David's voice boomed across the broad landing. 'How else did he die? Tell me that, eh! The doctors gave him weeks still, and I leave for a couple of days and come back to find him stiff and cold in his bed. By God, you'll rot in hell for this, woman. I'll take you there myself if I have to: by all that's damnable, I know the way well enough.'

As though on cue, another roar of thunder welled up and struck the house, followed almost at once by the brightest lightning flash I've ever seen, and for a moment I might have believed the Devil had stepped out on stage to snatch us all down to some gaping pit built specially for the inhabitants of Trevelyan Priors.

In the flash, I could make out everything at once: the great staircase sweeping away from us to reach the marble-flagged hall below. The lines of classical busts — Caesar, Cicero, Tiberius and others — on pale marble pillars. The great Gobelins tapestry by Boucher that had always dominated the top of the stairs was sharply etched on my eye. As for the rest of the walls, they were thickly hung with oil portraits from several schools and periods.

The giant window that stretched from top to bottom of the stairwell was lit up as though a row of searchlights had been planted behind it. Or flares, I thought, for this must have been how it was when flares lit up the midnight battlefield.

David and Marion were only inches apart now. He had his back to the staircase, and she was coming to him, her arms out-sretched, as though to... I strained to see what was happening, but at that very moment the darkness snapped back into place again.

There was a scream. A man's scream, as far as I could tell. It was followed within a heartbeat by a series of cracking thuds, then by a piercing woman's scream. I swept everywhere with my lamp, trying to see what had occurred, but the light was next to useless, a bedroom nick-nack designed for cosy fire-lit rooms.

Next thing, I bumped without warning into Marion, who was crouching on her hands and knees near the head of the stairs. I lifted her and took her hand. She was like a doll in my grasp. One by one, we went down the stairs together. I could hear a bustling of servants far off, but we had our own time to move in, and our darkness.

And, next moment, our light, for the thunder raged and the lightning flared up again. David was lying on his back, stretched across several steps. In the few moments I had, I hurried down to him and, as the darkness returned, made a rapid examination.

Marion was beside me moments later. I took her hand again.

'I think he's dead, Marion. As far as I can tell, his neck is bro-ken.'

'Serves him bloody well right,' she said. 'He was drunk as a lord.'

I never saw what happened in that dark interval, whether he fell or she pushed him... or whether something else happened. Somewhere in the back of my mind, I remember that I saw a shadow that should not have been there, stretching toward both of them. It's hard to be a judge, of course, when the elements are at their wildest and nothing remains stable. There was something there, why would I have doubted it, in that house of shadows; and there was something in Marion's posture, and something in her voice immediately afterwards. And if I thought she seemed broken-hearted in the days that followed, I do not believe she wept for my uncle, and I am sure that, for a time, she was jubilant for herself.

A Last Visitor

Simon Lysaght's Journal in old age

12 October 1994

I never saw Marion again. In time, I lost all contact with
Cornwall. I didn't write — Marion had warned me not to. There
was a new career ahead of me, then a family to establish, and, as
always, horrors to be forgotten. No, not entirely forgotten, not
even now. Least of all now.

From time to time, Marion would write to me, short notes
devoted in the main to William. She never recovered from his
death. It diminished her morning and night. I wondered at the
time how that could be, but now, knowing the world much better,
I think I understand. He was her one and only love. She was not,
after all, his true mother, and if there was any scandal in their passion, it can only have been on account of the difference in their
ages, which, thinking back, was not that great after all. I can't say
if he loved her in return, but her passion was only too visible in
those letters she sent me.

His memory was all she had left, she said later on, when the
Priors had become an almost empty shell, bereft of love or passion, where shadows walked all night long. As far as possible, she
kept to her little room downstairs, and listened to her life pass by
in silence. David's death left no visible trace on her, and she herself discounted it as something minor. And though it gave her
freedom, it could not buy her a path out of Trevelyan Priors.

A few months after the two deaths, she wrote enclosing a draft
for a considerable sum of money, which, she said, came from her
private estate. She'd been keeping it for Tom, she wrote, to pay
his way through university, and to set him up in whatever pro-
fession he might have decided on. And that is exactly what I
decided to do with it, in Tom's honour.

I had just arrived in York, where I had set myself up in general practice in partnership with a fashionable older doctor, when I
received a telegram (followed a few days later by a letter) from Dr
Quilty. He had moved to Truro, where he'd met and married the
woman who was now his wife. Marion had written to him,

giving him details of my medical success, and he had generously contacted me to offer any help he might. He told me he still kept in touch with some old patients in Porthmullion. He made no allusions to the past, save for one brief mention of Alice.

The marquis, he said, had already returned to his beloved France as soon as the war ended, in order to regain possession of his château, his estates, and his vineyards. Many of his precious artworks had been seized by the Germans and scattered to different destinations in Germany and Austria. Since then, I have heard rumours that he devoted his declining years to a hunt for these paintings and objets d'art, and that he succeeded in tracking down perhaps forty percent of them, in many cases being forced to pay a second time for their recovery.

I read of his death forty years or more ago, when I was living in Paris. There was a small paragraph in *Le Monde*, that spoke of his unsavoury reputation and his dabbling in ritual magic. It was said that no library, bookseller, or collector would buy the occult volumes from his massive collection. The rest of his library went to pay off debts he had incurred during the search for his stolen masterpieces. I tried to pity him, for he had been kind with me once or twice; but I could not find it in me to feel anything but revulsion for that horror of a man. During the Second World War, his remaining art collection was stolen by the Nazis and salted away in Bavarian mine-shafts, where it remains unrecovered to this day. As for the fate of his occult books, I know nothing and have not the slightest wish to know.

As I have written above, Marion stayed on in the house for the years remaining to her. As I think of her now, alone but for a tiny staff who worked at the Priors strictly during daylight hours, abandoning her to the house and its ghosts at night, I can scarcely bear to imagine it. Did she retain her sanity to the end? Did they ever give her peace? Or was she just so inured to her ghosts that she had the strength to face them for all those years?

I wonder now why she never went back to Clovelley, where she was born and brought up, and where her brother Cedric still lived with his wife and children. She had inherited David's fortune and the estate. She could have lived anywhere she pleased:

London, Paris, the South of France, Lisbon, Rome, Venice… She had so many choices. But she stayed on at the Priors, letting the gardens and the house rot around her. Cleaning was limited to a few rooms at first, then halted. Gardening had been discontinued long before.

She died of natural causes after the War. It had not been her war, of course; she'd sacrificed her son and her stepsons for that earlier, stupid war, and for her, as for so many of her generation, Hitler had meant little to her. There were no air-raids near her, and the reputation of the Priors meant no one thought to requisition it for military or medical use. Marion lived out the war in the splendid isolation she'd adopted all those years ago. Nothing disturbed her unquiet peace, nothing but her gaunt companions in that cold, echoing, bloody house.

Within two weeks of her death, I was contacted by her solicitors, a London firm that had worked for her family for three generations. They told me that the entire Trevelyan estate had passed to me. I was suddenly rich beyond my modest dreams. I was forty-seven and still in general practice, wondering what the coming National Health Service would mean for me. And not just for me, but for my small family. I was still married to my French wife Nicole, I still had two children, a dog, a cat, and a large house in York, which I had bought out of my success as a doctor. A modest success, be it said.

News of my good fortune brought all these matters to a head, for, if the truth be told, I had never been truly suited to a provincial doctor's life. As I approached fifty, I discovered myself to be just another middle-aged man bowed down with his discontent and his fear of the future. Yet, had it not been for the money, I'd have gone on till I put down my stethoscope or worked too many late nights to see myself into an early grave.

Trevelyan Priors was mine too, of course, but I'd vowed never to set foot in it again — a vow I plan to break only in the course of this last visit. From York, I saw to it that any remaining staff were paid off properly and given handsome bonuses for their loyal service, or small pensions where that was appropriate. And I gave instructions that the house was to be locked up and the keys sent directly to me.

Nicole and I had stumbled along for years, scarcely recognising one another. She'd had a brief but steamy affair with a deacon from the Minster, a descendant of my mother's favourite, Upham Pope, and they'd come close to causing the sort of scandal that might have rocked the church. I have never blamed her for that. I ought not to have married her in the first place. She never knew the truth, that throughout our marriage she'd played second fiddle to a dead girl, a girl who never changed or grew old.

I think I've already mentioned that I've seen Morwenna from time to time, always as pretty as when I first saw her, always standing gazing from a little distance away, smiling. On my honeymoon, she sat on the edge of the bed and amused herself greatly at our clumsy attempts at lovemaking. I assure you, it's nearly impossible to make love to a living woman when a dead one watches, offering more. I have seen her increasingly in recent years, and I know she's waiting for me somewhere. It's not her that I fear.

Over the years, men in dark suits have approached me, asking if I'd be willing to sell Trevelyan Priors, and always I've said no. But they're a tough breed these developers, and won't take no for an answer. Even in their present state, the house and its lands together form what is called a 'prime property'.

The general plan seems to be to redevelop the building into some sort of fancy hotel and health spa, along continental lines. One of these gentlemen, an American from Florida, intends to open up Nancledre Sands, that stretch of inaccessible shore I never set foot on. Should I tell him it was there they found Old Matthew's fish-eaten remains, vomited up by a current that has its origins at the foot of the Shot Tower? Or that my mother's corpse, identified only by what shreds of clothing were left clinging to her flesh, was carried on a long journey by the currents and returned at last to that same strand?

Nicole and I parted in the end, then divorced a year later without much rancour. I pay her a generous alimony, and I have settled the rest of my wealth on the children, Neville, then fifteen, and Thérèse, then thirteen. They are much older now, of course, and married — happily, I think — with children of their own. Neville is a consultant thoracic surgeon, Thérèse a barrister specializing in European tax litigation (as far as I can understand what it is she does!). They will have whatever remains of my money when I die, and that is where it will end. They know nothing of Trevelyan Priors or my history there, nor do I wish them ever to be told in my lifetime. Once I am gone, these pages will serve to explain much to them, and to warn them.

Nicole herself knows next to nothing of these events, other than that I spent some time in Cornwall when I was young and that I inherited my wealth from the people with whom I stayed. She never asked to meet other members of the family, or to go down there for a holiday.

So I have come here alone, in order to fulfill an old vow to myself. I've seen the Priors from the outside, and the gardens, overgrown with weeds and once-domesticated plants, run wild. The years lie over it all like green glass. I'm writing this in the cottage that once belonged to poor Peter Tregaskis or his father, where I was taken to be dried and comforted after my mother's death and Peter's fatal rescue bid. I was the ghost young Rachel saw, in my old-fashioned clothes and staring eyes. My beginning and my end have caught one another, and all I have to do now is wait.

No, that is not quite true. There is still time for one more thing. I must visit Trevelyan Priors for one last time. I must take my key and unlock the door and go all the way inside.

14 October

I have been to the house and I have confronted the past. This time, of course, I went well armed with the information I have set out in these pages, information gleaned from other people's letters and journals, and from my own memories. On reflection, I might have been better without all that. I am not a courageous man at heart, and only went up there because I knew — or thought I knew — what to expect.

I asked the local taxi to leave me at the gate.

'Aren't planning to go up there, are you?' he asked. 'It's been empty for years. If you don't mind my saying so, sir, a man of your great age should be indoors looking after himself, not traipsing about the countryside, putting hisself in mortal peril.'

'I have business here. It may take a little while. Could you come back for me in about an hour? Meet me here at the gates.'

I pushed down the handle on the door, but he put his hand on my arm.

'What sort of business, if you don't mind my asking? You look too frail to be out anywhere on business. No one's lived in the Priors since old Lady Trevelyan died. She was the last of the family, they say. Or maybe there was others, I wouldn't know. None of them would have dared set foot inside the building, no more than I'd set foot in there now. And I'd advise you to think the same, mister. No good can come of your going up there, whatever business you may have. Knock it all down would be the best thing, in my opinion. I pity anyone ever had to live there.'

'You think the house is haunted, then?' I asked. I couldn't resist it. And I genuinely wanted to know what the locals thought of the Priors.

'No doubt of it, sir, no doubt at all. Ask anyone round these parts. It's been known as a haunted place for as long as it's been here. My old grandmother, why she frightened us kids at night just talking about it. Things have been seen there, believe me. Let me take you somewhere else, sir, if it's sightseeing you've come for. They've reopened the tin mine down at Carharrak, and installed a super exhibition with history and such, sir. Would you like me to drive you over?'

I shook my head.

'Afraid not, tempting as it sounds. Maybe another time. When did the shot tower break in two, do you know?'

'Top half fell down about thirty year ago. The stones are half in the sea, half on the beach below. There's about fifty feet of the tower left.'

'What a pity. There aren't many surviving in this country. Well, I'll not keep your meter running.'

I handed him his fee and told him to keep the change.

'Thank you, sir. That's very kind. Take care up there, sir, and whatever you do, don't set a foot inside. Would you like a hand with that case? It looks terrible heavy.'

'Certainly not. I have my little trolley, it's very neat and compact, and I don't have far to walk to the doors.'

I watched him drive off, and only when his car had vanished from sight and the sound of its engine swallowed up in silence, did I start up the drive that led to the front door. I was dragging a little luggage trolley to which was strapped a large suitcase. The case was heavy, very heavy, and I pulled it behind me with the greatest difficulty, wheezing, panting, stopping frequently to recover my breath and my strength.

In spite of that dreadful weight, I felt as though all my years had been stripped away, and that I was once again a young boy about to enter the unknown world behind those doors.

October had come in cold after a mild September. The grounds were wearing their first carpet of leaves, and the trees were a restless patchwork of leaves and branches tossed and bent by a high wind. It was bitterly cold, and though I had wrapped up warmly, I was an old man, and old men do not fare well in wind or ice.

Halfway along, I looked up at the upper storey where the attics were situated. Just for a moment I was certain that a face appeared at one of the windows, only to withdraw again, as it had when I first came to Trevelyan Priors.

I stood at the front door at last, gasping for breath, fishing for the key in an inner pocket. Please don't misunderstand — I was not the cool, dispassionate man I may have portrayed myself to be. I was steeling myself to go ahead with my plan, and every minute that passed saw me put it off to the next.

I stood like that for a long time, waiting for my troublesome heartbeat to grow more regular and my breathing to calm itself. Finbally, I slipped the key into the lock.

To my surprise, it turned with little trouble, and the door opened to a wretched series of creaks and cracks. When I did finally step inside, I realised that I was scared stiff. What I saw that day on the beach would have caused anyone to doubt the base fragility on which the world of the human soul is built. In a world that allows such things, how can a man judge between right and wrong, for the devil is never further away than a glance over your right shoulder?

I unstrapped my case from the trolley and opened it. From it, I took a powerful electric torch, one of these smart black metal things I'm told is called a Maglite. One of my nephews gave it to me as a present last Christmas, but this was the first time I'd found a use for it. He'd have a shock to find me here, putting it to such a terrible purpose.

Even though it was daytime, not much light found its way through the dirty windows and into the great hall.

There were cobwebs everywhere, some visibly old, others new. Dust lay on every surface like a shroud that was renewed minute by minute. Even as I thought it, I knew that the image of a shroud was apt. The house was dead. Not simply uninhabited, but dead, its heart gone, its lungs shrivelled, its eyes and ears the delicacies of crows and soft sliding ghosts.

An ordinary man, burdened with my knowledge, might without blame have turned on his heels and fled. A property developer would have stayed put just long enough to make a quick evaluation of what needed to be done to the interior, before leaving noisily, slamming the door behind him and whistling the theme music to that ridiculous American film, *Ghostbusters*. Of course, property developers are not ordinary men.

I, however, for all that I'm perfectly ordinary in most ways, have never had an ordinary relationship with Trevelyan Priors. It had long had a destiny in mind for me, and I, at last, had one for it.

I stood in the Great Hall, connecting myself to the house once more, but this time I had come, not as a supplicant, but as its rightful owner. All the emotions of the first day came rushing back, and were followed by others more specific to the people I'd lived with there. Aunt Marion, my uncle, the sinister marquis, my cousin William, and, above all, my cousin, friend and playmate Tom.

I heard a voice whisper in my left ear. *A morte? La muerte? La mort?* Something like that. Something obvious. Already the house was playing games with me, already its voices laughing at me.

Before I had time to respond, a second whisper came from far down the room. Silence followed, then a child's laugh. The same voice as before? I could not be sure. I took a step forward. There was another whisper, louder than the first, then another and another until I was being pursued by voices, children's voices, centuries of voices, sad, bewildered, frightened. Mostly frightened. After hundreds of years, some of them still didn't know they were dead, while those that did had no clue as to where they were, or why. Some called on their fathers, some their mothers, a few on God. They hadn't been answered in centuries, but as long as they wandered through Trevelyan Priors, they would keep on pleading and crying.

But it was that first voice that stayed with me throughout, for the joke it made was serious beyond belief. I mean the voice that had whispered 'Death' gently in my ear. I knew the answer too, from Botto's poem: '*És tu, senhor dos meus olhos.* 'It is you, lord of my eyes...' Just let him watch, I thought: it will be my joke in the end.

I went through all the rooms on the ground floor. Most were as I last remembered them, apart from the cobwebs and the dimming of the light. The schoolroom had not been touched or altered in any way since the day Tom walked out. On the blackboard, just discernible beneath a thin film of dust, was the lesson Conor Fitzgerald had presented to us, that disastrous lesson that had ended in Tom's angry and misplaced flight.

I came at last to the library and opened it with the old key that had belonged to my uncle, and which Marion had left for me in a sealed envelope. The books had, in many cases, rotted on their shelves. Cobwebs reached from the ceiling to this shelf or that, forming an interlocking network in which spiders crept like soldiers on patrol.

As I ventured to set foot inside, the voices round me changed in tone and character. Fear now became the dominant feature, and I noticed that new voices had entered, all speaking in Latin. Church Latin, if you wish to be precise.

I touched a single strand and the web began to shake, proving itself to be a single web that stretched from one end of the vast library to the other. My touch set the spiders on edge and sent them scurrying to some presumed centre of their world. I could see them gather, and almost imagined them chattering to one another, or sending messages from one edge of the web to the other through the movements of their long legs and the silken strands they were still weaving.

I stepped inside and closed the door, pausing only to lock it behind me, stealthily. If my presence in the house had not been known before, it was now.

New voices joined the Latin speakers. Pleading for help, for mercy, for an end to the long fear. And then, above them, came a deeper sound, like the beating of a bass drum, and I knew I had indeed awoken something within or beyond the library.

I went upstairs to the bedrooms. It was dark in the corridors, for little light got through the single windows at each end. I played my torch beam everywhere. My room was there, William's nearby, Tom's not far away. I turned in the opposite direction.

My mother was standing near the stairs to the attic. She was wearing the dress she'd worn on the day of her death, that had dragged her down beneath the waves. To see her, I might have thought her newly drowned. What startled me, however, was how young she looked, and how attractive to an older man's eye. She frightened me all the same. I had read her account of the time she spent upstairs in the attic, the account you will have read by now, and now, I thought, she had come to stop me going up there myself.

'It's all right, Mother,' I said. 'I know what I'm doing.'

'You mustn't go up there,' she said, and it sounded as if she was speaking through cold water.

'I have to go, Mother,' I said. 'I have no choice. Look at me. I'm an old man now, and I know I don't have long to live. So what have I got to fear?'

'There are things far worse than death,' she answered. 'And many of them dwell in this house.'

'Why the house? Have you discovered that?'

She hesitated. Had she been here all the time, I wondered, leading some thin, ghostly existence, communing with the dark? If so, what had the dark told her?

'I know very little,' she said. 'This isn't a school. There are no teachers. But I do know that something happened when a priory still stood on this site. There were young friars, some little more than children. They'd been sent to the priory by parents who couldn't provide for them. Just as you were sent here by me, and for the same reason. One year, a prior came here from the French mother house. Soon some of the children began to disappear. Many years later, evidence was uncovered to suggest that Prior Anselm had engaged in demonic magic, and that he'd used the children in his care as sacrifices in his rituals. He was burned at the stake, but refused to renounce the Devil even while he was burning.

'After that, they say he was sometimes seen in the priory grounds and inside the building itself, so that friars feared him everywhere, but, above all, at Mass, where he would appear next to the altar, as he had been at the time of his death, his blackened bones showing through melted flesh.

'Even then, they say, children went missing. It's said that, in time, the entire priory was given over to diabolic practices, though that may well be a Protestant exaggeration. And then all that ended when Henry embarked on the dissolution of the monasteries and religious houses.

'And after that? Well, you know the answer to that yourself. The house is heavy with its young dead. And older deaths too, for the evil in this place is not discriminating. There's nothing you can do to stop it, Simon, dear, absolutely nothing. But you risk everything if you go up there.'

'It's all right, Mother. This is something I swore to do a very long time ago. It will make things right for you, right for all of us.'

I made to kiss her, but she was no longer there. Swing the torch as I might, I could not again pinpoint her in its beam. I sighed and prepared myself to climb to the landing where the attics began. I closed the case and lifted it as before, and it felt heavier than when I began. As I put one foot on the stairs, I was bent over and already groaning from my exertions. Perhaps the taxi driver had been right, perhaps I should have brought help. But one sight of my mother would have sent him scurrying back outside and into his taxi. I kept on carrying: without the case and its contents, all this would have been in vain: my living so long, my returning to this place.

It was exactly as my mother had written. I felt confidence drain from me and fear strike up like a hideous string quartet. With every step upwards, my legs felt weaker, and the burden I carried heavier. As ever, the light crept in through a thickly coated sky-light.

As I opened the baise doors into the first corridor, I noticed that the voices that had accompanied me thus far suddenly ceased, and with them the sound of the deep-throated drumming.

I sensed it from the first moment, and I thought it must be an all-encompassing chill of pure evil. On reflection, I think I understand it better now. It was not some inherent evil, born in the depths of eternity and transplanted here to rule a small kingdom with a rod of fear and misery. This was worse than that. This was good gone wrong. Piety turned to blasphemy, charity to hate, love to scorn, hope to despair, brightness to darkness, angels to demons, lovers cold self-abusers, runners cripples, day night, childhood a warped old age, life death, death putrefaction, from order to order, tossing, tumbling until heaven's child becomes hell's blackest and ugliest imp.

I walked down the empty corridor to the pedestal and its cob-web-wrapped vase, then turned as my mother had turned. A few steps later, and I knew I had reached the door, the one she had not opened.

In the following moments I went through all my mother had endured at that spot: black despair, a strong wish to die, great fear. My head hurt, my chest ached as though my heart would give way at last, my eyes grew blurred. This was the heart of things. I set down my burden like a sinner setting his heavy baggage down, and my arthritic hands ached intolerably.

On the door, as my mother had written, was a label, an old label with scarcely decipherable handwriting. I looked closely at it and realised there was, after all, a name on it, and that it had been written backwards, thus: SUMLESNA. Reversed, it simply read ANSELMUS.

But when I opened the door at last, I found myself in the plainest of rooms, bathed in the greyest of light, dulled to all sound from the outside. I lugged my case across the floor. A single chair sat in the middle of the room, and on it sat my cousin Alice, smiling.

'Simon,' she said, and her voice was very pleasant to the ear. 'I've been waiting for you for a long, long time.'

'Long enough,' I said. 'Long enough.'

'What brings you back to Trevelyan Priors?' she asked, and already her voice was changing.

'Surely you know,' I said, all the time struggling to conceal my intentions from her, or from whatever mind now dwelt in her phantom shape.

'Without people, the house is silent,' she said. 'There are no new children. I have no new playmates.'

'You were the last,' I told her. 'There can be no children here after you.'

'I don't understand you, Simon. Why can't there be as many children as we like? You could join me. We could run this house and they would join us here.'

I saw him take shape behind her, black, tall, and monstrous. He, better than anyone, could guess what I had in mind. He stepped out from behind her, angular and menacing. One hand was bone. I could almost smell his charred skin. Was he in hell? I wondered. *Why this is hell*, I remembered, *nor am I out of it…*

'It's time this came to an end,' I said. 'You cannot be in hell and out of it at once, for ever. It's time to go back. There's been too much anguish, too much fear.'

'It will never end!' he shouted in his broken voice. 'I won't let it end. You have no right to be here.'

'I have every right,' I snapped. 'I am the owner of Trevelyan Priors. This is mine to do.'

Saying that, I turned the case flat on the floor and snicked open the catches. That done, I unscrewed the cap on the can of petrol I'd brought. It was a large can, several gallons in capacity, and it had worn me out to carry it up here concealed in the case. I upended it and spilled petrol across the floor. I followed that with a match, and as the petrol burst into flame, I made my way slowly and painfully out of the room. The tiny explosion of petrol was the most satisfying sound I have ever heard.

What other solution was there, after all? I ran as fast as my old legs would take me through the corridor, and behind me I could hear the clear voices of little boys and girls. Children long dead, their unreal existences stretched out by one man who had only ever cared for himself. And I heard my uncle's voice, and that of his French master, two more men who had lived for themselves only. And I tried to find myself in all this, and I couldn't. But I felt no pain at last, and that was good, after so long.

On the bedroom level, I set fire to three more pools of petrol, leaving the main staircase free for my escape. I went down it once the flames had taken hold, and when I looked back I saw an army of children following me.

I used the rest of the petrol on the ground floor, took a last look at the old place, and went out through the main door, leaving it open for the children to make their escape.

I watched the house burn, each floor succumbing to the flames in close succession to the one before. With wonderful dignity, the old house submitted to its fate. Within ten minutes, it was a huge pyre that would never come to life again.

Soon, there was the sound of sirens. I thought it prudent to withdraw. I walked down to the old swan lake, taking it for a vantage point from which to watch the flames rise and fall, to watch them tear Trevelyan Priors apart, just as it should have been destroyed centuries before.

The burning went on throughout the afternoon. I watched until I grew cold. As I was about to leave, I heard a cry far up in the air. Others followed it, then others, and when I looked up I saw a flock of white swans flying like ghosts through the still grey air.

It was time to pay one last visit, to make my last break with the past. I walked back in the direction of the house, then veered and took a path through the weeds and the wild flowers that brought me by faltering steps to the enclosed garden and the summer-house. Most of the little house had collapsed, the victim of high winds and unforgiving storms. Some of the walls still stood, some of the glass remained miraculously intact.

I walked down to the little pond. It was not as I remembered it. I sat down on a stone. From where I sat, I could still make out dark smoke rising from the ruins of the house. In truth, I felt half dead. My head was splitting from my exertions, and my limbs ached everywhere. After perhaps half an hour, I felt somewhat recovered and took my notebook from my pocket in order to write these last notes. When I had reached this point, I heard a sound, a human voice.

'Simon.'

I recognised the voice at once, my dear Morwenna's voice, and when I lifted my head she was standing right in front of me, unchanged and beautiful, wearing the same dress she'd been wearing when we first met. I put down my pen.

'It's done, then,' she said.

I nodded. I could not take my eyes off her.

'It's time for you to come with me,' she said.

'Where are you taking me?'

'A place where we can be alone at last for as long as we want.'

'I still have things to do.'

She shook her head.

'None of that's important.'

'Morwenna, I'm an old man now. You fell in love with a boy.'

'Not a boy — a young man. And you'll be young again,' she said. 'Believe me.'

I laughed.

'It seems unlikely.'

'So is love.'

She bent down and kissed me on the forehead.

'I'll go over there,' she said. 'Finish your journal. Tell everyone what happened here.'

So I wrote again, and now it is time to lay my pen down for good. I won't be missed or mourned. But she's beckoning to me. It's time to go.